I0720450

A MEMORY MADE REAL

A MEMORY MADE REAL

❖

THE SEQUEL TO A TANGLE OF DREAMS

NICOLE ADAIR

Copyright © 2023 by Nicole Adair. All rights reserved.

This novel is a work of fiction. Names, characters, organizations, places, events, or incidences are products of the author's imagination or are used fictitiously. Any resemblance to actual events, locales, organizations, or persons, living or dead, is entirely coincidental.

Published by Validation Press, LLC

No part of this book may be reproduced in any form or by any electronic or mechanical means without written permission from the author, except for the use of brief quotations in book reviews or articles.

Cover designed and illustrated by Paige Poppe.

*This book was written for Brooke,
but it was also written for me and you
and everyone else
who has had to say
goodbye too soon.*

*Hold on to your magic.
This isn't the end.*

Like stars
we choose a slow descent
to dust,
the memories we trail so vivid
another wishes on the fragments
of ourselves we leave behind,
believing magic exists
in our fading pieces.
Left alone
we disappear between blinks,
all of existence narrowing
to one final gleam,
until a single glance captures our essence,
their gaze mapping our outline,
each look defining
the silhouette of our story,
crystallizing the pattern—a new
constellation.

—LYNDSI EARLE

CHAPTER ONE

GEMMA

A HAND BRUSHES against my cheek, the touch feather-light. Fingers tap a gentle rhythm across my face—my eyelids, my nose, my upper lip.

"Ollie?" My voice comes out scratchy and raw. I sound like I've been screaming.

The soft touch continues; cold, wet, spattering. With my eyes still shut tight, I slowly rub the moisture from my face, and with that gesture, the last of my impossible daydream is wiped clean. There is no hand brushing against me, no fingers tracing patterns in the freckles on my skin.

"Oliver?" I whisper again.

Nothing.

My eyes fly open in a flash only to be greeted by a muted morning, the sky covered in dark, brooding clouds. It's raining. The sun bleeds over the top of the mountains, but I can barely see it through the suffocating gray. The rain plinks noisily on the tin roof of the garden shed, the drops soft in the moist soil. I slowly look to my left and my right, my heart pounding recklessly with the hard-to-shake hope that maybe I'll catch sight of him lying next to me, his hand reaching out to mine.

But instead, I'm left blinking at what's left of my backyard. I stare at the vacant stretches of scorched and trampled down grass. He's not here.

How can he not be here?

The last words Ollie said to me ring in my ears. *"I love you,*

Gemma. Always have. Always will." A promise, a goodbye. The never-going-to-see-you-again finality in his voice. The look on his face when he held my thread in between his hands as he slowly, so slowly, let me go.

I blindly grasp the front of my dress, my fingers twisting in the soft cotton as if I could tear through the fabric and pry open my chest to search inside for my magic. But after a moment, my hand goes still. There's no point in wondering. There's no reason to search. With every breath, I feel the empty space between my ribs expanding. The empty space where my magic used to be.

I roll over to push off the ground, bits of damaged stone and wood digging into my palms. With a groan, I'm on my knees. Every inch of me aches like I've been hit by a truck.

"Gemma! You're here, you're all right." This time the hands I feel are real. Milo grips me by the shoulders and pulls me to my feet. "Gem." He throws his arms around me, squeezing so tight it's hard to breathe. "You're okay, you're okay," he chants while absently patting me on the back, brushing off the dirt and debris clinging to my stained white dress.

Another set of arms wraps around me. "Gemma girl, don't ever scare me like that again," my mom says as she leans into me, the tremor in her voice matching the shaking of her arms. Her forehead sinks against my shoulder as she lets out a long-held breath. I shift against her weight; it's hard to tell whether I'm supporting her or she's supporting me. All I feel is our mutual heaviness.

Milo finally releases me and rubs a hand over his face. "When Ollie took that mixing, I wasn't sure what would happen—"

"Have you seen him?" I ask, clutching his arm, my voice dry and brittle. "Ollie. Is he here?"

"What? I thought he was with you." Tipping his head to the side, Milo looks over my shoulder as if expecting to see Ollie hiding behind me in the wreckage. "You both vanished for a couple of hours," he says, his frown deepening. "We were all freaking out. Where did you go? What happened? Where's Ollie?" He barely pauses in between each question.

Mom tightens her hold on me, her eyes still fixed on mine. I drop my gaze to my feet and stare at my worn-out sneakers where a few drops of blood have dried on my right shoe. I try to scrape it off with my heel. The rusty color makes my stomach turn.

"So where's Ollie?" Milo asks again, this time with a little more urgency. "Teresa and Matthew were here, but they just left. They wanted to be back at their house in case he showed up." He pulls his phone out of his pocket and checks the screen. "Did he already run home?"

At the mention of Ollie's parents, I turn away sharply. I think I'm going to be sick.

"Tell us what happened," Mom implores, placing a warm hand on my cheek as she tries to get me to look up at her. "Tell us how we can help you."

I feel the words pressing against the back of my throat, all my hurried explanations and desperate excuses climbing higher and higher with every silent-soaked moment until my mouth is full of all the things I can't bring myself to say.

He's gone.

I messed up.

I don't know what to do.

I'm sorry I'm sorry I'm sorry.

My breath hitches in my chest. Milo and Mom hold perfectly still as if they're afraid that one single movement from them will startle me and send me running. I know they're waiting for my response. I can feel it in their hesitation, in the pause that's just begging to be filled.

"Gemma?" Mom asks quietly, her shaking arms still laced around my shoulders.

I swallow everything down, even the apologies because saying them out loud would make it more real, and I refuse to believe that he's gone for good, that I can't fix this. I know I have so many things to apologize for, but losing Ollie won't be one of them. So I ignore the stinging in my eyes and the sharp pain in my rib cage just waiting to be acknowledged.

I can break down later.

I can fall apart after I bring him home.

"I need more of that mixing." I spit the words out as quickly as I can and turn toward the house, kicking aside a tipped-over lawn chair in my rush to get back inside and out of the yard. Everything around me is a brutal reminder of what happened last night: the charred and ripped-up lawn; the fence, splintered and scattered; the pool, half-drained and dull in the gray morning light. The hollowness in my chest expands, like the yawning entrance to a deep, dark, and lonely place. I grit my teeth and shudder against the feeling, running even faster.

"The sleep mixing?" Milo calls after me. "Why? Gemma, stop, wait up—" I hear him and Mom stumbling in their efforts to keep up, but I don't slow down my pace until I nearly run straight into my Aunt Libby.

She's seated on the back patio, her posture stiff with her knees tucked tightly into her chest. A plaid blanket hangs off one shoulder as if someone draped it over her but she never bothered to pull it up around herself. I stare at the fallen corner of the blanket, limp and lifeless. Libby's eyes flick up to mine, and I freeze. The moment her gaze catches mine, flashes of red color my vision—a blurry, confusing snare of nightmare and ruin.

I want to squeeze my eyes shut, but I know that won't help the images go away. I see the shape of my grandmother's body falling to the ground, her hand tapping once on her chest, just over her heart, the way she always did when she looked at me. I feel myself back on the floor of the Dreamscape, crawling away from the trailing ends of the red thread, trying to outrun its coaxing lure to take hold and just be done with it.

Break the Claimings, it hissed relentlessly. *Unleash us unleash us unleash us.*

I shake my head to rid myself of the noise, but the whispers are gone. The only voice inside my head is mine; there's no magic left in me to sing, scream, or sigh. The last image I see is of Ollie holding the thread of my magic, that far-off look on his face as he undid the knot that tethered me to the Dreamscape, and to him, the whole scene painted sloppily in red.

No.

But this isn't a nightmare. I know that because no matter how scary a nightmare is or how awful and unending it feels, I always wake up in the morning. I lie there in my bed with the leftover fear clinging to me, hot and sticky, and with every relieved blink of my eyes and every shallow breath in my chest, I repeat in my mind: *you're safe—it wasn't real.*

But this is. I can't pinch myself awake or sink into my pillows with a sharp and shaky sigh. This is a nightmare that's bled into my waking hours. All it takes is just one look at Libby's hollow expression, and I'm reminded of the reality of everything that I've lost. The hard facts, the inarguable truths.

I am awake and Ollie isn't here.

I am awake and my grandma is gone.

My breath stutters as I open my mouth, willing myself to say something to Libby, but she looks away before I have the chance to form any kind of sentence. I jump when Milo grabs onto my arm. He pulls me away from Libby who's returned to staring off at the mountains vacantly.

Mom comes up behind me and squeezes my hand. "Why don't you take your sister inside," she says to Milo as if I'm not even here. "Have her sit down and get her something to drink."

"Then we'll call the Cades and have them come over," he adds. "Ollie can help Gem."

My throat squeezes shut at the sound of his statement said so confidently. *Of course Ollie's home. Of course he can help.* I open my mouth to correct him, to tell him the truth, but the words get lost again, too hard to set free in the face of Milo's surety.

Mom offers me an anxious look before crouching down to talk to Libby, her voice a soft and soothing murmur in the background as she tries to coax her back into the house. The rain falls harder as her eyes fill with tears.

I let Milo pull me through the back sliding door, flinching as the cool air from the kitchen washes over me. "I need more of that mixing," I start to say, but my words and my feet stop short at the sight in front of me.

Pots are still stacked next to the burners, crusted over with leftover mixings and congealed imaginings that Grandma never got to finish. Half-baked ideas and concocted schemes. Her jars are lined up neatly on the counter, ready for labels with inventive names to confuse the reader and make her laugh; funny ways to flash her magic without showing her hand, like a clever card trick to the untrained eye. I keep expecting her to round the corner, halfway through a reprimand meant just for me, her busy hands reaching for her gingham apron.

The kitchen table creaks as I lean heavily against its side, waiting for the room to stop spinning. My hand recoils when it grazes the cold edge of one of her knives left out next to a cutting board covered in piles of ginger peels and garlic bulbs. I take in deep lungfuls of the fragrant air, wondering what she was in the middle of making.

"Should we maybe..." Milo starts to say, his voice low and gravelly as he gestures to the mess in the kitchen.

"Don't," I whisper. "Please. Not now." For once, I don't know what to say to him. I don't know any words of comfort or how to offer any kind of apology that will erase what's been done. I glance to my other side, expecting to see Ollie. He would already be looking at me before I'd even turned my head. He had that way of knowing when I needed him before I knew it myself. Call it years of friendship, call it empathy and awareness—I just call it Oliver.

He would know what to say.

"Gem, come on." Milo takes me by the shoulders, his tone toeing the line between concerned and frustrated. "You've got to talk to me. Nobody knows what's going on. I'm trying to remember..." He pauses, screwing up his face as he concentrates. He closes his eyes and inhales sharply before letting the air slowly escape from between his lips in a drawn-out sigh. I pull against the strength of his grip until he quietly says, "All I remember is... the bonfire last night. And seeing you and Ollie together..." His shoulders stiffen as he cracks his eyes open to look at me warily.

I glance down at my feet, unable to meet my brother's gaze, my cheeks flushing at the mention of the memory.

Milo clears his throat. "And James," he rushes on. "I remember James coming here and saying all this crazy stuff about you and magic and—" He stops talking when he notices me stiffen. "Hey, it's okay," he says, wrapping his arm around me.

All I can do is shake my head. I can't stop picturing James's glowing green hands grabbing onto Grandma's shoulders, or the rage on his face and the madness darkening his eyes.

"There hasn't been any sign of him or his creepy friends for hours." Milo's expression hardens into something fiercely determined. "I won't let him come near you ever again, okay?"

I wish I could believe that.

After a quiet minute, he steps away and rubs his jaw, looking exhausted. "But that's all I remember, Gem. That's when things get fuzzy. I can't pull out the details. All I know is I was poisoned, you were poisoned, Mom flooded the backyard, and Grandma..." His voice cracks at the end, and he doesn't cover it up or cough it away; he lets it splinter right on the edge of the word. "Well, you know." He blinks rapidly, looking around at the mess in the kitchen. "I just don't know *why* any of this happened."

His gaze drifts over my head to where Mom is still on the patio trying to get Libby to answer or get back on her feet. It's strange to see Milo's normally laughing face so serious. I hardly recognize him in the sharp edges of his expression, the downward tug of his mouth. "So tell me what happened," he pleads, his focus landing back on me.

My heart thumps erratically, filling my body with a frantic hum and a new surge of tentatively fragile hope. Because for the first time since I woke up, it hits me: Milo still can't remember the Dreamscape and all its magic, but *I can*. I remember everything. My mind spins, tumbling over the possibilities of what this means. If I can remember the Dreamscape, then maybe I still have my magic. Maybe the magic that Ollie took from me was just the Elemental, Casting, and Mixing magic that never belonged to me in the first place.

Maybe I can go back and make things right. My fragile hope rattles around inside me, making it nearly impossible for me to think about anything else.

I grab onto that hope with both hands and refuse to let go.

With an impatient gesture, I tug on the corner of the envelope sticking out of the back pocket of his jeans, the word *Dreamscape* scrawled across the front in my messy handwriting. "There's no time to explain, just read this." I push myself roughly away from the table and rip open the pantry door.

The smell of the long and narrow room hits me right in the face, more forceful than any slap. Everything in here smells like her. I swallow thickly and breathe in deeply. *One, two, three...* The lingering scent of sage when she would tie a scarf around her knotted hair... *four, five, six...* The familiar feel of her hands, rough and stained, offering me a wooden spoonful... *seven, eight, nine...* Her eyes finding mine right before she—

Ten. No.

I can break down later.

I can fall apart after I bring him home.

My jaw aches from holding it all in. A human body wasn't made to contain this much feeling. It needs an escape, a release. My eyes want to break first, the tears want to fall, but I'm afraid if I let them out, they'll never dry up. I inhale slowly through my mouth, avoiding all the assaulting scents of memories. Of home.

I slowly walk down the length of the pantry, pausing to read each label on the countless number of jars, but I hardly register a word. All I see is her cramped scrawl, so similar to mine. I grab jar after jar, carefully cradling each one in my hands—everything from allergy remedies to stain removers. I pass vials full of ultra-violet liquids with labels boasting promises ranging from uncontrollable laughter to the cure for a woman's "monthly woes." A frustrated noise escapes my mouth. It's impossible to find anything in here. Grandma's organizational system only made sense to her, and she liked it that way.

"I remember now," Milo says from behind me. I glance over my shoulder to see his tall frame filling up the entrance to the pantry where he carefully folds the letter back inside its envelope and slides it into his pocket. "I remember the Dreamscape and the threads..." He trails off, looking at my now-empty wrist that used to be circled in green, purple, and gold—the colors of the three branches of magic. "I remember when..." He shuffles his feet, looking uncomfortable.

When you let everything unravel, he means to say, but he doesn't. He won't blame me. He's a better person than I am; he's always been that way. I'd be raging. I'd be smashing bottles and screaming that it's all his fault.

"So what happened to that magic?" he asks, pointing at my wrist.

I stare down at the blank stretch of skin along with him before tucking my arm behind my back and muttering a quick and emotionless, "It's gone."

"What do you mean—"

"I need to find more of that mixing," I mumble, more to myself than to him, spinning on my heel and returning to my search of the shelves that line the walls.

"But why? You just got back. Besides, that was the last bottle." He points to an empty spot on the shelf right above my head. "There aren't any left."

My stomach drops. "Are you sure? There has to be more." I stand on my tiptoes and reach a hand up onto the dusty shelf. Nothing.

Milo pulls me to a stop, his evident exasperation matching mine. "Were you the one always messing around in here, or was it me? Trust me, I know her inventory."

"I need to fall asleep *now*. I need to get back to Ollie!"

Milo's hand falls limply back to his side. "What do you mean you need to get back to Ollie? He's still in the Dreamscape?" he asks, his brow puckering.

The words start to come, but soon enough I'm choking on them. I stutter, then close my mouth again. A branching darkness cracks through me. It starts in my chest and spreads through my limbs, rooting me to the spot. "Yes," I confess. My entire world seems to hinge on that one little word. *Yes*, he's still there. *Yes*, it's my fault. *Yes*, I'm going to bring him home.

A sudden trilling sound fills the room, startling me. I slide my phone out of the pocket of my dress and stare at the screen as it continues to ring. Milo grabs the phone out of my hand to see who's calling, but the knowing expression on his face tells me that he already knows. The ringtone blares through the stuffy space. I'm surprised it doesn't shatter every glass jar and vial with its piercing, unending song. Neither of us moves to answer the call.

Milo's phone rings immediately after mine finishes. I force myself to look up. His amber eyes are sharp on my face, his mouth a tight thin line. "We'll figure this out," he says quickly before tapping his phone and holding it up to his ear. "Teresa," he states quietly. No hello. No goofy preamble. Milo cutting himself short is like salt in an open wound.

The sound of her frantic voice surrounds me. I can't hear the words, but I can hear the tenor: worried and anxious; she sounds just like Ollie when he's in one of his fretful states. My whole body goes cold at the thought. Milo turns his back on me and speaks softly into the phone.

Mom leans into the doorway of the pantry. "Do you want to eat something and then we can talk?" she asks, her voice thick with concern. "You look like you're about to topple over, honey. Come on, I'm going to fix something for Libby—"

I listen to my brother quietly talking on the phone, delivering the bad news to Teresa that her son hasn't come home. Over my mom's shoulder, I watch Libby slowly sink into a kitchen chair as far away from Grandma's empty seat as possible, her head tucked into her arms and resting on the table.

Defeated. Everyone is utterly defeated.

Desperation flares through me hot and wild. I can't just do *nothing*. I can't sit around here and wait until I fall asleep tonight. I spin around and grab the phone out of Milo's hand. "Hey—" he starts to say, but I'm already halfway out the pantry door.

"Teresa," I say quickly, "here, talk to my mom. It's going to be okay, I promise."

I don't wait to hear her response. I toss the phone to my mom who shoots me a confused look before pressing the phone to her ear.

"Come on," I say to Milo, yanking him by the arm down the hall and up the stairs at a sprint.

"What are we doing?" he says in between labored breaths. "You're acting crazy."

I only stop running once we've reached my bedroom where everything is precisely the way I left it. My bed is still unmade. The laundry remains unfolded in the basket on the floor. Even my music is still playing on the speaker I forgot to turn off yesterday. An old jazz standard croons through the silence of my bedroom; it's a song Ollie used to sing with his mom when they did the dishes together. I used to tease him about it.

I unplug the speaker with a single tug of the cord, then slam the door shut and turn to face my brother. "I need you to put me to sleep. Right now."

CHAPTER TWO
GEMMA

For once my brother is truly speechless. He stares at me blankly, his mouth pulled into a worried knot of a frown. "But... I don't know how."

"I want you to cast inside my mind and make me fall asleep."

Milo reels back, shaking his head. "Whoa, no way. You know I can't do that."

I flop down on my bed, grabbing one of my pillows and hugging it tightly to my chest. "Says who? Entering someone's mind is only frowned upon if it's done without permission, right? Well, you have my permission."

"That's not the only reason, and it's not just 'frowned upon,'" he mutters with a slight roll of his eyes as he sits down on the end of my bed with a sigh. "It's just not something Casters are supposed to do. The kind of casting that begins in one mind and ends in another is dangerous. Basically, the possibilities for what could go wrong are endless."

Casting has never made sense to me. And the more Milo explains it, the less I understand. I try not to let my impatience show as I grip the edge of the blanket on my bed and say, "If it's so dangerous then how come you and Libby went inside Teresa's and Matthew's minds to restore their memories?"

He tilts his head to the side, his dark blond hair flopping over his forehead. "Well, it was easier and safer then because they were sedated. If they would've shown any resistance, that day could've gone in a very different direction. If you're trying to mess with someone's mind while they're conscious and not so easily compliant, things get a lot more complicated. Besides, I was there strictly to observe, not to change anything. Libby was the one doing the heavy lifting."

I'll never forget watching her break the casting over Ollie's parents' memories. How her hands shook, her breathing fast and ragged. The way she sank into her chair, completely wilted, after it was finished, too tired to even be shocked by the hard-earned truth that Ollie was adopted.

My bed creaks as I sit up swiftly, swinging my feet over the edge to sit next to my brother, dropping all semblance of patience. Every second away from Ollie feels like another second wasted. "But once Aunt Libby went into Dad's mind—she told us herself—and everything turned out fine!"

Everything turned out fine! The words are so untrue it's almost laughable. The night that Libby looked inside our father's mind and found a confusing tangle of obsession, a volatile mess of justification and regret, was the same night that our dad went into the Dreamscape and never came back. I squeeze my pillow more tightly to my chest, hoping that Milo isn't remembering the same haunted look on Libby's face that I am.

He scoffs. "Libby was lucky, not to mention way more experienced than me."

I open my mouth to retort, but before I can, there's a knock at my door. Milo and I both stiffen, our faces frozen in twin expressions of dread. If Mom overheard our conversation, she's absolutely going to lose it.

"Are you two all right?" she calls through the door.

Thankfully, she just sounds concerned, not suspicious. Milo deflates in relief. I shove myself off the bed and crack the door open. "We're fine, Mom."

She tries to push the door open wider, but my foot holds it in place. "Can I come in?"

"We're just talking."

"I can talk with you if you'd—"

"We just need some space right now." I force myself to say the words even though I know they'll hurt her.

Sure enough, Mom's face crumples, her chin quivering as her hand falls away from the door. "I see. Well, you know where to find me."

I want to throw my arms around her neck and sob. I want her to tell me it's going to be okay even though it doesn't feel like it will. I want my Mom to swoop in and save the day, but instead I'm on one side of the door and she's on the other.

After another long look at me, she starts to walk away but stops before she reaches the end of the hall. "The Cades asked for you and Milo to come over as soon as you can," she adds. "Don't make them wait." And with that, she rounds the corner and disappears.

I stay by the door, listening for the sound of her feet on the stairs before turning back to Milo. He's collapsed on my bed with his hands pressed to his face. "You know Mom will go ballistic if she finds out what we're trying to do," he mumbles. "Mind magic is serious, Gemma."

Guilt makes my words sharper than I intend them to be. "Then let's make sure she doesn't find out. This is Oliver we're talking about," I say emphatically. "It's worth the risk. You know he'd do the same for us."

Ollie—always cautious Ollie—would do anything for us. He would push his fear to the side, he would dream up impossible magic.

He already did.

Milo sits up and releases a shuddering breath. "You're right," he says quietly, coming to stand next to me. "We need to at least try."

He doesn't tell me to lie down or give me any explanation about what he's going to do; he doesn't even warn me that he's about to begin. He just squares his shoulders and reaches his hands out, grasping the sides of my head in his grip, the soft golden glow from his fingertips illuminating the grim but determined look on his face. Rain patters gently against my window, but I can hardly hear it over the pounding of my heart.

Milo mumbles a stream of words in the Language, his eyes closing. The moment his casting begins, my vision starts to blur. Everything in the room seems to darken, taking on a strangely muted hue. Panic sears through me, white-hot and crackling. My feet shift restlessly on the rug as if begging me to bolt. My stomach churns as the current from his casting passes from his hands and into me like static electricity.

"Gemma, hold still and concentrate," he admonishes with his eyes still closed. "You've got to let me in. Don't block me out or this will never work."

"I'm trying," I whisper, my mouth suddenly going dry. I close my eyes, hoping that with fewer distractions I'll be able to focus, but if anything, the darkness is worse. Milo's magic relentlessly tugs on me, the humming sound of it ringing in my ears and leaving my skin crawling.

"Don't think about me, think about Ollie," he says, but this time I hear his voice inside my mind rather than out loud. My back goes rigid, and I try to jerk my head out of his grasp. "Try to relax."

But the more space his casting occupies inside my head, the more impossible it is to relax. The stronger his presence becomes, the harder it is to hold onto myself. I know Milo isn't trying to hurt me, I know he's just doing what I asked him to do, but everything about this feels wrong. I feel too seen, too exposed, too raw and ripped open. All the overwhelming guilt and grief that I've carefully packed away rises to the surface, unboxed and out in the open, their contents spilling out all over my thoughts for my brother to see.

My eyes snap open. "I can't do this," I say, trying to take a step back.

"It's okay, Gem," Milo reassures me, but his voice sounds strained. His eyes are still squeezed shut and sweat is beading on his forehead. "I've almost got it."

Then he mutters a word in the Language that I don't understand, but it sounds exactly like how it feels to fall asleep—slow and heavy, lavender-scented and sweet. My body stills as the word washes over me, quieting my panic and calming my urge to run. My eyes strain against the sudden onset of exhaustion, every blink growing longer and longer until the silent hush of my room slides into the liquid space of falling asleep. My mind gives one final lurch, one last feeble attempt at staying awake, but my eyes stay closed, and then...

Total darkness.

I open my eyes, but I can feel that I'm still asleep. A feeling of lucidity washes over me from head to toe. It's that strange awareness of knowing you're in a dream while it's happening—not quite there, not quite here, but in between.

Everything is gray and misty as if a slow-moving fog has rolled in with no plans of leaving any time soon. I turn my head from side to side, trying to get a better look at my surroundings, but there's nothing else to see. It reminds me of how it felt to wake up inside the Dreamscape, only this time, it isn't iridescent and covered in stars. This time it's nothing but muted stillness. Even my heartbeat sounds sluggish and dull. My skin looks mottled and lifeless in this light, less substantial than smoke.

"Ollie?" I call out. But the sound seems to die before it even leaves my lips. "Are you here?"

Silence.

"Ollie!" I call out again. I try to run but there's nowhere to go. My limbs feel numb and useless as I slog through the mist, unable to see if I've even moved at all. "Ollie, where are you?"

More silence.

My breath hitches as fear sinks deep into the pit of my stomach. It's not just the lack of color or the muffled silence. It's the creeping feeling of dread that's snaking its way up my spine, leaving me feeling cold and completely alone.

This is a place of nothingness.

Every part of me wishes this was just a dream, that I'd fallen asleep and my brain had gifted me this chance at peaceful oblivion. I want to pretend that this place isn't real, but somehow I know that it is. Because I can *feel* what's out there, even if I can't see it. The hum is there, a slight pulsing undercurrent that's nearly undetectable.

Magic.

The hum is faint but familiar, like the touch of Ollie's hand on the small of my back or the soft press of his lips against mine. I can barely feel it, but it's enough for me to know that he's out there. The tips of my fingers tingle in recognition, and that's when I know for certain: I'm on the outside of the Dreamscape. I'm not allowed in, but I'm not allowed to leave either.

I'm here, I'm there, I'm nowhere—and it feels like a punishment.

I swat at the half-shadows, scrubbing at them like a fogged-over mirror, but nothing changes. I try calling out Ollie's name again, but the gray gloom swallows it whole the second it falls from my mouth. The back of my throat starts to ache and my eyes sting from all the unshed tears.

It feels like I've been trapped in this colorless place for hours, but it's impossible to tell how long it's been. I scream for Milo to wake me up, to stop his casting and get me out of here, but he doesn't answer. That tiny flicker of hope I'd held onto starts to waver the longer I stand here motionless in the fog. I'd foolishly clung to the belief that if I could remember the Dreamscape, then maybe I could still go back, maybe I could still right this wrong and bring Ollie home.

But I was wrong.

Instead of a sky full of stars and his arms thrown around me, I'm here in a half-place that hardly exists at all, with my own arms folded tightly over my chest because that hollowness inside me has expanded past the point of containment, and if I don't hold myself together, who will?

All I wanted was more magic. So I took it, and then I lost everything. Now I'm suffocated by the very walls I used to hold up. The pale mist swirls, obscuring my sight and pressing against me as solid as if I was standing in front of a door, looming and locked—a door to which I used to hold the keys.

The irony isn't lost on me.

I start to laugh, the sharp sound breaking free from my chest, but by the time it reaches my ears, it's a sob. I sit down in the nothingness and wrap my arms around my knees, waiting for it to be over.

Just breathe, Gemma girl. Just breathe through it. It'll pass, I imagine my grandma saying to me. I can almost hear her whisper sliding against my ears.

No, it won't, I want to yell back. It won't pass.

I inhale, I exhale. I inhale, I exhale. And the night stretches on.

There's still no sign of Oliver.

With a gasp, I open my eyes. It takes me a moment to realize where I am. I feel groggy and muffled, and the way the weak light filters in through my curtains, painting my room in various shades of gray, makes my mouth go dry. I'm lying on my bed in my white dress with my sneakers still on my feet. My eyebrows pinch together; why did I fall asleep with my shoes on? I stretch out my legs and groan. My muscles ache as if I'd just finished running a marathon.

My desk chair tips over with a loud thud as Milo jumps to his feet. "You're okay," he breathes, rushing to kneel by the side of the bed. "I was beginning to wonder if you'd ever wake up." He tries to make it sound like a joke, but his face is too drawn to find any humor in it. He looks completely worn out.

Then I remember: the gray place, the nothingness, the failed rescue attempt.

"What—what happened? How long was I out?" I rasp, propping myself up on my pillows.

He hands me a cool glass of water that was sitting on my nightstand, then rests his forehead against the side of the bed and sighs into my comforter. "After you fell asleep, I carried you over to your bed because I wasn't sure how long the casting would last, and I wanted to make sure you had enough time to do whatever you needed to do..." He pauses and waits for me to fill the silence with an explanation.

My stomach clenches at the thought of describing where I went and what I saw, the cold, overwhelming emptiness that surrounded me. I shudder before taking a long sip of water, draining half the glass. "What time is it?" I ask, avoiding his questioning gaze.

"6:30."

"AM or PM?"

He stands up and twitches my curtain to the side so I can see the lengthening shadows covering the mountains along with the heavy blanket of thick, dark clouds. "In the evening. You've been asleep since I did that casting on you this morning."

I nearly slept the whole day away. My eyes widen as I sit up straighter. "Where's Mom, did she—"

"She came back and checked on us a bunch of times, but I just told her you were sleeping," he says, chewing on the inside of his cheek. "Which, technically, you were." His shoulders sag under the weight of his lie. "She bought it, of course, since you looked like the walking—" He snaps his mouth shut and stares at his feet, looking abashed.

You looked like the walking dead is what he meant to say. But those aren't the kind of things you say when death has just passed over your home, when it's still hovering on the periphery of every thought and clinging to every shadow.

"Anyway, she was worried about you, but she's also trying to help Libby out too. It's a lot," he says, rubbing his forehead anxiously as he paces around the room. "Gem, you really scared me. When you didn't wake up, I thought that I must've done something wrong with the casting and that maybe I put you in a coma or—"

"Milo, I'm fine," I say, setting the glass of water back down and running a hand through my damp hair. My other hand plucks at the fabric of my dress; I'm completely drenched in sweat.

"After a couple of hours, I tried to wake you up," he says, "but you kept rolling away and thrashing around. You were burning up, almost like you had a fever or something. And you were talking in your sleep." His mouth puckers into a frown. He's looking at me with the same expression he usually reserves for our mom when she's trapped at the bottom of one of her own nightmares. Memories of the two of us taking shifts with her as she cried in her sleep fly past me in a single blink.

I swallow roughly. "What did I say?"

"You kept saying his name."

I avoid his eyes and he avoids mine as old secrets and freshly hurt feelings stretch out between us, leaving us awkward in the soft evening light. We still haven't talked about how I hid my feelings for Ollie from him or how I snuck around behind his back all summer. It shouldn't even be an issue after everything else that's happened, but here we are, trapped in a silence too full of all the things we left unsaid.

"Did you see Ollie?" Milo's voice sounds small.

"No."

"Well, what did you see?"

It's a harmless question, and one that I was expecting him to ask, but his apprehensive face makes me feel like the walls of my room are closing in on me—I have to get out of here. I take a breath and stand on aching legs, looking around for my running shoes.

"Gem? What did you see?" he asks again, this time more firmly.

"I don't want to talk about it." I crouch down next to my overflowing laundry basket and pick through the clothes, searching for a pair of running shorts and a tank top.

"Gemma." Milo tugs on my arm and pulls me back up, turning me to face him, his cheeks stained a frustrated shade of pink. I try to shove him off, but he only tightens his grip.

"I said, I don't want to talk about it." It's getting harder to breathe. Claustrophobia leaves my heart pounding and my palms sweating. I can't handle being in this house for another second. I can't stand here and tell Milo that I don't have any magic left in me. I can't find the words to tell him that I have no clue how to bring Ollie home.

I just can't.

"Well, obviously something was wrong with my casting. Maybe tonight when you go to sleep, you'll—"

"No, it's not your fault. You didn't do anything wrong." I hesitate before forcing myself to say the words. "It just didn't work."

"But why didn't it work?" Milo releases my arm and walks back over to my desk, picking up the Dreamscape letter. "I thought you went there every time you fell asleep?"

"I do—I did—I don't know anymore." I yank open my top dresser drawer and search through the chaos of mismatched socks for a pair I can run in.

"Come on, you've barely said a word since you woke up!" he says, pulling me away from my dresser and shaking me slightly. "You have to give me *something*—" His words are cut off when a hot flare emanates from his palm, sending a flash of amber sparks flying out of his fingertips.

"Stop!" I choke the word out, unable to say more. I jerk away, my heart in my throat as I stare at the nearly singed straps of my dress.

Milo holds his hands up, this time his face flushing with embarrassment. "I'm sorry, I'm sorry." He shoves his still-glowing hands into his pockets. "I'm having a hard time controlling myself after... after everything," he finishes with a defeated shrug of his shoulders. "But I would never try to hurt you. You know that, right?"

I nod and turn back to my dresser, grabbing the first socks my hands touch and feeling ridiculous for my overreaction. I don't know how to explain to my brother that it's not him that I'm afraid of. That's not the reason my heart is beating out of my chest. I was afraid of the hum, the pulse I felt when the sparks flew from his fingers.

"It will end with the one who holds all magic in her hands." The words James said to me that night echo dully in the hollow place of my chest where my magic used to live. The frantic energy that I'd felt this morning—the urgency to act, to move, to make things right—slowly dissipates as my new reality sinks in with the setting of the sun. As all that grief I'd buried deep down comes bubbling to the surface.

I close my eyes, and for a moment, everything is red.

But when I open my eyes a second later, it's still just me and Milo, standing together in my room and feeling a million miles apart. He rubs the back of his head, messing up his hair and looking utterly miserable, which is so unlike him it makes me ache. I elbow him in the side to let him know he's forgiven.

"Nothing," I finally answer him. "I saw absolutely nothing."

He gives me a long searching look before turning and walking out of my room. I hear his door shut softly across the hall. Guilt sours my stomach. I better get used to the feeling; I don't think it's going away anytime soon.

My gaze lands on the neon pink of my trail shoes sticking out from under my bed. I grab my running clothes and change as quickly as possible, throwing that tattered white dress into the depths of my closet so I don't have to look at it anymore. Snagging a hair tie off my wrist, I gather my short dark strands into the elastic before shoving my feet into my shoes.

Avoiding all the squeaky floorboards, I carefully sneak down the hallway, nearly making it past my mom's bedroom, but her door is cracked open, and she must've been waiting for me because the moment my foot touches the top of the staircase, I hear her voice call out, "Gemma, come here."

I bite back my excuses and push her door open further, hovering on the threshold. Mom and Libby look up from where they're seated at the end of her bed.

"Did you sleep well?" Mom asks, her keen eyes examining. Her dark hair has fallen from its normally high bun, frizzing around her face from the humid rainy air. The lines around her mouth appear more pronounced than they did yesterday. Libby sniffs and wipes her face, looking sunken and small.

I feel exactly how she looks.

"Yep. I slept fine," I say through my teeth.

Mom stands and holds her arms out to me. I want more than anything to collapse into her. To have her tell me that it's not my fault and I'm not a monster.

But I wouldn't believe a word of it. It would all be a lie.

"I'm just going for a quick run," I say, my feet angling back toward the stairs.

"Why don't we go have some dinner? Or you could come in and talk for a bit?" She holds out her hand as an offering, but I back up another step, giving her a weak smile in return. She drops her hand.

"I just want to be alone right now," I mumble, which couldn't be further from the truth, but I know what I deserve.

Mom's face falls. She tries to pick it back up before I can see her disappointment, but it's there all the same. "I'm here," she says with a glance at Libby, who's staring at the rug on the floor. "We're *both* here for you."

Libby says nothing. She just turns her head in the other direction.

I give them one last stiff smile before thundering down the stairs. Rain pounds on all the windows in a steady, unrelenting rhythm. I find myself feeling jealous of the rain and the way it freely falls. I wish I could. But I don't trust myself to. The last time I fell apart changed everything.

I can't ever lose control like that again.

I yank open the front door and bolt into the downpour without looking back. My house is haunted now. Everything there reminds me of him or her, and if I don't get out now, I'll end up floating along like a ghost next to their memories. Not quite living, but definitely left behind.

So I close my eyes against the rain and do what I do best.

I run.

CHAPTER THREE

OLLIE

OLLIE?
Gemma's voice reverberates through the cavern, the surprise in her tone a lingering echo. I close my eyes and hold onto the sound of her saying my name until it fades away. Until there's nothing left but my breathing and my still-racing heart.

The sudden hush is deafening. Only moments before, the Dreamscape was shaking, stars were falling, threads were flying—it had felt like the world was breaking. But now? Everything's strange and eerily still, the sky an unbearably quiet midnight blue.

I used to think I liked the sound of silence.

Panic slowly spreads through my body, leaving me shaky and fumbling. There's a weird taste in my mouth, metallic and sharp, like the scent of pennies. I slowly lower myself to the iridescent floor, barely making it before my legs give out and I crash down in a heap.

I don't bother getting up.

I remember learning about adrenaline in my eighth grade biology class. The fight-or-flight response. I close my eyes and imagine the pages of my notebook, each one carefully labeled and transcribed. I mentally trace the shape of my handwriting as I go through the checklist in my mind: burst of adrenaline? Check. Shallow breathing? That too. Flushed skin, rapid heart rate, and trembling to top it off? Check, check, and check.

I'm clearly suffering from an adrenaline aftershock. Putting a name to what I'm experiencing almost helps it feel a little less overwhelming. Almost, but not quite. And it only solidifies my theory: Gemma and Milo—notorious adrenaline junkies—are insane. Why would anyone voluntarily *choose* to feel this way? I turn my head to the side, already opening my mouth to ask her, only to snap it shut a second later.

Gemma's not here, but that doesn't stop me from mentally playing out the conversation we'd have, like watching a performance on a stage. I'd tell her she's crazy, she'd tell me I'm too afraid, and then she'd laugh and dare me to do something stupid that she knew I wouldn't be able to refuse. And it's not just because I want to save face or appear braver than I am. No, that's not it at all.

It's because I can't say no when she looks at me like that.

I blink and the image fades away. The lights dim on the stage, the curtain swings shut, and no one comes out for an encore.

I shake out my hands, my fingers still tingling from the feel of her magic. From the feel of her hand in mine. Without me consciously deciding to, my mind replays my last memory of Gemma; her eyes glazed over and her mouth popped open in disbelief as I reversed the knot on her thread, releasing the hold her magic had over her.

Stop. Too much. It hurts. Retreat, my whole body signals to me. My chest constricts, making it harder to breathe, but this time I don't think it's from my fight-or-flight response. Left alone in the quiet, the whiplash of my impulsive decision leaves me feeling dizzy. I'm spinning like a top, trying to find a landing point, circling circling circling—

Only now my landing point is gone.

I sit up in a rush and slide my glasses off, rubbing my face with my hands. *What was I thinking?* I stripped Gemma of her magic, and now I don't know what's going to happen next. Obviously, I'm stuck here. I don't know how to leave the Dreamscape without her, and I don't know how to control it. The two of us were so intricately tied to this place that every time we fell asleep, we ended up here. It just happened—we never had a choice. *Magic calls to magic*, Gemma always said. As if that explained anything at all.

So how do I wake myself up from this nightmare?

It's not like I can remove my own magic. I'd need my magic to do so—a vicious cycle that never ends. I hang my head between my knees and sigh as a heavy feeling of resignation washes over me. I understand the weaving; I've held the threads in my hands and tangled my fingers in their power, so I know the kind of balance that's required for the Dreamscape to function as it should. The kind of balance that's required for me to be able to come and go.

It takes two—contain and release.

And without the two? Total lockdown.

Until when? Who knows—maybe whenever a new Threader is Claimed. I swallow against the painful tightening of my throat and choke out a strangled laugh. The magic will catch me in its grasp long before I ever see that day.

The steep cavern walls loom over me, the inescapable gleam of their silver threads shining on my skin, leaving me claustrophobic and clammy. I tug on the neckline of my faded blue t-shirt as the stars stare down at me in their stagnant state. It feels like the entire Dreamscape is holding its breath. A sheen of sweat covers the back of my neck and my stomach churns. All the peace I'd felt while executing my plan has completely vanished.

What was I thinking?

My heart pounds with the repetitive question, the only sound in this barren place. I just can't comprehend how I'm supposed to live under the crushing weight of this uncertainty. How do we exist from day to day and not know what's going to happen next? I marvel at the audacity of us humans, living our lives, playing our games and writing our tragedies, ambling along from one moment to the next and just... not knowing.

How do we do it?

I can't be here on my own. Maybe if I'd just—

Or if I—

I should've—

But it's impossible to finish any of those sentences. Maybes; what ifs. I'm going to drive myself crazy with thoughts like these. I rake my hands roughly through my hair and ask myself the only question that matters: is Gemma safe?

Well, she's not currently trapped in here or possessed by the red thread, so I'm willing to bet that yes, she's safe. And if that's the case, then that's all I need to know. I slide my glasses back on and nod to myself as if to signify that the issue is now closed.

But all the hairs on the back of my neck stand on end as I peer over my shoulder to see the small red tear glistening through the silver threads on the wall behind me. The violent shock of color looks out of place in the otherwise glittering and intact weaving. Even though the red thread has been quiet since the moment I removed Gemma's magic, just looking at it has me on edge. Right now, that thread is as thin and unassuming as a paper cut. A harmless irritation, unless it's left to fester.

Like an infection just waiting to spread.

I wish I could forget the way Gemma's voice sounded when the red thread spoke through her, how her eyes flashed scarlet when she looked at me. I hate that those are the last memories I have of her, lost and confused, possessed by something neither of us understood.

But can you blame us? Who can stay one step ahead of fate?

I try to summon an ounce of that courage I felt only a few minutes ago, that all-consuming clarity that I was making the right choice. Closing my eyes, I picture Gemma sprawled on the cavern floor, the red thread trailing behind her, whispering invitations of power and punishment. This time, I let my mind run wild. I don't shut down the memories or try to think of something else. I let myself remember every painful, crimson-colored second.

I knew that thing had been tormenting her for weeks, and still, I'd just stood by and watched as it slowly changed her. Chipping away at her defenses with meaningless offers and half-truths about breaking the Claimings. And the moment her grandmother died, the moment Gemma took hold of the thread and started to bind it to her, the whole truth became crystal clear. Fate wasn't offering unlimited magic for her to take, it wanted to reclaim everyone's magic for itself. It just needed a body to do so.

It needed Gemma. And it would've taken her and filled her up with magic until there was nothing left of her, just an empty shell of the girl I love. I don't understand everything that happened last night—not even close—but I do know that if the red thread had succeeded in binding itself to Gemma, that would've been the end of her. My mind conjures an image of her wide brown eyes transforming into something new, something foreign and shockingly red.

Why didn't I do more to help her?

I shake my head until the startling images vanish and my heart stops pounding. *Too far. Too much.* Breathing in slowly through my nose, I decide to employ a different strategy. I close my eyes and allow myself to remember how it felt to hold her gleaming silver thread, to see her life unfolding in bright vivid colors, every part of her radiantly rich and so full of magic. I exhale in relief. *That's* the Gemma I know, and she needed my help. So I gave her the only thing I could offer—an escape.

I did what I had to do.

But any right decision can start to feel wrong if you think about it too much. And I've got nothing but time to think. I suppress a groan; I'm dead where I stand. This is why I can't be left alone with my head. We don't get along all that well.

Pushing off the floor, I clamber back to my feet and stare up at the sky, expecting the stars to blink back in agreement with me. A billion tiny little nods of *yep, you're a goner*, but everything holds still as if it's waiting to see what I'll do next. I've always assumed the Dreamscape was alive, but I've never felt it so keenly before. My neck prickles with the sensation of eyes on me as I spin in a slow circle.

When Gemma was here, the sky was a mirror of her mood, a

reflection of her calm and her chaos. When she was mad, the air charged with electricity, the clouds billowed, and the stars fell. I remember a night when the sky was rosy and golden, cloudless and bright. It looked like a sky in love.

At least that's what I liked to tell myself. But now that she's gone and I'm here alone, the solidity of those memories feels more fragile. Like if I move too quickly, I'll outrun them. Or if I turn too sharply, they'll scatter.

After our first kiss, I never questioned Gemma's feelings for me. Not once. I trusted her fierce gaze and every stolen moment we shared. Even when she started to lose herself to the threads and the magic, I still believed in her. In us. But now there's a quiet voice, too loud in the silence, whispering through my mind and demanding to be heard: *If she really loved me, would we be in this mess? If she truly wanted me, would I be left wanting?*

I rub my palm roughly against my forehead, annoyed at how quickly I went there. If I had a watch, I'd glance at it and say, *"Well, that took all of five minutes for me to go into total dark mode. A new record."*

But I don't have a watch and time no longer exists, so there is no other mode but dark mode.

"Magic always has consequences," I mutter, then wince, marveling at the fact that I'm already talking out loud to myself. It's not a very reassuring sign. "Stupid, stupid consequences."

I stand there feeling sorry for myself for so long, even I don't want to attend my own pity party anymore, so I decide to circle the Dreamscape to see if I can finally map this place out. If I'm going to spend the rest of my life here, I might as well know the square footage. Gemma and I tried a few times before but never for long. Why would we when there were other things we could do together—

Don't go there, I beg my masochistic brain. *Please.*

The echo of my footsteps punctuates the quiet in a forcefully aggressive way.

You.

Are.

Alone.

With a sharp inhale, I start listing every U.S. president in order. After I finish that, I move on to the fifty states. Then the capitals. I run list after list of every useless trivia fact I can think of. Anything to avoid the painful truths.

I tilt my head back, my eyes roving over the complicated pattern of the weaving, searching through the threads of magic that are always within my reach but never truly in my grasp. None of this magic belongs to me, and it never did. I'm just a Threader, a gatekeeper of sorts, always on the outskirts. I chew on my bottom lip while my hand twitches at my side and let my mind wander to the quiet corners where I allow myself to wonder what would happen if I Claimed some of that magic for my own.

No, I remind myself firmly. *You saw what happened when Gemma took what didn't belong to her.* I shiver against the memories of how the magic always backfired, how it cracked her open and left her empty, ready to be taken over by the red thread. I quickly quash the thought of taking more magic before it can fully transform into an idea. A desperately foolish idea.

But clearly, I am both desperate and foolish as the disquieting stillness of the Dreamscape reminds me. Like the calm before the storm—a quiet pause that threatens more than it reassures. "No," I say again, this time out loud, with a glance over my shoulder at the dark tear in the weaving where the red thread lies silent and still. I don't want to open that door again.

I focus on putting one foot in front of the other and go back to making my mental lists.

Maximize, qi, etaerio, muzjiks.

I make lists of Scrabble words, categorizing them by point value, difficulty, number of letters, and on and on and on. But the list-making doesn't help this time. Because now there's a tiny thought left in a narrowly protected space in my brain, too delicate to handle, too translucent in its hopefulness. I try to ignore it, to dismiss it for the wishful thinking that it is, but I can't fully let it go no matter how ridiculous it might be.

Maybe there's a way out of here.

I walk for hours, or at least what feels like hours since I have no idea how time works here. I add that to my mental checklist: master the concept of time. It's impossible to know how far I've gone or if I'm just walking in an endless circle. There aren't any significant landmarks to track, and the stars are still as unchanged as a photograph. I look up at the tiny pinpricks of light, my mouth tugging into a frown. I've never seen the Dreamscape respond like this. It's never been so still for so long, and it's fraying my nerves.

I square my shoulders and keep pushing forward while that tiny, pathetically hopeful thought nestled deep inside me grows louder with every step I take.

Maybe there's a way out of here.

Maybe.

But if that was true, if there really was a way out, wouldn't my birth father have found it in the seventeen years he was trapped here? I think back to the night of my Claiming, how Ben's eyes were glazed over and white, his mouth full of whispered words, ancient and heavy, totally incomprehensible in his mutterings. The memory of him trudging through the Dreamscape with the colorless threads clinging to his body makes me shudder. He looked stooped with age, like he couldn't stand up straight under the strain of all that magic. And even once he relinquished his role as a Threader, the threads never released him. They swallowed him whole.

With a blink, the picture of my father changes to one of me, hollow-eyed and vacant.

I clench my hands into fists, my nails digging into the skin of my palms, and start listing every Major League Baseball team I can think of. But as soon as I start thinking about baseball, Milo's face flashes before me. I shake my head—baseball is not a safe subject—and scan my brain for another topic, but it's too late because now I'm thinking about home and my dad and—

The memory of my parents' faces comes crashing down on me, causing my eyes to sting. *No, not them. Don't think about that.* But the damage has already been done. My mind found the crack and now everything's spilling out: my parents sitting at the kitchen table, staring at my empty seat. Milo hugging my mom while she cries. Gemma consoling my dad with her arm slung around his shoulders.

But then the image shifts. Now they're all sprawled out on the couch, watching a Saturday baseball game. Milo hogs the bowl of chips and Gemma complains about it. My parents exchange an indulgent look that says, *kids, right?* And no one mentions me. Not even once.

My magic makes it impossible for them to fully remember me. Milo, my parents, even Gemma—eventually, they'll forget about me. It'll happen slowly at first, but then one day all the little details of our shared experiences will finally drift away until there's hardly a scrap left of me to hold onto. And maybe when they pass a guy on the street who kind of looks like me, they'll pause and feel the reverberations of a memory. Like an itch they can't quite scratch. But then they'll shrug and move on and live their lives and—

My breath leaves my lungs in a shallow huff of air. *Please, no more*, I beg myself.

The quiet sound of my footsteps fills the cavern as I trade all my wants and wishes for another mental list.

Periodic table it is.

CHAPTER FOUR
GEMMA

EVEN THE MOON is gone tonight.

The clouds have finally cleared, revealing a deep indigo sky tinged with streaks of orange from the leftover remains of a sunset already come and gone. The spiny ridge of the Superstition Mountains is sharp and unforgiving as I climb higher and higher, letting the curve of the trail lead me on. But I'm getting tired; my feet turn sloppy and slide on the wet gravel—still slippery from the day's earlier rain—sending me teetering toward the edge and dangerously close to the steep drop-off. My heart plummets in my chest, but for once it's not a thrill.

I scramble back from the incline until I'm safe on the other side of the switchback. Closing my eyes, I lean against a large outcropping of rocks and try to catch my breath. Below the mountain, the city lights sparkle throughout the valley, their yellow gleam a vague reminder that I'm not alone, even though it feels like it.

I don't remember climbing this high. Losing track of the miles was easy once my brain switched off and my body took over. I vaguely remember noticing the sun dipping lower and lower in the sky, but I hardly remember anything else about my run, just an incomprehensible blur of color. But the ache in my legs and the gnawing hunger in my stomach tells me I've been running for hours.

I go to check the time, but it's only then I realize that my pockets are empty. In my rush to get out of the house, I've left everything behind, including my phone and my earbuds. For the first time since I started running, I register the absolute silence of the desert around me. It's too quiet. I fidget on my feet as the stillness pokes and prods, willing me to give in and give up.

I feel like I've been sleepwalking. Between the dull ache of missing Ollie and these new sharp pangs of loss, my body hardly even feels like my own anymore. I've been torn open and ripped apart, and I wish I wanted to stitch myself back together again, but I'm having a hard time remembering where all the different parts of me belong. I wish I could remember the shapes and sounds of who I used to be, but the things that once mattered don't anymore. I'm not sure what to do with these new empty spaces, these unrecognizable voids. Add a piece here, throw in another there—what does it matter?

I'm a mess regardless.

Just as my heart rate finally begins to slow, I hear the sharp snap of a twig nearby, sending my pulse skyrocketing again. My back digs into the rough surface of the rock behind me as I press myself further into the shadows.

This isn't me. I've never been scared to be out alone in the desert before, but tonight it feels unfamiliar and lonely in its vastness. Going too close to the edge freaked me out, but what scares me even more was my reaction to it. I never used to be afraid of heights or edges or any kind of jump, but everything feels different now.

Risks aren't as glamorous as they used to be.

I wipe my face with my sweaty tank top, wishing the warm September air was cooler. Shaking out the stiff muscles of my legs, I reach down and touch my toes, sighing into the stretch. My legs are going to kill me tomorrow... and so is my mother. She won't be happy I've been gone so long.

I tighten the laces on my shoes and begin my descent of the mountain. But this time, the darkness makes it impossible for me to zone out as I run. Every shadow seems to linger, every noise has an echo, and I suddenly cannot be alone for one more second. The starlit miles seem to drag on and on before I finally make it to our pothole-ridden road. I hobble past the familiar houses, trying to avoid looking at the one directly across from mine, but a light in one of the front windows makes me pause.

The Cades have Ollie's room completely lit up and his curtains thrown open wide as if they're afraid he won't be able to find his way home in the dark. Like they're trying to guide him back through this simple gesture alone. I can see the deep blue walls of his bedroom, his bed made and pillows fluffed. My gaze catches on the teetering stack of paperbacks sitting patiently on his nightstand, still waiting to be read. My whole body goes numb at the sight. I quickly turn on my heel and face my own house.

All the lights are out.

I push through the front door, mud-covered and thirstier than I've ever been in my entire life.

"Gemma Fitzgerald, where have you been?"

I look up at the sound of the voice. It's not my mom scolding me, it's my brother. I almost roll my eyes at his use of my full name. "I'm fine, Milo, calm down," I croak, leaning against the door and trying not to show how badly my legs are shaking. "No need to go all paternal on me."

He's sitting alone in the dark on the living room couch, his glare illuminated by the greenish glow of his phone. "Seriously, what were you thinking? You've been gone for *hours*."

"I go on long runs all the time."

He scoffs and tosses his phone aside, blinking at me through the darkness. "Yeah, but not *all-night* runs. It's nearly 11 o'clock. How are you even still standing?"

My right leg starts seizing as if to emphasize his point. "I didn't mean to be out this late, I'm sorry," I mumble, kneading my knuckles into the muscle of my thigh.

"And you didn't take your phone or anything. We didn't know where you were or if you were okay. Did you even stop to think about how that might make us feel?" Milo's not yelling, his voice is barely above a whisper, but the sound of his quiet anger still makes me wince.

"I know, I'm sorry. I just lost track of time." I pry my running shoes off and limp over to the couch, plopping down next to him with a groan. I think my legs are officially broken. "Where are Mom and Libby?"

"They're asleep. Mom was trying to wait up for you, but she could barely keep her eyes open. I told her I'd do the honors." He scowls at me, his shoulders bunched up tight under his t-shirt. He raises his eyebrows and looks at me expectantly, releasing a sigh when I stay silent. "So, do you need anything? We can talk or—"

"No, I'm fine," I lie through my teeth, leaning back against the plush cushions. I don't know if I'll ever be able to get off this couch again.

"Then I'm going to bed. This has been one of the longest days of my life, I'm so tired—" My stomach growls loudly, interrupting him. Milo's face softens, and he shakes his head. "Come on. Up, up." He offers me his hand and pulls me to my feet. "We need to feed you."

"I'm fine, just go to bed," I protest, but he ignores me. Tucking his arm around my shoulder, he all but carries me into the kitchen, flicking on the lights with a wave of his hand before easing me onto one of the tall barstools. I try not to flinch at his casual use of magic, but Milo's knowing expression makes me think that he noticed anyway.

First, he fills up a glass of water and slides it across the counter to me. I drink the whole thing in three swallows, and he fills it up again, muttering under his breath about dehydration and electrolytes. Then, he goes to the fridge and pulls out a plate carefully wrapped in tinfoil. He sticks it in the microwave and the smell of pot roast fills the kitchen, leaving my mouth watering. "Mom made way too much food for dinner, even too much for me," he tries to joke, but his smile only lifts one corner of his mouth. "I think she just wants to keep her hands busy, you know?" The microwave *dings* and he pulls out the plate, handing it to me with a fork.

I stare at the carrots swimming in a pool of gravy and blurt out, "I'm scared to go to sleep."

Milo leans against the counter, lowering his voice to the point that it's barely audible even though we're the only ones in the room. "Does this have anything to do with what happened earlier? The mind magic?"

I swallow, and push the plate away, suddenly losing my appetite. "Yes," I whisper.

Milo pushes the plate back to me. "Eat."

Grudgingly, I pick up my fork and spear a potato while my brother stands there watching with his arms folded.

I want to tell him everything, I do. I just don't know how.

I want to tell him about the gray place and how I spent all day trying to outrun it, but then I'd have to tell him about what happened in the Dreamscape with Ollie. How it felt when I saw him standing there, holding my thread in his hands. How the magic leeched out of me, slowly, slowly until suddenly it was gone and everything felt wrong and empty.

I felt wrong and empty.

But I'd be lying if I didn't also say that I felt a little relieved.

Because trailing behind me was the one thing I couldn't outrun: fate, stark and red; its siren call to break the Claimings, to bind myself to it and become something else, something more. Someone who could take control. Someone who could punish those who deserve it. Someone unbreakable.

But when Ollie turned to look at me with my thread in his hands, his eyes brighter than the stars, his face the most determined I'd ever seen it, I wanted him to take it all away.

I'd never felt so split down the middle, so torn over two different feelings—wanting my magic and being afraid of it. I rub my hand over my chest, convinced there's a crack running right through me, but my hand just catches on the fabric of my tank top. There is no crack, it's just the guilt that's tearing me up now.

Milo waits, chewing on his cheek and looking like he wants to say something but knows he can't. This is my story to tell, and I'll tell it when I'm ready to.

And that's not tonight. The words aren't here, and I'm too exhausted to find them.

Milo's shoulders droop as if he read my mind. Maybe he did. Or maybe it's the closed-off set of my face or the curve of my shoulders, sunken in defeat. But he doesn't push me. He just waits and makes sure that I eat every last bite of my dinner, filling up my glass of water three more times. I keep my gaze fixed on my plate because if I look up at him, at all that anxious, patient concern, my dam will break.

But when he tries to fill up my plate with a second serving of pot roast, I drop my fork with a clatter and hold up my hands. "Milo, stop. I'm so full, I don't think I'll make it up the stairs."

"Please, like you were ever going to make it up anyway. You can hardly walk." He rounds the corner and offers me his arm. I take it gratefully and hop off the barstool, my breath hissing through my teeth. "Come on, Gem. Just one step at a time."

Tears prick at the back of my eyes. I don't deserve him.

We silently and slowly make our way up the stairs, my hand gripping my brother's arm as we make the climb and turn down the hall. "Wait here," he says once we reach the door to his room. He darts in and comes out a moment later with his pillow and blanket in hand. His arm loops under my shoulder as he steers me through my bedroom door.

Without another word, he shakes out his blanket and fluffs his pillow before flopping down on my floor. The tears I'm barely holding back blur my vision as I turn away and collapse onto my bed, shoving my face into my own pillow and inhaling sharply.

"I'm here if you need me," Milo whispers from his spot on the floor.

I don't answer, and I hate myself for that. I should say, "I'm here for you too," but that wouldn't be true. How can you be there for someone when you're not even there for yourself? I'm like an empty cup, all poured out and smashed on the floor, the pieces too sharp and jagged to be put back together again.

Broken.

A mere minute later, Milo's snore cuts through the quiet. I stare out my window, wondering if I can make it to sunrise, hoping I can skip the rest of this night altogether.

Just a few days ago, I was lying on my bed, unable to fall asleep because of the swooping sensation in my stomach, that almost agitating excitement from knowing I was about to see Ollie. I would fall asleep with a grin on my face and my hands twisted in the cotton of his worn-out t-shirt that I always slept in, knowing I was about to tumble headfirst into him and the Dreamscape. And now I'm lying here unable to fall asleep for a completely different reason.

Shivering, I tug my blanket up over my legs until I'm completely cocooned. I stare at the ceiling, willing myself to stay awake, but my body is so overly tired that fighting against sleep is impossible. The sound of Milo's breathing cuts through the quiet as the darkness wraps around me. I don't remember closing my eyes, but when I open them, all I see is gray.

We fall into a new routine.

Every night, I dream without dreaming. I go to the gray place and wander around aimlessly, calling out Ollie's name and waiting for the night to be over, while the hum of what used to be washes over me. Every morning, I wake up to see Milo sprawled on my floor with the Caster Chronicles cracked open on his chest like he fell asleep looking up spells. After that first night, he dragged his mattress across the hall and left it on the floor of my bedroom without me asking him to. And every morning when he wakes up, the second his eyes open, he asks me if I saw Ollie. My answer is always the same.

No.

Every day, I run until my legs give out, and every day I imagine Ollie running with me. I can almost feel him, his elbow knocking into mine as he tries—and fails—to pass me. The brush of his hand, the heat from his body, the sound of his steady breathing mixing with mine. It's all so clear, I can almost convince myself it's real. But remembering makes me feel unbearably fragile, so I turn up my music and run until the image of him drifts away, blurring into the shadows along the edges of the trail as the sun dips below the horizon.

I try to do a better job of taking care of myself so no one else has to. I remember to eat three meals a day and drink plenty of water. I make sure to take showers and help with the chores. I nod along when someone talks to me, contorting my mouth into the semblance of a smile when I have to.

Milo's a whirlwind. He's folding laundry and picking up groceries; he's doing inventory at The Mage & Sage, packaging up the last bottles of Grandma's mixings that she'd made to sell at her store. He eats standing up at the kitchen counter, not even pausing to sit down, the Chronicles propped up against the jug of orange juice while he reads in between bites. When he's not reading, he's on the phone talking to relatives or planning funeral arrangements with Mom. He looks taller. Or maybe just older. Like he aged ten years overnight.

The house is bursting with flowers of every kind as Mom gathers her best and brightest blooms for the services. She enlists me to help her out in the garden, but it's obvious that's just her excuse to try to get me to talk to her. Out under the glare of the sun, our conversations always stutter to a stop before they ever really begin. I know she's worried and that she's only trying, but this family has never been good at emotional deep dives. We'd rather laugh and cover it up with a joke or movie quote or some other evasive maneuver to distract from whatever's actually going on. Milo's practiced, I'm an expert, and my mom's the one who taught us everything she knows.

It's not her fault, not really. I know her memories are a jumbled mess after my dad. She couldn't remember his magic as a Threader and his connection to the Dreamscape, or his obsession with changing his fate. He became a phantom, a barely remembered figure who flitters in and out of her consciousness like a butterfly unwilling to land. But still, I grew up fatherless, and we barely addressed the issue at all. If that's not dysfunctional, then I don't know what is.

Sign us up for family counseling. We desperately need it.

When Mom's not in her garden, she's camped out in the kitchen, fluttering back and forth as if she's unsure what to touch or which appliances to use—this was never her domain. But she can't seem to leave this room. She wears one of the spare aprons, leaving Grandma's soiled gingham one on the hook next to the pantry door. Every day, the kitchen is overpowered with the sickly-sweet smells of cookies and brownies, layered cakes that tilt on their stands. Mom's a flour-covered sweaty mess, but she bakes as if she's determined to fill the void my grandma left behind with a mountain of cupcakes.

Everything remains uneaten on the counter.

And Libby stays in her room. Mom has me carry up trays of food to leave in front of her door, but Libby doesn't answer when I knock. Each time I walk away feeling the tiniest bit relieved that I didn't have to force my way through another stilted conversation full of awkward pauses and gaps that can't ever be filled.

How did this become our new normal?

One morning, Milo meets me in the hallway as I'm coming out of the bathroom. He blocks me in the doorway, his arms crossed and his expression resolved. "We need to go talk to the Cades, Gemma. It's been a week. They want to see you. They want to know what happened."

And so do I, I know he wants to add, but he bites his tongue and sighs instead. "I can't keep telling them you need more time," he says, lifting one shoulder in a half-shrug. "Teresa asks for you every day, you know."

My chest tightens painfully. How can I face Ollie's parents after what I've done? How can I answer their questions or offer condolences when I have no solutions, and it's my fault we're in this mess in the first place? And an even worse thought: what if *they* want to comfort *me*?

But then I think of Ollie. What would he do? After his usual cycle of avoidance and discomfort, I know he'd show up. He'd put on a brave face and quit thinking only about himself. Can't I do the same?

"Fine," I mumble, turning to follow him down the stairs. I slide my feet into my sandals while eyeing my dirt-caked running shoes waiting for me by the front door.

"Not today," Milo says, shoving me forward. "They need us."

I scowl and march past him, partially shutting the door in his face before he walks through. He coughs behind me, and it sounds an awful lot like *"rude."*

It almost makes me laugh.

I've been avoiding looking at the Cades' house all week, but now that I'm standing in front of it, I can't stop staring. Every inch of this house is covered in memories. There are three small sets of handprints in the driveway from when Matthew repaved it when we were five. There's the tidy desert landscaping where we were forced to pick weeds as punishment after we once egged Scott Tillman's house down the street. Ollie accepted the punishment even though it wasn't his idea to terrorize the neighbors, it was mine. Scott had made fun of my haircut and I was out for retribution. Ollie was the one who was freaking out the whole night that we would get caught; Milo couldn't have cared less. But that's Ollie for you—worried and loyal to a fault.

I catch my smile with my teeth before it grows into something real. My eyes flicker over to his bedroom window where the light is still on.

Milo nudges me in the back and points to the Cades' front porch. "After you."

My foot snags on the last step, and I nearly bang my shin

against the wood just like I did on the night Ollie's estranged uncle, James, followed me out on my run. The night before everything changed. I can still feel the rain, cold and dripping down my face as I scurried to get away from him. My pulse starts to race as I remember him calling after me, *"The thread told my father about you."*

I lean against the doorframe, trying to breathe through the panic, but my heart won't slow down.

"You okay?" Milo asks, holding his hand out to knock.

We never used to knock.

"I'm fine," I say, though it comes out like a whispered wish.

Milo looks unconvinced, but he knocks anyway. Ollie's mom answers in less than a second. It's as if she's been standing there, waiting for her son to walk through the front door. I try not to gape at the sight of the always immaculate Teresa Cade looking unwashed and disheveled, her auburn hair hanging limply over her shoulders, the deep frown lines etched into her face stark reminders of her worry.

Her tired eyes land on mine, and I freeze. She takes us by the hands and pulls us inside, shutting the door behind us. "Gemma," she whispers, throwing her arms around me. "You're okay. We've been so worried." She pats my back over and over as if reassuring herself that I really am here.

The guilt sends my stomach rolling; I'm definitely going to be sick. I gently push her back. "I'm sorry. I can't do this." I glance between Milo and Teresa just as Matthew comes running into the entryway, his face lit with a tender sort of hope that makes me feel even worse. I wrap my arms around myself and slowly back away, shaking my head. "Ollie should be home. Not me." I quickly turn and yank open the door so hard it slams against the wall, knocking one of their framed family photos to the ground with a shattering crash.

I run down the porch steps, tripping over the uneven mound of dirt that still sticks out weirdly across their yard from when I tried to use the Elemental magic that wasn't mine. Just more evidence of my mistakes. As if I need any reminders.

"Gemma, wait—" Teresa's soft cry rings in my ears for the rest of the day and long into the night. I swear, I can even hear it in my sleep.

In the gray place, alone as always.

Gemma, wait—

But I've never been good at waiting.

CHAPTER FIVE

OLLIE

WELL, I'VE OFFICIALLY exhausted myself.

After cycling through every topic I could possibly think of, reciting fact after fact while aimlessly wandering around the Dreamscape that never seems to end—stars and threads, threads and stars—I collapse in the middle of the cavern floor and scowl up at the dark sky, shoving my glasses up onto my forehead to rub my eyes. "You could at least give me a Claiming to tie or something," I mutter, my voice hoarse from disuse.

The stars don't even blink in response.

It's not just the depressing fact that my life is basically over that's killing me, it's the sheer boredom of waiting for *something* to happen. That's what's really going to do me in.

I sit up and cross my legs under me, tapping my fingers restlessly against the pearlescent floor, its silver light dancing under the rhythm of my touch. My gaze flits over the cavern walls, which gleam brighter than a full moon.

A slow and sorry sigh slips from between my lips. I've been avoiding the inevitable. But what's new?

I push off the floor and stand on my feet, squaring my shoulders. My steps drag as I approach the wall glistening with the threads of Gemma's magic. I pace back and forth, debating my next move. And as I stare at the wall, I finally allow myself to unpack the tentative hope I've been suppressing for who knows how long.

Maybe, just maybe, I can find my way home.

I rub my hand across my jaw as I carefully examine each fact, a meticulous study of my magic compared with Gemma's. Here's what I know: any power that I have belongs to the weaving in the stars, to the threads that bind us to magic. My magic requires me to stay here, to tie more Claimings, to succumb. My magic is like an anchor weighing me down; it doesn't provide a single escape route, and the longer I stay here, the harder it will be to leave—of that I am sure.

But Gemma's magic was different than mine. Hers wasn't dependent on the Claimings; her magic was the Dreamscape itself. It's what held me up and kept this place from collapsing every time I whispered the words, *"Tied and bound, I seal your fate."* Our magic was separate but complementary. Together, we provided the warp and weft, the impossible balance of holding on and letting go.

So if I want to get out, I'm going to need to find a crack in her magic, not mine.

With my hand extended, I slowly edge closer to the shimmering wall where the thin silver threads cascade like a waterfall. What's the worst thing that could happen? I don't find any secret backdoor and I'm stuck here forever, doomed to play out the same fate as my father before me.

That's already happening. I'm already living my worst-case scenario.

But as I hesitantly inch closer to the threads of Gemma's magic, I realize the hidden lie in my ruminations: the actual worst thing that could happen is the crushing disappointment I'd feel if I let my hopes get too high.

I honestly don't know if I'd survive that.

My hand hovers as I mull it over, weighing my extremely limited options until I inhale sharply and mumble to myself, "Come on, man. Don't overthink this." A tiny shiver of recklessness grazes against the back of my neck, sending my outstretched hand into the gossamer threads dangling in front of me.

The Dreamscape flares with a sudden burst of light as the luminescent threads latch onto me, crawling up my hands and trailing along my arms, wrapping around my chest in tight, crushing movements. Jerking back, I try to shake them off. A high-pitched buzzing fills my ears like static on a radio turned all the way up. I sway on my feet as Gemma's magic crashes into me, tangling with mine. My whole body shakes with the effort to stay upright; it's too much for one person to hold onto.

The buzzing intensifies as my hands move to pull the threads apart, but the strands are so bound together that it's nearly impossible to sort through the jumbled mess. I let out a strangled yelp when I see even more silver threads dragging behind me. They wrap around my legs and my hands, these ones falling from the sky above, so thin and translucent, it's no surprise I didn't notice them earlier.

I'm like a tiny insignificant fly trapped in the middle of the world's most intricate spiderweb.

Gemma's magic and mine.

For the first time, I truly understand why the Dreamscape needs two Threaders. Clarity consumes me even while the magic threatens to engulf me. The Dreamscape requires balance, and I'm the only one here to settle it. The scales are left tipping, sending the weight of her magic and mine tumbling into me with more force than I can handle.

"I don't want this!" I yell through the static, my stomach dipping as Gemma's magic pushes against mine in a strange and unfamiliar way. "Let me go!" I clench my jaw tightly and resume shaking the threads off, but that only makes them tighten their grip on me.

Holding my breath, I go perfectly still, trying to find some sliver of steadiness amongst the chaos as the threads continue their slow and steady strangling of me, like a snake constricting its prey. But I hold my ground and focus on the magic, *my* magic, sitting in my chest. Then with a heavy exhale I wrap one hand carefully around a fistful of gleaming silver. *"Let me go,"* I say quietly this time, the words of the Language surprising me, their cadence strange but familiar as they roll off my tongue.

At the sound of my voice, the threads start to loosen. With shaking fingers, I pry the remaining ones off before scrambling away from the wall and sprawling on the floor with a groan. The threads shimmer brightly back at me, winking under the starlight as if to remind me they're not going anywhere, and neither am I. It's only a matter of time. I turn my head and close my eyes in a feeble attempt at blocking out the overwhelming glare of the threads. But instead of the peaceful oblivion of darkness, my mind conjures the image of Ben's face when he was trapped here, his eyes milky white and unseeing, all the threads dragging behind him like shackles. Too much magic for one person to hold.

It's only a matter of time.

A bright light filters through my eyelids. Cracking my eyes open, I see one star shining brightly overhead. In a blinding flash, it bursts, and a single sky-blue thread falls slowly from its center, arcing in its downward spiral.

A Claiming waiting to be tied.

I jump to my feet, my hands flexing by my sides, tingling with the feel of magic and the urge to reach out and grab hold of the threads. Half of me wants to dismiss the feeling, to ignore my duty to the weaving and any obligation I feel to tie the Claimings. To cross my arms and turn my back in silent protest for everything that's happened to me. But the other half of me craves to feel the magic I *know*, even if I don't understand it as well as I thought I did.

I shouldn't want to get lost in the weaving, but I do.

Another thread tumbles down, this one a gleaming bright purple, and my mind is overtaken with a scattered handful of buzzing anxious thoughts, each one flying by too quickly for me to answer. *What if this is the moment the magic overtakes me? What if I can't remember how to free myself from the weaving?*

What if I don't want to?

The truth is I don't know what's going to happen, and that scares me. But the monotony of loneliness scares me even more.

I lunge forward and grip both threads in my hands, wrapping them swiftly around my forearm. They snap against my skin, giving me goosebumps, but this sensation feels mercifully familiar after that tumultuous rush I felt when Gemma's magic tried to bind with mine. I take a deep breath and prepare myself to enter the weaving, to plunge headfirst into the wonder of someone else's life.

Someone full of hope and new beginnings.

Instantly, the Claiming sweeps me up, enveloping me entirely until I feel as if I've left my body. I see a girl standing before her family, her green eyes lit by the flames of a nearby fire. She shivers with anticipation. I pull the threads together, winding them this way and that, my fingers deftly tying the knot that binds her to her magic.

And as I move the threads, her life flashes before me in a blur. I see her as she began, a tiny infant in her mother's arms, and I see her as she will end, old and gray, with withered hands and a final breath. Her magic spreads between each moment, creating a new beginning even though the ending always stays the same.

The girl beams at the small circle of people surrounding her, waving her glowing purple hands and shrieking with delight, thrilled with the limitless possibilities before her. Her magic is like an open door, a ceaseless invitation to become something more.

She's a Mixer, just like Grandma Ellen. As soon as her name crosses my mind, a new vision explodes before me, interrupting the Claiming I was witnessing.

I'm in the Fitzgeralds' backyard. There's a cloud of smoke, hissing fluorescent steam. James chokes for air on the ground at Ellen's feet. *"You make your own fate, Gemma girl,"* she whispers. Then the smoke clears, and James stumbles forward. He reaches for Ellen's shoulders, his face twisted in anger, his hands glowing a dark and sickly green. Ellen's eyes search for Gemma's one last time. She rests a hand right over her heart, tapping once just before she falls to the ground, lifeless.

Withered hands and a final breath; the ending always stays the same.

I grit my teeth against the pull of the memories. The loss of Ellen weighs heavy on my chest, making it difficult to breathe. And even worse, I can't stop thinking about the pain Gemma and Milo must be feeling right now and how I'm not there to do anything about it.

I yank on the threads, trying to return to the peace of the weaving where everything doesn't have to hurt so much all the time. The cavern shakes violently, the floor trembling beneath my bare feet. More and more silver threads snap off the walls, swaying back and forth as a swift wind kicks up, whipping my hair and my t-shirt. Ominous black clouds billow overhead and lightning forks in the distance, the eerie stillness of the cavern now completely vanished.

The Dreamscape knows she isn't here.

The purple and blue threads burn on my wrist, singeing my skin as they try to tug me back to the magic waiting to be Claimed, to the girl with the glowing purple hands, her green eyes round and expectant. But Gemma's magic keeps pulling me back out, those trailing silver threads wrapping around my wrists and ankles and dragging me back to my reality.

Me, alone in the Dreamscape. Me, unable to satisfy the demands of our magic. Me, spiraling, as usual.

I don't know how to hold down the rest of the threads while also tying off this Claiming. I can't do both jobs. The tug of war is endless, and my resistance feels futile. I wonder how Ben survived all these years—how did he do it? Then I scoff at the thought; Ben didn't survive. Only his body did. All that remained was a vessel, an instrument. Something for the magic to wield.

The Dreamscape hums as if waiting for me to make up my mind, to just give in already and get it over with. It presses around me in a suffocating way, engulfing all my thoughts like the crashing of a white-capped wave, urgent in its endless rising. The longer I'm here, the more everything swells—my missing, my wishing, my feelings of stupidity and recklessness.

Higher and higher, up and over. Like the swelling of the sea, the rush of a roiling river.

I close my eyes, and the memory of another wall of water looms over me. Vivian's wave washes me clean, leaving the salty taste of pool water on my lips. And with that wave, the rest of the details of that night fall into place—Vivian's voice shaking as she yells for her children to run; Milo ignoring her and staying by her side; James sweeping his wet hair out of his face and climbing to his feet—

And Gemma, reaching for the red thread, a sob caught in her throat.

It's too much.

I stop fighting and let my hands fall to my sides, the blue and purple threads of the girl's Claiming still caught on my wrist. My magic thrums in my chest and my hands clench into fists as the silver threads of the Dreamscape wind up and around me, trying to find something to hold onto.

It's too much.

Contain or release, contain or release—my magic can't decide what to do. I throw my hands up, pushing Gemma's magic out to the cavern walls as they begin to tremble, threatening to close in on me when I begin to work the threads of the Claiming once again, finishing the knot I'd already started. It's a monumental task, trying to be in two places at once.

And I can't do it anymore.

My entire body vibrates as I hang my head in defeat. And with a roaring crash, all of the Dreamscape's magic rushes up and over me. I let my last thoughts be of her.

The shape of her mouth when she smiles at me, the way one corner tugs up before the other.

Tied and bound—

The way she tucks her hair behind her ears when she's concentrating on something.

I seal your fate.

Her eyes, red—

No.

—brown and fathomless, warm and unguarded.

"Tied and bound, I seal your fate." The words spill out of me as I grasp the completed knot in my hands.

Gemma.

She wanted the magic more than she wanted you. A whisper brushes up against my ear, softer than a sigh, as the threads slice into the skin of my wrist, blood beading along the edges of the thin wound.

"That's not true," I whisper back. "It's not."

You weren't enough for her. She got bored. She needed more.

"That's not true," I say again, shaking my head, desperate to be right. I don't know if the whispers come from the red tear in the weaving or from inside my own head; neither option is comforting. My grip on the Claiming relaxes as I let the newly bound thread slip through my fingers, drifting lazily back amongst the stars to rejoin the rest of the weaving.

The Dreamscape shakes roughly, barely holding itself together. "You win," I mumble, as more silver threads slip from the wall and wind around my legs, clinging to me and offering no chance for escape. The cavern shudders once more, and then everything goes still. "Let's just get this over with."

The threads oblige me and wrap more tightly around my arms, pulling me deeper into the magic. A jolt of guilt slams me right in my stomach as the reality of what I'm doing hits me. But I barely have a chance to register the guilt before it fades away into a swirl of color and sound as all the faces of the people I love slip out of focus, and everything that made me Oliver starts to disappear.

Now there is only magic.

Because what else do I have?

CHAPTER SIX

GEMMA

I'VE NEVER LOOKED good in black.

I straighten my dress, tugging it roughly as I stare at my reflection in the mirror. The fabric feels stiff and itchy, too formal and fussy. But it's the dress my mom laid out for me on my bed next to a pair of shiny new black high heels. I rip the price tag off the dress and gingerly slide my bruised and blistered feet into the shoes; I've lost more than one toenail from all the extra running I've been doing.

With a huff, I turn toward my closet, determined to find something else to wear, something that doesn't scream *"I'm going to a funeral!"* even though that's exactly where I'm going.

My fingers fly through the mix of clothes hanging up in my closet. I don't have a ton of dresses to begin with, but the ones that I do have are like a highlight reel of the worst moments of my life. The white dress from the night she died. The red dress she gave me the night everything changed.

I rip the red dress off its hanger, crushing the soft fabric in my hands as I reach down and grab the white dress from where I threw it onto the floor a week ago. After digging around for a minute, I find a wrinkled old shopping bag under a pair of worn-out running shoes. I shove the dresses inside and throw the bag to the back of the closet with a thud that sounds like its own kind of ending.

Maybe after today, I'll quit dresses altogether.

I turn back to my reflection in the mirror and run my hands

over the itchy black dress one last time, pulling the hemline down so it covers my knees, which are still scabbed over and healing after running through the desert, falling in the gravel, crawling through the grass...

Why can't I turn it all off, just for a moment? It's like my traitorous brain is dead set on bringing up every painful second of that night, each replay a visceral reminder that I chose wrong.

That I trusted in the wrong things.

The wrong person—me.

I shake my hands to rid myself of the lingering sensations of magic and impulsiveness and the feeling of Ollie's fingers laced through mine. I can't think about that right now. Not if I want to make it through the day.

I lift my chin, my hair swishing against my cheeks, and look at the girl in the mirror. I hardly recognize her. Her eyes are dark and flat with purple shadows underneath, her black eyebrows slashing across her face like an accusation. I've never seen someone look this exhausted with herself.

Milo shuts his door behind him at the same moment I walk into the hall. The corner of his mouth flicks up into a shadow of his former smile. I look down at my shoes. We haven't spoken much since I ran out on the Cades yesterday. He still slept on the floor of my room last night, but I could tell just by the set of his shoulders that he was disappointed in me. He didn't yell or offer me a lecture; instead, he said nothing at all, which might've been worse.

Wordlessly, Milo straightens his tie, as black and formal as my dress, and holds his hand out to me. A peace offering I can't refuse. As we slowly make our way down the stairs, my mind takes me back to the night of our Claiming, my hand in the crook of his arm, the two of us bouncing down the stairs, eager and anxious for what was to come next. Back when all we had to wonder and worry about was which of the three branches of magic would Claim us.

I wish I could go back in time and pull that painfully naive

Gemma by the arm and make her stop. I want to hold her to me and warn her about what's going to happen next. To tell her that she has a beautiful life and not a single thing needs to change. Everything she could ever want is already right in front of her.

I grip Milo's arm tightly and sway on the final step. He squeezes my hand. "We can do this. For her."

I nod stiffly and plant my feet more firmly beneath me.

I can do this.

Mom and Libby wait for us in the kitchen, both solemn in black dresses of their own. Libby stands hunched and small, halfway hidden behind my mom. Her posture is so timid and childlike that the sight of her makes my throat feel too tight. The house is unbearably quiet as the four of us stand there and stare at each other, each of us waiting for someone else to say the right thing.

No one breaks the silence. Not in the house, not in the garage, and not in the car.

The drive to the cemetery passes in a blink, and before I know it, I'm sliding out of the car and trudging over the uneven grass to the hole in the ground where I'm supposed to say goodbye to one of my favorite people.

But all I can think about is how much Grandma would hate this. She would want us to wear bright colors, play loud music, and throw back some of her mixings that make everything topsy-turvy just because it's fun and would make her laugh. She wouldn't want pressed dresses or silent car rides. She would hate how Milo's head hangs down and the way Libby sniffs loudly, avoiding everyone's gaze.

Chin up, Gemma girl, I can almost hear her say. Almost as if she were standing right next to me.

I haven't been to many funerals. Ollie's grandpa died when we were seven years old, and we went to the services with him. I remember that we had to stand up and sit down a lot and that the priest droned on and on. I remember having a hard time sitting still, but wanting to be there for Ollie, so I stayed. He had sad eyes and a puckered mouth that made me think he was trying not to cry, so Milo and I each squeezed in on either side of him, whispering in his ears until he could smile again.

Funerals for the Claimed aren't that different from Nons. Lots of black, lots of crying, lots of condolences. But there isn't a priest or someone officiating. Anyone is allowed to speak and share a memory. We call it the Remembrance. After the memories are shared, everyone in attendance that is Claimed releases a small bit of magic to carry the departed soul to whatever's next.

At least that's what Grandma always told me. I don't know what to believe. All I know is that I don't like thinking about her floating around in some void, waiting for the magic to push her onward... whatever that means.

Our neighbors and other people from town line the graveside, a quiet parade of somber faces. I doubt there are usually this many Nons at a funeral like this, but Grandma had a lot of loyal customers and people she was friendly with. For how much she harped on Milo and me about keeping the One Unbreakable Rule—stay away from Nons and never reveal the truth about magic—she sure spent a lot of time with them. But that was typical Grandma—what rules can we bend but not break?

The setting sun paints the cemetery in burning shades of orange and yellow, casting long shadows over the scattered gravestones that stretch out past where I can see. The golden hour—Grandma's favorite time of day. She always said that magic was at its strongest right when the sun came up and just before it set. I don't know if that's true or if it's just something she made up, but the memory of her face turning toward the kitchen window with her eyes closed and a soft smile on her lips as the golden light poured through makes me think that maybe she was right.

That *was* magic.

Mom has me help pass out flowers to the people gathered around. She brought all of the most fragrant blooms from her garden carefully tucked into large wicker baskets—peonies, gardenias, lilac, and jasmine. Using her magic, she sends a slight breeze through the crowd, stirring the heady scent into the late evening air. Then she turns to me with one final flower in her basket. A sunflower, Grandma's favorite.

Mom gives it to me and cups my cheek with her hand. "This one is for you, Gemma girl."

I try to thank her, but my mouth is suddenly too dry to speak, so I just throw my arms around her instead. She sways as I cling to her, running her fingers through my hair. After a minute, she leans back and asks, "You ready?"

"No." But I follow behind her to line up with Milo and Libby around the gravesite, clutching the sunflower in my hand so tightly it's shaking, dropping bright yellow petals to the ground, like tears made of sunshine.

The polished wood of the dark walnut casket gleams in the golden light. I scan the crowd of mourners so I don't have to look at it while we wait for Mom to finish greeting people. There's the delivery man who worked with Grandma for ten years, holding his hat in his hands, his brow furrowed as he stares at the barren plot of earth. Then there are the neighbor kids that live down the road from us, only four and six years old, holding onto their mother's legs and peering at the casket, their faces openly curious. Grandma used to make them batches of bubbles that took hours to pop.

The younger sister, Lydia, keeps catching my eye, and I can't help but feel a flash of annoyance every time I feel her gaze on me like a spotlight. I don't want to be gawked at. But what else are funerals good for except the chance to stare at the ones who got left behind? I tug at my dress with my hands and try to fix my features into something other than a grimace, but all I can manage is pursing my lips into a tight thin line.

I know people are curious. We had to be vague and withholding when it came to announcing Grandma's death, and I'm sure our lack of information has led to a lot of whispering and darting glances. How else could we explain what happened?

So instead everyone murmurs about "old age" and "health

problems," which I know for a fact would irritate Grandma end-lessly. She always used to say she was as fit as a fiddle or as healthy as a horse. Insert any idiom of choice about good health and longevity, and I'm sure my Grandma has said it before.

The crowd finally settles, quieting as Mom steps forward. She clears her throat and softly says, "To Ellen Mae Fitzgerald," usher-ing in a moment of silence. Everyone bows their heads, and a hush falls over the cemetery.

A bead of sweat trickles down my back; it's still too hot for mid-September. I rock back and forth on my heels in the brittle summer grass. I can't hold still. I know how important this moment is, but the feeling of needing to bolt seizes my legs so strongly that my feet jerk a few inches. Milo shifts next to me and puts a hand on my shoulder with a tiny shake of his head.

I feel someone staring at me again. Four-year-old Lydia's light blue eyes look sad and confused just like Ollie's did at his grandpa's funeral all those years ago. She's just a little kid. She doesn't understand what's happening here today.

I barely do, so how could she?

This time when Lydia peers at me, I hold her gaze. *What would Grandma do?* I think to myself.

I don't have to think very hard; she would try to make Lydia laugh. She would be making all of us laugh. So I take a deep breath, and when I release it, I cross my eyes and stick out my tongue. A startled hiccup of a giggle escapes Lydia's mouth. She smiles timidly at me before darting back behind her mom's legs to hide with her brother.

Milo raises his eyebrows at me, and I'm suddenly filled with the inappropriate urge to laugh, like *really* laugh. A stomach-aching, chest-heaving, laugh. I bite down on my cheek so hard it nearly starts to bleed. Milo lightly elbows me in the ribs and throws me a narrowed-eyed glare, but that only makes me want to laugh even more.

I can't stop looking at everyone here and thinking of things to tell Grandma. My mind catalogs all the funny things I've noticed or the details I know she would love. I'm developing a twitch with how often I've glanced over my shoulder, expecting to see her standing there.

That's the worst part about funerals. You can't stop thinking about all the things you want to tell the one person who isn't there. It's so mind-numbingly awful that all I want to do is laugh. Because crying sounds so much worse.

Once the moment of silence is over, Mom eases back to stand next to Milo and me, and with shaking steps, Libby takes her place at the head of the graveside. She stoically places a hand on the dark wood of the casket, her head dipped low and her black hair swinging over her face. My heart thrums against my ribs. I haven't heard Libby say a word in over a week.

She takes a single, steadying breath, lifts her chin, and says, "My mother was the craziest person I ever knew." Her voice cracks at the end.

And then so do I.

I lean forward and laugh so hard I'm convinced my body's going to break into a million little pieces from the force of it. Mom and Milo both flinch, startled by my outburst. The rest of the crowd shifts uncomfortably as they wait for my laughter to die out.

But it doesn't. Libby stretches her small frame to its fullest height and slowly turns to look at me, her hand still resting on the casket. My shoulders shake as I clench my teeth together, trying to tamp down my laughter, but my jaw relaxes once Libby offers me a wide grin. She's laughing too, a small chuckle compared to my breathless cackling, but a laugh nonetheless.

"She was so crazy," I choke out. "Totally crazy."

"A little bit batty," Libby adds, wiping her eyes.

"And brilliant," Mom chimes in softly.

"And wonderful," Milo says next to me. "She was the most amazing person I've ever known. And I'm going to miss her every day." His face falls, and he turns into my shoulder and starts to cry, his tears soaking through the fabric of my stupid, itchy dress.

I laugh and I laugh until my laughter finally turns into crying, and I feel so relieved to let it out that I'm grinning like a maniac as I pat my brother on his back in the same soothing circles that Grandma used to do when we needed help calming down. Milo's arms go around me at the same time mine circle him.

That's better, I can almost hear her say. *You're going to be just fine, my loves.*

Libby wraps my mom in a hug. "I'm not going anywhere, Viv," she whispers, loud enough for Milo and me to hear too. "I'll be here."

The four of us, which used to be the five of us, cry and laugh until we're all wrung out and wasted. I sniff self-consciously and wipe my face, feeling completely emptied, but ready to be filled up again. After that, everyone shares memories of Grandma that range from touching to hilarious. Some anecdotes are familiar and well-worn, stories I've heard countless times throughout my childhood. Other tales are rare little things that I clasp tightly in my hands. New and unexpected pieces of my grandma I never knew existed that I now get to keep with me forever. I tuck the memories away, gently folding each one around me until I'm sur-rounded by her.

A line forms next to the graveside where family members and friends each wait with a flower to place on the casket. By the time it's over, my stomach aches and my throat is raw, but I feel better than I've felt all week.

Once the last memory is shared, Mom steps forward. She places both hands on the glossy surface of the casket, and they glow a soft shade of green. I glance nervously toward the Nons, wondering what they see. But Libby's mumbling a steady stream of words, her golden gleaming hands gripped tightly behind her back as she walks amongst the crowd, casting spells to send the Nons on their way. A few neighbors share confused looks before turning and leaving, their eyes hazy and unfocused; others check their watches as if only just remembering they have somewhere else to be. The rest amble off through the iron gates of the cemetery, climb into their cars and leave, the staggering pile of flowers left behind on the casket the only evidence they were ever here.

Now it's just the Claimed that remain, ready to add their magic to the ceremony. But after a quick scan of the group, I realize that Ollie's parents are still here. My stomach twists at the sight of them holding hands and hanging back, quiet and unsure.

Milo joins Mom and places his hands next to hers on the casket with Libby standing on the other side. The three of them collectively turn back to look at me. My chest tightens when I realize they're waiting for me to complete the circle. I look down and hold out my empty hands in a shrug. I have no magic to offer, nothing to give to help my grandma move on. Even if I don't know what to believe about the afterlife, the thought of simply watching while the rest of my family gives her one last gift is completely unbearable.

My face flushes with shame. I take a few steps back, but Milo grabs hold of my arm and shakes his head. He pulls me forward to stand in between him and Mom, each of them taking one of my hands in theirs. The spaces between my fingers glow from their magic, thrumming with the silent power radiating between them.

I try to pry my hands away, but the weight of my family and their unified magic presses against me, pinning me in place. Milo, Libby, and Mom close their eyes as their magic flares, sending a jolt up my hands and through my skin. My heart pounds at the close proximity, my breath coming out ragged and uneven. I blink back fresh tears and hate myself for allowing another wave of fear to wash over me.

My eyes stay wide open.

Milo and Libby whisper their castings. At first, it doesn't look like anything is happening, but then I see the small carvings taking shape across the lid of the casket. Flowers and stars, the cycle of the moon, and climbing vines, all etch their way onto the surface of the dark wood. I recognize my brother's handiwork in the carvings of the small animals scurrying across the lid, looking as if they could crawl out of the wood at any moment.

Mom turns her focus to the sweeping desert willows and the sprawling ironwood trees that grow alongside the fence of the cemetery. She raises her hand, and the trees begin to sway, their branches singing a mournful tune that catches on the edge of the breeze and drifts its way over to us. The sound of it makes my bones ache. The flowers scattered over the gravesite stretch and grow, each one weaving into the next, creating a long chain that circles the grave until the casket is nestled in a blanket of beautiful blossoms. The rest of the Claimed join hands and add their magic, flashes of purple, green, and golden light. The pulse shakes the earth beneath my feet and sends a chill up my spine.

Out of the corner of my eye, something flickers. It's silver and gleaming and the sight of it sends my heart racing. A thread. A single silver thread.

I watch, mesmerized as it slowly sways back and forth near the edge of the grave. It wraps around the casket in a steady spiral, until the entire surface is nearly surrounded by the twinkling thread. My hand twitches beneath Milo's as if it wants to reach out and touch it, but I'm afraid if I break the connection with my family, it will fade away. So I just stand there and stare with my heart in my throat as the single thread arches across the box that holds the remains of my grandmother.

I don't blink. I'm too scared I'll miss something.

Milo and Libby whisper the final words of their castings, and Mom's eyes come back into focus, her grip on my hand finally relaxing. I lean forward, my whole body tense from waiting as the thread finishes wrapping with a bright flash. A thin, dark purple thread emerges, tangling with the silver.

The casket begins its descent into the earth. I peer over the edge and watch as the end of the silver thread ties itself into a simple knot, a single loop around the purple thread.

Tied and bound, I seal your fate, I think to myself. I hardly dare to breathe.

Mom waves her hands in a smooth gesture, and the large

mound of freshly dug earth shifts, tumbling over the side and into the grave.

"Wait—" I try to say, but it's too late. The silver and purple threads are gone, making me wonder if I imagined the whole thing in the first place. This seems like the right moment for me to experience some kind of grief-induced delusion.

I grab Milo's wrist, clutching it tightly. "Did you see that?" I mutter under my breath.

"See what?" He sniffs and rubs his eyes with the back of his free hand.

"It was nothing," I say more to myself than to him. "Forget it."

I wipe my hands on my dress and wait for my heart rate to slow down. I probably didn't see anything anyway. Maybe it was a trick of the light or a glare from the still too-hot sun that's roasting me in this horrible dress. It could've been anything. I swallow roughly, trying to shake off the fear that's still hovering over me and making my palms sweat.

Mom lowers her hands with a small but satisfied smile. There's already a patch of soft, bright green grass growing over the top of the grave. It looks lush and out of place against the sun-bleached and tired-looking lawn that covers the rest of the cemetery.

I back away from the graveside, eager to leave this place and go for another run. That outburst of emotion has left me feeling off-center and hopelessly bare. I tug at the sleeve of my dress, but everything's in place. No wardrobe malfunction could explain why I feel so exposed.

It's the missing her. And the missing him. That's what's rubbing me raw.

"I'll meet you at the car," I say to Milo without waiting for his response. I walk with my head down, frowning as I march through the dry grass; my heels keep sinking into the soil.

"Gemma," a familiar voice says nearby. I look up too late and slam right into Teresa Cade. She places her hands on my shoulders to keep me from tipping over. "Whoa, hold on there." She smiles, one side of her mouth turning up higher than the other, and it looks so much like Ollie that my eyes immediately fill up with tears.

I duck my head, not in the mood to completely lose it again. I've had my fill of tears for the day, for the month, and probably for the rest of my entire life. "Hi, Teresa," I finally say. "I'm sorry about yesterday, I shouldn't have run out on you. It's just so hard to be there without..." I'm such a coward. I can't even say his name.

"That's okay. You've got a lot going on, and I know it's been difficult. Milo's been keeping us in the loop." She squeezes my shoulders one last time before dropping her hands. She looks tired and anxious, and why shouldn't she? Her son has disappeared, and I've offered next to no explanation.

Teresa tucks a strand of her long auburn hair behind her ear and stands tall, planting her feet like she's bracing herself for something.

My heels sink into the grass and my heart sinks into my stomach.

"I have something for you."

CHAPTER SEVEN
OLLIE

Tied and bound, I seal your fate.

Tied and bound, I seal your fate.

Tied and bound, I seal your fate.

And with every Claiming tied, I seal mine.

CHAPTER EIGHT
GEMMA

I HAVE SOMETHING for you.

Teresa's words seem to echo in the space between us. I stop fidgeting with my sunken shoes in the grass, letting my body go completely still. "What is it?" I ask, my eyes finally meeting hers.

She glances over her shoulder at her husband who's standing a few feet away under the scant shade of a mesquite tree. He gives her a brief but reassuring smile before turning away to give us more space. Teresa hesitantly reaches into her bag, sliding out a small piece of paper folded in half. It has a soft, wrinkled look to it like she's been holding onto it for days, maybe longer, worrying it between her fingers. She fiddles with a slight tear on the edge, the paper scraping lightly against her nail.

"When Charlotte—" Her voice catches on the name of her cousin—Ollie's birth mom. She pauses and clears her throat. "When Charlotte left Ollie with us, she left this behind as well. She put it inside an old book we used to read together when we were kids, one she knew I would always keep." Teresa pinches the paper right on the crease as if trying to further seal its contents away. "She tucked it inside and told me to use it if her spell ever broke and Ollie Claimed his magic. To give it to him if he needed her."

A few tears roll down her right cheek and off her face, landing on the sorry-looking lawn beneath our feet. You'd think this cemetery would have greener grass with how much it's watered. Shouldn't something grow out of all these broken hearts?

I take a step forward with my hand outstretched and my pulse thrumming. Teresa twitches the paper in my direction, but it stays held within her tight grasp, her hand stopping at the halfway point between us. "Of course, I didn't remember that she'd left this with me, not after she'd altered my memories. For Ollie's whole life, I didn't know. Not until the day Libby brought our memories back."

The day Ollie's life was turned upside down—the moment he found out his parents weren't actually his birth parents. I remember sitting there next to him, my hand gripping his under the table as we watched Aunt Libby break the casting over Teresa and Matthew, the one that prevented them from knowing the truth.

Two spells were cast by Charlotte, both designed for forgetting. Ollie's magic was Shadowed, and his parents' memories were erased, all in the hopes that it would keep Ollie safe. From his magic, from the Dreamscape, from her family, maybe all the above. I swallow the bitter taste in my mouth, wishing I didn't feel like adding myself to the list of things Ollie should've been protected from.

Teresa's shoulders droop and her face falls, slipping into an expression that looks oddly familiar. "I thought I'd have more time," she says.

As she bites her lip and glances down at the paper held between her hands, I realize why I recognized the look on her face. It's guilt. Something I've become well-acquainted with this past week.

"I was too afraid to give this to him myself. I was scared that I would lose him." Her tears fall in earnest now, the last rays of the setting sun glinting off her wet cheeks. "But I lost him anyway."

"You didn't lose him," I reassure her, even though I've been thinking the exact same thought for days.

"Then why isn't he home?" She rubs the spot between her eyebrows, squeezing her eyes shut. "Why can't I remember where he is?" she asks, her voice fracturing on the word *remember*. "Why?"

I want to tell her everything about the Dreamscape, about

how the stars would shine in Ollie's blue eyes, the way his mouth would soften when he held onto the threads. How he would sink to the floor after tying a Claiming, totally overwhelmed and at a loss for words.

"It's beautiful, Gem," is all he could ever manage to say. *"It's incredible."*

I want to tell her, but what's the point? She'd forget by tomorrow, and then I'd have to start all over again, and I don't think I'm strong enough to do that. And if I tell her everything, she'd never look at me the same way again. Because then she'd know that I'm the reason she tosses and turns in her sleep, that it's my fault she has to leave the light on in Ollie's room all night long, waiting for him to come home.

"Some magic doesn't want to be remembered," I whisper, wincing at my lack of explanation, but it's the only one I know how to give. I wrap an arm around her back and tuck myself into her side, taking on the impossible task of holding up a mother who's missing her son. "But I made a promise to you, remember?" I say, hating myself for bringing it up again. "Everything's going to be okay."

She blinks rapidly a few times and wipes a hand across her face, smudging what's left of her mascara. "He really loved you, you know," she says softly, looking down at me.

I stare back at her, and the words slip past me before I realize what I'm saying. "Love. He *loves* me. Oliver could never be past tense."

I chew on the inside of my cheek, feeling awkward after saying something like that out loud, especially to his *mom*. But even though my face is flushed and I can no longer meet her gaze, the truth of what I said slams into me, knocking my breath right out of my chest.

He loves me.

Teresa's blush mirrors mine, and her eyes fill with new tears. "Of course, of course. I didn't mean—" She stops and shakes her head, then places the folded sheet of paper gently in my hand.

"Take this. Maybe it'll help," she says, tugging the straps of her purse more firmly onto her shoulder. "Maybe *she* can help." Her words are so faint, I'm not even sure I heard her right.

"And you take this." Milo's voice comes from over my shoulder. He pulls a beat-up envelope out of the pocket of his suit jacket, smoothing it out with his hands before lightly tossing it to Teresa; I glimpse the word *Dreamscape* scrawled on the front. "I left one at your house on the kitchen counter too. Read it as many times as you need to, okay? We won't forget him."

I raise my eyebrows at Milo.

"Duplication casting," he mutters. "Very handy. And it saves on printer ink."

I can't decide if I'm impressed that he thought to make copies of my letter or annoyed that I didn't. But mostly I feel relieved that the Cades can each keep an explanation in their pocket. It's better than nothing, which is all I've offered them.

Teresa stares at the envelope in her hand, her finger tracing over the unfamiliar word. She shivers once and delicately slides it into the front pocket of her purse. "Thank you," she says to Milo and me. Then she squeezes my hand one more time before walking over to her husband, who's still waiting for her under the scattered shadows of the mesquite tree. Matthew gives me a wave and a small but steady smile before taking Teresa by the hand and pulling her toward the cemetery gates.

Milo and I look down at the folded note. The paper feels light in my hand, but heavy somehow, too. Full of secrets and promises.

And maybe even a little bit of hope.

"So, what is it?" he asks, moving to stand closer to me.

I lift my chin and flip the paper open.

It's a name.

And an address.

I stare at the faded blue ink, my heart thrumming wildly in my chest.

"Gem?" Milo nudges me, and I startle. I'd nearly forgotten he was there. "Let's go find Mom," he says urgently, already on the move.

I nod and carefully fold the note up, holding onto it tightly with both hands. As we weave through the crowd of black-clad figures, I keep my face in a permanent half-smile and try to avoid all eye contact. A few hands reach out and squeeze my arms or pat Milo on the shoulder, but we don't stop until someone tugs on the back of my dress.

"Gemma, wait." My second cousin Sylvia wraps me in a crushing hug and sobs into my neck. "I'm so sorry about Ellen," she moans as more tears gush out.

I try not to cringe over the contact; we aren't nearly close enough for this kind of display. "Thank you," I sigh, pushing her blonde hair out of my face, still searching the crowd for my mom.

"Isn't it your Claiming soon, Sylvia?" Milo's voice cuts in over her noisy sniffling. He loops his arm through mine, gently extricating me from Sylvia's tear-soaked hug.

She wipes her nose on the sleeve of her black dress and hiccups. "Yes, it's actually tomorrow. But I understand if you won't be able to make it," she says in a rush.

"We'll be there," Milo answers solemnly. "What's more important than family?"

I stifle the urge to stomp on his foot. "Speaking of family, I think Mom's looking for us," I say a little too loudly. We mumble our goodbyes to Sylvia as she runs off to her parents—her whole and unblemished family—still eagerly awaiting her Claiming and the day she'll hold magic in her hands.

I remember what it felt like to be her.

We finally find Mom standing with Libby in the middle of a group of great aunts and more cousins. And cousins of cousins—lots of people I know but don't *know*. Milo starts to push his way through the crowd, but I pull on his sleeve to hold him back, thinking of Sylvia's shuddering hug. "Maybe we should just wait for her by the car?"

A knowing look flits across his face. He doesn't argue but

glances back over his shoulder and sighs. "I guess so. Looks like it could be a while."

We turn and cross the lawn littered with gravestones, pausing to look back at Grandma's patch of grass once more. I have to squint to see it through the dusky light. In the lengthening shadows, it just looks like another grave among the many. Nothing special.

"You didn't have to be rude to Sylvia, you know," Milo says, breaking the silence. "She didn't do anything, she's just sad."

I try not to snort. "Sylvia barely knew Grandma. She saw her maybe once every other year and—"

"It doesn't matter, she was just trying to be nice."

"But I'm so sick of it!" I lower my voice when a few heads turn in our direction. "I'm sick of having a reason for everyone to feel sorry for us," I say, gesturing to the flock of mourners surrounding Mom and Libby. *Like a murder of crows*, I think to myself.

"I know." Milo exhales heavily and folds me into one of his best hugs with his chin resting on the top of my head. "But we just need to be strong, and—"

Anger zips through me, hot and uncontainable. "Stop it, Milo. Just stop. I can't take this anymore." I shrug out of his hug and march through the rusty cemetery gates to the parking lot where our Jeep is waiting on the hot, cracked asphalt.

"Oh, so now you're mad at me," Milo says, his brow furrowed. I open the car door, but he quickly shuts it again, leaning against it to block me from getting inside. "For what, trying to comfort you?" He glares at me under the orange glow of the streetlights that flicker above us.

Tears prick at the back of my eyes. I rub them roughly with my palms. "No." I pinch my lips together, trying to shove my frustration back down, but it's too late; it rises to the surface in a painful, sharp burst. "I mean, *yes.* I'm mad at you for doing everything right. You keep saying the right things and doing the right things. You're the man of the house, taking care of everything. I mean, you practically planned this entire funeral by yourself."

He crosses his arms over his chest. "And that's a problem because..."

"Because it's not you!"

It's been torture watching him—his resoluteness, his stiff shoulders, his refusal to joke or cry or yell. All week long, I waited for him to get mad at me, to take me by the shoulders and tell me to snap out of it, but he never did. It's one of the reasons I could hardly stand to be at the house. Nothing felt like home. I know it isn't fair of me to be mad at him about that, but the truth is I miss my brother. The one that teased and fought and annoyed me when he was bored. The one who always slept in too late, wasting half the day away. The one who could still act like a kid because that's exactly what he is. I hardly recognize this new responsible, always reliable version of Milo.

And I'm just so tired of missing everyone.

Milo looks away and clenches his jaw.

"Say what's on your mind." I cross my arms to mirror him. "Go ahead."

He whips his head back to me, all frown lines and angry eyes. "Of course I've had to take care of everything, Gemma, you haven't been here. And we needed you. *I* needed you." He runs a hand agitatedly through his hair, mussing up the back; yet another thing the old Milo never would've done. He always liked to keep his hair perfectly tousled just so. "What are you going to do when we get home? Lace up your running shoes?" he asks, his voice an accusation.

My face flushes with guilt, but I straighten my back and try to hold his gaze.

"You keep leaving me to carry it all on my own. And I'm doing my best to pick up the pieces, trying to cast protection spells around you and the house because I don't know where you are or if you'll make it home again. I can't quit imagining James finding you out there alone in the desert—" He cuts himself off, shuddering.

"So yeah. Someone needed to step up," he says, his voice cracking. "Libby wouldn't come out of her room, and Mom won't quit baking. Who else is left?" He shrugs one shoulder, his mouth curling down. "It's just me."

He's not even yelling at me, but I wish he was. Somehow, I think that would feel better than his quiet disappointment, his shrugging defeat.

"You're scaring me, Gem. It's like your fire's gone out." He shakes his head and scuffs his black dress shoe against the asphalt. "You just woke up and Ollie was gone, and now you won't tell me anything. You're distant and closed off, and you have this look on your face..."

"What kind of look?" I ask, even though I already have a pretty good idea of what he's going to say.

"Like you've given up. Like your magic's gone."

All I can do is look down and nod, my heart thudding dully. He's more right than he understands.

He taps me under my chin, forcing me to look up. "Remember when we used to tell each other everything?" He offers me the ghost of a smile.

The lump in my throat makes it nearly impossible to speak. "I remember."

He stares up at the sky for a long moment as if he's counting the few stars that are visible. "I miss him too, you know," he says faintly. "You're not the only one who lost their best friend."

I stumble back as the rest of my righteous anger evaporates off me in an instant. Shame tugs on my stomach; we still haven't talked about what happened at the bonfire—Ollie's lips on mine, his hands on my waist, and Milo stepping between us.

I'm not the only one who's hurting.

I deflate against the side of the Jeep, shoulder to shoulder with my brother. "I'm sorry, Milo," I say, burying my face in my hands. "And you're right. About everything. I haven't been there for you."

He doesn't answer for a while. The silence stretches on for so long that it forces me to peek between my fingers at him.

His face softens. "Well, of course I'm right. I always am." He nudges me with his elbow. "But to make it up to me, you can generously offer to do all my chores for the rest of the year."

I choke out a laugh, feeling immensely grateful for the hint of his smile and the start of forgiveness. "Sure sure," I mutter, "but first there's something we need to take care of." I hold up the piece of paper still held in my hand, flipping it open at the crease. "I know you miss Ollie too. So let's bring him home. You and me."

Then I take a deep breath, let it go, and tell Milo everything that happened that night in the Dreamscape. I tell him about how the red thread called to me, and how I didn't know how to stop myself from answering. I tell him about Ollie holding onto my thread, his grip sure and steady, and how my magic slowly slipped away.

Milo listens patiently until I get to the end, and then he asks in a low voice, "Your magic really is gone?"

"Yes," I answer quickly, trying to stay detached from such a small but heavy word. Admitting it out loud feels even worse than I thought it would.

"Oh, Gemma." Milo lightly bumps the back of his hand against mine. He doesn't tell me he's sorry because he knows I've had my fill of sympathy. But with that simple gesture, his empathy shines through. "So, because you're not there, Ollie can't get out? And you can't get back into the Dreamscape because he took your magic from you. A catch-22."

I knock my head back against the window of the Jeep. "Basically."

He rubs his hand across his forehead and sighs. "Oliver, you noble, well-intentioned idiot."

"Basically," I say again, with a small laugh that I catch between my lips before it turns into more blubbering. "And I don't know what would've happened to me if he wasn't such a wonderful idiot." I sniff and wipe my nose with the back of my hand, letting that all too familiar feeling of guilt settle itself more heavily between my ribs.

Milo taps his foot and squints through the growing darkness. "I need you to be honest with me, Gem. Can you do that?"

Without meaning to, I take a few steps away, as if to put more distance between myself and his question. My back stiffens against the painful realization that a few months ago, my brother never would've had to make a preface like that. Not to me.

"But I just told you every—"

"What do you see when you dream at night?" he asks, carefully watching my face.

Honesty. He wants honesty. A shiver slides down my spine. "Everything's gray and cold and empty. I think it's the outside of the Dreamscape." I swallow. "No, I *know* it's the outside of the Dreamscape. I can sense it, but I can't see inside."

Milo presses his mouth into a thin line, his expression smooth, revealing nothing. "Hmm," is all he says in response.

"'Hmm' what?"

"I'm processing. Give me a minute."

I only wait another ten seconds before I open my mouth again, ready to start badgering him for answers when Mom and Libby walk up to the Jeep looking exhausted. I hear the sound of car doors slamming and last goodbyes as the rest of the straggling funeral attendees finally exit the parking lot.

"Let's get out of here," Mom says, wrapping her arms around Milo and me, hugging us close. Her eyes are red-rimmed and puffy. Mine probably don't look any better. "I'm starving."

"Please no more cakes, cookies, brownies, or any other treat that needs to be baked," Milo groans as he opens the door. "Wow, I can't believe I just said that. Who even am I?" he mutters as he climbs into the backseat with me.

Mom laughs lightly and takes her seat behind the wheel, her dark topknot bobbing on her head. "You're right. Time to give it a rest with the baking."

Libby buckles herself into the passenger seat. "But what about pancakes?" she asks hesitantly.

I reach my hand out, lightly resting it on her shoulder. "Only if we use Grandma's syrup. I love that stuff."

"Me too," Libby says, nestling into her seat with a sigh, her long black hair shielding her face from view, but it sounds like she's smiling.

The four of us just sit there for a moment, testing out our new dynamic in a silence that doesn't feel uncomfortable but isn't quite lived in yet either.

I know it's just pancakes, but it feels like more than that, too. It feels like potential, like a tiny sliver of a new beginning but with extra chocolate chips thrown in.

Mom's tired eyes find mine in the rearview mirror. "Let's go home."

CHAPTER NINE

GEMMA

ALL THE STARS are out by the time we make it home, each one a tiny pinprick of light winking in the wide black sky.

Milo and I spent the entire car ride locked in a heated but whispered debate over how to tell Mom about Teresa's note and the hastily formed plans we were still in the middle of making.

I watch Mom as she pulls into the driveway, how she holds her head up high with her hands tight on the steering wheel, like her firm grip is the only thing holding this family together. The way she carefully talks to Libby as if she's afraid of saying too much too soon.

Milo meets my eyes, dipping his head in silent agreement, his mouth set in a grim line. There's one thing we know for sure: our mother is not going to take this news well. We have to play this right if we're going to get her to agree to anything. We need to present our well-thought-out argument calmly and reasonably. No need to rush into anything.

But Milo and I are not exactly known for being calm or reasonable, so whatever patience we had in the car evaporates the minute we step through our front door.

We corner Mom in the kitchen, both of us talking too loudly over each other, our words spilling out in a confusing garble. She flinches back from the noise—things have been pretty quiet around our house for the past week. "Slow down," she mutters as she sinks into a chair at the table. "One at a time, please." Mom gestures for us to take the seats across from her then leans her elbow on the table, tucking her chin into her hand.

"What's that?" Libby asks, pointing to the folded sheet of paper still clutched in my hands. She pulls out a chair to sit next to Mom, her eyes darting to the empty seat at the head of the table.

Milo tries to grab the paper from me, but I'm too quick. I slide it across the scarred surface of the table to Mom and Libby and say in one giant breath: "Teresa gave us this address that Charlotte left behind, and we need to go and find her so we can see if she knows anything that would help us get Ollie out of the Dreamscape. It's kind of our only lead right now."

Mom's hand hovers over the note. "Ollie's birth mother? And get him out of the—what?" she asks, her brow puckering.

This time Milo's the one who rolls his eyes. "How do you deal with this?" he mumbles to me out of the corner of his mouth. "It's so annoying."

"You have no idea." But he's on a high horse for someone who needed to be reminded what the Dreamscape was on the drive home from the cemetery. I'll probably have to tell him again within the hour.

"Hang on," Milo says before running up the stairs two at a time only to thunder back down less than a minute later with an envelope in his hand. "Here." He slides another perfect duplicate of my Dreamscape letter across the table and sits down next to me.

Mom leans back in her chair and begins to scan the letter, with Libby reading over her shoulder. My leg bounces up and down, my foot tapping noisily on the tile floor. As I wait for them to finish reading, I'm left with nothing to do except fiddle with the edge of Teresa's note, the single scrap of paper that contains all my barely-there hope.

Charlotte Lowell
1877 East Edgewood Lane
Bakersfield, California 93307

"I'm too hungry to wait for pancakes," Milo says, loosening his black tie and heaving himself out of his chair.

I smile at the back of my brother's head shoved in the fridge. Lately, he hasn't had much of an appetite. Everything's upside-down right now, so I'm desperate for any sign of normalcy. And the sight of Milo's head bent over a Tupperware container full of leftover chicken is so unbelievably normal that it makes my whole head throb with the effort of not breaking down in tears again.

When I turn back to see if Mom's finished reading yet, my gaze lands on Grandma's empty chair beside her, and for a moment, I forget how to breathe. How can I when her absence is constantly shoved in my face like that?

I take a deep breath, forcing myself to keep my eyes on the empty chair and imagine her telling me to count to ten, to focus on grounding myself when it feels like everything's spinning out of control. We all deal with heartache in different ways, don't we? *One, two, three...* I'm the one who runs and runs so she won't have to think. *Four, five, six...* Libby favors solitude, hiding out in her room until she feels safe enough to try again. *Seven, eight, nine...* Milo rises—he organizes and takes charge; and apparently, my mother bakes. *Ten.*

There's no right way to be sad, is there?

Libby finishes reading and gives me a long look before saying, "I think we need chocolate chips in the pancakes." And with that, she starts rummaging through the cabinets under the stove, looking for the griddle.

"Try the one on the left," I call out. The metallic clatter of her wrestling Grandma's pots fills the kitchen before she makes a triumphant little noise.

Mom's chair scrapes against the tile. She stands and neatly folds the letter back into the envelope, setting it down on the table and trading it out for the slip of paper with Charlotte's address on it. There's a crease between her eyebrows as she reads. Her fist tightens around the note, crushing it slightly. "No. Absolutely not."

My stomach clenches. I knew this wouldn't go well.

Milo spins away from the fridge nearly dropping his armful of food. "What do you mean 'no?' We *have* to go. Tonight. We need to—"

"I know you two just want to help and believe me, I want Ollie home too. But Teresa shouldn't have given you this," she says, her expression hardening as she reads over the address again. "You're just *kids*. I'm not about to send you off on some mad dash hundreds of miles away to go see a woman none of us know. If she's even there," she adds, her voice rigid with finality. She grabs her purse that she'd tossed on the table and pulls her phone out, shaking her head. "Not happening."

Milo slams a casserole dish on the counter, and a greenish-brown sauce splatters all over his white shirt and suit jacket. He doesn't even notice. "We're going," he says, crossing his arms over the mess on his chest. "We have to."

"No," Mom replies.

My cheeks flush with heat as I jump out of my seat. "But Milo's right. Just let me explain—"

"I said no," Mom interjects.

It's so strange to feel something other than sadness taking up space in my body for the second time tonight. It's been so long since I've felt anything other than numb that I almost don't recognize the buzzing sensation of defiance shooting its way through me. I dart my hand out and try to take the address from Mom, but she slides it into her bag before I can even touch the paper.

She dials Teresa's number, her fingers tapping quickly on the screen. "I'm going to talk to the Cades. You two have been through enough. We'll figure something else out."

"*Mom!*" I try and fail not to whine, my heart climbing up my throat. Now that I have this possibility, this thin, hardly visible, crescent moon of a chance to act, I can't just keep sitting here and doing nothing. I can't.

My mother's fierce gaze locks onto mine, a challenge I don't dare look away from. "I will not lose another member of my family to this magic. I refuse," she says, her forceful enunciation leaving no room for misinterpretation. She turns on her heel and presses her phone to her ear. "Teresa," she exhales. "We need to talk." The downstairs office door slams shut, cutting off the rest of her conversation.

My shoulders hunch as I turn to face Milo. "What now?"

He chews on his lip as he watches Libby quietly mixing the pancakes, her expression closed off and thoughtful like she hasn't heard a word any of us have said, aimlessly stirring and staring into the batter as if it holds all the answers to life's greatest questions. "Well, pancakes, I guess," he says, his mouth still pinched in a frown.

I flop onto one of the tall barstools across the counter from Libby. Milo looks down at his shirt and grimaces as if just realizing there's something resembling leftover enchiladas all over him. He chuckles darkly. "Well, I was never going to wear this suit again anyway," he mutters, shrugging out of his jacket and tossing it on the other end of the counter before sliding onto the stool next to mine.

Libby throws another handful of chocolate chips into the batter, humming quietly to herself. I fidget on my stool, swinging my legs back and forth and trying to ignore the clammy sort of awkwardness I've been feeling around her lately. Maybe she doesn't think what happened to Grandma is my fault—I wouldn't blame her if she did—but I don't really want to stay in the room long enough to find out whether or not that's true. With Libby hiding away all week, I've been able to avoid those hard conversations. But now? I flinch and shift my stool closer to Milo's, feeling grateful he's there to unintentionally act as my buffer.

But when Libby catches my eye, she just wordlessly hands me the bag of chocolate chips, nudging the bowl toward me. I dump the rest of the bag in. Now the batter looks like pure chocolate with a side of pancakes.

"Perfect," she says, tapping the spoon on the side of the bowl.

She gives me a smile that's small but genuine, and I feel my posture relax just slightly.

We watch her greasing the skillet for a minute, her gestures practiced and familiar. She looks like someone who's spent a lot of time in the kitchen, which surprises me since Libby usually forgets to eat most days if she's too busy reading. "Mom used to trap me in the kitchen all the time when I was growing up," she says as if reading my mind. "She used to call me her sous chef. I think she was secretly hoping I'd be Claimed as a Mixer like her. Well, not so secretly, I guess."

She laughs once and scoops a generous helping of batter from the bowl before pouring it onto the cast-iron skillet resting on the stove. The rich warm smell of chocolate instantly fills the room, conjuring a thousand different memories with just a single inhale. Countless mornings filled with bedhead and squinty eyes and Grandma slapping a stack of perfectly round pancakes onto a plate in front of me, then drizzling the syrup with a flourish.

I stare at the bottle of syrup sitting on the counter, the glass glinting under the kitchen lights, but all I can think about is the patch of green grass growing over her grave.

"Libby, can I ask you a question?"

"You can always ask, but I might not have an answer," she says, glancing over her shoulder, her expression a little more guarded than it was only a moment before.

I almost tell her to forget it, but then my eyes flick over to the bottle of syrup again and I find myself asking, "Where do we go?"

"Excuse me?"

"When we die. Where do you think we go?"

Milo quits picking at the food on his shirt and sits up a little straighter in his seat. Libby slowly turns away from the griddle where the pancakes are softly sizzling, the spatula in her hand drooping to rest on the counter. She blinks a few times at the two of us before clearing her throat and saying with a shrug, "Beyond, I guess. We go Beyond."

I lean forward, resting my elbows on the counter, and frown.

"That's what Grandma always told me. But what's that supposed to mean?"

"We go beyond all of this." Libby waves the spatula around the room, gesturing to the back sliding door as if the exit to the Great Beyond is just on the other side of our patio. "We move on to something else. At least that's what my mom always said when I asked about my dad."

My grandfather died of a heart attack when Libby was very young. My hand twitches like it wants to reach across the counter to take hers, but I don't. I don't know how to talk about missing fathers and empty chairs at the table. I should, but I don't.

I wrinkle my nose. "That sounds like the kind of answer you give when you don't know what you're talking about. Like the kind of thing you tell a kid when you want them to stop asking you questions."

"We're well-versed in those types of responses," Milo adds dryly.

Libby's smile cracks across her face, a little slow and jagged like she forgot what it feels like to give a proper grin. "Well, she did always follow it up with a cookie and a, *don't you worry about the Beyond, darling; worry about the here and now.*"

I laugh. It's short-lived and weak, but it's something. "That sounds like her."

Libby plucks two plates from the cupboard, then flips a stack of pancakes on each one before sliding them across the counter to us.

"I'm skeptical," I say as she hands me the syrup, "but I like the thought of her out there exploring some new terrain." I run my finger over the sticky label, snorting at the name Grandma called her concoction—*The Good Stuff*. "She was always sort of beyond this world anyway, wasn't she?"

"Indeed she was." Libby spirals the syrup out of the bottle over her own stack of pancakes, flicking her wrist with a flourish just like Grandma always did.

Milo drizzles some over his stack rather than dumping half the bottle like he usually does, his carefulness yet another reminder that we only have so much of her left.

The three of us eat in silence at the counter, but the quiet feels soft rather than strained. It feels like a tribute. I slowly chew my food, tasting the sweetness of the pancakes while Grandma's magic works on me, sending a handful of other sensations running through my body: the feeling of gravel under my feet on a mountain trail, the sound of Ollie's best and loudest laugh, and the smell of Grandma's hands, lavender and sage.

I slowly put my fork down, trying not to outwardly shiver as the magic drips through me—sticky and sweet as the syrup.

Suddenly, I'm not so hungry anymore.

I scoot back from the counter and hop down from my stool. "I'm going to go change."

"Me too," Milo says through his last mouthful. He tugs at his tie and points to my black dress. "We should probably just burn these clothes."

"Probably."

I go to clear my plate, but Libby takes it from my hands and stacks it with hers and Milo's, that far-off look clouding her eyes once again. "Let me clean up. Please," she says quietly. She starts the water running in the sink and turns her back on us. Her hasty retreat makes me wonder what she felt when she tasted the syrup.

I glance toward the office door; Mom still hasn't come out. "We need to talk to her, Milo, I can't—"

"I think I have an idea," he says as if he didn't hear me talking. "But it might be stupid." He pauses and scratches the back of his neck. "Strike that. It's definitely stupid."

We start trudging up the stairs, both of us worn out from such an unending day. "Well, what is it?"

He turns down the hall that leads to our rooms. "It probably won't work," he mumbles, more to himself than to me, "and you're not going to like it, but it's worth a shot."

"Milo, come on, are you going to fill me in anytime soon, or are you just going to continue having a conversation with yourself?"

"I'm still formulating. Give me a sec." He stops in front of his bedroom door. "I'll meet you in your room. Five minutes." Then he turns and shuts the door in my face with a lazy wave of his glowing hand.

I stiffen and wait for that familiar feeling of annoyance to wash over me, but it doesn't. I'm too busy trying to decipher his cryptic words and whatever he means by, "it's definitely stupid." Dread sweeps over me as I push open my own bedroom door. Milo's bad ideas and idiotic plans never used to bother me. I was usually egging him on or already one step ahead of him.

But that was before.

And trying to squeeze myself into the shape of who I used to be—a girl who was unafraid; a girl who liked to skirt the rules and walk the line—makes my skin feel uncomfortably too tight. Like I don't fit in here anymore, but *here* is me, and I have nowhere else to go.

I rip the itchy black dress off, unceremoniously ball it up, and throw it into the darkest corner of my closet before digging through my pile of clothes on the floor, frantically searching for the pajamas I've been wishing for all day. My hands go still on the soft, worn-out fabric of Ollie's old baseball t-shirt. The one that's way too big on me in the best way, with long black sleeves that dangle over my wrists. I hold it up to my face. It still smells like him.

Like citrus and sunshine.

I slip his shirt over my head, pull on a pair of the slouchiest sweats I own, then crawl onto my bed to wait for Milo to reappear. After only one minute of lying there by myself, my legs won't quit bouncing and every creak of the house makes me jump. I grab my phone off my nightstand, just for something to do with my hands, and as the screen glows to life, I see the tiny little red bubble over the phone icon. The one that tells me I have over a dozen voicemails.

I take a steadying breath, and before I can talk myself out of it, I tap on the first message, left over six months ago.

"Gem! It's me—"

The sound of his voice fills my ears, leaving my eyes pooling with yet more tears, hot and pulsing and so utterly miserable. I hastily hit pause; I don't know if I can listen to another word.

But the silence afterward is just as painful, if not more.

"Gem! It's me—" echoes on repeat until I can't take it anymore, and I tap the screen once again.

"—I just saw the funniest thing—" he breathes, his laughter cutting off his sentence. There's a muffled sound like he's moving his phone to the other side of his face. I close my eyes and I can picture him, his grin lifting higher on one side, his cheek pressed against the phone to pin it in place.

His muted laugh fills my ear again, and then so does another familiar voice. *"Don't listen to him, Gemma!"* There's a scuffling sound like Milo's trying to wrestle the phone away from him. More laughter and someone's grunt.

Ollie had this ridiculous habit of leaving messages. He was obsessed with "the lost art of the voicemail," as he liked to call it, and I had about twenty waiting messages on my phone as proof. I always pointedly ignored them to show him that people actually *didn't* want to listen to a rambling voicemail, but that never deterred him. If he called and I didn't answer, a voicemail was there, blinking and waiting.

I've never been so thankful for long, rambling, pointless voicemails. Now it's the only way to hear his voice, his humor, his warmth—I can feel it radiating through my phone speaker. So I lie there and listen to all his voicemails in order. Some are old stories I've already heard before—many of which are the countless ways Milo has humiliated himself for the sake of a girl, but a few are about his parents, and others are about a book he's reading that he "just needs to talk about before he explodes."

There's one voicemail that's less than two weeks old. I save that one for last.

"Hey, it's me." I wish I could make fun of him for saying that every single time. As if I wouldn't know it was him.

"I'm about to go to bed, so I'll see you in a few minutes," he says, sounding tired but happy. *"But I couldn't wait. I guess I just wanted to say that: it's never enough, Gem. I'll never get enough of you."* He pauses and breathes into the phone. *"Okay, that's it. You probably won't even hear this because of your stubborn refusal to revive 'the lost art of the voicemail—'"* I mouth the words along with him, *"—but I needed to say it anyway. If you do hear this, I'm sure you're rolling your eyes or maybe you're calling me a sap."* Another laugh. *"But I don't care. I am a sap, a sentimental sap, and it's all your fault. You made me this way. See you soon."*

The line goes dead just as Milo shoves open my door and walks into my room. I hurriedly drop my phone onto my bed and rub my face with my hands. I wish I would've answered the phone that night. I wish I would've listened to that voicemail and called him right back to tell him that I love him too.

"You okay?" Milo asks, one eyebrow raised at me and the phone on my pillow.

"No, but I will be." The words sear through my chest as I realize the truth in them. I sniff and sit up, feeling the first rush of determination I've felt in what seems like a very long time. "Now, tell me your big idea. I don't care how stupid it is—I'm in."

CHAPTER TEN

OLLIE

T IME IS AN easy place to lose yourself.

It's expansive and wide, curving around me like a spiral of ribbon, soft and flexible. It shimmers across my skin, effervescent in its unending newness. On one end is the beginning, so far away and faint it's impossible to make out. But still, I know it's there, warm and golden, immaculate in its contentment. The other end trails off into the darkness of unknowns, calm and quiet like a sudden silence after a loud noise. A sought-after exhale, a tender relief.

Life, death, and every moment in between.

It's too big to take in all at once, yet everything is distilled to this single moment; a contradiction just begging to be pulled apart and examined. None of this should make sense, but somehow it does.

I hold perfectly still needing nothing and no one, not even myself. I don't ever remember wanting anything other than this—here, now, yesterday, and tomorrow.

Was there anything else?

The question confuses me, a brief irritation before dissolving into nothingness, like dust motes swirling through the sunlit air until it's gone gone gone.

All I see is the weaving. All I know is the magic.

Time is an easy place to lose yourself.

Every now and then, something tugs on me, something urgent that demands to be remembered. But the tugging is easy to ignore when everything else surrounding me is so much brighter and heavier and *here*.

Then, a flash of purple, like a distant fork of lightning. Something about it is familiar in a way I can't describe. Awareness hovers on the edge of my consciousness, grazing against who I used to be with a feather-light touch, never fully landing.

Another flash of purple and a low rumble of thunder. The sound nudges against me, insistent in its need to be heard. It's round and ringing, too full for me to hold onto with both hands, too strange for me to grasp.

But it sounds so familiar.

There's a purple thread trailing through the stars and flickering in and out of view. My hand twitches when I hear the sound again.

Oliver.

So familiar.

A tingling down my spine tells me to reach out and touch it. I try to stretch out my hand, but it's too hard to move. Every inch of progress feels slow and labored, so by the time my fingers wrap around the purple thread, I can hardly remember why I wanted to take hold of it in the first place. Then it hits me: the scent of lavender and sage mixed with the hint of something sweet. Like chocolate.

And I see her—Ellen. I see her body lying broken in the grass just as clearly as if I were standing there next to her again. But then the moment reverses, and like a videotape rewinding, Ellen's life flies through my mind at warp speed. It burns in my eyes like the afterimage of a firework—too bright and too fast for me to focus on any single detail, but I can *feel* her. There's a strength about her that's impossible to ignore.

Her thread feels like laughter and lightning. I can see her hands in the soil, the way she plucks a leaf and smells it before placing it in her apron pocket. Now her hair's frizzing from standing over the hot stove, her mouth mumbling as she stirs a bubbling pot full of something pale pink and shining. Then she's rocking her babies—her grandchildren, and her children before them—her mouth tucked into a smile so small and quiet it feels like a secret. It's the kind of smile that makes me feel like I know absolutely nothing. And it makes me wonder if I ever will.

I hold my breath as her very nature unfolds before me. My mind feels pulled in so many different directions that it's hard to focus and maintain my grip on the thread.

But I remember Ellen. And when I remember her, I remember Gemma.

And then I remember everything.

My head breaks the surface and I gasp for air. The faces of everyone who's ever mattered to me suddenly come crashing to the front of my mind. My parents, Milo, Vivian and Libby...

Gemma.

What am I doing? I think to myself. *How much time have I lost?*

My heart stutters when I see that I'm hovering at least ten feet off the ground, suspended by the silver threads that wrap around me, holding me in place. Everything is dark and still, the stars barely visible from this point of view. Every few seconds, the Dreamscape trembles, shaking more silver threads loose with a cracking sound like the snapping of a sail in the wind. It's as if all this magic is literally trying to jump ship, but where would it go?

I watch as a handful of glittering threads gracefully arc across the dimly lit cavern until they land on me, wrapping around my legs so gently I hardly feel a thing; another link in the chain of the silver shackles that bind me.

Smothering panic presses against my chest, making it difficult to breathe. I struggle against the threads, but it just makes them wrap around me more tightly. After a few minutes of ineffectual wrestling, I remember how Ben used to relax into the magic until he could control it enough to find his way out. Closing my eyes, I try to breathe deeply, focusing all my energy on loosening the threads. But as soon as I do that, more magic pours into me—Gemma's magic and mine.

It feels like I'm barely treading water in a churning, relentless, unforgiving sea. The magic rises higher and higher, up and over my head as it tries to swallow me whole. I lose all sense of where I am. Of who I am. It's just too much. I try to come up for air, but another wave crashes over my head, nearly sending me tumbling back into the weaving, into the deep blue of oblivion.

Then, three words that I feel in my bones more than I hear in my ears: *drop my thread.*

"What?" My voice is dry and raspy. I wonder how long it's been since I've spoken out loud. My hand tightens instinctually, clutching Ellen's thread to my chest. I'm afraid to let go; I'm afraid of forgetting again. Gemma's brown eyes swim in and out of focus as I cling to the only lifeline I have.

Ollie, let it go.

The sound of my nickname loosens my grip. Her deep purple thread slowly drifts out of my fingertips until it's just another tiny flicker of light, a single star in a sea made of millions. But I can still hear her laugh, crashing like thunder as the Dreamscape shakes and more silver threads unfasten from the wall, licking at my ankles like the start of a roaring flame.

Now let them all go.

As if on cue, one star overhead shines brighter than the rest, a single pale yellow thread falling from its center, coming to a stop right in front of me. Then another thread tumbles down from the weaving, this one dark green—Elemental magic ready to be Claimed. I blink at the swaying threads, each one pulsing with light, feeling stupid and slow.

Let them all go? But how?

My magic tugs at my hand, pulling me forward until I nearly touch the two threads hanging in my face, but I yank my arm back at the last second. "Let them all go," I repeat back to myself as I stare at my hands. The lingering sound of Ellen's laughter and the vague hint of her whisper have vanished in the wind, leaving a heavy silence behind. Did I just imagine that whole thing? I wouldn't be surprised if I was completely losing my mind at this point.

I slide some of the looser threads off me, slowly sinking back down to the cavern floor. Even though they feel lighter than air, the more threads I peel off my body, the more I realize how heavy their weight actually is. My muscles ache from the strain of carrying it all.

I land roughly on the opalescent floor, nearly falling on my face. My legs shake and my feet stumble over each other; it feels strange to stand on solid ground again. But the further away I get from the threads and the Claimings, the more clearly I can think. I turn my back on the stars and close my eyes as I replay Ellen's words.

Let them all go.

Did she mean to stop tying the Claimings? Is that even an option? My stomach lurches at the thought, leaving me feeling sick and confused. The truth is, I don't feel capable of stopping. I don't know how to leave it all behind.

But the sound of Ellen calling out my name is still fresh in my ears, reminding me of who I am.

Reminding me of home.

Whether it was imaginary or not, it woke me up. And the last thing I want to do is go back to sleep.

My magic thrums in my chest with every beat of my heart, the tips of my fingers prickling as I tuck my hands into the pockets of my jeans. I turn back around and face the stars, tipping my head back so I can see them clearly. They flicker, they wait, they sigh with impatience.

"I'm done. Find someone else."

CHAPTER ELEVEN

GEMMA

M ILO'S SHOULDERS ARE tight, and his jaw is set as he nervously paces the length of my room before flopping next to me on my bed. He drops something heavy onto the mattress—one of the Caster Chronicles. The leatherbound book hums with energy, filling the space between us with a frantic buzzing sensation that makes my skin crawl.

I try to discreetly scoot a few inches away, but my bed frame creaks loudly the second I decide to move, basically throwing me under the bus.

Milo watches my attempts to distance myself from the book with a knowing look on his face. "Well, this is exactly what I was afraid of."

I pull my legs up to my chest, resting my chin on my knees. "What do you mean?"

He taps his fingers on the old book, nudging it toward me. I try not to, but once again I flinch. "*That's* what I mean. You're afraid of my magic." He says it matter-of-factly, pulling the book into his lap with an apologetic twitch of his mouth. "Which kind of ruins my plan."

Heat crawls up my neck and into my cheeks. "You're so dramatic. No, I'm not." I focus all my concentration on keeping my voice steady. He watches me carefully, reaching for the book as if he's about to toss it onto my lap. I swat his hands away and give him the best eye roll I can manage. "Milo, stop. I'm *fine*. Just tell me what your plan is."

He purses his lips, clearly unconvinced. I've never been good at lying to him and he knows it. "Okay, here it is: I want to go back inside your mind."

My face blanches. "But I thought you said it was too dangerous."

"Well, it is, but it went all right last time," he says, his gaze keen and searching. "Right? I mean, the casting worked and everything..."

The memory of his magic seeping into my brain has me clenching my hands into fists. I bury them under my pillow. "I guess so," I say, my voice coming out too small. "So what are you going to do?"

"I've been thinking about what you told me earlier. About the gray place." My stomach flips uncomfortably the second he mentions it. "I *knew* something was up with you. I knew you weren't just having nightmares."

The way he says it makes me think it was more than just twin intuition that led him to this belief. "How did you know?"

He traces a finger down the worn-out spine of the book. "Every night after you fall asleep, I read. Don't look so surprised," he says, with a smirk, not even looking up to see my raised eyebrows. "Contrary to popular belief, I do know how to read, you know."

I snort.

Milo flips open the book, and the pages flutter as if a swift breeze just blew through my room. The words dance across the yellowed paper, each one so heavy with magic I can feel the weight of them without even needing to hold the book in my hands. Every time I try to focus on a single word, it makes my eyes hurt. It's like the magic itself refuses to be pinned down in writing—it's nearly impossible to capture. The energy humming from the pages makes all the little hairs on my arm stand on end. I lean back as far as I can without alerting Milo.

"I've been reading through this, trying to get some idea of a casting that might... I don't know." He runs a hand over the back of his hair, smoothing it down in a familiar gesture. "To be honest, I don't know what I'm looking for. I just want to do *something* to help. But every night when I'm reading, I've noticed that you look sort of... dim."

I blink at him. "I look dim?"

He sits up straighter and pulls the book onto his lap, his hands running absently through its pages. "Yes. Before, when you used to go to the Dreamscape, you faded away. But now when you sleep, you're still here, but it's like your whole essence is muted. Darker. Almost like you're covered in—"

"Shadows," I finish for him, swallowing roughly. Because that's exactly how it feels when I'm in the gray place. Shadowed—halfway between something real and imaginary. Insubstantial. Nearly nothing.

"Yeah, shadows."

We sit in silence for a long moment, both of us lost in thought.

"Like Ollie? How he was Shadowed?" I finally whisper. I think back to the day when we discovered that Ollie had been Shadowed his whole life. He'd always had the potential for magic, but Charlotte had blocked it, hoping to cover it up so effectively that his Claiming would pass him by entirely. Aunt Libby said it could've diminished his power until it was too weak to be Claimed. But the moment Ollie was called to the Dreamscape that first night, the Shadow casting was broken, and then nothing was the same.

Milo frowns and flips through a few pages, passing our family tree and the record of each Claiming. "Not exactly. But something similar." He points to some words on the page, every slanted edge and rolling curve of the letters illegible to me. "There isn't a specific record of a Shadow spell in here, which means that no one in our family line has attempted it. And for good reason," he says. "That's the kind of casting that delves deep into another person's mind, and things could go downhill pretty quickly if you go too far. Honestly, it's kind of amazing that Charlotte was able to pull it off. I don't know how she did it."

He absently taps his thumb against his chin. "But I've been thinking that maybe it has to do with how well you know the mind you're entering and whether or not your intent is good, then maybe the magic cooperates a little better, you know? Even though Ollie was just a baby, Charlotte *knew* him. Same with Libby and Dad; I think that's how she was able to see snatches of the Dreamscape and protect her memory of the name and the place." He fiddles with the edge of the book, his expression sheepish. "Never mind. When I say it out loud, it sounds so stupid."

"No, it doesn't." I've seen magic at its source, and Milo's right. It's far more alive than any of us understand—more flexible, more fragile, more complicated.

"I guess some magic really does defy logic," he says. Then he scoffs and cocks his head to the side. "Well, technically, I guess *all* magic defies logic, right?"

"You could say that again."

"But anyway, all of that has given me an idea." Milo shuts the Chronicles gently, the pages folding into each other with a sound like a sigh. He takes a deep breath and when he exhales, he says, "I was thinking I could do some kind of spin-off of Libby's casting on Dad, something similar like a mirrored version..." He pinches the bridge of his nose, looking tired. "If I can go inside your mind, maybe I can help you see what's on the other side. I know it's not much of a plan, but until we go find Charlotte, it's all we've got."

The sound of Ollie's voicemail is still ringing in my ears, his voice soft and quiet and tinged with laughter—

see you soon, see you soon, see you soon.

There's nothing I want more than to make those words come true. "Okay," I say, my voice coming out higher than usual.

"Okay?"

"Let's just try it and see what happens." I collapse ungracefully on my bed, trying to look braver than I feel even though my hands are starting to shake. "So what do I need to do?"

Milo grabs my desk chair and drags it over to the side of my bed. "Just try to relax, remember?" He sinks into the chair and stares at his hands as if they'll reveal all the answers. "Don't worry, I've got this."

My stomach dips at the sound of his hesitancy.

He cracks each of his knuckles one at a time like he's trying to drag out the moment, avoiding my eyes as he rolls his shoulders. "Try to empty your mind of everything except the Dreamscape. And Ollie." He clears his throat and rubs the back of his neck. "I mean, just think about him in the Dreamscape, that's all. You don't need to, like, *think* about him any more than that—but whatever. You know what I mean."

My cheeks turn a bright shade of pink as I say, "Okay, okay. Got it," before he can embarrass us both any further. But now that Milo's all but opened the door that leads to my memories of Ollie, it's nearly impossible to shut it. I *cannot* let my brother into my mind when I'm thinking about Ollie like this—it would be completely humiliating for both of us. I inhale sharply and try to clear my mind of swirling stars and first kisses, but the more I try not to think about it, the harder it is to stop. Ollie's blue eyes are piercing as he leans in closer, his lips brushing against mine...

Milo's going to kill me.

"Okay, go." I barely get the words out.

He snorts. "This is a little more complicated than putting you to sleep. I can't just snap my fingers and dive into your mind, you know. Give me a minute to find the right words."

"Some prodigy," I mumble out of the corner of my mouth.

"I heard that."

The soft amber glow of my brother's hands filters through my eyelids like the flickering sway of a candle flame, and the closer the light gets, the harder my heart pounds. I exhale deeply, trying to calm the mounting panic in my chest, to focus on the Dreamscape and bringing Ollie home, but it doesn't help. All my hard-won certainty has abandoned me, leaving me feeling more alone than ever.

"I can't do this," I pant through painfully short breaths. "I can't. I can't."

"Breathe, Gemma. It'll be fine," Milo mutters. It sounds like he's gritting his teeth.

The heat of his hands hovers right above me, the sickly yellow glow bleeding through my closed eyes until the warm color darkens to a red so deep it's nearly black. My breath catches in my throat, rough and stuttering. "Wait, stop—"

But I'm not fast enough. His fingertips land on the crown of my head, sending a sharp shock traveling through me all the way to the tips of my toes. I yelp and sit up, roughly brushing his hands away. "I said, *stop*."

"I didn't even do anything yet!" Milo groans, but he pulls his hands back and shoves them into his pockets. "What's the problem?"

The pulse of his magic reverberates through me, matching the frantic pounding of my heart. I try to find the words to explain, but my mouth is too dry to speak, so I just shake my head.

How do I explain this gnawing knot of fear that's stuck in my chest? How do I describe how its roots are spreading, latching onto all the empty spaces that used to hold my magic and my want for it? It pulses like a gaping wound, still fresh and bleeding.

Red.

Why it is always red?

Milo nudges me on the knee with his fist. "Look, if it's about you and Ollie—" His mouth tightens into a thin line, but he holds my gaze. "We don't need to talk about that right now. Let's just see what we can—"

"No, it's not that." But that definitely wasn't helping the situation.

"Then what is it? It's not like I'm going to go rooting around in there." He taps the side of my head and gives me the start of a smile. "I'll just see what you want me to see."

I shove my pillows aside and sit up, sliding quickly off the bed, my muscles tense and loaded like a spring. "Milo, it's more than that." I think about the anxiety that climbed through me, hot and unexpected at Grandma's funeral. The way my pulse skyrocketed when everyone started whispering words of magic. I didn't feel that familiar pull, that longing for more that never seemed to subside. Instead, I just felt this spiky, dizzying fear.

"You were right," I say, pacing back and forth across the rug. "I *am* afraid to feel it. The magic. The last time you went inside my mind, it was almost unbearable. Your magic was completely inescapable, and I didn't like how it made me feel."

Milo doesn't gloat about being right. He just watches me pacing from his perch on my desk chair, his expression thoughtful. "What did it feel like?"

I don't pause to think through my answer. "Terrifyingly out of control," I blurt out. "The last time I held magic..." Like a movie I can't quit watching, the scene replays in my mind. Milo, his face mud-spattered and afraid as he watched me wrap the red thread around his arm in a swift circle. I rub my forehead as the memories of that night tug me deeper into the dark, lonely places of shame. "I tried to take your magic from you, Milo."

Give us the magic. All of it, the thread whispered.

Understanding dawns on his face, but he doesn't cower like I think he should. He looks at me with his amber eyes—Grandma's eyes—and says, "But that wasn't you. It was the thread."

"You don't understand—"

"Listen to me, Gemma. You made mistakes. I made mistakes."

"What do you mean *you* made mistakes? You didn't do anything."

"Yeah, I did." He releases a heavy sigh as if he's been trapping that breath inside him for a very long time. "*I'm* the one who started the fight. *I'm* the one who provoked James." He ducks his head and says, "If I would've just kept my mouth shut, maybe..."

Maybe. At the sound of that weighted word, new possibilities unroll before me, alternate paths not taken. Maybe if Milo hadn't lost his temper, then maybe Grandma wouldn't have needed to defend us, and maybe I never would've taken hold of the red thread. Maybe I would've realized that I already had everything I could ever want. Maybe I could've let that be enough.

I let the possibilities fade away before they're allowed the chance to fully take shape inside my mind. We made our choices, and these are the consequences. Maybes and what ifs—none of that matters now.

"It's not your fault, you know," I say quietly.

"Then it's not yours either."

We stare at each other in a silent standoff, each waiting for the other to back down first. Finally, Milo tosses one of my pillows at me and says, "Truce?"

I make a noncommittal noise as I lay back down on my bed, clutching my pillow against my chest and closing my eyes. "Just tell me this: what's the worst thing that could happen if this casting goes wrong?"

He pauses for too long. "Well, I could get stuck inside your mind and never find my way back out again, and we'd probably both go insane."

"Good to know," I say, sinking deeper into my pillows. I don't bother telling him that I already know what it's like to hear voices inside my head, to feel like I'm losing my mind.

"But seriously, that's not going to happen."

"Also good to know."

Milo scoots forward in his chair and raises his hands. "Ready?"

"Not in the slightest," I answer back at the same moment his glowing hands land gently on my temple. I try to clear my mind of everything except Ollie.

I'm coming, I want to whisper. *I never should've left you*, I want to say.

My shoulders tense as that same tingling rush of magic enters my skin. Something brushes along my consciousness. At first, it feels unassuming and feather-light, barely enough for me to register it. But soon it grows insistent and smothering, like that feeling when someone stands too close to you and there's no room to back away.

"Try to breathe, Gem," Milo mutters. "You're locking me out."

His hands shake as his magic nudges against my mind again,

like a pair of eyes boring into the back of my skull. I breathe through it, just like Grandma taught me, letting my memories fade into a sea of stars and swaying silver threads shining like moonbeams. And in the hazy glow, I picture his face.

Ollie. He's waiting for me.

Milo's hands shine even brighter as he whispers a few words in the Language, the slippery sound of his casting sending a shiver up my spine. In the corner of my mind, there's a flash of light and a crash of noise, like the sound of a backdoor flying open and slamming into the wall. Then a crackle of energy and suddenly—I'm not alone.

Milo. I can't see him, but I can feel him. His presence is undeniable; it's like I just let a golden retriever loose in my house. But under his familiar enthusiastic energy, there's an edge to him that surprises me. A depth that almost feels unknowable. It makes me wonder how much of himself he hides behind all his jokes and easy smiles.

Even from me.

Having him inside my head is unbelievably uncomfortable and awkward. It's as if the two of us have been shoved into a small closet only big enough for one person. It's all elbows and craning necks and a muggy, claustrophobic feeling that makes me want to run, to find the wide open sky and never look back.

Slowly, a muted fog seeps in until it washes everything out, its long tendrils wrapping around me like clinging, pale fingers. I suppress a shudder and tuck my arms around myself. I hate this place, I hate this feeling, and I hate that my brother's here to watch me hate it.

"Whoa, where are we?"

I nearly scream when Milo appears next to me. He waves his hands in my face, looking not quite solid, not quite see-through. He gives me a strained smile. "See? Prodigy," he says. His voice sounds echoey and far away like it's coming from underwater.

"This is bizarre," I mumble, trying not to let on how uncomfortable his presence is making me. But I'm sure he can feel it. He is in my mind after all.

The grayness flickers like a TV screen covered in fuzzy static. Milo glances up, his mouth pulled into a frown. "You need to concentrate, Gemma. You're too focused on me right now. Just think about the Dreamscape and Ollie. I'll see what you see."

I stumble forward into the nothingness. "But there's nothing to see!" I call back over my shoulder, but no one is there—Milo has vanished.

"Focus." His voice slices through my mind, forcing its way around my other thoughts, the sound of it piercing and foreign as it filters through the surrounding mist.

I try to make some kind of forward progress, but it's impossible to tell which direction I'm moving in. "Ollie?" I cry out, just like I do every night. "Ollie, can you hear me?"

There's a pulse humming through the static, low and steady, the sound of it vibrating under my bare feet. *"Follow it,"* Milo commands, confirming my suspicions that there's magic somewhere out there. *"And hurry,"* he adds. *"I don't know how much longer I can hold onto this."* The sound of his casting drifts past me, making it hard to focus on anything other than the shape of each word.

The humming grows louder as I start to run. I stretch my hands out in front of me, reaching through the heavy mist until my fingers tangle into something almost tangible. I stiffen, my fingers snagging on the hint of something cool and vaporous. It's how I'd always imagined it would feel to run my hands through a cloud—like a whisper you could touch. The humming intensifies, sending chills racing up my arms.

"What is it?" Milo asks, his voice passing through my mind like one of my own thoughts.

"I think it's..." I pause, holding my hands as still as I possibly can. "Threads. I think I found some threads." They're not as solid as the ones I remember from the Dreamscape, but the feeling is too similar to deny.

"Are they... are they leading anywhere?" Milo's question staggers as he fights to catch his breath; he sounds like he's barely holding on. His whispered casting grows louder and louder as I stumble forward, trying to make my way through the misty fog and the heaviness surrounding me—all the things keeping me from seeing Ollie.

"I don't know, I can't see anything." I grip the threads in my hands, wrapping the impossibly thin strands around my wrist. I can hardly feel them against my skin. Frustration mounts in my chest and climbs up my throat, hot and agitating.

"Focus, Gemma," Milo warns me, his voice slipping in and out of my subconscious.

"On what?" I yell back. "It doesn't matter how much I concentrate or how often I think about him. I'm still here, and he's still there!"

Milo doesn't answer, but his quiet determination is palpable. It shines a light on my thoughts, searching for solutions in forgotten corners of my mind that I wouldn't think to look into. I close my eyes and rub my face, and the first thing I think of is the night of our Claiming, the way Ollie was trapped in the shadows. He struggled against them, trying to escape, but he couldn't do it on his own. He needed me.

"Ollie," I sigh into the night, sending out a whispered plea, the bare beginnings of a spell.

Isn't that how all magic starts? With a wish?

My voice combines with Milo's, blending into a single note that gives me goosebumps. The shadows bleed out of my hands like steam evaporating into the cold with a hiss as the gray nothingness grows darker and darker until it transforms into a deep midnight black.

My breathing stops when I see it.

The Dreamscape.

CHAPTER TWELVE

OLLIE

"**D**ID YOU HEAR that?" I yell pointlessly into the void. "I'm quitting! I'm finished! I'm going to find a way out of here!" My pledge bounces off the cavern walls, loudly at first, but quieter with every echo; it sounds feeble by the time it makes its way back to me. "I'm coming home, Gemma," I whisper. "I'm coming home."

How? I have no idea. Not a clue. But for the first time since I ended up stuck here, I feel a sense of purpose, a bold persistence in changing the course of my fate. I don't know how much time I've lost, but I do know that I don't want to waste another minute of it.

Not another second without her.

The Dreamscape shakes and the stars shoot through the sky, a chaos of color. It's as if the cavern has heard my declaration and is pulling out all the stops to try and change my mind. The threads of the Claiming still hover in front of me, bobbing gently up and down and dipping into my line of sight.

My magic surges forward, willing me to touch it, to start the Claiming. My hands tingle with such an intense buzzing sensation it's almost painful. I cross my arms tightly over my chest, which makes me feel childish and stupid, but what other choice do I have? If I lose my focus for the slightest moment, I know what'll happen. I've seen it all play out already. I'll start the Claiming, and that will be the end of me.

Magic only needs a vessel.

The cavern trembles violently under my feet, the floor aglow with the silver threads still shaking loose, like some sort of mythological creature that's been asleep for centuries only to be woken once more. Hungry and ready to devour. More silver threads snap free from the walls until everything feels like it's about to cave in, like the crumbling of a sheet of paper, compacting and crushing more with every movement.

I take a few steps back, but the threads of the Claiming only follow. I make sure not to touch them, tucking my arms more firmly against myself because I don't know what else to do. If I just stand here, the threads will get me eventually. I try not to think about the seventeen-year-old boy or girl who's standing there waiting to Claim their magic, waiting for me without knowing it. I shake my head back and forth, trying to dislodge the guilt that's burrowing inside my brain, but that doesn't help.

So, I start to run.

It feels strange to run without Gemma's silhouette in front of me. I'm so used to seeing the outline of her shape, always a few paces ahead of me, that my mind keeps imagining her here, her black hair flicking to the side as she looks over her shoulder and laughs.

My lungs fill with the stagnant air of a cave long forgotten as I pump my arms and legs faster and faster, running with no destination in mind, just simply to get away. I run until I can't run anymore, until I fall forward with my hands gripping my knees and my chest heaving. A flicker of light shines just over my head, and without even needing to look up, I know exactly what I'll see.

A Claiming demanding to be tied.

It seems I can't outrun who I am.

Time for Option B.

I slam my hands down on the wall in front of me and grab onto a fistful of the silver threads before they have the chance to latch onto me. Then I swiftly wrap them around my fist and give them a hard tug. The whole cavern shudders and I stumble on my feet, but I don't let go. I pull the threads closer to my face and watch the shimmering lights dance across my skin, marveling at how different they feel. Strange and foreign, like another species. It's not the full magic that I've held in my hands, waiting to be Claimed. This magic is inflexible and unyielding, metallic in color and feeling. Powerful but also empty.

This cavern constructed from these shimmering silver threads—brighter than the stars and lighter than air—is actually just a beautifully constructed cage built for two.

And now just for one.

Without Gemma here to hold the Dreamscape, everything's unstable and weak. So I run past the sloping walls, yanking handful after handful of threads, uprooting them from their rightful places. My magic recoils against the destruction; it feels wrong in every way to break the one thing I'm supposed to protect.

Protect and honor the weaving, my magic whispered to me on the night of my Claiming.

Break the Claimings, she used to say.

I rip up another fistful of threads, their silver gleam a soft glow in my hand. The Dreamscape tips from side to side, like a head shaking back and forth.

No no no, it seems to say.

"Then make me stop!" I yell back.

None of this makes any sense, and I am sick of it.

In a flash, I remember the night I took Gemma's magic from her, how the memories of former Threaders danced around us, half-formed and hazier than a dream. Each of them fighting over this magic and how to balance it. Fighting over fate itself, damaged beyond repair.

The Threaders of magic, two ripped at the seams.

In that same flash of memory, the solution is suddenly crystal clear to me: I need to undo what's already been broken.

I try to think with my magic, not my brain. I picture the silver thread trailing from my chest where my magic resides, leading to the rest of the weaving. My right hand reaches out and hooks it with my fingers as my left hand grabs another silver thread dangling off the wall. My magic in one hand, Gemma's magic in the other.

I tie the two together in a simple knot before sliding them swiftly across my forearm, leaving a small slash on my skin. The threads glisten with the dark stain of my blood. The Dreamscape stills for just a moment as if it too is remembering that night long ago when Lillian and Atticus gathered the silver threads in their hands and unknowingly bound us all in a curse of forgetting. The same night Cora broke the red thread, changing everything.

"Help me fix it," I whisper. *"Please."*

Words fill my mouth, heavy and hopeful, and before I even register what I'm saying, they're tumbling out in a steady flow, rhythmic and haunting.

> *"By blood, we balance.*
> *By blood, we change.*
> *What once was broken*
> *no longer remains.*
> *Stripped of these chains,*
> *freed and unbound,*
> *the Threaders of magic,*
> *when two become found."*

My voice sounds nothing like my own; the words ring with an authority that I certainly don't possess. There's a finality to them that shakes the ground below my feet.

My heart thuds in my chest as I wait for the consequences to reveal themselves. But nothing happens. All that remains is a moment of stillness, a quiet so profound it makes me wonder if I've ever truly heard silence before. Because this silence goes beyond just what I can hear—I can *feel* it.

The threads of our magic, mine and Gemma's, dangle limply in my hands. My grip relaxes and slowly the silver threads slip through my fingers.

What else is there to do but let go?

The stars flicker once, twice. I remember when I was twelve, I heard that most of the stars in the sky were actually dead, but because they were so far away—lightyears and lightyears away—their light just kept on shining for us until one day—*poof.* Death caught up in a single second, and they vanished. I remember looking out my window at the night sky and feeling a strange sense of dread that I didn't understand. How could stars like that even die?

I couldn't sleep. I couldn't stop obsessing over it. All I could think was this: if something that big and that beautiful could go out in a blink, what does that mean for me, an ordinary boy, just a speck in this big wide universe?

I only later learned that it isn't true. Most of the stars in the sky are alive and well and will still be shining long after I'm gone. But sometimes when I can't sleep at night the thought of it still haunts me.

Poof.

Death caught up in a single second.

I look up at the weaving and wait. The stars flicker again. And then one by one, they start to go out.

I close my eyes. And that's the moment I hear her.

"Ollie."

CHAPTER THIRTEEN

GEMMA

I T FLICKERS IN and out of sight like a distorted view from behind a gauzy curtain. It's hard to make out the details of what lies beyond. It's not the Dreamscape I remember but rather the *idea* of it. Like a brand-new thought, uncertain and wavering, it refuses to fully form.

The stars are weak and far away, not the brilliant galaxy that used to make me tip my head back in wonder. Lightning streaks across the sky in distant bursts, but I barely register it. My heart pounds as I lean forward to get a better look, but I'm immediately met with resistance. It feels as if I'm standing on tiptoe and pressing my nose against a window, trying desperately to see through the foggy glass. Countless threads curl around me, dark and unfamiliar as they wind around my wrists and ankles.

A soft sound brushes against my ear, like a secret caught in the wind. The words are muffled and faint; they slide across my skin, rough and uncertain.

...the Threaders of magic,
when two become found.

I don't understand what it means. The threads that were wrapping around me go still, and all I hear is the sound of my breath. The air suddenly has a stagnant quality to it as if I've just entered a space that's been left alone for far too long. A place forgotten.

"Ollie!" This time I don't whisper. This time his name comes loud and clear like the ringing of a bell. I squint through the darkness, scanning through the emptiness, searching for any sign of him.

"Gemma? What's going on? Are—okay? I can't—you... anymore—" Milo's voice cuts in and out like a cell phone with bad reception. I feel a tugging sensation, sharp and abrupt in its attempt to pull me back out, but I shake it off and keep pushing forward, calling Ollie's name over and over again.

The stars flicker, still fuzzy in their lack of form, more like pale blinking smudges of light. And I don't know if I'm imagining it, but it looks like they're starting to disappear.

The stars. One by one.

My hands catch on handfuls of threads, insubstantial as air as they slip through my fingers. I shove down the panic that threatens to choke me. Nothing about this feels right—the threads, the stars, the aching quiet.

Where is he?

Then, a cracking sound tears through the silence like a gunshot. I flinch against the suddenness of it, stumbling back a few steps. The noise ricochets around me, splintering into a hundred other sounds that leave me feeling shaken and small.

And in the middle of the chaos, at the heart of it all, I finally see him.

Oliver.

He's here.

My heart surges as I see him standing there, hunched over, his hands resting against the worn fabric of his jeans, his dark head of hair dipped low as he stares at what used to be the floor of the Dreamscape, but is now a gigantic crack that zigzags across the cavern at a dizzying speed. His brow is puckered, his mouth tucked into a puzzled frown, and when he looks up to watch what's left of the stars blinking, I notice that he's lost his glasses.

But he's *here*, and for the first time in weeks, I feel like I can breathe.

"Ollie!"

He turns in the direction of the sound of my voice, his blue eyes wide and shining.

"Gemma?" he says in disbelief. His voice comes out gravelly and deep like he hasn't used it in a while. He clears his throat. "Where are—how—"

The ground shakes again, sending him sprawling to the floor as the crack below him stretches further and widens deeper, yawning like it's preparing to swallow him whole.

"Ollie, move!"

He scrambles to his feet, nearly tipping over again as he breaks out in a sprint. His arms pump as his bare feet slide across the stone floor, but he's not fast enough. I don't think anyone or anything could be fast enough.

I stretch out my hand uselessly; I don't even know if he can see me. But he must because, with a wildly determined look on his face, he stretches out his hand toward me.

I imagine his fingers lacing through mine. I imagine pulling him through to the other side of this nightmare—to home and family and *us*. I imagine it so vividly, the picture so clear in my mind that I can almost feel the warmth of his hand in mine, his pulse pounding as he grabs onto me and sighs in relief. I imagine it so forcefully that I swear I can see through the sheer impossibility of it.

As I watch him run, I imagine it all.

A graze of skin. A flash of heat.

Ollie.

Then a searing pain rips through my skull.

OLLIE

She's here.

She's here?

I'm running toward her but my mind can't make sense of it. For a second, I worry that I've totally lost it, that I've conjured a mirage of Gemma out of loneliness and desperation, but then she says my name again and the sound of it is more real than anything I could've ever imagined.

She's here.

She's indistinct in the half-light with her hand reaching out to mine, but even through the growing shadows, the sight of her makes my breath stutter and stop. Every single one of my earlier doubts feels shallow and meaningless now. How could I ever have questioned the way Gemma feels about me? *She loves me.* I see it in her eyes and the shape of her mouth, the urgency in how she stretches out her hand.

Whatever else might've happened, whatever mistakes were made between us, she still loves me. I hold onto that feeling tighter than I've ever held on to anything in my life because it's only in this moment—a moment filled with absolute perfect clarity—that I realize my belief in her is the one thing that's going to get me home.

Even as the stars blink out of existence and the cavern itself threatens to eat me alive, all I can see is her.

The Dreamscape shakes again, and in a roaring rush, the branching crack finally catches up to me. My foot snags on the silver threads that trail through the crumbling pearlescent floor. Hot air rises up to greet me, like whatever waits below is boiling over in its rush to escape.

My hands grip the edge of the crevasse where the floor has split wide open, my feet dangling below me.

Why did I think I could fix what was broken?

The cavern rumbles in reply, shaking my hands loose until my vise-like grip grows slack. I throw my head back as I fall, hoping for one last glimpse of Gemma, but all I see is the slow fade of the stars overhead. They stare impassable and immovable, reproachful in their coldness and their inability to care about what happens to me.

After all, they needed me, and I refused.

Magic always has consequences.

"Gemma!" I cry out like a last Hail Mary. "I'll find you!"

As the Dreamscape crumbles around me, I feel like that twelve-year-old kid again: if something that big and that beautiful could go out in a blink, what does that mean for me, an ordinary boy, just a speck in this big wide universe?

Darkness.

CHAPTER FOURTEEN
GEMMA

HE'S GONE.
One second Ollie was there, calling out my name, and the next...

Nothing.

"No," I whisper. "No." I crane my neck, trying to get a better view of the widening gash in the floor where Ollie vanished in a single second, but the threads where I stand are wild and reckless, whipping back and forth and blocking my path.

The Dreamscape folds in on itself, the floor buckling as the walls cave in like they always threatened to every time Ollie tied a Claiming. And I'm not there to hold them up, to keep him safe. I choke out a sob and try to push through the fraying edges of the gray place, but no matter how hard I try, no matter how hard I shove, I just can't make it to the other side. Because to be on the other side, you have to have magic, and I don't. I still don't have the right keys to the door.

A frustrated groan slips out my mouth as another bolt of pain rips through my head. It feels like claws are tearing me to shreds from the inside out. I want to break through the rest of these barriers and run through the cavern; I want to find Ollie and bring him home, but this pain is making it hard to think. My vision swims and the Dreamscape wavers in and out of view. I feel like I'm going to be sick.

I close my eyes and massage my forehead with my knuckles. "Milo, something's wrong," I say, my jaw clenching.

No answer.

"Milo!"

There's a fluttering motion to my right and a sound like a tea kettle boiling over, high-pitched and whistling. What's left of the Dreamscape shudders out of sight as my concentration and connection to Ollie are spread too thin. Like the sudden blowing out of a candle, everything goes dark.

I hunch my shoulders and scream as Milo's grip on my mind tightens like he's trying to white-knuckle his way out of here. Snatches of his thoughts interrupt my own, passing too quickly for me to process, but they all have the same sharp edge to them: fear.

"Gemma, I'm here, I'm here. I'm trying—I can't —" Milo's faint voice sounds as pained as mine. The high-pitched noise intensifies until it's all I can think about. It rings and it rings like a warning bell—absolute and undeniable.

We're out of time.

A heavy, smothering pressure makes it hard to breathe. I try to hold onto myself, to cling to the things that make me Gemma, but Milo's presence presses too heavily for me to remember anything clearly. My likes, my dislikes; the things that make my heart burst, and the things that make me cry—all of it slowly slips away as if it was never there in the first place. There isn't enough space in my mind for two people, and there never was. That fact seems incredibly obvious now. I guess I should've known this wasn't going to work from the very moment he'd said, *"Well, I could get stuck inside your mind and never find my way back out again, and we'd probably both go insane."*

Hasty plans with stupid beginnings tend to have stupid endings too.

Suddenly, the squeezing pressure shifts, and I feel a hand grabbing onto my arm, pulling me out with a hurried tug. Everything narrows and spins until I'm convinced that right here, right now, I am going to die.

And then I open my eyes to the sight of my bedroom walls

washed in moonlight. The clock on my nightstand flashes the time in neon blue numbers. *1:58 am?* Milo was inside my mind for over six hours. That realization makes my head spin even more. "Milo?" I croak, panicking when I don't see him in the chair next to the side of my bed. He groans from somewhere on the floor in response.

A small hand grabs me by the chin, yanking my head up. "Gemma, can you see me? Are you okay?" Libby hovers over my bed, moving my head from side to side and tracking my movements, glaring at me with brown eyes so dark they're nearly black. She's out of breath and absolutely furious. "Please tell me you're okay," she says through gritted teeth. "Please tell me you're okay so I can properly berate you without worrying you're about to pass out or throw up in the middle of it." Her voice is pure acid. I've never seen her this angry.

"Yeah... yeah. I think I'm okay." I rub my hand across my head to make sure it's all in one piece. Only seconds ago it felt like my whole body was about to split down the middle.

"Good." She drops her hand away from my face. "Now, what were you *thinking*?" she asks, sinking onto my bed, her posture stiff and unforgiving, my Dreamscape letter clasped tightly in her hand. She's wearing Grandma's fuzzy purple bathrobe; it looks out of character and far too large on her small frame. As if reading my thoughts, Libby tugs the tie more firmly around her waist with a scowl.

"Aunt Lib, we were just—" Milo tries to stand, but his shaking legs give out and he tumbles back to the floor. His pale green t-shirt is soaked in sweat.

She turns her glare on him. "Don't even start with me, Milo. You *know* better. You *know* how volatile and risky mind magic is! I thought you had a better grasp on your magic than this. I thought I could trust you."

Milo grimaces and smacks the back of his head against the floor, closing his eyes.

Libby stands again and paces the room, her hands heavy on

her hips. "If I hadn't heard the two of you screaming your heads off and come in here to fix everything, you both could've died. And you're lucky it was me who found you and not your mom. What do you think that would do to her if something happened to either of you? Did you even stop to think about that?" She narrows her glare, and Milo and I both shrink away from her. "No mind is meant to be shared for that long. You two have *no* idea what you're doing. This is magic that cannot be messed around with."

Milo's head dips, his hair flopping sadly over his forehead like a worn-out flag of surrender. "We shouldn't have done it, I know—"

"Yes, we should've," I cut in, sitting up straighter. If Milo's posture is a study of defeat, mine was made for battle. I feel like I've been slapped in the face or had a bucket of icy cold water dumped over my head. Seeing Ollie has jolted me awake. "Milo, it *worked*. I could see inside."

He sits up in a rush, his expression hesitantly hopeful. "I couldn't tell. There was too much for me to focus on with the casting. It felt like I was trying to hold a roof up with my bare hands." Libby practically snarls at him, and he flinches. "Did you see him?" he asks quietly.

"Yes, I saw him," I whisper.

Milo exhales and deflates back onto the floor with his hands over his face. "So he's okay." A short, sputtering sound that could almost be called a laugh bursts out of him. "He's okay," he repeats into his hands, the tone of his voice painfully relieved. "So what's next? How do we get him out?"

Libby chews on her lip as she listens to us, clearly torn between wanting to continue her lecture and wanting to hear more about what happened. She crosses her arms and raises her eyebrows expectantly in an unspoken invitation for me to continue.

My stomach twists into knots over what I have to say next. "Well, he *was* okay—"

"Wait, what do you mean 'was?'" Milo's newly formed smile twitches, the left corner of his mouth turning down.

My eyes prick with the hint of new tears. I take a deep breath and let it out in a rush. "I don't know, something's wrong. I was able to see through to the other side of the Dreamscape, but it was... different." I think back to how the stars refused to shine, the way everything collapsed in on itself like it couldn't hold the weight of it any longer.

Or maybe Ollie couldn't.

"The floor ripped, right down the middle. And that's where he fell." My eyes aren't just stinging now. I wipe at the tears that made their escape and are trailing down my cheeks, carving out new rivers made of grief and regret. "Oliver's gone. And I think the Dreamscape is... broken."

Milo hangs his head, all his temporary elation forgotten. Libby sinks back onto the bed and wraps an arm around me. "I'm still mad you two did something so stupidly reckless and that you didn't ask for help, but I am glad that you could see him. Even just for a moment."

She rubs her hand up and down my arm in a gesture of comfort, but her kindness is lost on me. I want to shake her off; I want to kick the door in; I want to scream. What was the point of it all? To endure that magic, to have Milo scraping down the inside of my mind? What was the point of seeing Ollie only to have him ripped out of my reach once again?

It feels like a cruel twist of fate to have caught a glimpse of him only to watch him tumble headfirst into the darkness seconds later. I know what happens when magic swallows you whole: you never make it out alive. That's what happened to my dad, to Ben, and to every other Threader who lost their way.

I don't know what's on the other side of this magic, and it's killing me.

Libby drops her arm from around me and reaches for the Chronicles still lying on my bed. "Maybe we can find a casting to..." She trails off, uncertain.

Find a casting to what? To go back in time and fix this mess? I watch as she thumbs through the crinkling pages. I want to knock the book out of her hands and tell her it's no use. We're not going to find any answers in there, not when we don't even know what questions to ask.

My head is throbbing. I rub a knuckle right over my eyebrow, kneading the skin until that pain is sharper than my headache. I can't stop replaying the image of Ollie reaching out to me, his hand grasping for mine in the dark, and then—

"Wait, what is this?" Libby mutters, her startled tone bursting through my memories like the sudden popping of a bubble. She leans in closer over the open page of the book, her nose nearly skimming the words—which shimmer as if they're etched in silver ink—and she begins to read, her voice rhythmic and clear.

> *"By blood, we balance.*
> *By blood, we change.*
> *What once was broken*
> *no longer remains.*
> *Stripped of these chains,*
> *freed and unbound,*
> *the Threaders of magic,*
> *when two become found."*

"What—what did you just say?" I shudder involuntarily as the power of the Language, the indisputable magic in each word carefully chosen and delivered, washes over me.

"It just... *appeared*, almost like someone was standing over my shoulder whispering the words into the book themselves," she says, her voice tinged with excitement and a hint of disbelief. "I've never seen the books behave like this, I—" She stumbles over what to say, completely at a loss. "Do you know what this means?" she finally asks. "Have you ever heard this before?"

I look once more at the squiggling words dancing across the page, the silver writing glistening like the threads of the Dreamscape. "No, I'm not sure what it means," I say, slumping against my pillows. "But I have heard it before—just the last part."

The Threaders of magic, when two become found.

Those were the strange words that I heard in the gray place only moments before I saw Ollie tonight. I can still hear the sound of the Language echoing through the shadows while the stars looked on just beyond my reach.

The world around me fades as I remember the last time I heard words similar to those in a memory lost to time and the Dreamscape, standing side by side with Ollie, our hands clutched between us.

By blood, we balance.
By blood, we curse.
What once was given,
must now be learned.

Pictures fly through my mind of Cora breaking the red thread of fate, of Lillian and Atticus trying to stop her, and the curses and consequences that followed after meddling with magic that didn't want to be messed with.

Tied and bound
but only in dreams,
the Threaders of magic,
two ripped at the seams.

I close my eyes and try to think through the pounding of my head. I feel as if I'm standing on the deck of a ship in the middle of a storm. Everything sways back and forth as I try to right myself against another wave. And another. And another.

My eyes fly open in a flash. "Milo, tell me what you know about the Dreamscape."

He sits up and rubs his face. He looks as if he wants to question me but is far too tired to fight me on it, so instead he launches into a perfectly clear explanation of the Dreamscape and mine and Ollie's magic.

I stare at him openmouthed, then reach across the bed to where the Dreamscape letter sits next to Libby. I toss the worn envelope onto his lap. "You didn't even need to read this, but you still remembered anyway."

Libby and Milo both sit up straighter and look at each other in disbelief. "Whoa," he says. "So do you think that means—"

"That Ollie broke the curse when he broke the Dreamscape? Possibly... 'What once was broken no longer remains,'" I repeat the words slowly, skeptically, too afraid to get my hopes up.

By blood, we balance. By blood, we change...

What did you do, Oliver?

"I think I'll be able to remember from now on," Milo says confidently. "It doesn't feel so hazy anymore. It's getting clearer." He taps the side of his head, then winces, massaging his forehead like me. "It's all up here, safe and sound." He flicks the envelope on my desk with a satisfied smile. "Good riddance—I'm so sick of reading that thing."

"Same here," Libby says as she flips through the pages of the Chronicles in a flurry. She's hardly listening to us; all her anger over the mind magic seems to have temporarily vanished in the face of her discovery. After the last week of her silence and solitude, it's a relief to see her animated once again, to see her hunched over a book and lost in thought.

I run my hands through my hair, wishing I could scrub away all this confusion and the headache promising retribution. *Stripped of these chains, freed and unbound...* If Ollie's gone and he's not there to tie the Claimings, what does that mean for the magic? For all of the Claimed?

Pushing off the bed, I hop to my feet and nudge Milo's leg. "Hey, when is Sylvia's Claiming?"

"Tomorrow," he says. "Well, actually today," he amends once

he catches sight of the time on my clock. "Why? I thought you didn't want to go?"

I didn't. But that was before. Now the Dreamscape is broken and there are no Threaders to release the Claimings. Now I need to see what happens when magic doesn't have someone holding its leash.

A small but bright fire smolders deep inside me, hot embers against the irresistible darkness of everything else. The darkness of quitting, of feeling too small to make a difference, of crying until there's nothing left. This flicker of fire isn't strong enough for me to call it hope, but at least it's *something* when before there was nothing.

I lift my chin and look at my brother, trying to keep my voice steady as I say, "Go pack your bags. I think we need to take a little road trip."

CHAPTER FIFTEEN

OLLIE

THE SUMMER I turned twelve years old, I went through a phase where I couldn't fall asleep at night. What started as existential dread quickly escalated into me lying there for hours, tossing and turning, staring up at the glow-in-the-dark stars on my ceiling, so desperate to fall asleep that sometimes it would bring me to tears.

Insomnia. I wouldn't wish it on my worst enemy.

My parents tried everything. Too much light? Blackout curtains. Too dark? Leave the light on in the hall. White noise machines, soft music, my dad sitting on the floor next to my bed reading out loud to me from his most boring legal briefs—none of that helped. They even dragged the TV from the living room down the hall and into my room in the hopes that maybe a favorite movie playing in the background would finally lull me to sleep.

Nope.

Instead, I would stay awake for most of the night until the early morning hours just before the sun came up—that in-between time of day when the gray light of dawn still clings to the navy blue of a midnight come and gone. Only then would I succumb to sleep in a fit of pure exhaustion.

But twelve-year-old kids don't survive very well on two hours of sleep every night. After a while, not even Milo could tease me about how tired I was, which is when I knew I was officially pathetic. He saw the dark circles under my eyes—purplish and bruise-like—and the way I would stare off blankly. I was basically a zombie.

With a bleary gaze, I watched the clock all day long, too tired to do anything but dread when I'd have to try to fall asleep again.

My mom took me to see a therapist. He had me draw pictures while he gently asked what I was worried about. I drew a black sky full of stars, pressing so hard on the crayon that it snapped in half. I looked up at the nice man in the wrinkled sweater vest and square-frame glasses and told him that one day we were all going to die and that I wanted to stop thinking about it, but I didn't know how, and all he did was blink at me sadly a few times before nodding and saying, "Yes, Oliver. One day we will all die."

The next time my mom tried to take me back to Mr. Sweater Vest I refused to get in the car.

Logically, I knew it was stupid. I wasn't even really afraid to die, so what was the big deal? I felt broken and strange, obsessive and weird. My parents were totally distraught; they begged me to talk to them. But after the therapist and his matter-of-fact, *"Yes, Oliver. One day we will all die,"* I didn't know how to bring up those gnawing worries again.

I just waited for it to go away.

One night, as the sun went down, I opened the front door to see Gemma and Milo standing on my porch dressed in their pajamas and with sleeping bags rolled up in their arms. They camped out in my room for three days—that must've been when my parents hit rock bottom. Nothing screams desperation like inviting more pre-teens into your home after hours.

We built a giant blanket fort, rolled out our sleeping bags, and binged on all our favorite movies and junk food. But every night without fail, Milo would peacefully drift off mid-sentence, and Gemma would start snoring softly from where she was sprawled out next to me, her legs twitching even in sleep, and I would be left alone, wide awake in the quiet.

On the last morning of our epic sleepover, Ellen showed up at our house with a light rapping on our door and a knowing smile on her mouth. She sent the twins home, then huddled in the kitchen with my parents, her sleek silver hair tucked into its usual tight bun. I barely registered their whispers and worried glances from where I sat at the table, trying to summon the energy to lift my cereal spoon. Their words floated over to me, hardly pausing to land before fluttering away.

"It's an old family recipe," Ellen said. "I think it could help."

My bloodshot eyes fell on the small glass bottle in her hand. I remember how the sun from the kitchen window caught on the curves of the glass, throwing the swirling contents into sharp relief. I squinted at the bottle, unable to determine if it held a liquid or a gas, the dark purple a shade so deep it looked like sleep itself bottled in a jar.

I sighed so loudly that the three of them looked over at me.

After a hopeful nod from my mom, Ellen walked over to the kitchen table where I was slumped in my seat. She reached out a stained hand and pulled me from my chair. "Come with me, Ollie boy. Let's get you to bed."

I didn't reply, I just clung to her hand and marched obediently after her.

Before we'd made it down the hall, the front door flew open and there was Gemma. "Can I stay? *Please?*" she begged her grandma, her round eyes flicking back and forth between the bottle held in Ellen's hand and me.

Ellen shook her head ruefully and chuckled. "Fine. But only if you hold still and stay quiet."

Gemma nodded solemnly and followed behind us. Once in my room, Ellen pulled my curtains shut, then flipped my striped comforter down with a flick of her wrist before glancing over her shoulder to see me still standing unsure in my doorframe. "Well, why don't you lie down, Oliver?"

Gemma took me by my elbow and pulled me over to my bed, giving me a little push onto my pillows. Ellen held up the small bottle in her hand and shook it a few times until the contents were swirling. In my sleep-deprived state, I could've sworn it began to glow.

I rolled over onto my side, scrunching my face into my pillow. "It's no use," I mumbled. "I don't know how to sleep anymore." The words were heavy and thick on my tongue like syrup, making my mouth clumsy and awkward. "Maybe there's something wrong with me." I couldn't think of another thing to say, so I just let my admission hang there in the air.

"There's nothing wrong with you, Ollie. You just need help remembering, that's all," Gemma quipped.

Ellen shushed her, but then said, "Gemma's right. All you need is a little help, my boy."

"And what makes you think *you* can help?" I said into my pillow, ruder than usual and not bothering to care.

"Oh, I think this will help. I made it myself." Ellen tugged on my shoulder, rolling me off my side until I was lying flat on my back again, her mouth curled into a wry smile. "Don't you want to try?" She waved a small teaspoon back and forth a few times. *Like a witch waving a wand*, I thought to myself.

I pinched my eyes shut and shook my head with my lips pressed tightly together, refusing to even entertain the thought of successfully falling asleep.

"Come on, Ollie," Gemma whispered.

Even when bone-tired, I couldn't seem to turn off my people-pleasing tendencies, so I opened my eyes and held out a reluctant hand. "Whatever."

Ellen made a small noise somewhere between a laugh and an exasperated sigh as she poured a portion of the bottle onto the spoon. "You can thank me tomorrow. I like brownies."

"Me too," Gemma added. Ellen shushed her again.

I gulped down the mouthful, surprised at its sweetness and how icy cold it was. I dropped the spoon and shivered as a feeling of euphoria washed over me, along with a tingling sense of anticipation. All the colors in my room momentarily flashed brighter before everything started to fade, the edges of my bookcase blurring until it looked more like a mirage than anything solid. Ellen switched off the lamp on my nightstand and all the stars on my ceiling began to glow.

I turned to her with what I'm sure was a goofy smile on my face and hiccuped a laugh.

"Are you giggling, Oliver Cade?" Ellen asked with a laugh of her own before fluffing my pillow and pulling my blanket up to my chin. Gemma leaned over her grandma's shoulder and grinned down at me.

Every time I blinked, their faces swam, looking disjointed and inside out, all their colors wrong but not in a scary way. I laughed again. "This must be what dreaming feels like," I sighed. "It's weird. It's nice. I like it."

Ellen's smile flipped into a frown. "What do you mean?" She paused, her eyebrows arching. "Have you never had a dream before?"

I closed my eyes and all the colors stopped spinning, but they still danced behind my eyelids. "Nope. Never never ever."

"Never ever," Gemma repeated. "It's true."

"Hmm, that's odd," Ellen said, more to herself than to me.

"You're odd," I replied with a yawn. "And you always smell like you've just been struck by lightning."

Ellen snorted the same way Gemma does when something funny sneaks up on her. "Is that right? Well, Ollie, I think you'll be glad for my oddness come morning. I don't think you'll have any more trouble with that pesky insomnia again."

"Why?" I breathed out, my eyes still closed. My pillows felt like marshmallows, soft and swelling and warm; I'd never felt so comfortable in my whole life.

"Just trust me," is all she said. She ruffled my hair before standing up, both of her knees popping loudly in the quiet.

"But what about the stars?" I asked, peeking my eyes open.

She glanced up at the ones glowing on my ceiling. "What about them?"

I flung my arm over to point out my window, the motion

heavy and lopsided. "They'll die. We'll die. It's all going to end someday, isn't it?"

Ellen and Gemma stared at my window where the curtains were shut, blocking the mid-morning sun.

"Nothing ever ends, Ollie. Not in the way you think. It just changes into something new, that's all." Ellen's words were soft but as matter-of-fact as Mr. Sweater Vest's.

"It just changes into something new," I repeated slowly, testing out the words on my tongue.

Of course.

"Sweet dreams," Gemma whispered before Ellen quietly closed my door with a soft thud, and that's the last thing I remember before I fell.

And I fell and I fell and I fell.

I'd never felt so keenly what it feels like to fall asleep before. Sure, I drifted off every single night, but did I really *feel* the drifting? The out-of-body aimlessness that takes us over in one final arching swoop? It's that hazy place where reality melts into illusion, fluid and shapeless in its refusal to actually exist.

That's what it felt like as I fell through the Dreamscape. I fell through that strange crack in the floor only to slide head-first into sleep. Sweet, soft, rolling oblivion. That last piercing moment of consciousness before everything, absolutely everything, goes dark.

I should feel afraid, but I don't. Instead, I just feel relief.

There are no stars. There are no threads.

There is only me and this moment and Ellen's whispered words: *"Nothing ever ends, Ollie. Not in the way you think. It just changes into something new, that's all."*

Something new.

CHAPTER SIXTEEN

GEMMA

"**B**UT I THOUGHT you didn't want to go to Sylvia's Claiming?" Mom peers at me in the rearview mirror. "Correct me if I'm wrong, but I believe when I brought it up a few days ago, you said, and I quote, 'I'm not going, and you can't make me,'" she says, one dark eyebrow raised in accusation.

"I changed my mind." I shrug one shoulder and look out the window, watching the Superstition Mountains shrink in the distance until they're nothing more than a purple smear across the horizon. Milo snorts from the front seat but doesn't turn around. "And why does Milo always get to sit in the front?" I ask, smacking the back of his headrest.

"Because I'm the oldest."

"By *four* minutes."

"Plus I'm the wisest and the funniest, and definitely the best-looking—"

"And certainly not the most obnoxious," Mom interjects.

"Not to mention," Milo says, ignoring her, "my legs are, like, twice as long as Gemma's." He sprawls his long legs on the dashboard, and Mom swats them back down with a flick of her hand and a scoff.

"Short people should still be allowed to sit in the front, you know," I say with a sniff.

"Yeah, maybe with a booster seat—"

"*Enough,*" Mom groans. She sounds annoyed, but the look on her face says otherwise. She has this sort of fragile happiness about her that makes my throat feel too tight. It's the way she smiles softly, looking back and forth between Milo and me, her gaze open and tender. It's the kind of look that can't help but be hopeful. One that says, *maybe we'll be okay after all.*

She rolls down her window, sending a sharp blast of cool air through the Jeep. She's lighter than I've seen her all week, humming along to herself, letting the breeze play through her hair. It seems the return of her children's bickering plus the promise of colder temperatures and pine trees has brightened her up like nothing else could. She grew up in the mountains of northern Arizona, and I think that no matter how much she loves the vastness of the desert, it will never truly feel like *home.*

I turn and stretch out my legs on the empty row of seats. Libby decided to stay home. She told Mom she wasn't up for another family gathering so soon after the funeral. But just minutes before we left the house, she found Milo and me in the garage, loading up the Jeep for our overnight trip to Flagstaff.

"You packed more than me, and I'm a girl," I muttered to Milo as I tossed his heavy duffle bag into the trunk before slamming it shut. "Just who exactly are you trying to impress? Great Aunt Beatrice?"

"I always dress to impress," he said with one of his old smirks. "You never know who's going to show up to one of these things."

"Except we do. Lots of cousins."

"And maybe their attractive friends."

"You are impossible. I can't take you anywhere." I rolled my eyes and shoved past him to the garage door at the same moment Libby swung it open.

She clutched one of the Chronicles to her chest, looking back and forth between Milo and me. "We need to talk."

"Did you need something?" Milo asked as he rushed forward,

his voice overly earnest. His head was bowed, and his hands were all but clasped together in penance. Obviously, he was still feeling guilty about the mind magic incident.

Which was exactly what Libby was there to talk about. "Look, I didn't tell your mom about what happened last night," she said quietly. She tossed Milo another glare, and he took it with grace and a solemn frown. "I should've. And I still might. But I didn't want to add more to her plate. She's got enough to worry about right now."

That was the truth. All morning Mom had either been on the phone with relatives or doing inventory for the store. And through it all, she somehow managed to never take her eyes off my brother and me as if she was just waiting for us to make a break for it and start driving to California. When we asked her what happened during her phone call with Teresa last night, all she did was purse her lips and say, "We'll discuss it later."

It was maddening.

There was no conversation about Charlotte's address or what to do about it. And there was no mention of the Dreamscape either. I kept watching her, wondering if her memories were coming back like Milo's and Libby's had, waiting to see some kind of recognition in her, but she never brought it up, and neither did we.

"Anyway," Libby said with an agitated sigh, "you both have to promise me that you won't do anything reckless at the Claiming. No more mind magic. And call me the second something happens. I'm going to do some more research while you're gone to see if I can find anything else that will help."

"Great idea, Aunt Lib." Milo flashed her an enthusiastic thumbs up in yet another attempt at getting back on her good side. "And we'll behave, I *swear.*"

"Where have I heard that before," she mumbled. Her tight mouth and stiff shoulders did not seem to believe him. She turned her scrutinizing gaze to me.

"The second something happens, you're our first call," I agreed.

Throwing her arms around Milo and me, Libby squeezed us in a quick but suffocating hug, sniffing loudly. "Good. Just don't be stupid, okay?" And with those touching departing words, she turned on her heel and went back inside.

"So, what's the plan for tonight?" Milo asked the second the door shut behind her.

"There *is* no plan. We show up to the Claiming and see what happens, which could be nothing." I gave the garage door opener a stinging slap with my palm. "But this is the best connection to Ollie we've got besides Charlotte's address—"

"Which Mom has confiscated and isn't giving back any time soon," he added. For a moment, the lines of his face sharpened, hardening his features into an unfamiliar mask made of frustration and disappointment. But I blinked once, and everything softened, his expression clearing until he just looked like Milo again.

We stared at each other across the Jeep. Then—

"But I memorized it," we both blurted out at the exact same time.

We've only been driving for an hour and already I feel restless. It takes all my self-control to not turn into the classic cliché and ask my mom every ten minutes, *"Are we there yet?"* My legs bounce against the seat; I can't seem to get comfortable no matter what position I fold myself into. And the biggest issue of all: I can't turn my mind off.

All morning I allowed myself to be propelled forward by Milo and our newly-found momentum. I was calm as I packed my bags and scrambled some eggs for breakfast. I was cool and collected as I showered and pulled on my jeans and striped t-shirt. It felt good to finally be taking some kind of action even if I wasn't sure yet where that action would lead.

But now as I sit here in the backseat of the Jeep and the desert flashes by outside my window, bleeding into dizzying shades of tan and blue, reality has caught back up with me, and I realize that I'm still afraid. I'm trying to trust my instincts, but tapping into that part of myself feels like tapping on the shoulder of a stranger.

"Why don't you play some music, Gem?" Mom says into the silence.

I pull out my phone with a sigh and stare at the picture on my lock screen. It's still the photo from our birthday in July, the three of us sunburned and grinning, our sombreros tipped back on our heads and street tacos littering the small table.

"Gemma?" Mom prompts again. I don't look up, but I feel her eyes on me with Milo's joining a second later.

"Yeah, hang on," I mumble as I swipe the picture away and scroll through my playlists. Normally, this is something I love to do—taking charge and finding the perfect song to fit the mood. Something that everyone can sing along to as they lean back against their seats and watch the sun sinking over the mountains, the car painted gold as it flies down the freeway.

Going through my playlists is like flipping through an old photo album, snapshots from another time when the world was less confusing and a little bit brighter. I have playlists for running, playlists for driving, and playlists breaking down each of my favorite musical eras. But today, none of them feel right. I scroll and I scroll, looking for something to fill the silence, but all I see is him.

I see Ollie in the front seat complaining about the indie music that he hates. I see him hijacking my phone to play one of the handful of songs that the three of us actually agree on. And when I see him like that—smiling, laughing, thoughtful, and watching—it just reminds me of how I saw him last night—alone, confused, scared, and falling.

Seeing Ollie like that didn't lessen the loss of him, it only intensified it. A glimpse of him wasn't enough, and it never will be.

Yet somehow I'm supposed to get my act together and come

up with a plan. Somehow I'm supposed to pick out a playlist and carry on. But how can I make a plan when I have no idea what I'm doing? How can I play any music when every single song I've ever heard sounds like him?

My shaking thumb hovers over the screen of my phone, but before I can make myself pick something, Milo switches on the radio and tunes it to a station that's playing his beloved generic pop music. Trilling vocals and a heavy bass line pulse through the car, rattling my teeth. Mom winces and reaches out to change the station, but Milo slaps her hand away. He winks at me in the rearview mirror before going back to looking out the window, softly singing along in his horribly pitchy voice.

Who says twin telepathy isn't real? I sink into my seat and thank the stars and everything good in this world that Milo Fitzgerald is my brother.

We pull up to Sylvia's house right as the moon is rising in the indigo sky, parking on the slanted driveway near the cluster of other cars that have traveled to see the Claiming. I see license plates from Arizona, Colorado, California, and New Mexico. The house is nestled in the mountains, its tall and narrow frame resting on massive wooden beams, elevating it off the ground.

Cold September air rushes to greet me the moment I open the car door. I tug on my sweatshirt and pull the sleeves down over my knuckles, pausing to marvel over the simple gesture as anyone from Arizona does the first time they put on a sweatshirt after a long, hot, unending summer.

Even though the temperature back home has finally started to dip, you'd still never know it was fall. But up north in the mountains, even in the pale light of the rising moon, I can see the leaves starting to change, their colors shifting to yellow, orange, and burning red.

Milo shuts his door and elbows me in the side. "Here she goes," he says quietly, gesturing with his chin toward Mom, who's just stepped out of the car. "How many times is she going to mention the fresh air while we're here? Five bucks she can't even make it to the front door without trying to inhale the whole mountain."

Mom's boots crunch in the gravel of the driveway as she circles to the back of the Jeep. The pine trees lining the path to the house seem to shake out their branches and stand up straighter as if trying to impress her. She pauses and looks up with a small, satisfied smile. Tipping her head back, she says, "I'm happy to see you too," and the pine trees sway in response. Then she opens the trunk and pulls out our bags, tossing them to us one by one. "Would you smell that mountain air? Just smell it!"

Milo grins into his shoulder and mouths *"Told you"* as we follow her up the creaking wooden staircase leading to the dark green front door. He holds out his hand as if waiting for me to slap a five-dollar bill into it, but I ignore him. As if I would ever bet against Mom and her Elemental love of fresh air and new plants to play with.

Mom raps lightly on the door, still breathing deeply. I'm sure she wanted to come and support our family for the Claiming, but mostly I think she wanted to make the trip to Flagstaff because she needed to get back to her roots, to feel grounded once again. And who could blame her? This is the place where she grew into her magic.

The door swings open, and Sylvia's mom, Emily—our second cousin twice removed, or something like that—greets us with an enthusiastic hello and too many hugs. After we've extricated ourselves from her embrace, she ushers us to separate rooms so we can change for the Claiming. "Hurry," she urges us with a glance out the dark windows lining the back wall of the house where the muffled sounds of the backyard party filter in. "You never know when the ceremony will start!" And with that she bustles off, greeting more family members on her way out the back door.

My heart thuds in my chest as I peel off my sweatshirt and

dig through my bag, searching for the one remaining dress I have that doesn't have any painful memories attached to it. I shake out the light blue fabric and pull it roughly over my head, but when I glance in the bathroom mirror, I don't look at the dress or check to see how it fits. All I see are my flushed cheeks and my dark eyes, wild and wide. I grip the counter and stare at my reflection, trying to breathe deeply through the mounting panic.

I don't even know if this Claiming will begin.

And if it does, then what? My mouth goes dry as I think about the magic and the possibilities and the choices I'll be forced to make. A soft sound like a murmur, twisted and tangled, wraps around me, raising the hairs on the back of my neck and sending a chill down my spine. I close my eyes and see a flash of red.

No.

But when my eyes fly open, all I see is the reflection of a scared girl in a blue dress, breathing too fast. There are no other voices, not a whisper to be found.

It's just me.

CHAPTER SEVENTEEN

GEMMA

MILO TAPS ON the bathroom door, and I nearly jump out of my skin. "Let's go, Gem, I'm starved."

I run my shaking hands through my hair once before giving up and grabbing my bag without another glance in the mirror. Nudging the door open, I find Milo waiting for me in the hallway, already loosening his tie.

"I smell hamburgers," he says hopefully.

The back deck is full of food and family. Mom's off to the side, animatedly talking to her cousin Emily. They're laughing and reminiscing as they poke through Emily's garden boxes growing under the windows, each one full of the prettiest flowers I've ever seen. Mom tenderly cradles the blossoms, her hands glowing a soft green as a violet petal falls onto her palm. I smile at the sight of the two Elementals gushing over the plants, at the matching smudges of dirt caked under their fingernails.

There are twinkle lights strung through the arching branches of the trees surrounding the house, but beyond the carefully manicured yard, the forest is dark and looming. Small round tables are scattered across the sprawling lawn where Sylvia stands in the middle, chatting with some of her guests. Her frilly dress is so pink, I can see it sparkling from here. She waves excitedly when she sees me. I hesitantly wave back with what I hope is a genuine smile, but it feels forced on my lips.

Everything is so beautiful that, in a way, it almost hurts. The night is crisp, the stars are shining, and every single person here believes in magic and the certainty of it. I brace myself against the railing surrounding the wide wooden deck; everything feels too loud and too bright.

Milo's already at the long buffet table, piling his plate high with the spoils. I stare at the impressive display of food and wish that I could find comfort in a plate full of hamburgers like he can, but my stomach is too twisted into knots to even think about eating right now.

Every inch of my skin feels stretched too tight to the point of transparency. Like if anyone looks too closely, they'll see everything that's happening inside me. I count my breaths and scuff the toe of my sneaker on the weathered planks as I search the crowd, waiting for something to happen and dreading the moment it finally does. A single thought replays in my head on a continuous loop like a vinyl record caught in a groove, the needle scratching in its effort to escape.

Now what?

Now what?

Milo balances two cups and a towering plate of food as he makes his way back over to me. He hands me a plastic cup of lemonade and scans the yard, chewing on his lip. I assume he's looking for any signs of magic until he asks, "So who exactly are we related to?" He points to a couple of giggling girls clinging to Sylvia's arms.

A laugh bursts out of me, unexpected and full. My brother's worry over flirting with a cousin is just the distraction I need. My heart rate slows as I cross my arms over my chest and shake my head. "I've said it before, and I'll say it again: I can't take you anywhere."

He grins and tosses me a roll off his plate. We amble down the deck stairs to the yard, looking for a place to sit. Every few feet, we're stopped by someone who wants to talk about Grandma or ask us how we're doing. I recycle the same answers over and over again, mechanically sipping from my cup of lemonade and eyeing the empty table furthest from the crowd. Milo graciously gives

Hugs and slaps backs while his food grows cold and my patience wears thin. Slowly, we make our way over to the table at the edge of the lawn, its surface covered with a white lacy tablecloth and flickering candles.

I plop down on one of the folding chairs and tear off a piece of my roll, but it just feels like cardboard in my mouth; I can hardly swallow it. I glance over at Milo, expecting him to be making out with his pile of burgers, but instead he's staring at the other tables, his hands resting beside his untouched food.

"It's weird," he says.

"What's weird?"

"It's weird being here with all of them and pretending like everything's okay. I don't like it."

Pretending? Is that what he's been doing this whole time? It bothers me that I didn't recognize that his smiles were fake, that his jokes were forced. It bothers me, but it also makes me feel just a little bit closer to him with the realization that we're both players in the same game. Actors who don't even need their scripts—we've got every line memorized.

"Tell me about it." I choke down another bite of my roll and chase it with a swallow of lemonade.

Milo sighs, then finally digs into his food. I keep up my constant scan of the yard and the back deck, my eyes flicking over to where Sylvia is standing every few seconds as I watch and wait and watch and wait. Everyone's milling around, completely oblivious to the tension as they congregate around Sylvia, making predictions about which branch of magic will Claim her.

The chair to my right is pulled out with a soft scraping sound. "A quiet table, how marvelous." A tall blonde girl I don't recognize sits down next to me. "Can I steal this seat?" She plunks her leather purse on the table without waiting for my response.

Milo perks up and drops his fork, his mouth popping open. "I don't believe we've met. I'm Milo." He reaches across me and extends his hand. "And that's my sister Gemma. Please tell me we aren't related," he says, his gleaming smile more dazzling than the silver moon overhead.

I snort into my cup.

"No, I'm a family friend from out of town. I'm Zoe," she answers, tossing her long icy blonde hair behind her shoulder and squeezing his hand.

Milo's transition from sad and listless to suave and cool in the blink of an eye has me rolling mine. I don't want to say that my brother has a type, but he most definitely does. And Zoe is precisely his type. Leggy and blonde and batting her eyelashes—check, check, and check.

I really hope she's a cousin. I could use a good laugh.

"So, where are you from?" he asks, leaning an elbow against the table and tipping his head to the side, his gaze on Zoe fixated and bright.

She giggles and opens her mouth to respond, but I don't hear a word she says, because the way Milo's looking at Zoe forces all my tucked-away feelings for Ollie to the surface. Like a punch to my stomach, the pain is swift and demanding as it knocks the air right out of me. Missing him is so tangible that the weight of it feels like its own presence. Everywhere I go it follows me. I can almost feel his hands on my waist or his nose running down the length of my neck as he whispers in my ear.

It's like living with a ghost.

The ache is almost unbearable. My breathing comes out fast and shallow as if even my lungs can't work properly without him here. I dig my fingernails into my palms and try to catch my breath, letting the wave of missing him wash over me until I'm completely submerged.

This feeling scares me. But not feeling it scares me more.

"Gem, you okay?" Somehow Milo has managed to drag his eyes away from Zoe and is now peering at me with concern. His pity only tightens Ollie's invisible grip on me, like fingers flexing against my skin.

Zoe joins Milo in his gawking. She looks at me curiously, her eyebrows scrunched and her mouth puckered as if I'm a puzzle she's trying to figure out.

I turn away, my cheeks reddening under the weight of their questioning stares. "I'm fine," I mumble in Milo's direction. I bite the inside of my cheek and look down, willing myself to not start crying in front of my brother and the girl he's flirting with. That's the kind of rock bottom I'd rather not experience.

"Wait, did you see something?" Milo asks under his breath. "Any threads or a sign from Ollie—"

"*No,*" I hiss, my heart racing at the sound of his name. "I told you, it's nothing."

I glance at Zoe, hoping she'll pick up on my silent signal to please leave the table, but she's too busy digging through her giant purse to notice. I grit my teeth, worried that she's about to pull out a pack of tissues and hand them to me along with her condolences.

After giving me another long look, Milo turns back to Zoe, flashing her a smile. "When were you—"

But his question is cut off as the candles on the table flicker out all at once. The three of us stare at the smoke rising from the still-glowing wicks—there's no breeze. I look over my shoulder to see that all the candles on the other tables have flickered out too. With a sharp crackling sound, the bulbs from the twinkle lights flare brightly before going out in a blink. The only remaining light comes from the fire in the center of the lawn. It rotates slowly over the grass without burning a thing.

My neck prickles ominously as Sylvia claps her hands and jumps to her feet, her pink dress flouncing. "It's starting!" she cries out, prancing over to stand next to the fire. Her parents make their way down the stairs with a shared skeptical glance between them. They must feel it too.

Something isn't right.

I nearly jump out of my skin when Mom's hand lands lightly on my back. "Do you hear that?" she murmurs as she takes the seat on Milo's other side.

A low humming vibrates through the air, more of a feeling than a noise in the way it surges in its urgency. It vibrates through me, shaking my body and making it nearly impossible to stay in my seat. I grip the edge of the table and focus all my attention on Sylvia, who's twirling around in her poofy ballerina dress, still totally unaware. I want to grab her by the shoulders and tell her to hold still. I'm so afraid of missing something.

Then her hands start to glow, and she squeals. But her elated noise is cut off when the glowing suddenly dims, her hands flickering once more before extinguishing entirely. "Mom?" she asks, her quivering voice the first sign of uncertainty.

The fire next to her roars unexpectedly, the flames climbing higher in the air. Sylvia and her parents stumble back out of the way, the three of them huddling together in their shared confusion. Emily tucks one arm around her daughter and raises the other to calm the billowing fire. For a moment, her palms glow a soft green, but then nothing happens.

No magic.

Emily's brow puckers as she examines her fingers, her mouth popping open. She slowly lowers her hands and turns to face her husband, his concern a mirror image of her own. Their worried whispers are drowned out by the rest of the yard's curious mumblings, everyone craning their necks, trying to get a better look at Sylvia and the fire and what was supposed to be her Claiming. A bead of sweat trickles down my back.

Something isn't right.

"I'm assuming this is the sort of weird Dreamscape reaction we're supposed to be looking for, right?" Milo asks in a low voice.

I swallow and nod. "Yeah, something like that."

He rises from his seat, his eyes fixed on the growing flames, but before he can go anywhere Mom eases him back down into his chair with a firm hand. "Stay here," she says to us. "I'll be right back."

He looks ready to argue, but Mom has already run off to help Sylvia and her parents, leaving us behind. He frowns and stares at the unlit candles on the table, thin tendrils of smoke still spiraling from the blackened wicks. A stream of unintelligible words slips from his mouth, his hands glowing amber. But a moment later, he cries out and jumps to his feet, ripping his suit jacket off and patting the now-smoking cuffs of his collared shirt.

An acrid metallic smell fills the air, like a recently blown fuse. Without thinking, I grab my cup and dump the rest of my lemonade onto the scorched edges of his shirt. "What were you *doing*?"

Milo's blush is visible even in the dim light, his cheeks flushing pink as he darts a look at Zoe, who's staring at him open-mouthed. "I was just trying to relight the candles, that's all." He tucks his soaked arms behind his back. "It's not just Emily's magic that's acting weird. Something's up with my casting."

Zoe pointedly scoots her chair away from him. "This feels weird, I don't like it." Slinging her bag over her shoulder, she fumbles for her phone, nearly knocking over Milo's cup in her rush to get away. She steadies it with a shaking hand. "Tell Sylvia I—I don't know. Tell her I'm sorry, but I'm leaving."

Before either of us can say another word, she takes off across the yard with her phone pressed to her ear, her blonde hair a flash in the darkness. She's not the only one who's leaving. The family has divided into two groups—the overly helpful who are running around and offering assistance, trying in vain to fix a problem they can't even see, and the confused and the skeptical: those who slowly back away and fade into the night, shaking their heads and clutching their magic close. I hear mutters of *"Skipper"* as they leave. They must assume that if the Claiming isn't working, if something strange is going on, then Sylvia must be the start of a new Skipper line with no magic.

Across the yard, Mom tries to control the rising flames, but nothing she does is working. I watch as she attempts to summon some water, but instead is rewarded with a swift wind that blows cold and crisp, sending the flames up in a rush of orange and blue.

The way the magic is behaving is eerily familiar. My hands tingle as I remember what Ollie said to me after I'd taken more magic from the Dreamscape, after I'd tied all three branches to me. *"You're using magic that doesn't belong to you. It won't work for you."*

I cross my arms and clench my hands into fists. But doesn't this magic belong to them?

I watch Milo who's still tugging at the smoking sleeves of his shirt and Mom who's struggling against the mini tornado she unintentionally summoned. Across the yard, I hear other cries of confusion as more of the Claimed realize that their magic isn't cooperating, that it seems to have a mind of its own. When I look at them, all I can see are the stars of the Dreamscape slowly flickering out one by one.

"Magic always has consequences," Ollie had whispered to me. *"You're the one who taught me that."*

Off to the side of the fire, Sylvia's frozen in the grass, staring anxiously at her hands. The sight of her standing there all alone while chaos erupts around her propels me out of my chair.

"What are you doing? Do you see something?" Milo asks, knocking over his chair in an effort to keep up with me.

I don't answer because I have no idea what I'm going to say or do, but I can't just sit there anymore. I remember what it felt like to be lonely and isolated on the night of my own Claiming—the night my life was supposed to transform into something glittering and new.

As I move quietly through the crowd with Milo on my heels, the memory of that July night wraps around me so viscerally it's like I can feel the grass from my backyard under my bare feet, the crush of red fabric against my skin. By the time I reach Sylvia, I can hardly hear anything but the words from my Claiming still echoing in my ears: *"Laws that govern, threads that bind. The knots that tether us to time."*

I shake my head, trying to clear it. "Sylvia, are you okay?" I ask, reaching out my hand to lightly touch her shoulder. She flinches, and when she turns to face me, her tear-streaked face shining in the light of the fire, I gasp.

I can *see* her heart beating in her chest, her pulse keeping time to the low humming that fills the night air. There's a dim glow coming from inside her, a barely lit flame compared to the fire raging next to her. "Milo," I say, grabbing him by the sleeve and pulling him closer. "*Look*. Do you see that? Look at her."

Milo squints and frowns. "See what?" he mumbles near my ear. "She's... glowing."

Sylvia watches us whispering and begins to cry again. "I know," she wails. "Everyone's saying I'm a Skipper."

I shake my head, offering her a weak smile. "I don't think that's the problem."

I raise my hand to my chest and press it against the soft cotton of my blue dress, remembering how it felt during my own Claiming, like the magic had climbed inside me and settled itself in, right next to my heart. I remember how Libby told us that every one of the Claimed has the potential for magic and that it grows in strength until we turn seventeen. Until we're old enough to be Claimed. I remember that she called it *the core of who we are.*

Sylvia has the potential, and somehow I can see that. But the magic refuses to Claim her because there's no one there to bind it.

There are no Threaders.

I reach over and take Sylvia's hand in mine and say the words I was so desperate for someone to say to me on the night that everything went wrong. "Listen, it may not feel like it right now, but everything's going to be okay. You're not alone." I squeeze her hand and repeat the words, "You're not alone, Sylvia."

She nods her head up and down as a few more tears spill onto her cheeks. "Thanks, Gemma," she says in a quivering voice, wiping her face with her sleeve. She throws her arms around me in a quick hug before running off to stand next to her parents.

Something flickers near the base of the flames. A small green thread tangled around a golden gleaming one, with a dark purple thread looped around the middle. The threads are so thin, they're nearly translucent in the light of the fire, but their power is obvious and strong. I think back to all those nights I spent holding up the Dreamscape, my arms shaking and my magic pulsing as Ollie tied each Claiming and sealed it with his blood.

Contain and release, contain and release. Now it is only release, release, release.

A mess of magic with nowhere to go.

I crouch down closer to the flames to get a better look, my breath coming in sharp, jagged bursts. It's not just the threads of the three branches of magic, there are countless silver strands clinging to them, too. The threads latch onto each other before springing apart, again and again in a senseless dance. They writhe as they twist through the yard, wrapping around everything they come into contact with. A single purple thread wraps around Sylvia's wrist only to recoil a second later. There's a silver thread looping around Milo's leg, and another wound through my mom's fingers. More threads trail through the shrubs lining the yard and even more climb the pine trees swaying in the night breeze, the air so cold my breath forms little white clouds with every exhale.

"Okay, please tell me you can see *that*," I say, turning to Milo and pointing to the thread winding around his ankle.

"What are you talking—whoa," he exclaims, wiggling around like he'd just discovered a trail of ants crawling up his pants. Milo's hands give off a burst of amber light before flickering out, his eyes meeting mine in a flare of panic. He gives his leg another shake, and the thread finally relents, releasing him and slithering away in the grass.

"What do we do, Gem?" he asks, his chest heaving as we watch the thread rejoin the rest of the tangled magic—a disruption, an anomaly, a swirling storm about to break.

Break the Claimings.

I suppress a shudder as the memory flutters through my mind, faintly at first, but louder with every passing second—the hissing sound of the red thread murmuring in my ear: *"Unleash us unleash us—"*

"Gemma!" Milo shakes me by the shoulder, peering intently

into my face. "Did you hear me? What are we going to do? What's the plan?"

"I—I don't know," I stammer. A plan—I was supposed to have a plan. But now that the moment is here, my mind is blank and my heart is racing. I don't know what to do; I don't know how to help. A chill runs down my spine as a single silver thread slides past me through the grass. My hand twitches as if it's about to grab onto it, but before I can, it flies past me, disappearing into the night.

A deafening crack splinters through the yard and several people scream. Milo grabs my arm and points to a massive pine near the edge of the forest. It's black and smoking and split down the middle, every branch startlingly bare as if it was struck by lightning. Mom covers her mouth at the sight of the tree so mangled and broken.

The threads have vanished. It looks like the mess of magic finally found a place to land.

The yard goes quiet as everyone stares at the tree, slowly gathering around its base like the scene of a car crash you can't look away from. My phone rings loudly in my pocket, making me jump. I slide it out of my dress, glancing at the screen before answering. "Hey, Aunt Libby," I mutter, turning away from the tree and trying to keep my voice steady. After all, I did promise I'd call her the second something happened.

But before I can offer any sort of explanation, she interrupts me "Gem, something's wrong. My magic—it's..."

My heart lurches. "It's what?" I ask, gesturing Milo over.

The silence is staticky; I press the phone harder against my ear, holding my breath.

"It's not working," she says quietly. "I can't read the Chronicles."

CHAPTER EIGHTEEN

OLLIE

AWARENESS HITS ME with a sharp shock.

First, there's a series of soft clicks followed by a loud vibrating hum that sounds mechanical, like a machine roaring to life. Then, the sensation of something shrouding my body. Thin and nearly weightless, it wraps around me, trapping me inside like a caterpillar nestled in its cocoon.

I don't fight against it. Something about it feels vaguely familiar. Something about it reminds me of home.

I open my eyes to see a strange green light shining dimly overhead. I squint and instinctively reach out for my glasses, my hand roving blindly through the darkness, searching for my nightstand before I realize the absurdity of what I'm doing.

There is no nightstand.

But then my fingers slide across the smooth surface of the wood until they wrap around the familiar shape of my glasses. They're in their usual spot, right where I always leave them before I go to bed—on top of a book and next to a glass of water.

There shouldn't be any glasses.

I hesitantly put them on, blinking once, twice, three times before the strange green glow solidifies into the pointed shapes of the glow-in-the-dark stars hanging on my bedroom ceiling.

Nightstand. Glasses. Glow-in-the-dark stars.

All of these pieces make sense individually, but together equal something impossible. Because together that would mean that I'm lying on my bed in my room back at home.

I sit up in a flash and kick off my sheets, which were close to mummifying me. The sound of the air conditioner rattles outside my bedroom window, working overtime in the warm summer air. The clock on my nightstand flashes the time in neon numbers: 4:12 a.m.

"I did it," I whisper in the dark with a grin. Elation floods my body as I realize that somehow, impossibly, I've made it home, safe and sound.

I stare up at the glow-in-the-dark stars, and they stare back at me.

My smile slowly slides off my face; I took those stars down from my ceiling years ago.

Leaning over, I flip on my lamp and search the nightstand, my hands frantic as I look for my phone to call Gemma. But there isn't any phone. All I see is a stack of paperback mysteries I was obsessed with in eighth grade.

A dull pulsing pain has started in my head, just above my eyebrows, like a slow drip of dread. I shove my pillows aside and tumble out of bed, my bare feet landing soundlessly on the carpet. "Mom?" I call out, my voice sounding higher than usual. "Dad!"

I lunge for my bedroom door, and my hand slides through the handle as easily as if it were made of nothing. As if it was an illusion, or maybe just a delusion. I grasp onto the door until the entire thing dissolves into trailing smoke that slowly curls upwards and nowhere.

"Wait!" I call out, barreling through the smoke and into the hallway as the carpet below me fades away. Instead of finding myself running toward my parents' bedroom, I'm falling

falling

falling

again.

My knees buckle as an old sagging couch slides up behind me, forcing me into a seated position on the worn plaid cushions. I squeeze my eyes shut and clutch the edge of the couch with a white-knuckled grip, way too freaked out to even take a peek at my new surroundings. But after only one second of sitting on the scratchy old cushions, the same ones I've sat on a million other times, I know exactly where I am—in my backyard, in the old detached garage.

I'm in the Grotto.

I crack my eyes open and momentarily allow myself to relax, to let the couch support my weight as I sink back in relief. Everything in the Grotto is exactly as it should be: the record player in the corner with the carton of vinyl stacked neatly next to it, the ancient TV with its permanent layer of dust, the twinkle lights strung through the rafters, Milo's favorite beanbag in the corner.

The side garage door flies open with a *bang*, making me jump. "I *told* you he'd be out here," Gemma says to someone over her shoulder. "Why do you never listen to me?"

Milo pushes past his sister. "Maybe because you never shut up, so there's too much for me to filter through."

I'm completely frozen as I watch their skirmish unfold, a ritual as familiar to me as breathing. All I can do is sit there and stare as the two of them throw elbows and sling a few half-hearted insults until Gemma hops over the back of the couch and sits next to me, her feet landing lightly in my lap. "So, did she text you?"

I swallow roughly while she waits for me to say something, but I seem to have completely lost the power of speech. I'm too scared to move, too afraid to even breathe just in case it scatters the moment away, disturbing whatever this is—real or not. I want it to be real, more than I've ever wanted anything. Because Gemma's sitting here with her feet in my lap, smiling and happy to see me like this is just any other day. Her dark eyes are clear and bright, gleaming at me in the dusky light of the Grotto while the twinkle lights shimmer over her smooth black hair. If I squint hard enough it would almost look like she was swimming in a sea of stars.

She's so beautiful. My memory did not do her justice.

"Gemma." I lunge forward, throwing my arms around her, unable to stop myself for another second. I hold her tightly to my chest, resting my cheek against her hair and breathing in the sweet vanilla scent of her shampoo. "You're *here*." My hands tighten against her back, pulling her closer until I can feel her heart beating against mine.

She stiffens in my arms. "Ollie?" she asks hesitantly, transforming my name into a question.

At the sound of her voice, the Grotto starts to shimmer, all the colors shining a little too brightly—unnaturally, even. My grip on her loosens, and within the span of a blink, I'm back in the same position that I started in, seated on the couch with Gemma's feet in my lap. The shimmering has stopped; everything appears dim and normal, all the colors back to a reasonable level of saturation.

If I was afraid to move before, now I'm truly petrified.

"So, did she text you?" Gemma asks again. She waits for me to answer, her expression expectant and untroubled as if the last few seconds never even happened.

My mind is reeling, still trying to recover from the shock of seeing her in the first place, not to mention the weird reversal in time. "Who?" is all I can think to say.

She leans forward only a few inches away from my face, and my breath completely stops when she grabs me by the chin, shaking my head from side to side. "*Samantha*, Ollie. Did she text you?" She tries and fails to raise one eyebrow. "We need an update."

I feel strangely lethargic, totally incapable of keeping up. Like that feeling when everyone else is in on the joke except for you. It makes the skin on the back of my neck prickle.

"Let's check his phone," she calls back to Milo who, up until this point, I'd completely forgotten was there. Gemma smirks and drops my chin, waggling her fingers in the air like she's about to start digging through the pockets of my jeans.

"Samantha?" I choke out. "Why are we talking about her?" Because out of every bizarre thing that's happened so far, Gemma bringing up the girl I had a short-lived crush on sophomore year is by far the weirdest.

Milo and Gemma share a skeptical look that lasts for too long, turning into a silent conversation in which I'm not a participant. The Annoying Twin Thing. The walls of the Grotto start to tremble, the wooden rafters shaking dust into the space between us as the twinkle lights flare brightly.

Finally, it hits me. *Samantha.*

My stomach lurches as I look at Milo and Gemma more closely. Their faces are a little softer, a little rounder. How did I not see it before? They're *younger.*

Milo's hair is shaggy, swooping over his forehead before flipping out over his ears. Gemma's hair is longer too, straight and smooth and brushing her collarbones. This was how she wore it until a guy in her algebra class told her that boys only liked girls with long hair. The next day, she showed up at school with a chin-length haircut and a narrow-eyed smirk.

That happened when we were fifteen years old, which is exactly how old Milo and Gemma are right now.

I stare down at my hands, at my arms poking out of the sleeves of my white t-shirt; I look much ganglier than usual. I run my hands along my chin and through my closely cropped hair as the evidence piles up in front of me. I'm in the body of my fifteen-year-old self, too.

This is a *memory.* I remember it now.

Milo pokes his head up from the mini fridge with an apple in his mouth. He grabs a giant bag of chips off the shelf above the fridge and yells in a muffled voice, "Is my boy getting some action? Nice!" He spits the apple out and tosses it to Gemma who grimaces and lets it fall on the couch.

"Gross," she says, rolling her eyes. She reaches over my head to grab a handful of chips from the oversized bag in Milo's hands. "And save your celebrating, it might be premature. For Ollie to get some action he would actually have to *do* something, you know. Like, make a move. And that's next to impossible." She winks at me and pops a chip in her mouth.

"Fair point." Milo picks up his discarded apple and eats it in three bites. "He *is* notoriously slow," he mumbles through his mouthful. "Maybe I should tell Samantha that she should ask him out first. Help him out a little." They both tip their heads back and cackle in unison.

"Would you guys *please* stop talking for two seconds!" I say with a groan. The couch's ancient springs give a tremendous creak as I stand in a rush, running my hands through my hair. "I don't know what's happening right now, but look! I'm *here*, I'm home!" I gesture wildly to myself. "I got out of the Dreamscape somehow, and I—"

My voice is drowned out by a fuzzy, incoherent sound, like the crackling of static on a radio. The low hum of other voices travels into the room, the pitch of their whispers scraping against the inside of my ears. For a moment, everything in the Grotto freezes. Even the dust motes slowly swirling in the air come to a sudden halt as if time itself has decided to stand still in the hazy golden evening light.

But Milo and Gemma don't seem to notice any of this. They're tossing snacks back and forth and ceaselessly chattering on and on about Samantha.

"I think you're ready to take this to the next level," Milo says, pouring the end of the chip bag into his mouth and sprinkling crumbs onto his shirt like snowflakes made of fake ranch and food dye. "So let's go to her house! Maybe Mom will let me drive the Jeep if I stay on the back roads." Gemma nods along, already halfway to the door at the mention of a joyride. Milo crumbles up the empty chip bag and aims for the small trash can in the corner. "Let's go see if I can work my powers of persuasion."

I don't even have to look to know he'll miss the shot because now I remember everything about this moment. I remember Milo's hastily formed plan to "borrow" the Jeep when Vivian told him no, he couldn't take the car out on his own with only a driver's permit. I remember how we never made it to Samantha's house because he hit a gigantic pothole, got a flat tire, and then was forced to make the phone call of shame to ask his mom to come and save us. I remember how he was grounded for three weeks—Gemma too, for going along with his schemes.

I remember how I went on a grand total of two dates with Samantha and talked about Gemma the entire time.

If this is a memory, how did I end up here? And what do I do now? Do I just go along with it? I spin in a slow circle, searching for any sign of magic, any clue as to where this extremely precise hallucination is coming from as that feeling of stumbling one step behind continues to press down on me.

Milo flings the Grotto's side door open wide and races outside. "Come on, guys!" he calls out, his voice growing distant.

"You coming, Ollie?" Gemma must sense my hesitation because she pauses at the door and looks back at me, just like I knew she would. Only this time my hesitation to follow isn't due to teenage angst and short-lived crushes, this time it's a full-blown *what on earth is happening to me* crisis.

I shove my mounting panic aside and take a few steps forward, wrapping my hand around her waist and pulling her to a stop. "Gemma, wait."

She inhales sharply, the stuttered sound of her breathing the only sound in the room. My hand tightens around her as I tug her closer. "Please, I need your help," I whisper near her ear. I know asking a memory for help is a long shot, but it's the only shot I have. And memory or not, it's still Gemma—that has to count for something.

I run my other hand through her hair, marveling at the softness of it, the way the silky black strands glisten in the fading light. She shivers and looks up at me, her lips parted and her cheeks flushed bright pink.

Fifteen-year-old me would *never* have been so bold. He thought about it. A lot. But he definitely wouldn't have ever touched Gemma like that.

He would've pulled her hair instead.

I lift her chin with my finger and her eyes widen, but she doesn't move away. The ground rattles beneath my feet, tipping me closer until my mouth is only a breath away from hers. But before our lips touch, before she ever says a word, her shape starts to waver, every line and curve of her dancing in and out of view until only an impression of Gemma is left behind, like a barely-there footprint in the sand. The walls of the Grotto collapse in on themselves, folding over and over again like a heavily creased note until all that remains is the single garage door, its golden handle glinting at me strangely.

"Wait, come back," I call out, grabbing for the handle with flailing hands. The moment I step out the door, the ground falls out from under me, everything vanishing. And I am falling
    falling
    falling
    again.

CHAPTER NINETEEN

OLLIE

"*T*HIS MUST BE *what dreaming feels like.*"

Those long-ago words seem to linger in the air, the echo of my twelve-year-old voice faint and breathless, stretched thin over time.

I'd always wondered why, for my entire life, I'd never conjured a single dream. Why every night when I fell asleep, my mind was just... empty. A void. I used to feel like I was broken, like maybe that part of my brain couldn't be accessed or something.

But if this is what dreaming feels like, a memory—crisp and clear until it's not—a feeling—comfortable and safe until it changes—I think I might've been better off sleeping in my endless state of nothingness.

Because this?

This is a nightmare.

One blink later and the sun is beating on me like a spotlight, too hot and too bright, revealing a brilliant blue and cloudless sky. I shield my eyes against the light, but I can't quit staring. I can't even remember the last time I saw the open sky so endlessly vast and free of stars.

I'm running, but I don't know why. All I know is that my muscles are burning and my lungs are screaming for air. The scenery flashes by in a senseless blur; only the sharp edges of the rust-colored mountains overhead are clear. Heat radiates off my sweat-slicked skin as my shoulders crash into a dozen other sets of shoulders, jostling and sweat-soaked like mine, the ground rumbling under our feet like a miniature earthquake. With a ragged breath, I glance down at my mustard yellow racing jersey and my worn-out trail shoes.

I just fell into the middle of a cross-country race.

The desert trail winds behind the back of my high school, skirting along the edges of the Superstition Mountains. Giant saguaros loom overhead, casting long shadows on the ground. It's a windy day, but the scorching air provides zero relief from the heat. Instead, it just makes me feel as if I've got a hair dryer blowing in my face. The spindly ocotillo plants are bent in the breeze, their wiry branches shaking from the force of it, orange blossoms falling to the ground.

I stumble over a loose rock, and the runner behind me grumbles in annoyance, shoving off my back to break away from the pack. Slowing down, I try to ebb the flow of adrenaline coursing through my body by focusing on the familiar motions of running—the pumping of my arms, the breath sliding through my chest, one foot in front of the other.

Wake up, I plead with myself.

But this isn't a nightmare, is it? It's a memory. An already lived-through event remembered in perfect, agonizingly crystal-clear detail.

A sharp elbow nudges me in my side. "Man, Ollie, why'd you make me sign up for this? I *hate* running." Milo shakes his hair out of his eyes and grimaces dramatically. "I'm never listening to you again," he pants before disappearing back into the mass of moving bodies, the cloud of dust trailing behind them obscuring everything in my sight.

"Milo, wait!" My legs finally give out as my panic surges, sending me sprawling on the trail. But when I crawl to my knees, the ground below me shifts and hardens, cooling under my touch until it's transformed into the square shape of beige kitchen tile under my hands. Suddenly, I'm in my house, crouched under the table, my body much smaller and younger.

"Did you find it, Ollie?" My mom's warm voice calls from

overhead. She peeks under the table and grins at me. "Or are you hiding the missing tile in your pocket, hmm?"

I frown and open my right hand, which was clenched in a fist, and stare down at the Scrabble tile resting on my palm. She laughs and motions for me to climb out.

I clamber out from under the table and pull myself up using the chair across from my mom. Her auburn hair is long, and her smiling face is smoother—the younger version of my mother I only remember from photographs. She raises her eyebrows and points to the Scrabble board lying on the table. "All right, Ollie boy, it's your turn."

"Mom!" I scatter the tiles as I bump into the table and throw my arms around her neck. She smells like chamomile tea and safety. Her hands land lightly on my back as the kitchen's colors sharpen and the room begins to sway. I have no idea what memory this is or how old I am. It could be any ordinary day, one of the many countless hours I spent playing board games with my mom. A small slice of time lost in the normalcy I used to take for granted.

But it's home, and I don't ever want to leave it again.

The tiles on the table rattle as the floor begins to shake. "Mom, make it stop. Please make it stop." I bury my face in her shoulder so I don't have to see the walls unfolding or the image of her beginning to fade.

She chuckles softly, completely unfazed by the memory slowly peeling away. "Are you that afraid you're going to lose?" she teases, tousling my hair. The sound of static fills the space between us. I blink and I'm back in my chair, sorting through Scrabble tiles while my mom plays a word with a triple letter score. The memory continues to play out even while it falls apart.

I close my eyes and whisper to no one, "Make it stop."

But that only makes time travel faster, the feel of the memories more fluid than before. One second, I'm in my kitchen, and the next, I'm in the Fitzgeralds' pool, my face breaking the surface of the turquoise water with a gasp. Then I'm in the grocery store, running to catch up with my dad who's pushing a giant shopping cart, followed by sitting behind Gemma in my fifth grade classroom, her black hair tucked behind her ears as she doodles on the corner of her desk.

It's like how some people say they see their lives flashing before them when they think they're about to die. It's that same feeling—that mind-bending, timeline-jumping, free-falling feeling that completely engulfs me as I tumble headfirst through my life. Each memory wraps around me, enveloping me in too-vivid sensations, tying me down with electric colors until I'm pinned under the weight of remembering. I try to wrestle free, but where would I go?

It's a unique kind of torture watching your life unfold so rapidly. Seeing the people you love but always in the past, never moving forward. I wish it would stop; I never want it to end. Because if this is all I have left, then I'll take it. I'd rather be waterboarded by memories than have nothing at all.

Another blink and my memories send me back to the Dreamscape, but this time I'm not alone—it's the last night Gemma was here with me. The sky overhead is a bleeding red, the stars of the weaving barely visible. I look down at my feet to see Gemma tangled in the red thread, her eyes desperate and wild.

"Ollie," she breathes. "Help me."

My hands reach out for her, just as they did before, and the memory presses words into my mouth. "I'm here, Gem, I'm here. Let it go."

"I don't know if I can," she says, her voice breaking. "It's too tight. I've seen too much. I don't know if I can go back. I don't know if I can let it go." She shakes out her arms, trying to loosen the knots tied around her.

Why did my memories choose to snag on *this* moment, one of the single worst in my entire life?

But there's no time to wonder. The memory shoves my hands into action. I grab onto the red thread, flinching under its heat. The moment I touch it, there's a sudden torrent of whispers, a contradictory sound both gentle and grating. Even though I was prepared to hear it this time, the noise still makes my stomach drop. A cold layer of sweat breaks out across my forehead.

The thread screams for Gemma. Its broken promises of power and revenge are brittle and sharp and even worse than I ever could've remembered on my own. Just as before, the thread mostly ignores me as I try to untangle it from around her. But this time I hold on a little longer. The memory of the Dreamscape flares brightly around me, the red thread singeing the tips of my fingers.

Unleash us it hisses over and over again.

I don't know what compels me to tighten my grip on the thread. Maybe it's to combat that sense of helplessness raging through me. Or maybe it's the lingering wish to change the outcome of our fate. But whatever the reason is, this time I don't let go when the thread shows me the vision of Gemma possessed with magic, her eyes cruel and red, her mouth mocking.

This time I meet her gaze and say, "Take me instead."

At my words, the memory glares so brightly that I have to turn away. Unlike before, the red thread now turns its full attention to me. It's like feeling eyes on the back of my head, like pouring salt into an open wound. A stinging, chilling sense of dread that plunges into my chest the longer I hold onto the thread.

Oliver Cade, it slowly whispers, stretching out each syllable of my name. Quietly, thoughtfully.

Its whisper multiplies into an incessant stream of murmured words. They slither all around me, hissing like a sigh, like the longest, deepest exhale I've ever heard. I shiver at the sound, all the hairs on my arms standing on end until the red sky of the Dreamscape vanishes as the memory of that night is finally ripped from my hands.

I'm surrounded by darkness. I can't move my head or my arms or my legs. I don't even know if I have a body at this point. It feels like there's nothing of me left; nothing solid, nothing real.

Maybe I've been cracked open and spooled out, unwound like an endless thread.

No specific memory takes me this time. Now it's just the darkness mixed with flashes of color and snatches of sound. Like my life was thrown into a blender and is being poured out all over me. Maybe now I'm finally going to drown in it.

Homesickness—that's what this is.

But through the suffocating chaos, I feel a pair of unseen hands gently touch my shoulders.

"Who's there?" I call out blindly, my voice cracking like broken glass.

"Hold still, let me help you," someone breathes in my ear. There's a bright flash, and the dizzying spin of memories begins to slow, everything quieting as if someone finally turned the volume down.

"Think of somewhere safe, somewhere familiar," the voice commands. "Somewhere you would be alone. Picture it. Think of nothing else."

It's hard to calm my mind down when there's a stranger in the darkness giving me instructions I'm not sure I should follow. But the idea of *somewhere safe, somewhere familiar* is too tempting to ignore. I take a deep breath and focus on an image, concentrating on that place with everything I have until my heart rate slows and my anxiety subsides.

Another blink. And then—

I'm outside in my backyard on the patio looking out over the mountain range. The air is crisp and cool, the sky a rosy shade of early morning pink. The polished wood of the deck chair I'm sitting in feels sturdy and smooth against my back. I tip my head up and stare at the sunrise, inhaling deeply, gratefully.

When I turn my head to the side, I let out a startled yelp. There's a woman sitting in the chair next to me, her hands folded in her lap, her wide eyes hesitant and sad. I recognize her immediately. Her dark simple dress shimmers, and her pale skin glows pearlescent in the soft light of the rising sun.

The last time I saw her was inside a memory given to us by the Dreamscape. She was fighting with Atticus over what to do about her sister, Cora, the red thread dangling between the three of them.

"Let fate unfold as it will," she'd pleaded.

She was a Threader, just like me.

"Hello, Oliver," Lillian says quietly, her voice wavering like her ghostly form. "We finally meet."

CHAPTER TWENTY

GEMMA

I CAN'T QUIT staring at the tree.

Its blackened branches give off the smell of a campfire recently doused, smoke still rising from the splintering cracks. The small group of relatives that stayed behind all mutter quietly to each other, their gazes also fixed on the charred remains. Parents tuck their children under their arms and pull them away as if the decay is contagious.

"Gemma?" Libby's voice breaks through the silence on the other end of the phone. "Did you hear me? I said I can't read the Chronicles." Her voice has transitioned from quiet and small to borderline hysterical.

"Yes, I heard you," I say, tightening my grip on the phone.

"I don't know what's happening. I was in the library reading when all of a sudden the words wouldn't hold still on the page. It was like trying to read without my glasses except so much worse. None of the words made *sense*." She pauses, breathing softly into the phone. "But there's more. It's not just that I can't read the Language—I can't find the words I need for casting either. I can barely string together the simplest of spells," she says miserably. "It's like my magic is... fading away."

Or burning out like a star collapsing.

A Claiming undone, a weaving unraveling.

She doesn't say it and neither do I, but the truth of the situation lies in between every unspoken word—it isn't just the new Claimings we need to worry about.

It's all of them.

I think of Libby curled up in one of Grandma's cushy armchairs, the way she tucked herself in with the Caster Chronicles surrounding her. How she pored over each leather volume, searching for new castings, piecing together our history with painstaking affection.

I can't imagine Libby without her magic. And her silence on the other end of the phone tells me she can't imagine it either.

There's a crackling sound overhead, and the twinkle lights flicker back on, but the candles remain unlit, the wax dripping down their sides long since hardened. Milo pokes me on the shoulder. "I think it's over," he says with a look of relief. "I think my magic's okay now."

Over? I have a feeling this is only the beginning, I want to say, but I can't get the words out. I can barely admit it to myself. "Libby needs to talk to you." I hold the phone out to him.

"Hey, Aunt Lib," Milo says, pinning the phone to his shoulder with his cheek. He mumbles a word of casting and waves a glowing hand over the singed candle wicks on the table next to us. Tiny yellow flames flicker to life, the light dancing across the table, illuminating the discarded plates of food and tipped-over cups. There's a blooming stain of something dark and red in the middle of the tablecloth. I shiver once and look away.

"What do you mean you can't read the Chronicles?" Milo says into the phone, all the color draining from his face. A few curious cousins turn in his direction, so he ambles off to the other side of the yard to talk to Libby, listening intently.

After circling the dead tree a few times, Great Aunt Beatrice declares that we should do some kind of Elemental ritual to exorcise the magic from the decaying tree. She waves a wrinkled hand to the few Elementals in the crowd, but no one volunteers. No one's ever seen anything like this happen at a Claiming before. There's a nervous edge to the group made worse by the sight of the black sap leaking from the tree, the tar-like substance dripping down its trunk like tears.

It's not just the damage itself that's shocking, it's the unexpectedness of it all.

Mom shakes her head, her gaze still trained on the tree. She isn't just sad about losing something so beautiful and ancient, it's more than that—she's afraid. She rubs a hand roughly across her forehead, her brow furrowed and tight. And when her eyes finally leave the tree, they land on mine. She looks at me long and hard, and I swear in that moment she can see right through me. I break eye contact first and stare fixedly at my feet in the grass, my heart racing.

I wonder what she sees when she looks at me.

Mom turns and extinguishes the fire in the center of the yard, which finally complies with her magic. She takes Emily and Sylvia each by the arm and steers them into the house with the promise of tea and chairs to collapse in. The rest of the family files up the stairs behind them, offering Sylvia unsolicited explanations or words of sympathy. A few of the stragglers even mention other Skipper lines they know that are doing "just fine without magic." She winces and stoically nods along, looking like she wants to burrow into the ground and stay there forever.

I pace back and forth on the now-quiet deck, waiting for Milo to finish talking to Libby. Other than the massive blackened pine tree, which looms unmistakably in the silver light of the moon, the rest of the yard is peaceful.

Milo crosses the lawn, pausing at our table to grab his abandoned dinner. He jogs up the short set of stairs and hands me my phone. "Libby's really freaking out," he says, his voice grave.

I shove my phone into the pocket of my dress and wrap my arms tightly around my stomach. "I don't blame her."

We stare out at the dark forest beyond the yard, each of us lost in thought until Milo takes a swig of his lemonade, pulling a face. "Man, this stuff is sour."

I grab the cup out of his hands, waving at the plate of food he has balanced on the deck railing. "Unbelievable. How can you even think about food right now?"

"Because I'm *hungry*, and every time I try to eat I'm interrupted," he huffs, straightening to his full height. "Not to mention, I just found out that I might be losing my magic. Now, can you please let me eat my sad cold hamburger in peace?"

I set his cup on the railing next to his plate, bumping into him with my shoulder. "I'm sorry," I whisper, wishing I had something better to offer him. The empty space where my magic used to be pulses along to the rhythm of my heartbeat.

He doesn't reply, he just takes a giant bite of his soggy burger and sighs. He swallows and looks down, staring at his hands, which are pale under the shadows of the trees. "What if this doesn't get better? What if it's permanent?"

"That's why we need to leave," I say, my voice low and urgent. "We need to go find Charlotte. I don't know if she can help us, but finding her is the only lead we've got. She's our only connection to Ollie. And we need to leave as soon as possible—this could be happening to other people too. Not just at the Claimings, but everywhere. To anyone with magic."

Milo finishes his hamburger in two bites and nods. "Whatever that was, I don't want it to happen again." He tosses his plate into a nearby trashcan and leans against the railing of the deck, looking out at the night sky. "My magic felt... *wrong*."

"What did it feel like?"

"Like I was wearing my shirt inside out."

I almost laugh. "That's not very dramatic."

The corner of his mouth lifts. "Yeah, except instead of a shirt it felt like *I* was inside out. I don't know, it's hard to explain. It felt weird; I didn't like it." He tips his head back, staring into the blackened branches of the tree. "It scared me. For the first time, I felt how fragile it is—my connection to my magic."

In my mind, I see the thin, delicate threads of the Dreamscape, weaving in and out between the stars, connecting the Claimed to their magic.

Impossibly fragile is right. And now it's torn open with no one there to protect it.

Mom opens the back door of the house and calls us inside.

"Tonight," I mumble the moment she turns away, "after Mom falls asleep."

We both look down, neither of us stating the obvious. We've snuck out before. We've broken rules and made her worry, but this? This feels like crossing a line.

"We have to," Milo says, once again reading my mind. "She'll never willingly let us leave."

Inside, the rest of the family is trickling out the door. A hint of awkwardness hangs in the air. Even in a family surrounded by magic, nobody likes to be confronted with the unexplainable. After the last hug has been hugged, the door swings shut with a lonely sort of sound, but I can't help but feel relieved.

Mom's in the kitchen filling a tea kettle. As she clicks the burner on, she says to Emily, "We should go. I'm sure the three of you need some time and space after everything." Again, her eyes land on mine, her mouth tight with tension before she fixes her gaze back on Emily. "I know we talked about us staying for a few extra days, but we don't mind getting a hotel and heading home tomorrow."

Emily shakes her head, reaching into the cabinet to pull out her stash of tea. "Nonsense. You're not going anywhere. We've got the guest room made up for you and Gemma, and Milo can sleep on the couch in the study. We want you here. Besides, I'm sure Sylvia could use a friend to talk to."

But Sylvia was already running up the stairs, and the resounding slam of her bedroom door seemed to say otherwise.

Emily rubs a hand over the back of her neck and asks, "How does peppermint tea sound?"

"I'm going to do some reading before bed," her husband Thomas says, picking up a large book with a worn leather cover. He taps the spine absently and says to himself, "There's got to be something in here."

"Can I check it out with you?" Milo asks, his voice eager. "I've never seen another family's Chronicles before."

Thomas runs a hand over his receding hairline and smiles distractedly, motioning Milo to follow him into the study. Milo glances back at me over his shoulder one last time before turning down the hall. I nod once.

My stomach churns with guilt and fear of the unknown, but it doesn't change my mind. I know what we need to do.

We leave tonight.

I'm lying in the dark, staring up at the guest room ceiling and counting my breaths when the door finally creaks open, and Mom quietly shuffles in. She's been sipping tea with Emily for hours. I slow my breathing down and relax my face as I peer at her through my lashes. Her features are shadowed in the slanted stripes of moonlight bleeding in through the blinds in the window, but even in the bad lighting, I can tell she's been crying.

She sniffs quietly as she changes into her pajamas and slides under the sheets on her side of the bed, which already feels crowded from too many pillows. One of her bare feet brushes against mine under the covers. I have to remind myself to keep my eyes shut, to not flinch from the sudden coldness of it.

After a few minutes of silence that makes me think she must've drifted off, she whispers, "You don't have to pretend to be asleep—I know you're awake."

Even as my heart stops, my mouth curves into a guilty half-smile, and I turn onto my side to face her. "What gave it away?"

Her eyes are round and solemn even as her own mouth cracks into a grin. "Everything."

I snort into my pillow.

We breathe into the quiet for another moment, and then she says, "I know what you and your brother have planned. I know you're leaving."

I pull the soft cream sheet up to my chin. "What gave it away?" I ask again, this time in a small voice with no trace of humor.

"Everything," she repeats. "I know you." She says the statement simply, like that's reason enough, and I guess for a mother it is. "I know that no matter how badly I want to, I can't make you stay, but can I say something before you leave?"

I nod my head, too caught off guard to give a real answer.

Mom rolls over so she's flat on her back, placing her arms under her head like she's gazing up at the stars rather than the popcorn ceiling of an unfamiliar guest room. The corners of her mouth are still turned up like she's on the edge of a smile, but something's holding her back. "I'm starting to remember, you know. Just bits and pieces. But it's more than I remembered before. About your dad."

My breath catches in my throat, and I don't dare to move. I don't want to risk breaking whatever spell has been cast. My mom never talks about my dad. I used to think it was because the memories were too painful or because she missed him too much, but after my Claiming, I realized it was because she literally didn't remember the truth about what had happened to my dad.

It was only when Libby told us her story, when she'd finally shared that sliver of memory she'd taken from my father's mind on the last day they saw him, that I realized the extent of the damage done to my mom.

"When I first met your dad, when I first met Noah—" She cuts herself off with a sharp inhale like she's surprised by the sound of his name. "Noah..." she says again softly. "He knocked me off my feet," she finishes with a small laugh. "I'd never met anyone like him. The summer we met I was staying with a family friend, and Noah lived nearby. You know how it is—even though we try to keep a low profile, sometimes the Claimed can't help but gravitate toward each other."

I think about Ollie and me ending up across the street from each other, and I nod.

I've never heard my mom tell the story about how she met my

dad. Not once. Questions bubble up inside me, ready to spill out at any moment. I try one out, the taste of it foreign on my tongue. "What was he like?"

Her response comes quick and easy. "He was like the sun."

I let her answer settle onto me. *The sun.* Bright and warm; difficult to ignore and impossible to live without. I squirm restlessly under the sheets, testing out the feel of the weight of her memories on me. Could I bear it? Could I hold onto them knowing how this story ends?

"I'd been Claimed the year before, and he was Claimed the year before that. I'd been struggling to get a grip on my magic. That summer I caused multiple snowstorms, and I was constantly flooding the backyard. The Nons on the evening news couldn't stop talking about the 'unseasonably strange weather' we were having." She shakes her head ruefully.

It's hard to imagine my mom not having control over her magic. Snowstorms and flash floods—I can't even visualize it.

"My mom got tired of the mess and the drama, so she sent me off to practice with an old friend in the valley who was also an Elemental." She sighs and her mouth hardens into a thin line. "Both of my parents were Casters and they liked things a little... quieter. Especially my mom." Her mouth softens, and a laugh tumbles out, surprising me. "The funny thing was, I brought Noah home with me at the end of the summer, and he was far louder and wilder than I ever was. They didn't know what to do with us."

"Well, that plan backfired," I say, laughing along with her. "So that means you met..." My voice lowers, dipping into that tender place of sadness that lives inside my chest. "You met Grandma that summer." The gentle sound of our laughter fades.

Mom's shoulder presses against mine as she exhales. "If Noah knocked me off my feet, then Ellen picked me back up again. I used to tell your dad that, sure, I liked him, but I only fell in love with him after I met his mother." She picks at the patterned quilt lying over us. "My mom and I were never close. And Ellen filled that gap, that hole in my heart. She was a strong-willed, single mother with an energy that was just unfailing."

I close my eyes as a flood of memories washes over me, each one featuring my mom and my grandma working together side by side, taking care of Milo and me. Grandma knew how hard it was to raise two kids all alone, so she was there for my mom, every day through every year.

Unfailing.

With the memories comes the pain. I'm not surprised, I expected it. But this time when it hits me, it doesn't knock the wind out of me. It's not the tearing open of a still fresh and ragged wound. This time, it's a slow puncture, a needling pain. It hurts, but I can breathe through it. It hurts, but the pain reminds me that she was here. I guess sometimes pain needs to be felt in order to remember.

I'm stronger than I thought. The realization catches me off-guard, but the more I think about it, the more true it becomes. I can bear the weight of this. And I'll do it gladly if it means I get to keep the good parts too.

Mom sniffs and says, "I remember how your dad used to try to describe the Dreamscape. I was so drawn to the mystery of it, to the elusiveness of his magic."

I sit up and shove the heavy quilt off my legs. "So you *do* remember the Dreamscape now. I was wondering."

"Something's changed, hasn't it?" she asks, her gaze far-off and thoughtful. "I remember so much, but it only comes in snatches, like the details of a half-remembered dream. It's the pieces of a puzzle, but never the completed picture." She rubs her forehead absently. "At the Claiming tonight, a memory wandered into my mind out of nowhere. One second, I'm trying to calm the fire down, and the next, I'm thinking about your dad and the sound of his voice when he would describe the stars and the threads. All that magic."

"The curse is broken," I whisper into the darkness. I think about those silver threads I saw snaking their way through the grass tonight. I think about the floor of the Dreamscape torn open and gaping, Ollie's hand grasping for mine. "Somehow Ollie broke it. And the Dreamscape along with it."

Mom frowns and sits up too. "I think you've got some explaining to do."

I grab a pillow and wrap my arms around it, hugging it tightly to my chest. And then I tell her everything—well, almost everything. I tell her about my time in the Dreamscape, about how I held the place together while Ollie tied the Claimings. I tell her about the memory of Cora, Atticus, and Lillian. I grit my teeth and stumble through the parts that include the red thread, my words clumsy and rushed. Mom stays quiet and never interrupts, but her eyes are round with barely suppressed alarm. When I get to the memory of Dad and Ben in the Dreamscape—how they fought over the broken red thread, how Dad tried to fix it and bind it to himself—I pause and chew on my lip, unsure if I should go on.

Mom grips her own pillow, her face grim but determined. "It's okay," she says. "I'm okay. Keep going."

So I tell her how it broke him, how he muttered to himself and laughed, the hollow sound of it still ringing in my ears. Then I finally tell her how the tear in the weaving swallowed him whole, trapping Ben alone in the Dreamscape for the next seventeen years.

Trapped, just like Ollie.

Her face is even paler after I've finished, but there's an unexpected air of relief around her too. "It finally makes sense," she mumbles. "I feel like I've been trapped in the haze for so long." When she looks up at me, tears are tumbling down her cheeks. "I'm so sorry, Gem."

My throat tightens, making it hard to swallow. "But why? None of this is your fault." I take her hand in between mine and give it a squeeze.

"I know, but I'm still sorry all the same. I'm sorry you had to grow up with a mom who was only half there, stuck somewhere in between what was real and what wasn't."

We're both quiet for a moment. My phone buzzes, probably with a text from Milo asking if the coast is clear, but I ignore it. "Can I ask you a question?"

"I think that's only fair," she says with a short laugh.

I tuck my hair behind my ears and look down. "What are your nightmares about?"

All those nights when she would cry in her sleep, and Milo and I would run down the hall to sit with her, I always wondered if they were about my dad, but I didn't know how to ask.

Mom lifts her eyebrows. "It's strange actually. They aren't so much about anything as they are… a feeling. I wish I could tell you more about what I see, but it isn't really a place. It's *nothing*. It's cold and gray and—"

"Empty," I finish for her, and she nods. Goosebumps cover both my arms.

My mother's been dreaming about the gray place; the space between here and the Dreamscape.

"I remember that last day with Noah," she says, her eyes going fuzzy as she thinks back. "How he came into the nursery and told me his plans. He said he was going to fix it. He was going to fix the red thread and fix the Claimings so we could move on with our lives, so our kids wouldn't have to deal with this magic. But I was confused, as I always was every time he brought up the Dreamscape. I couldn't remember. I read his letter again and again, but it was never enough." Her shoulders curl in on themselves like she's about to fold in half. "Libby was right."

"About what?"

"That casting your dad did. He was trying to give me a memory of the Dreamscape. I think…" she hesitates, tugging at the hem of her t-shirt, "I think he went inside my mind. I think he used mind magic, only it didn't work."

I stiffen at the mention of mind magic. "Is that why your memories of him are—"

"Such a mess?" She shrugs. "That's probably one of the reasons."

And the reason she sometimes dreams of a place of nothingness. A broken piece of magic, jagged and sharp and wrong, placed inside her mind by a desperate man who only wanted her to understand.

"I think Noah was tired of living inside a secret. He used to light up when he talked about the Dreamscape. He used to love the wonder of it, even the exclusivity of it; I think it made him feel special. But as the years went on, he grew resentful. The magic called him away every time he fell asleep, and he couldn't control when it would bring him back. Sometimes he was gone for days. Other times, only hours. He became agitated and restless. He wanted *more* for his life."

I jerk back, her words hitting me like a slap.

He wanted *more*.

You could have more. You just have to take it.

The phantom whispers of the red thread wrap around me until I can hardly breathe. My fingers twist into the quilt, clutching and clinging, searching for something to hold onto.

"Gemma, are you all right?" Mom leans over and takes my face in her hands. "Breathe, honey, you're okay." Her words sound reassuring, but she looks so scared.

My phone vibrates next to me on the bed again. And again. Milo's waiting for me.

I brush her hands away. "It's just that... I'm no different than Dad. I wanted more too. And look where it got him. Look where it got me."

Mom's face softens as she wraps her arms around my shoulders and pulls me into her like she's done so many times before. "Oh, Gemma girl, there's nothing wrong with wanting. To be human is to want. The trick is learning to want what's good for you. What's right. And that takes time and patience and a life full of choices. There's nothing wrong with wanting more. And there's nothing wrong with you."

Her words unlock the tightly sealed box I'd shoved all my most broken parts into. A sob breaks loose from my chest. Then another, and another, and another. I cry into my mom's shoulder as she rubs circles on my back and reminds me over and over again that I'm okay. There's nothing wrong with me.

And for the first time since I touched the red thread, I believe her.

The door slowly opens to reveal Milo standing in the hall with his duffle bag in hand and his backpack slung over his shoulder. He glares at me until he realizes that Mom is sitting up next to me wide awake and currently watching his every move.

"Um, I was just checking on you guys," he mutters, quickly throwing his bag down the hall. "Yep, everything looks good in here," he says with a glance around the room. "So, I'll just be off to bed then."

"You can drop the act, Milo," Mom says with a shake of her head. "I already know."

"You *told* her?" he all but screeches at me.

"She already *knew*," I say back, crossing my arms.

Milo huffs, looking back and forth between us as if trying to gauge the strange mood in the room. His eyebrows dip as he notices my sniffling and puffy eyes. He drops his backpack on the floor and sits on the bed. "It's time; we need to leave," he says quietly, looking at Mom and not at me. He takes a deep breath like he's about to plunge into the deep end of a pool. "You saw the Claiming tonight. If we don't find Ollie, if we don't fix this, who knows what will happen to everyone's magic—"

"Milo," Mom interrupts. "I know. I have to let you go."

She raises her hand to her mouth, pressing her fingers to her lips as if she's trying to shove the words back inside her. As if her freely granted permission shocks even herself.

Milo clamps his own mouth shut and darts a glance at me. He scratches the side of his head as Mom leans over, plucking her purse off the nightstand and pulling something out of the inside pocket.

It's the note with Charlotte's address. "You'll need this," she says.

Neither Milo nor I mention the fact that we'd already memorized the address. There's no need to reemphasize the fact that we were about to sneak out, steal the Jeep, and drive to another state unaccompanied.

Milo's eyes widen as he takes the slip of paper and carefully slides it into the pocket of his hoodie. "Thanks," he says softly.

"And you'll need these." She tosses him the keys to the Jeep. "I'll have Libby come get me. We'll figure it out. Now go," she says with a tremor in her voice, "before I change my mind. Gemma will fill you in."

Milo stands and swings his backpack over his shoulder in that easy way of his. "You ready, Gem?"

"As I'll ever be." I grab my own bag from the foot of the bed and follow him down the hall.

Mom trails behind us wrapped up in the large quilt. She looks so small, standing there in the cold night air, huddled in the deep folds of the blanket as she opens the front door. She hugs us both, but she doesn't tell us to be careful, and she doesn't ask when we'll be back. All she says is, "Bring him home."

I wonder which *him* she's talking about.

I hold Teresa's note tightly in my hands as Milo backs the Jeep down the steep driveway. He cracks the windows, and the crisp autumn air fills the space between us. "Let's hit the road," he says, punching the gas.

I roll my eyes. "Who actually says that, Milo."

He grins back at me, obviously glad to be back behind the wheel with the wind rushing through our hair and the moon shining down on us. He taps the address into the GPS and starts to wind his way through the curvy back roads that lead down the mountain.

"Wait, I made a new playlist." I reach into my bag to pull out my phone, but before I do, I see the brief stunned look on my brother's face. "It's a good one," I say as I connect my phone to the car's speakers.

"You always say that."

"And I'm always right."

The music swells, clear and bright like the night before us. Milo turns the volume up and tilts his head to the side, listening. "Yes, this definitely sets the mood for the 'on the hunt for my boyfriend's magical birth mother' trip we're taking." He knocks my arm off the center console, hogging the whole thing.

I snort, but when I turn to look out my window, it's with a small smile on my lips. I want to tuck it away and save it for later; that's the first time he's ever referred to Ollie as my boyfriend.

He doesn't make a big deal out of it, so neither do I.

But still. It matters.

I'm coming, I'm coming, I whisper like a wish.

Like a promise.

CHAPTER TWENTY-ONE

OLLIE

THIS DREAM JUST keeps getting weirder and weirder.

Lillian blinks, waiting for me to say something. When all I do is stare at her, she straightens in her seat, grimacing at the wood beneath her. "These chairs are not very comfortable. This place—is it your home?" Her dark eyes rove over the mountains, still a pale purple under the first blush of sunrise. "Why is it already so hot when the sun has not even risen?" She runs a hand under her dark hair wrapped in a knot at the nape of her neck as if wiping off sweat.

I almost laugh, but I'm too stressed out to even crack a smile. "Yes, it's hot, and yes, this is my home. This is my backyard."

"And being home makes you calm. Good. You chose the right memory, Oliver."

I have so many questions, I can't decide which one to ask, so I blurt out the first thing that comes to my mind. "How do you know my name?" I try to keep my voice casual, like I'm totally fine with her sudden appearance. Like it's completely normal to sit and chat with a ghost.

"I have been waiting for you for a long time."

"Waiting for me? But—why—"

"Oliver, calm yourself."

"I *am* calm," I wheeze out, my breath coming too quickly.

She frowns and dips her chin, pointing to my white-knuckled grip on the armrests of my chair. "If you don't stay calm, you *will* get tangled up again."

"Tangled again? Tangled in what?"

"Your memories. That is how I found you."

My stomach clenches. The flashes of color, the whirlwind of sensation... Is that what that was? Was I literally tangled in my memories?

"How are you here? Why are you here? And where are we?" The questions tumble out of my mouth at a rapid-fire rate, giving her zero chance to respond. I shove my chair back and pace the back patio, the concrete warm against my bare feet. "Are you a ghost? Am *I* a ghost? Are we—" I stop talking when the ground starts shaking beneath me, looking over to Lillian in alarm.

She presses her hands down on her chair in an attempt to keep it from rattling beneath her. "Please, remain calm," she reminds me again with a wary glance over her shoulder, her pearly face translucent and hazy, the desert background slightly visible behind her. "Try to just be still and listen. This memory will not last much longer; we have already stayed too long."

There's a loud crashing sound, like stones scraping together. We both turn our heads to see the Superstitions quaking as if the mountains themselves are groaning in protest over our presence. I stumble on my feet as the memory slams me back into the deck chair, pinning me in the same position I started in. The moment I'm seated and still, the mountains stop their trembling, and the sun resumes its lazy ascent across the rose-colored sky.

Lillian slowly rises from her chair and takes a few steps toward me, carefully approaching as if she's afraid I'll get spooked and try to run off. "I am not a ghost, and neither are you. As you know, my name is Lillian. I was once a Threader, a keeper of magic." She says it slowly and emphatically, as if she's not just telling me, but also reminding herself.

She looks down at her semi-sheer form, her dress shifting around her ankles in the breeze. "But I am a barely-there version of myself, merely a collage of recollections. There is not much left of me to be remembered—you and Gemma are the last ones with any memory of me. And once I am forgotten..." She sighs, gesturing to the shimmery sheen of her skin.

I watch the way the early morning light makes her flicker like a candle flame. "You'll fade away, won't you?"

She doesn't say anything. Her solemn silence is answer enough.

"What about Atticus? Is he still with you?"

"No." She doesn't elaborate.

I chew on my lip and ask the question that's been pressing on my mind since the moment I saw Lillian sitting in one of my deck chairs. "Have you... have you seen my dad? Or Gemma's?"

She stares off at the mountains with a far-off look on her face. "They are trapped in the magic of their memories, lost to what was."

I sink back in my chair. I don't know what to feel when she tells me that. It's not like I was expecting to sit down and have a heart-to-heart with my birth father. I saw how he looked on his last night in the Dreamscape. He was the shell of a man, worn down by magic and solitude and a complete lack of hope. I don't think that's something a person can come back from.

"I am the only one left who has not succumbed to *Remembering*," Lillian says in a small voice, her gaze still trained on the craggy sun-kissed peaks of the Superstitions.

Her strange emphasis on the word sends a shiver running down my spine, like the trickle of ice-cold water on my bare skin. "What does that mean?" I swallow roughly, wishing I could just as easily swallow my fear. "Could you please explain what's going on?"

Gemma would scoff at my politeness. She would've already grabbed Lillian by the shoulders and tried to shake the answers out of her.

But Gemma's not here.

The mountains rumble again, this time the sky darkening in a flash like a sudden storm approaching. Lillian glances up at the billowing clouds with a frown. "We have already stayed too long," she mutters again before peering intently at me with her strange black eyes. "I will show you, but you must let go of this memory to truly see."

She points down at one of my hands still clenched tightly in a fist. I slowly uncurl my fingers to see a pale pink thread, the same color as a sunrise, flickering across the palm of my hand, the other end of it trailing upwards and out of sight.

"And I must warn you. This place, what I am about to show you..." She hesitates and runs her thumb across her chin, tapping it lightly. "It is not meant for us."

I shiver once again, filled with equal parts dread and anticipation. "Show me."

"Try to empty your mind. Focus on seeing, not Remembering."

I take one last look around my backyard, my stomach plummeting as the deck chairs vanish along with the patio and the desert landscape. I relax my grip, watching the colors fade. After a painful moment of indecision, I let the thread float free from my hand.

It's hard to let go.

"Clear your mind, Oliver. Take a deep breath. And Open. Your. Eyes," she says, her gaze flicking past mine and beyond the mountains. I follow her line of sight, and that's when I finally see.

We aren't in my backyard. Not really.

We are suspended in nothingness. A darkness so thick it's palpable. I can sense my feet resting on something, but I can't see anything below me. The darkness constricts around us, squeezing my chest and making it hard to breathe. It reminds me of the night of my Claiming when I broke through the Shadow spell to find Gemma in the Dreamscape. The darkness undulates, pulling me in deeper and deeper until a hand yanks me back.

"Oliver, calm your mind—you are slipping into another memory. Focus on what you see in front of you, not what you remember." Lillian's voice floats disembodied through the air.

I rub my hands over my face and take another look. Now that my eyes have adjusted, I can see that it's not as dark as I'd originally thought. My breath staggers as I try to take a step back, but my feet won't move, and there's nowhere else for me to go. I scan through the darkness, trying to get a sense of where I am, but my brain will only focus on one small detail at a time. I have this horrible sinking feeling that if I could see everything all at once, I wouldn't be able to handle it.

There's something out there—something moving. The sound of it brushes against my ears, soft and searching.

"Remain still, or they will overwhelm you again," Lillian whispers from next to me.

I can barely see her now. Her colors are muted, her edges softer; she's much more mirage-like than she was before. "Who will?" I ask, my chest tightening as I imagine a swarm of ghostly figures lurking in the shadows. More ghosts—that's just what I need.

"Not who. What," she says, pointing with a shaking white finger. "The memories."

Memories.

The word lingers in the air with a haunting hiss that sounds like the spray of the sea.

A pause. A breath. And then everything comes to life.

Dark swelling waves crash into each other, steel-gray and churning, the sheer power of each movement rattling my bones. But these waves aren't made of water, they're made of threads—countless silver threads that give off the strange sheen of every color imaginable, like light passing through a prism, refracted and ultraviolet.

If the Dreamscape was a vast starry night, then this place is a turbulent ocean.

It's unlike anything I've ever seen.

A few stray threads wrap around my ankles like the rush of the tide coming in. The moment I feel their touch, disjointed images flicker across my mind, snatches of half-remembered conversations filtering through my ears as the scent of something warm and spicy like Christmas morning fills my nose. The threads tug on me gently before letting go and drifting back to rejoin the others, taking the fuzzy pictures and muted sounds with them, all of it faint and familiar and just out of reach.

I gasp, swaying on my feet, feeling both too full and unbearably empty. "All of those threads… they're my memories?"

Lillian nods, her mouth forming a half-hearted shape between a smile and frown as her gaze follows mine. "Yours, mine, everyone's. This is where our memories reside. No matter where they begin, they all end here."

"But where is 'here?'" I ask, my voice teetering between desperation and exasperation. Her mysterious vagueness is really starting to get on my nerves.

"Do you not recognize it?"

She waits, saying nothing as I squint through the darkness, following the ebb and flow of the silvery threads. I exhale desperately and look up into the blackness, still half expecting to see the stars shining overhead in an otherworldly sky. But unlike the Dreamscape, there are no stars here. No stars for the threads to tumble out of; no constellations that form the pattern of the weaving. Instead, these threads seem to have a life of their own, everything wild and out of order, surging like a dark and endless ocean.

"Are we on the other side of the Dreamscape?"

Lillian nods once more.

In a sudden rush, as if my acknowledgment has sharpened their awareness of me, the tide of threads rises higher and higher, until the lip of the wave curls just over my head.

"Empty your mind, Oliver," Lillian warns.

I want to, but that's basically impossible since all I can think about is the looming wall of memories hovering over me.

"But I can't—" The wave breaks with a massive crash and the threads latch onto me, winding around my legs and trailing up the rest of my body. Each one tugs me in a different direction, the feel of them sharp and shocking as they snare on my clothes and pull on my hair. Memories fly past me at a reckless speed, leaving my head spinning. As soon as one wave breaks, another rises in its place. Claustrophobia traps me in its sweaty grip. It's too much, it's too fast, and there's no end to it.

This place is not meant for us.

"Breathe, Oliver." Lillian's voice cuts through the pandemonium, but I can't focus on anything other than the streaking swirl of colors parading through my mind. "I know it is overwhelming. But Remembering is the same as any other magic—you have to control it. Try to remain calm. You are Remembering too many things at once. Focus on one, and let the rest go. Try to return to your home."

I close my eyes and will myself to reappear in my backyard. I concentrate with everything that I have on the feel of the wooden chair beneath me, the concrete patio under my feet, the heady scent of heat coming off the small patch of grass, which looks as if my dad just mowed it and smells like the color green.

But no matter how hard I try, I can only maintain my hold on the memory of home for a fraction of a moment before it's seized out of my grasp and lost in the chaos once more. How can I keep my focus when every other memory is vying for my attention, all of them screaming for me to see, to feel, to choose them instead?

All the air in my lungs is sucked out as if I have literally been plunged underwater. I try to fight the cold force of it, but I can't tell which way is up. Am I swimming toward the surface or further into the depths of this unknowable current? I don't know if it even matters—it feels like I'll never come up for air again.

The threads tighten their grip on me, squeezing across my chest and arms and legs in a crushing, constricting motion. But even in my panic, a small part of me remembers to stay calm. It reminds me of my time in the Dreamscape and how the threads of the weaving would catch me in their grasp, unrelenting in their invitation to see, to feel, to choose to stay.

I remember relaxing into that feeling. I remember recognizing that the only way to gain any sort of control over it was to surrender. I remember thinking about Gemma and the way she would close her eyes and breathe when she was too wound up to hold still.

I imagine her standing there in front of me, inhaling sharply through her nose and exhaling deeply through her mouth. She repeats the pattern over and over again. I slow my breathing until it mimics hers. Until the roaring of the waves is gone and all I can hear is the sound of her breath mixed with mine.

I wonder what she used to think about when she closed her eyes and held still like this. A sharp twinge of regret unfolds inside me in a swift and painful burst. I wish I would've taken the time to ask.

There's a faint brushing against the back of my hand as a single thread wraps around my wrist and tugs me forward until I'm tumbling head over heels in a sickening, tumultuous rush.

I blink, and I'm in the Fitzgerald's kitchen. The sky is dark and gray outside the windows, the wind howling like a wolf. Gemma sits at the kitchen counter, her feet bouncing restlessly on the footrest of the barstool with a *tap tap tap*, her black hair swishing across her cheeks as she fidgets. She looks to be about sixteen years old, and this storm looks like a late summer monsoon.

"I just want to go for a run," she says, slumping onto the counter melodramatically. "Strike that—I *need* to go for a run."

The memory is so crisp and lifelike, it's as if I've never left this moment. It's a completely surreal, trapped-in-amber feeling. But now that I'm looking for it, I notice the hints of magic everywhere. Everything's shiny and slightly stiff, almost *too* perfect to be real. I peer more closely at the thin threads weaving the memory together, stitching my reality into a living, breathing thing.

The shape of the kitchen flexes around me like a snake preparing to suffocate its prey, the walls inching closer as if about to swallow me up before tossing me back into the sea of memories, completely untethered and all alone. My heart pounds and my legs buckle as I sit down beside Gemma, the barstool spinning slightly from my stumbling. The moment I take my seat, the scene smooths out, settling around me.

"But it's raging out there, which is why your mom said no." The words fall out of my mouth without any conscious thought. It's not *me* speaking to Gemma, it's the memory version of myself, repeating a conversation we must've had before. Now it's like a scene from a movie, and I'm one of the actors. Every line is memorized, every action already blocked out and chosen.

If I focus too much on the magic, it all starts to unravel. But if I let the memory play out the way it's supposed to, the way it did before, maybe it will let me stay.

I have to be present. I have to believe it's real.

I have to believe that *she's* real.

Gemma swivels to face the window. "It's not *that* bad," she mutters. A streak of lightning cracks across the dark sky in a flash, illuminating the messy kitchen. Ellen's pots are stacked chaotically near the stove, most of them crusted over with some kind of lime green paste that smells like oregano and burned hair.

"I don't know... I'd say that's pretty bad."

Gemma turns to me, her eyes already rolling. "Of course you think it's bad. You worry just as much as Mom does. Maybe even more." She swings her legs back and forth, spinning my stool with the toe of her shoe. "I need to get out of here. I can't stay trapped in the house for the rest of the day."

I hold up my phone with its glaring flash flood warning and she scoffs. "I know, I know," she sighs heavily. Then she closes her eyes and breathes in slowly through her nose, just like I remembered. And it's like I'm not even there anymore; she's gone to a different place where she can stay calm and slow her body down. A place that only exists for her.

"Gemma," I ask suddenly, breaking the steady silence. "What do you think about when you're counting your breaths?"

Her eyes fly open. "What?"

The kitchen starts to look warped and bloated, the image of it swaying in and out of focus. I take her hand in mine, slowly lacing our fingers together. Her mouth pops open, but she doesn't pull away. "I want to know what you see when you close your eyes."

I've gone completely off-script from the memory—a rash and foolish move—and I know I'm going to pay for it. But my breathing hitches when Gemma's hand unconsciously tightens around mine. She chews on her bottom lip while she thinks, considering me. "I count to ten. And I…"

Gemma drops my hand as her voice slows and slurs, fading into a faint hiss barely discernible from the downpour. The wind blows harder, shaking the house and spattering the rain noisily against the kitchen windows as if the memory is trying to wash away any remains of my question and my sticky, stubborn hope.

"Come on, Gemma," I say urgently, reaching out and touching her face, grazing her lips with the tips of my fingers. "Finish what you were saying."

A hand flexes around mine, but this time it's not Gemma's. Lillian pulls me off the barstool as the Fitzgerald's kitchen tumbles around me, cabinet doors slamming, pots and pans flying, the refrigerator door swinging open and shut. Gemma doesn't react to any of this; she's gone completely still, as vacant and lifeless as a faded and forgotten photograph.

"You cannot alter the past, Oliver," Lillian says, her voice quiet but firm. "You cannot add to a memory that has already written itself. That will weave something different, something new. That is a magic few can comprehend."

I shake my head, backing away from her and bumping into the counter. "But Gemma started to answer me! She was changing the memory—it was working!" I'm scrambling, too afraid to let the memory go, too afraid to lose her again. But when I turn and reach out for Gemma, my hands grasp pointlessly through the empty air.

She's gone, and in her place, a burgeoning darkness blooms.

Lillian's gaze narrows as she tugs me by the hand, plucking at a gossamer thread wrapped around my wrist that's the exact same shade as the rain dripping down the windows, and the rest of the memory scatters like smoke, revealing the swelling sea of memories behind her. "You must let each memory unfold as it will," she says, releasing the thread from her grip.

I frantically reach out, trying to grab hold of it, but it's already lost to the deep. Just another indistinguishable thread among the countless others.

"You know better than most the price you pay when using magic that does not belong to you. We cannot alter a fate that does not want to be changed, Oliver. Remember that."

CHAPTER TWENTY-TWO

OLLIE

ONCE AGAIN, LILLIAN and I are balanced on the edge of nothing with the angry sea surging around us. I try to keep my mind clear, to not let it zip from one thought to the next like an out-of-control ping pong ball, but I can already feel a sense of dread, urgent and heavy, spreading through my stomach. It feels like I've just been shoved out of a moving plane, forced to go sky-diving when that was the last thing I wanted to do.

I grab hold of Lillian's elbow and shudder at the contact; touching her is like plunging my hand into icy-cold water. "Well, who does this magic belong to then?" I try to keep my voice quiet as if that will keep the threads from finding me, but the tempestuous waves are so loud I nearly have to shout. "And how are my memories even *magic*? It's just stuff that's happened to me, it's—"

"I used to be like you. I had so many questions," she muses, her careful attention fixed on the sea. "But I have been down here for a very long time, so I no longer wonder." Her voice grows so quiet I can hardly hear her. "Sometimes I miss it, the wondering." She shakes her head as if trying to clear it, and her focus turns to me, her gaze piercing even in the dark. "All memories are magic, Oliver. Every word said, every touch given, each sunrise and sunset. Every single moment is magic manifested, we just refuse to see it. Does it not seem obvious to you now?"

All memories are magic. I let her words settle inside me, warm and solid like hot stones pressed against my chest. It does seem obvious, now that I think about it.

"You need to practice controlling yourself, or you will get stuck again. Last time, you let your runaway mind be in control, you let your feelings decide for you. You brought us into a new memory because of *her* rather than choosing for yourself."

I try not to bristle against her accusatory tone. "So, you're saying I'll get stuck... inside a memory?"

"If you are lucky. Or you will get trapped in *all* of your memories, all at once. Which is exactly how I found you." Her expression is sharp and full of warning. "And if you are stuck for too long, it is nearly impossible to escape," she says with a visible tremor. "You will be trapped inside your own mind, never free from the magic. A fate worse than fading."

My stomach drops. "Is that what happened to Atticus? To Noah and Ben?"

She doesn't answer for a long moment. "Sometimes I think I hear them," she finally says, staring out at the endless sea. "Sometimes I hear their whispers. There are voices, so many voices." Her mouth tightens into a thin line as she sways, lost in thought. The sea grows choppy and white-capped, her own memories rising to meet her, waiting to devour her in her moment of distraction.

I try not to freak out over the dead look in her eyes, but it's hard not to panic at the thought of the both of us drowning. "Lillian!" I shake her arm, and she startles as if she'd forgotten I was there. After a few slow blinks, she stiffens at the sight of the sea surging around us and closes her eyes, inhaling sharply until the waves settle into a gentle ripple. A temporary calm.

"Whoa, how did you do that?" I ask, marveling over the swiftness of her self-control.

"A lot of practice." Her mouth twitches into the start of a smile.

"Has that ever happened to you? Have you been trapped in your memories?"

Her small smile flickers into a frown. "If it had, then I would not be here with you."

"But why are you here anyway? And *how* are you here?"

Lillian lifts her chin. "Because someone must fix what has been broken."

The image of a torn red thread, its edges frayed and unraveling, comes unbidden into my mind. The swelling sea responds to my train of thought, rising overhead with a massive tangle of threads ready to barrage me with an endless stream of painful and confusing memories.

I fix my attention back onto Lillian, trying to ignore the lure of the memories calling to me like a siren song that never quits playing. I grit my teeth; there's a mounting pressure building inside my head, just behind my eyes. "But the thread was already fixed!" I yell over the roar of the sea, thinking about Noah and how he'd reattached the missing piece of the red thread. *"I can fix it, I can fix it,"* he'd said over and over again.

The lip of the wave curls threateningly over me, loose threads trailing across the back of my neck.

"You and I both know that repairing that thread did not fix anything," Lillian says flatly.

I look away, childishly clinging to the belief that if I ignore her, I can ignore the truth. But I know she's right. Of course it's not fixed. If anything, it's more damaged than before. Stronger and more determined.

The thin ridge we're precariously balanced on gives a little shake, and Lillian grimaces. "We have been here too long. Take us to another memory."

"Can't you? I don't know how." I shuffle back a step, anxious to get away from the rising waves, but there's nowhere else to go.

"If you do not learn to control yourself, Oliver, we will never fix anything."

"But how am I supposed to fix anything?" I ask with a groan, throwing my arms up in exasperation. "All I want to do is go home."

She flinches at the word before straightening her shoulders. "Then let me help you. Let me show you what I know." She holds out her pale hands imploringly. "Please, Oliver, I know it is not enough to make up for my mistakes, but my memories are all that I have to offer. And you cannot go inside them unless you learn to Remember. So, if you want to go home, then go home. Think of a specific time and place. Practice."

Home. I glare at the sea, at the snarled mass of threads, at the way they shimmer, iridescent and beautiful even in their chaos. I glower at the silvery sheen reflecting off each one like scattered starlight. It's annoying that something so disordered could still make my breath catch. Rubbing the space between my eyebrows, I stare at the sea; something about it is familiar, but I can't place it. I let my eyes wander and my mind drift until it snags on a nearly-forgotten memory.

A few years back, my mom was looking for a new hobby and briefly got really into embroidery. One day she came home from the craft store with bags full of soft, silky threads in every color of the rainbow. She had stacks of sturdy wooden embroidery hoops with swatches of white fabric stretched tightly over their frames and tiny square packages of needles. For the next couple of months, she sat stitching on the couch every single night while my dad and I flipped through the TV.

She loved it. She said it was relaxing to move her hands and focus on something small and achievable. The more she practiced, the tidier her stitches became. And even though I was a ten-year-old boy who was extremely uninterested in embroidery, I couldn't help but be impressed with her finished products: gardens bursting with flowers and forests teeming with life, quippy quotes and words to live by.

But when I flipped the finished hoops over, I was shocked to see the twisted mess on the other side. For every neat and polished stitch on the front, there was a chaotic swirl of color and knots on the back.

That's exactly what this place looks like. If the Dreamscape was a weaving, then this is the tangled mess on the other side.

"Well done, Oliver." Lillian points to the tidal wave tipping overhead where a thin thread, soft and sky blue slowly uncurls from the rest of the sea and hovers near the back of my hand. "You are Remembering," she says, nudging me forward. "Go ahead and take it."

This time I know what the memory will be. I can feel it brushing against me, relentless in its invitation to tumble down into its depths. As my hand wraps around the thread, I can practically see my mom sitting on the couch next to me with her legs folded beneath her. My mouth tugs up as I remember how her eyes would cross in concentration as she pulled the blue string through the white cloth—a cloudless stretch of sky appearing before her.

This time, I'm prepared for the sensation of falling. The darkness shifts again, shuffling like a deck of cards with me in the middle until everything stills and the scene slowly sharpens like the lens of a camera focusing. I blink against the sudden brightness, the overwhelming flood of awareness.

I'm at home with my parents, the sky the black of night outside the large windows in the family room. The air smells like slightly burned popcorn and something else I can't quite name. Something I used to not be able to smell unless I'd been away from my house for a really long time.

"Ollie, could you hand me the scissors?" The sound of my mom's voice feels more like home than anything else in this room ever could. I stare at her profile, lit by the glow of the TV in front of her. "The scissors, Ollie," she says again, holding out her hand without glancing up from her embroidery hoop.

"Here you go." I startle at the higher pitch of my voice, at the smaller shape of my hand as I pass the scissors over to my mom. Leaning back against the couch cushions, I pluck at the pajamas on my scrawny frame. I'm back in the body of ten-year-old Oliver.

Dad yawns from his chair across from the TV, the brown leather worn and supple beneath him. "You can stay up for the extra innings, Ollie." He looks at me over his shoulder with a grin before turning back to the screen. "But just this once," he says, like he always did every time a baseball game went past my bedtime.

It's just an ordinary evening at home with my family. So ordinary it's almost boring. So ordinary it was lost in a sea of a thousand other nights just like this one.

But now it feels unbelievably priceless.

My eyes blur as I sink into the familiar feel of my couch. Maybe I could just stay here. Maybe I could just let my life replay and that could be enough.

I'm just so tired.

"You cannot stay forever, Oliver," Lillian says quietly from next to me on the couch, my blue thread held loosely in her hand.

I jump; I'd all but forgotten she was here. My heart races as I glance quickly at my mom sitting on my other side.

"She cannot see me." Lillian sighs. "This is your memory. I am merely an observer."

I nod imperceptibly and sniff into my shirt sleeve. This time I'm careful not to disturb the scene. I cross my arms and stare at the TV, hopeful that if I ignore Lillian long enough, she'll leave me in peace. Mom continues to cross stitch, her hands busy and quick as she hums to herself. Dad tosses another handful of popcorn in his mouth. Lillian watches a commercial for dog food flashing across the screen with a bemused expression.

After another minute of contented silence, she asks, "Can you feel it? The way your mind starts to wander?"

I don't answer, but my mouth tightens into a thin line. I don't want to admit that my grip on the memory has already slackened, that I've had to start concentrating on every detail to keep myself here.

"At first you think you never want to leave," she continues, her gaze still trained on the glow of the television. "That being here, being home, would be enough. But even in the moments you crave, your mind is still not satisfied. It wants to move *forward*, beyond what is already known."

My jaw clenches as I watch my mom's needle go back and forth, back and forth through the cloth. She looks up and smiles at me. I try to smile back.

"Soon it will drive you mad." Lillian's voice is small and tired as she sinks deeper into the pillows behind her. Something about her reminds me of a piece of sea glass found on the shore. Like she was once shiny and sharp, every edge of her defined, but after enduring the crashing of countless waves, she's now worn down and dull. Discarded. Forgotten.

Fading away.

The memory flickers and the family room shakes. No matter how badly I want to stay, my focus is wavering. I think about the churning sea of memories surrounding us and blanch—I don't want to go back there.

"It helps if you imagine the sea as something else."

"Wait..." My ten-year-old voice comes out with a squeak. "Can you read my mind?"

Lillian's mouth twitches like she's about to laugh, but she doesn't. "No, Oliver. Your fear is written all over your face; mind reading is not required." She pries my hands loose from the thread as the peaceful picture of my parents at home vanishes like it never existed in the first place. "Remembering is too much for the mortal mind. It helps if you visualize the sea as something else, something safe and known. Do you have a place in mind that provides order?"

My heart is climbing up my throat, but I nod quickly.

"Close your eyes and think of that place. Remember it as vividly as you possibly can. Imagine that is where you are, and the chaos of the threads will organize itself around you."

I smell it before I see it—the warm, smoky scent of dusty paperbacks pressed gently together on a groaning shelf. Feeling the hint of a thread wrapping around my fingers, I let it tug me forward into a memory so structured that the threads will have no choice but to comply.

I crack my eyes open and squint under the sudden harsh glare of the fluorescents. I'm in my neighborhood library, in the quiet aisle between science fiction and mysteries.

And finally, I can breathe.

CHAPTER TWENTY-THREE

GEMMA

"CHEERS." I leave one hand on the wheel to clink my neon green energy drink against Milo's. He chugs the entire thing in three big gulps before tossing it into the backseat of the Jeep where it rolls noisily on the floor, clinking against the rest of our discarded cans—the graveyard of our sleepless night. I drink mine more slowly, letting the fizzy feel of the overly sweet drink work its magic on me.

"Do you remember what Grandma used to say about these?" Milo taps the edge of my can.

A small smile lifts the corner of my mouth. "She said that energy drinks were the closest that Nons ever came to bottling their own mixings. She said they were nearly as good as hers."

"High praise, coming from her," Milo laughed.

"The highest."

The sky up ahead is inky and star-scattered, but out the back window, the barest hint of light is creeping in as the sun begins its slow crawl toward morning. Every hour or so Milo and I trade places in the driver's seat, switching back and forth to let the other fall into a fitful sleep.

Each time I close my eyes, I go to the gray place—the space in between dreams. And even though I only sleep for a handful of minutes at a time, it feels longer. It's like time stops in that strange place, like it hardly exists at all. Without Milo there to help, I can't see past the endless mist and into the Dreamscape, so I wander around in the fog, half-heartedly searching for any sign of Ollie. But I know he's not there. Everything about it feels empty and cold—like loneliness come to life.

"We're almost there," Milo says, his voice gravelly with exhaustion. He taps his phone, lighting up the screen. "Less than two hours to Bakersfield now."

I grip the steering wheel tightly in my hands as my foot presses harder on the gas. "Eight hours," I mumble. "Can you believe it? She's only been *eight hours* away this whole time."

"I know."

"That'll kill Ollie."

Compared to the size of the whole wide world, Ollie's birth mother being only one state away is practically down the street in this scenario. I know he won't say anything about it when he finds out, but knowing Ollie, he'll agonize about that fact for weeks.

With the music turned off and the windows rolled up, the car is quiet except for the sound of the engine rumbling and Milo's foot tapping absently on the plastic floor mat. Maybe we're just tired, or maybe the excitement of being on the road has worn off, but both of us look wrung out and agitated now. The significance of what we're doing has started to sink in, leaving our minds occupied and our silences strained.

"Do you think she'll be there?"

For hours, we've taken turns asking each other that same question.

Milo shrugs and looks out his window. "Who knows. She gave Teresa that address a long time ago."

For hours, neither of us has come up with a real answer.

"Have you heard anything from Libby since last night?" I ask.

"No." Milo folds his hands in his lap, his jaw flexing. He doesn't need to say anything; I can tell just by looking at him how worried he is about the state of Libby's magic and what that could mean for him.

For everyone.

I catch a glimpse of my reflection in the side-view mirror. I look as tired as I feel with the smudge of dark circles already blossoming like bruises on the thin skin under my eyes.

I flinch at the blinding flash of light in the mirror as another car's headlights pierce through the gloom of the predawn hour. It's easy to feel alone out here, like Milo and I are the only ones left on the planet, slowly lurching toward our unknown destination. For the entire drive, I've felt boxed in by my worries, completely contained by the Jeep and the sound of my brother humming along to the radio and that feeling deep in the pit of my stomach that I just can't escape. It gnaws at me incessantly, reminding me of two simple truths I wish I could deny: one, my life is about to change again, and two, I still have no idea how to deal with that.

Another twenty minutes pass with both of us lost in the mess of our own thoughts. Eventually, Milo nods off, leaving me to watch the slow brightening of the horizon on my own, the sky turning a pale lavender the color of promises; morning will come soon enough.

I roll my neck and check the rearview mirror only to see that same pair of headlights winking back at me. "Milo... hey, Milo, wake up." I poke him hard on the shoulder. "Hey, wasn't that car at the gas station when we stopped outside of Kingman last night?"

Milo swats my hand away and mumbles something incoherent back at me. I leave one hand on the wheel and crane my neck over the side of my seat, trying to get a better look. The Jeep swerves into the other lane and Milo jolts up, grabbing the wheel with an exasperated sigh. "Ten and two; eyes on the road, remember?" He sits up straighter in his seat and rubs his face with his hands.

I ignore his comment. "That navy Volvo back there. Do you recognize it?"

Milo opens what appears to be his seventeenth granola bar and eats it in one bite. "How should I know?" he says through his mouthful. "We've passed a million cars. It's probably not actually the exact same car."

But we haven't passed a million cars. The highway has been

quiet, mostly vacant of other vehicles except for ours making the steady trek to Bakersfield.

"I guess," I agree with a shrug, but my focus flicks back to the Volvo. A strange feeling slowly slides down my spine, cold and dripping and impossible to ignore.

"Want a bar?" Milo asks, still unconcerned. He waves a golden crinkly wrapper in front of me.

"I'm good."

He doesn't argue. The words are barely out of my mouth before the granola bar is in his. "I need some real food soon, or I'm going to perish." He balls the wrapper up and tosses it over his shoulder before slumping in his seat.

I make a noncommittal noise, only half-listening as I change lanes without signaling. A moment later, so does the Volvo. My hands tighten on the steering wheel, my palms slick with sweat.

A green exit sign flashes by on the right. I jerk the wheel sharply and take the exit at the last possible moment.

Milo's head knocks into the window with a loud thud, and he mumbles something under his breath. "What are you doing?" he asks with a quick glance at his phone. "We're not supposed to exit here—"

"I want to see if they're following us."

"If *who* is following us? That random Volvo?" He twists in his seat to look out the back window. "Gem, you're acting crazy. Look, they aren't even slowing down. Quit being paranoid." The Volvo flies past us on the freeway, still heading west. Milo visibly relaxes in his seat and shakes his head with a chuckle. "No more caffeine for you."

I let the Jeep roll to a standstill at the stoplight at the end of the off-ramp. My heart pounds in my chest as I stare at the glaring red light, too bright in the dim purple haze of early morning. I suck in deep lungfuls of air, but it's just not enough. I don't think my body remembers how to breathe.

"If you make a left here, we can get back on the freeway—hey, what's going on?" Milo drops his phone in his lap and turns in his seat to look at me. "Gem?"

The light changes to green, but I still don't move. I just sit there, frozen in my seat, watching the light change from yellow to red.

Red.

It's always red.

The color bleeds through my mind until it's covering every single one of my thoughts, stark and shocking. Violent, even. The memories of that night rip me out of my seat and away from my brother as surely as if I was standing there in my backyard, wearing the white dress I used to love and watching everything fall apart. I can feel the heat from the red thread pulsing in the closed grip of my hand like a heartbeat, its ruthless rhythm racing.

Give us the magic. All of it.

Break the Claimings.

I can see him now, crawling toward me through the grass, his shaking fingers reaching up to grab the red thread, a look of pure, unabashed longing on his face...

James.

I can hear him, how he murmured, *"It's incredible. I wish you could see this, Dad."* But his reverent awe quickly changed to a howl of horror once the red thread latched onto him, tightly wrapping around his arm as it took away his magic. Slowly, like water circling the drain.

I remember the dizzying feel of it, how snatches of his memories flashed before my eyes. Now those images are burned into my mind, but I wish they weren't. I didn't want to know what he looked like as a little boy or that his dad used to hit him. I never asked for a closer glimpse of the slow-burning rage that lived inside him, so close to the surface and ready to consume everything in its path.

James.

"James." I spit his name out in between ragged breaths, my chest heaving painfully. My hand grasps the front of my sweatshirt, tugging at the fabric as if that will help me remember how to breathe. "I thought... maybe it was... James following us."

The stoplight transitions from green to yellow to red once again, each of the colors shining through the window and onto Milo's face. His eyes have softened, though his mouth remains a hard line. He watches me carefully, his gaze flicking from my impossibly tight grip on the steering wheel to the humiliating way I can't catch my breath. It's as if he's taking inventory of all the ways I'm a complete disaster.

A car finally pulls up behind us. We both flinch, but it's not the Volvo. An SUV honks twice before pulling around us, the middle-aged woman behind the wheel pausing to give us a dirty look before shooting through the green light.

My anxiousness escalates into a frenzy of words. "He's never going to stop, Milo. I *saw* inside his mind. He's obsessed with magic and proving that his family wasn't crazy. And now that I took away his magic, he's never going to leave me alone. I know he'll show up eventually, and when he does, who else is going to get hurt—"

"Pull over, Gem. Let me drive."

I take another shaky breath. "I'm fine, I can do it—"

"I know you can. But why don't you let me help you?"

The sound of his quiet voice snaps something inside me. It's the thing that makes me feel like I need to stand taller than I really am. The thing that only wants to bend but never break. The thing that makes me unyielding and stubborn and so completely exhausted

I'm just so tired.

Without another word, I pull over to the side of the exit. My fingers are aching by the time I peel them off the steering wheel and park the Jeep. Milo hops out of the car and walks around to the driver's side to swing my door open. Mechanically, I unbuckle my seatbelt and slide out of the car.

But Milo doesn't get in. He eases the door shut and runs his hands through his hair. "I'm scared too, you know."

I lean back against the car, slowly breathing in the cold air. "Yeah, but you can function," I mutter. "You can be scared without your body completely freaking out and shutting down. I mean, what *was* that?" I point behind me at the steering wheel. Shame colors my cheeks in a scalding shade of pink. "How am I supposed to help Ollie or fix anything if I can't even fix myself?"

"Who says you need fixing?" Milo leans against the car door next to me, his shoulder bumping into mine. "Who says there's something wrong with being scared?" I open my mouth to argue, but he silences me with a look. "Those are rhetorical questions, by the way. I'm not finished yet."

An uninvited smile tugs at my mouth. "Go on then."

He sighs and crosses his arms. "Gemma, we all went through something that night, not just you. You're walking around like you have this enormous weight on your shoulders, like you've got a monopoly on all the heavy stuff." I try to look down but he dips his head so I have to meet his gaze. "You're not the only one who's hurting or scared. You're not the only one who feels like they don't know what they're doing. You're not the only one who has a hard time breathing. When are you going to figure that out?"

His words feel like fingers pressing onto the pressure points of every single one of my insecurities. "Milo, I—"

"You're not alone. You don't have to figure this out by yourself. So stop pushing me away, and let me help you."

It's light enough outside now that I can see the sincerity etched into every feature of his face. I blink back hot tears and nod my head—slowly at first, then faster like a bobblehead that's determinedly trying not to cry. "Okay," I say with a sniff. "Okay, yes. You're right and I'm sorry. I need help." As soon as I say the words, the tightness inside me loosens slightly. I take a shuddering breath, filling the now-open space with more air. "I need your help."

Milo doesn't look smug at my admission; he just looks relieved. Like maybe he can breathe a little easier now, too. "Well, that's what I'm here for."

I nudge him in the ribs with my elbow. "When did you get so wise? And that's not a rhetorical question."

He shrugs and opens the car door behind me so I'm forced to move. "Maybe I've always been this wise and you just didn't want to admit it." He smirks and slides into the car, motioning for me to hurry up. "Let's hit the road."

"Do you really need to say that every time we start driving?" I snort as I pull my door shut and buckle my seatbelt.

"It feels necessary."

Kind of like you, I think to myself. *Necessary. Required. Needed.* I don't say the thought out loud, but Milo smiles at me like somehow he heard me anyway.

He signals and pulls the Jeep back onto the still vacant off-ramp. The GPS tells him to take a left back onto the freeway, but the moment before he turns, his expression shifts, rearranging itself from a determined focus to one of intense longing.

"Milo, what's up? Your face is all weird."

"I'm *starving*. Can we stop somewhere and eat?" He looks out the window with bleary eyes.

I glance at his phone; we're less than an hour away now. "I guess so." I doubt I'll be able to stomach any food, but if Milo doesn't eat a decent meal soon, who knows what will happen to him? He'll probably self-destruct before we ever find Charlotte.

The road stretches out in front of us, long and lonely in this one-light town. It looks like the kind of place that you'd only stop at on the way to somewhere else.

Milo's movements are agitated and sharp. He goes to turn into the parking lot of a fast-food restaurant, but at the last second, he jerks the steering wheel back and presses his foot down on the gas, peeling out onto the main road.

"I thought you were starving," I protest as my head slams into the headrest, but he doesn't answer. We pass two more places to eat without him even slowing. "Come on," I groan, "now's really not the time to be picky."

My brother is basically a human garbage disposal. In our entire seventeen years together, I've never once seen him be selective when it comes to what or where he eats. "Milo, just pick somewhere, and let's go through the drive-thru."

But still, he ignores me. He just keeps speeding down the road, hardly pausing to look at his surroundings. Then his hands begin to glow a soft golden amber.

"Are you casting right now? What's going on?" The sight of his hands, glowing and white-knuckled on the steering wheel, makes my mouth go dry. "Milo, please stop. You're scaring me."

He shakes his head, then looks down and yelps. "What the—" He tries to yank his hands off the wheel, but they don't budge. If anything, his fingers seem to tighten their grip. His eyes finally meet mine, wide and frantic. "Gem, listen to me. I cast a protection spell on us before we left Flagstaff." We both stare at his glowing hands. "It should only be triggered if someone else is trying to use magic on us."

"What do you mean someone is using magic on us?" Like an idiot, I whip my head back and forth, searching the car as if I'm going to find the culprit sitting in the backseat. My vision starts to tunnel; everything seems to narrow as all the edges fade to black.

"I can't stop driving," Milo mutters, "but it's not me." He takes a hard right and pulls into the nearly empty parking lot of a rundown diner, its tarnished chrome glinting in the morning sunlight.

And sitting in the nearly empty parking lot is the navy-blue Volvo.

The driver's door opens and a tall girl with an icy blonde ponytail steps out. "Is that... Zoe?" Milo asks, his voice rising an octave with incredulity.

"Wait, who?" My mouth is so dry, I can barely get the words out. The girl looks familiar in a vague sort of way, but I can't sit still long enough to focus on her. I'm craning my neck, trying to see if James is in the car too.

"Zoe," Milo says again, this time with a harder edge to his voice. "From Sylvia's Claiming last night?"

I freeze in my seat, my back a rigid line. He's right. It *is* the same girl. The one Milo was flirting with before the rest of the night went up in smoke when the Claiming started to unravel.

Zoe doesn't smile when she sees us. She leans against her car, watching us carefully, her facial features arranged to appear impassive.

"What do you think she wants?" I try to say the words slowly and evenly, but they come out too quickly and all on top of each other—a pile-up of panic.

Milo waves his still-glowing hands between us. "I don't know, but she's obviously the person who did this," he answers back roughly. "And I for one don't appreciate being summoned here against my will like a dog."

As if on cue, Zoe pulls a small glass vial out of the leather bag she has slung over her shoulder. She holds it up with one hand and gives it a little shake. The dark purple contents start to bubble. "We need to talk," she calls out, her voice muffled from the space and glass between us.

"Let's get out of here," I whisper. "Let's just leave." I can't stop looking at the vial in her hand or the heaviness of her bag, which is so obviously packed full of other bottles and jars of mixings. This girl clearly knows her magic.

"I *can't*," Milo hisses back. "Whatever mixing she used on me is keeping me here. It led me to her. I don't even remember driving here, it's like I was sleepwalking or something." He shudders. "Must be some kind of mind control."

Zoe shakes the bottle again and says impatiently, "I'll reverse the mixing, but first we need to have a conversation."

Milo mumbles something rude under his breath, then rolls down my window and leans across me to talk. "It's Zoe, right?" His question is met with silence. "You know if you wanted my number, you could've just asked me at dinner last night. I would have given it willingly. Gladly. Enthusiastically. But this whole thing," he waves his glowing hand between the Volvo and the

Jeep, "is a bit theatrical for my taste." His tone is pleasant and playful, but everything about his demeanor is closed off and guarded.

Zoe doesn't react. Not even a blink.

"Well then," Milo says, his plastered-on smile vanishing from his face in an instant. "Not sure why you're following us or why you've drugged me, but if you could stop now, it'd be much appreciated." He reaches his hand out toward the window. "I'll take that antidote now."

Zoe softly scoffs, tucking the tiny bottle back into her bag with a small shake of her head. But Milo must've been expecting that because less than a second later, he whispers a casting and her bag flies off her shoulder, the leather strap dragging on the ground just out of her reach as it sails through my open window.

She looks unconcerned as if she assumed Milo would do exactly that. She watches my brother as he roots through her bag, the glass bottles clinking against each other with a light tinkling sound. After a moment, he holds up a handful of small vials identical to the one with the antidote and makes a frustrated noise.

"Feel free to test those out on yourself," Zoe says, picking at her nail, the perfect picture of casualness. "But just to warn you, the side effects may vary, and you might not be too happy with the results. Only one of those is the antidote, and until you figure out which one it is, you're stuck with me."

I hold my breath, half-expecting Milo to say something stupid and unnecessarily flirtatious, but all he does is scowl and drop the vials back into the bag, the purple liquid so dark it's nearly black.

Satisfied that he's abandoned his search, Zoe finally looks up, her pale eyes blue and serious. "We need to talk about Charlotte."

The sound of her saying the name of Ollie's birth mom sends a sharp shock through me all the way to my toes. I don't even have to look at Milo to know that he's surprised too; it's practically radiating off him. "How do you know Charlotte?" I ask, unbuckling my seatbelt in one swift movement.

"It sounds like you're ready to have that conversation now,"

Zoe says, turning away from our car and toward the greasy diner. She holds one of the chrome doors open, waiting for us to follow.

But just before I climb out of the car, Milo stops me, tugging on my elbow. "Wait. Are we sure this is a good idea?" His gaze narrows as it shifts to Zoe.

I release a shaky breath and close my eyes, letting Ollie's face fill in all the empty spaces, every corner of the darkness stretching before me. "Of course I'm not sure. The only thing I'm sure about is Oliver."

Milo nods and pulls the keys out of the ignition, tossing them lightly back and forth between his hands, his expression thoughtful. "Well, I did say I was hungry." He gestures toward the diner, which looks like it should be closed for health code violations. "Shall we?"

I feel a small twinge of recklessness as I slam my door shut, like the barest hint of who I used to be. The echo of someone who took risks without thinking twice. Now all I seem to do is think.

Zoe holds out her hand before Milo passes through the door to the diner and he grudgingly returns her bag. "This time, you're not leaving without my number," he says as he brushes past without pausing for her reaction.

I suppress a groan and turn to Zoe. "You wanted to talk. So let's talk."

CHAPTER TWENTY-FOUR

OLLIE

I COLLAPSE ONTO the closest chair I can find—an uncomfortable orange plastic thing that I've never actually seen anyone sit on at the library, but I don't care. I've never been so relieved to be somewhere.

Lillian stays standing, her hands clasped behind her back. "You found a place of order?"

"Yeah," I breathe. "It's my library."

"You have a library?"

I raise an eyebrow. "No, it's a public library. You know, a place where they loan books out?"

Her face remains blank, but she nods along mutely. I wonder if she's ever been inside a library or if she had one in the time and place where she's from. Sometimes it's easy to forget how old she actually is.

I point to the rows of bookshelves on either side of us. "I've been coming here my whole life. My mom started bringing me when I was just a little kid. It's quiet and semi-comfortable. It's the kind of place you can lose a whole afternoon in." I adjust my position in the strange, plastic, too-modern-to-be-comfortable chair and look down at the thin thread—the same shade of cream as the crisp page of a book—weaving between my fingers. "And it's organized, which I believe was one of your requirements. So, what do you think?" I wave my arms out to the side like I'm some kind of tour guide.

Lillian toys with the cream thread in her hand, letting it slide across her palm. "This place smells strange, but if it provides order for you, then that is enough." She watches me settling into my seat, stretching out my legs in front of me. "But stay alert, Oliver. We are still in the sea of memories; the threads have merely responded to your visual. They are only organized because you wish them to be," she says, gesturing to the shelves of books surrounding us. "You must maintain your grip on this visual or the rest of your memories will break through." She nudges my feet so I'm forced to sit up straight. "Do not let your guard down."

As I look closer, I realize that she's right: everything's made of threads—the books and the furniture, even the speckled gray industrial carpet. The floor shakes beneath my feet like the ocean crashing against the shore, knocking a few of the books off the shelf, their pages fluttering as they fall to the ground and vanish in a splash of threads.

I reel back, stumbling into a rickety cart piled high with books ready to be returned to their proper places. The shelf behind me shudders as the cart smashes into it, threatening to collapse at any moment.

"*Remember*, Oliver. Focus," Lillian calls out, the cream thread held tightly in her hands.

I concentrate, holding perfectly still as I let my eyes run over the colorful spines, slowly and methodically drinking in every detail and willing it to be real. *I believe, I believe,* I chant to myself. Finally, the trembling stops, and the library goes still. I release a long-held breath that was trapped inside my chest. "Got it," I say, easing back into the plastic chair. "My guard is now officially up."

If I don't keep it together, this entire scene, the library and the safety it provides, will be dashed to pieces against the tumult of the threads just waiting to drown me once again. But clinging to this illusion feels like clinging to a hastily made raft composed of nothing but flimsy driftwood and whatever scraps of hope I have left.

I can't help but wonder if that will be enough to keep me afloat.

My gaze catches on the titles of the books closest to me. I lean in, squinting to read the curving words etched in silver, rising to my feet to follow the seemingly endless shelf with Lillian trailing behind me. Every title I pass by is shockingly specific, each book time-stamped and cataloged in my memory rather than the Dewey Decimal System.

Third Grade Spelling Bee, Fourth Round.

Christmas Morning, Volume 5.

Learning to Ride a Bike: Part II. And on and on and on.

"This is incredible," I say, running my hand along the pale wood of the shelf. "How is any of this real?"

Lillian's mouth curves into a frown; she looks truly perplexed. "What do you mean? It is *magic*. It is as real as you wish it to be."

"You make it sound so simple, so *easy*. Like I can just believe something and that makes it possible. Well, if that were true, I would've squeezed my eyes shut and wished myself home a long time ago. That's not how magic works. There are three branches, and each one has its own rules. There are *rules*, Lillian. '*Laws that govern, threads that bind. The knots that tether us to time.*'" I recite the words that I heard during my Claiming. "Sound familiar?"

Lillian chews on her cheek in a weak attempt at tamping down the rueful smile spreading across her face.

Irritation zips through me in a rush. "Why are you *smiling* at me? What could possibly be funny about this?"

"You just remind me of myself when I was a Threader. Back when I thought I understood everything."

I grunt in annoyance as I turn down the next aisle where we pass an entire section of books labeled *Daydreams About Gemma*, each one blurring with a soft silver gleam. I hurry past them, hoping Lillian doesn't notice my red cheeks, and wishing I could lose myself in one of those daydreams even for just a moment.

"Yes, there are laws," Lillian says, her smile creasing as her eyes flit over the titles etched onto the spines. She shakes her head and her smile wavers. "Yes, there are rules, but that is in the outside world where magic is tethered to a soul, where a body acts as a conduit for power. Here, it is different. Here, the magic is unbound. Surely you can feel it."

Of course I do, but I don't say that. "But what about the Dreamscape? There were so many rules I didn't understand."

Lillian pulls on the sleeve of my t-shirt, forcing me to stop. "The Dreamscape is only the gate—both the entrance and the exit—the weaving that holds it all together." She holds up her hands and intertwines her fingers, gripping them tightly to demonstrate. "But there is so much more to the story," she says, motioning to the shelves on either side of us. "Just like your books. It's as if you are reading a story with most of the pages torn out. You only have the ending. I had the middle. What we need is the beginning."

My brow puckers in confusion. "You've been looking for the beginning? Of what, magic?" I say it in an off-hand way, dismissive even, but Lillian nods her head solemnly in response.

"Yes. The beginning. I only have my memories of what I was taught, what I was shown by the Elders. But I think there is more."

More. My mind catches onto the word and refuses to let go. I want to crack it open and examine its contents. I want to pull it apart with my own two hands and search for every elusive *why* and *how*.

"But you've been down here for... a really long time," I say delicately, trying not to sound completely insensitive. I don't know how near-ghosts feel about the passage of time. "And you haven't found anything?"

Lillian bristles. "Magic has its secrets, and when it does not wish to reveal them, nothing can change that. But perhaps you can."

I snort. "And why on earth would you think that? I know a lot less about magic than you do. I think that fact has been established."

"Perhaps," Lillian agrees. "But maybe you know more than you think. Maybe this has always been your fate." An uncomfortable silence settles between us where the word *fate* seems to sit, awkward and heavy, right in the middle. After a moment, she clears her throat and quietly says, "We knew you would come. Eventually. We always knew this was how it would end."

"'*We*?'" I rasp out. "Who's 'we?'"

"Atticus and the other Threaders," she says with a shrug of her shoulders. "Those who have faded away."

I peer around the corner of the bookshelf, half expecting to see more ghosts—or memories, or whatever you want to call them—flickering in and out of view in the next aisle over, but it's still only me and Lillian, wandering an empty library packed full of my memories. I watch her drifting slowly past the rows of books, her feet barely touching the floor. "How have you made it this long?"

Lillian leans in closer, and for the first time, I see what she's kept hidden from me. The aging and the wear and tear that comes from living in a sea made of memory and magic. She's older and more translucent than I realized; she's not the same Lillian I saw in the memories with Gemma all those nights ago, she just wanted to appear that way.

"I told you," she says firmly, "I cannot fade until I fix this."

"So, what, you've survived on pure guilt?" I ask, sounding more than a little skeptical.

"Guilt is a powerful kind of magic, Oliver. Once it has you in its grip, it is nearly impossible to escape." She buries her face in her hands. "That is why I sent you and Gemma those memories in the Dreamscape," she says in a muffled voice. "I was trying to make amends, to work around the curse of forgetting that I helped unleash. I cannot fade before I fix what has been broken. I will never find peace until I do." Her form flickers precariously as if to emphasize the urgency of the situation.

"That was *you* sending us the memories?" I think back to those early nights in the Dreamscape when Gemma and I would wander around with no idea what we were doing. I think back to how nothing was revealed to us until Gemma accidentally spoke the Language, triggering a series of memories as the threads peeled off the walls and floated gently into her waiting hands. First, the memories of Lillian, Atticus, and Cora, and then the memory of our fathers.

"Do you have any idea how frustrating it was to only receive tiny slivers of information at a time? Hints and half-solved riddles—that's all we had to hold onto. We had no clue what we were doing! If you wanted to help, couldn't you have sent us more?"

We never knew the right words to say or which questions to ask. It felt like we were trapped in an unending guessing game. As I stare at Lillian, who still has her face in her hands, that same feeling of helplessness washes over me in a cold and sudden burst.

Not much has changed. I still feel like I'm in the middle of a game. And I still don't know the rules.

She slowly lifts her head, her dark eyes finding mine. "I wish I could have done more to help, but you have no idea how hard it is to survive down here."

I shuffle my feet like a sullen reprimanded child.

After a weighted pause, Lillian says, "When my sister Cora broke the red thread, fate itself was fractured." Her stare is piercing. "Do you understand what that means?"

I start to nod, then stop and sigh. I wish I could say that I understood any of this, but that would be a lie. So I shake my head instead.

"It means that when the red thread split, time or fate or destiny—whatever you choose to call it—*broke*." She shivers once, folding her arms around her stomach. "I saw it myself. And before it broke, I saw how the possibilities, the unceasing endlessness of it all, drove my sister absolutely mad. Fate used to unravel slowly and unhindered, but my sister—" Lillian's voice cracks, splintering the word into a thousand little pieces. "Or rather, *we*, all three of us, changed that. When she split the thread, it split right where you and Gemma enter the scene. And what came next was lost. Damaged. Altered. Fate itself became blind to its own future." She takes a steadying breath, then releases it. "The only thing fate could see was you. And her. The two of you together, and then... nothing."

Her words die out, slowly fading into the muffled silence of the library.

It takes me a minute to find my voice. "So that's why the red thread wanted Gemma."

"And why it still wants you."

A chill runs down my spine, and the bookshelves start to tremble. "Me? But why? And how do you know?"

"Before Atticus was lost to the thread, before he trapped me in the Dreamscape and set off a cycle that was doomed to repeat itself over and over again, he whispered things. He talked to himself. He was wild with longing for the thread, for the knowledge and power that comes with holding fate in your hands. That thread devoured Threader after Threader as it waited to get to the end of its line. It wanted its missing piece. And it wanted the two of you."

"I don't understand—"

"It wants the two of you because that is all it can *see*. You are the end of the road that was supposed to stretch on forever." Lillian paces around in an agitated circle. "The night I brought Cora into the Dreamscape changed everything. The history of the Claimed was lost, the legacy of the Threaders completely destroyed. Fate was altered and unable to play out in peace. We woke it up to our human frailties. It saw how incapable we are with our magic, so it decided to take it all back. To break the Claimings."

An image of Gemma with red fathomless eyes flashes through my mind, twisting my stomach into a knot. "So what can we do? How do we fix this?"

Lillian's shoulders sag in relief, like she's been waiting for me to ask that question but wasn't sure if I ever would. She gives me a small smile. "All I have left are my memories. I can show you what I know about the threads and the Claimings. The things you should have known from the very beginning if you had been properly taught." She hesitates, her jaw tensing. "But, Oliver, you must be careful. Going inside a memory that is not your own is complicated and dangerous. You could very easily become stuck in a time and place that does not belong to you, losing all sense of self and purpose. If you do not maintain your mind and manage your own memories, you will be lost to the magic."

My mouth flies open, filled to the brim with more questions just waiting to be asked, but Lillian's already turned away from me, her hand loosening its grip on the cream-colored thread of my library.

"Let it go," she says over her shoulder, pointing to the thread intertwined between my fingers.

I exhale deeply, taking one last look at all the colorful books stacked neatly in rows before slowly uncurling my fist and letting the thread float free. At the same moment, Lillian reaches back and wraps a dark brown thread around my other hand.

Immediately, the aisles of the library are teeming with life. The rows upon rows of bookshelves have been replaced with rows upon rows of plants of every shape and size—green bushes, brightly colored blossoms, and trees so tall they kiss the clouds. The sweet musky scent of old paper is swallowed up in the freshness of the suddenly crisp open air. I tilt my head back and stare up at the dimly lit sky, at the first pinpricks of light dotting the horizon. My feet rest in the dark earthy soil, still warm from the sun's earlier rays.

My library has transformed into a garden.

"This is how I organize the threads. This is how I make sense of the sea of memories," Lillian says, her voice unmistakably fond. "This was my father's garden."

"It's beautiful." My simple statement doesn't even come close to doing the lush garden justice, but it needed to be said regardless. This is the kind of place that would be hard to leave. It's the kind of memory that would be easy to get lost in.

Lillian's posture relaxes as she wanders down the rows, and I follow behind her, careful not to touch anything. After a moment, she reaches down and plucks something off a plant covered in tiny dark blue flowers. It's a thread the color of midnight, and it shimmers like the stars.

"If you want to see my memory, hold onto this thread and empty your mind. If your memories interfere with mine, you could get caught in between. And Oliver," she says, pausing until I meet her eyes. "Promise me you will not deviate from the memory. We are observers, nothing more."

"Okay, I promise." I hold out my hand, but just before my fingers brush against the strand, I hesitate. And in that moment of hesitation, all I can see is Gemma lunging for the red thread, her eyes wide and shining.

This isn't the same thing, I tell myself.

"Maybe. But it's still a little bit reckless," I imagine Gemma's voice whispering back.

And maybe it is. Searching through someone else's memories with the very real chance that I might get stuck there for good is definitely a risk. But I don't see what other choice I have. Maybe this is how I find my way home.

I take a deep breath and grab onto the thread Lillian's offering me, her expression wary as if she too is unsure how this will go.

In a blink, the garden vanishes. I try to keep my mind empty, but it's like the harder I try, the more my mind wants to wander. I can feel the threads of my memories, reaching out to me, snapping against my skin, begging me to take hold. I grit my teeth against the feeling and focus on the single thread in my hand.

"Just breathe," Lillian commands softly, "and empty your mind."

My body stills as the memory blossoms in front of me, solidifying with every second of my unwavering focus.

A midnight sky full of stars. A cold winter's night.

A Claiming about to begin.

CHAPTER TWENTY-FIVE

OLLIE

IT'S A CLEAR night, not a cloud in the sky. Shadows in the shape of great tall trees line the narrow path that winds below our feet, everything dusted with a light covering of snow. My breath comes out in little white puffs; the air feels too thin in my lungs. I wrap my arms around myself, shivering against the sudden chill, and wonder if I can ask Lillian for an imaginary jacket or something because it's seriously freezing.

"Hey, Lillian, could you—" I jerk back, the rest of my question cutting off as she turns to face me. This isn't the same woman I was standing next to only seconds ago. This version of her is younger, probably the same age as me. Her black dress and long cloak blend into the gloom, but her bright eyes shine through the darkness. She's just a girl. This is who Lillian was before all the heaviness piled up on her.

She holds up one of her hands and stares at the smooth, unblemished skin under the muted light. "I have not been inside this memory for a very long time," she says quietly.

Lillian may look younger, but something about the tone of her voice sounds the same—weary and rough and full of the kind of sadness that comes from being alone for too long.

After she speaks, the trees begin to sway, and the ground starts to shift as if it's about to fall out from under us. She purses her lips and crooks a finger, beckoning me forward. "Follow me, and try to speak as little as possible. We cannot deviate from the memory, or it will collapse around us."

I shiver, and my bare feet sink deeper into the snow. "And if that happens…"

"We will be thrown back into the sea to begin again." The stars whirl overhead as if to emphasize her point, shooting across the sky in dazzling streaks like tiny little exclamation marks.

Lillian takes a deep breath and closes her eyes, holding still as she Remembers. The cold air bites at my cheeks as the memory settles back into place. I fidget restlessly as I wait. I don't like how it feels to completely give up control, to let Lillian occupy the driver's seat. Inside her memories, I have no say, no ownership, and that loss leaves me feeling even more unsteady than I anticipated.

A moment later, Lillian's eyes fly open, and without another word, she turns and heads down the path, her footsteps muffled on the freshly fallen snow. I hurry to catch up, not wanting to be left behind in an unfamiliar forest inside of a memory that doesn't belong to me. We slip silently through the trees with Lillian walking confidently through the maze with ease. It's obvious she knows these woods. I, on the other hand, nearly trip over every other root I come across. It's impossible to see under the thick covering of trees blocking out the minimal light from the sprinkling of stars.

"Hey," I hiss, tugging on Lillian's sleeve. I know she all but told me to zip it when she reminded me that we needed to speak as little as possible, but I can't help it. I'm time-traveling through memories; I have a few questions. "Why do the Claimings always happen at night?" I ask, peering through the thick forest.

She doesn't look in my direction, but she whispers back, her mouth barely moving, "Because it is easier to believe in magic under the cover of darkness, is it not?"

She gestures to a clearing where the trees have thinned enough for me to see a fire blazing at its center with an enormous mountain range looming behind it, their snow-capped peaks a sharp silhouette against the night sky. They look vaguely familiar, like photographs I've seen of the Rocky Mountains, jagged and majestic.

Surrounding the fire is a small group of people in the loose shape of a circle, families huddled together against the cold, talking and laughing and warming themselves against the flames, all of them wrapped in thick, dark cloaks similar to Lillian's. The wiggly younger children slip in and out of the circle under the arms of their parents, chasing each other with sticks or holding hands and dancing around. A few of the women closest to the fire start to sing. The melody is unfamiliar, and I can't hear the lyrics of the song, but the haunting tone of their voices makes my chest ache and my eyes sting.

Even from where I'm standing on the periphery of the group, I can feel the excitement; the air is palpable with it. As I watch the scene unfolding under the light of a pale crescent moon and more stars than I can count, I have to admit that Lillian is right. On a night like this, it's easy to believe in magic. Because even though I've never been in these woods or met these people before, something about it still feels like home.

I follow Lillian to the edge of the circle, the crowd rippling with anticipation when they see her. As the group sways, I accidentally bump into a stocky man with a sleeping baby resting against his shoulder, and I find myself whispering a hasty *"sorry"* before I remember that nobody can see me. This isn't my memory—I'm just here to watch.

Lillian comes to a stop next to a middle-aged man and woman. She clutches hands with the woman who turns and smiles fondly at her, a smile made of recognition and love. The man puts his arm around Lillian and gives her a squeeze. She leans into him with a sigh, a great big exhale that sounds like the very definition of relief. On the man's other side is a blonde girl, just a little older than Lillian. She leans over and whispers something into Lillian's ear, and the two of them break out in giggles.

Cora and Lillian. Two sisters with their mother and father.

A family, whole and complete.

I step closer, peering up at their dad, the one whose death sent his two grieving daughters into the Dreamscape to search for a way to change his fate, to undo a terrible wrong. He has light hair like Cora, but his eyes are dark like Lillian's. He looks like an ordinary man; there's nothing unusual about him.

"Must it be so cold tonight?" Cora says through chattering teeth.

"It was much colder on the night of *my* Claiming," their mother says with a grin.

"Freezing to death is not a requirement for the ceremony, my love," their dad says with a wink. He chuckles and leans closer to the fire, his hands glowing with a soft green light as he captures a small flame. He uses his broad shoulders to pull his daughters in, tucking them against his chest and holding them close to the little flame cupped between his hands.

"Much better," Lillian sighs, the light from the fire dancing across her face.

He's an ordinary man, but aren't all fathers? That doesn't make them any less extraordinary to the ones who love them.

I think about my own dad back at home, and my throat tightens uncomfortably. I think about what I would do if I lost him, and I wonder if maybe I already have. Would I bend time and fate to bring him back?

To bring me back?

Cora leans over to Lillian, speaking quietly near her ear and forcing me to hover awkwardly behind them in order to eavesdrop. "Are you scared?"

"A little," Lillian admits.

"You should be."

Lillian blanches, her chin quivering just slightly.

Cora laughs and elbows her sister in the ribs. "It was only a joke," she says with a wicked grin. "You will be just fine, Lilli."

Even while Lillian huffs in annoyance, a laugh still slips out of her mouth. Her hand tightens onto Cora's. "Do you really think so?"

"I know so." Cora looks at her younger sister with fierce affection. "Maybe you will be a Caster like me. Think of the fun we would have." She slings her arm over Lillian's shoulder as the two of them face the fire once more with their parents on either side of them.

I take a step back, feeling obtrusive for listening in on their quiet moment. Watching them together like this—the way Cora teases, the way the two girls laugh together—it's easy to forget what happens next.

A father lost.

A rule that was broken.

And a fate forever changed, just not in the way they'd planned.

I wonder how it feels for Lillian to step back into these memories, knowing what she knows now. Knowing that she doesn't just lose her father to death, but her sister to madness as well. Hindsight is everything; isn't that how the saying goes? I guess that's true, even when it comes to magic.

"Are you ready?" Lillian's father asks in a soft voice. "Is it time?"

Lillian takes a deep breath and nods before extricating herself from the arms of her family, her gaze flicking to meet mine briefly before marching into the center of the circle to stand next to the fire.

"I am ready to Claim what is mine," she says in a steady voice. But when her eyes slip to her sister's, there's a slight timidness to them, a vulnerability she refuses to show anyone else.

Cora gives her a reassuring smile, and Lillian visibly relaxes.

In a sudden burst, the flames rise higher. The children closest to the fire squeal with delight before running back to their parents to hide behind their legs. In one fluid movement, the circle widens and everyone stills, the air growing thick with anticipation. There's a gust of wind and the sound of trees rustling. The cold air whips through my hair as I turn toward the sound. Three figures emerge from the dark wood, slipping into the circle quietly to stand near the fire. I blink in amazement and stare at the woman and the two men who seemed to appear out of thin air.

Long silver threads that shimmer like stars trail off each of them, but after I blink, the threads have vanished.

The circle erupts with excited whispering.

These must be the Threaders.

The older man appears to be around the same age as the woman. Both are gray-haired and self-assured in their steps. She is tall, and he is not. The other man with them is not so much a man as he is a boy. After one look at the dark hair flipping over his forehead and the impish grin he gives to Cora, I know exactly who he is.

"Atticus," I breathe. The Elders and the Threader in training.

The short man tucks his long dark cloak around himself more tightly and shudders. "What a beautiful night for a Claiming," he says, turning to Lillian, his voice low and gravelly. He shudders violently again. "Forgive me. I am not used to the cold."

Cora and her mother laugh into their cloaks, the black fabric muffling the sound.

The woman steps forward and brushes her long hair out of her face before taking Lillian's hand in her own. She raises their clasped hands and turns to the group. "Who here will offer some of their magic so that Lillian may Claim hers?"

"I will," her father says at once. He extends his hands, and they begin to glow.

"So will I," her mother adds, intertwining her free hand with her husband's.

"And I will too," Cora exclaims.

One by one, each of the Claimed calls out their support for Lillian, joining hands and adding their magic to the circle until the entire clearing is lit with a soft ethereal glow. A low hum pulses through the ground as the air is filled with an electric charge, smelling of lightning and the sharp clean scent of snow. I hold my breath and lean forward, forgetting the cold as I wait for what happens next.

But once the circle is complete, it's not as if something unbelievable happens. There isn't some grand display of magic or a loud impressive *bang*. No, the remarkable thing is more of a feeling, subtle but deep-rooted and far-reaching. It's that same feeling I got when I held onto the threads of the weaving. It's a sense of community and history. It's family and time and love and loss and the pure wonder that a group of people could gather together and say that they don't just believe in magic, they believe in her.

In Lillian.

It's something that was completely missing when I had my own Claiming. On the night I got my magic, I'd never felt more alone. But tonight, in this memory, that overwhelming feeling of isolation feels so far away.

The two Threaders step forward and reach out their hands, the female Threader pausing and quickly gesturing for Atticus to join them. He winks at Cora, whose blush is visible even in the dim lighting, before sauntering over to follow behind the Elders. The three of them slowly walk around the perimeter of the circle, their dark cloaks billowing behind them as they pause at each glowing hand. At first, I think they're just clasping hands in greeting, but then I realize it's more than that—the Threaders are taking the magic that was willingly offered.

Delicately, they unspool the magic from the upturned hands of the Claimed, pulling out long threads of purple, green, and gold, weaving the strands together into a beautiful and intricate braid. My mouth falls open as I watch, and when I hear the excited whispering of the younger kids in the group peering into the center of the circle, I know I'm not the only one who's impressed.

The two older Threaders are confident in their movements, their fingers practiced as they weave. Atticus stumbles behind them, looking unsure with every thread he takes, his eyebrows raised like twin question marks, but the Elders are patient as they demonstrate how they move their hands. The three of them balance the weight of the magic between themselves as they reach the end of the circle. Lillian waits patiently in the center next to the fire, her awe-struck face lit by the flickering flames.

The two Threaders extend their hands, and after a pointed look at Atticus, he raises his too. Then they grasp onto the two tallest trees extending over the circle, a pair of white aspens growing at the edge of the grove. With a creaking groan, the two trees bow toward each other, sending a flurry of snow down to the ground as their branches intertwine to form a sort of arch, like a simple version of a doorway. The woman begins to weave the braided threads through the branches of one of the aspen trees, and the man follows suit with Atticus trailing behind them and mimicking their movements in between shooting glances at Cora.

The trees shudder under the force of the added magic, but rather than buckling from the weight, they seem to stand a little taller. Their white trunks stretch as the radiant threads wrap tightly around them, turning them into one solid unit rather than two separate trees. It's an imposing sight.

"Laws that govern," the woman whispers.

"Threads that bind," the man finishes.

"The knots that tether us to time," they say together.

I've seen the threads tied into knots—I've tied them myself countless times—but I've never seen a weaving like this. It's an ancient sort of magic, maybe older than the earth itself, and just looking at it forms a lump in my throat.

"Woven in starlight," the woman starts again.

"Written in the sky," the man says, adding his voice to hers.

"Our fates tied together in a single line."

The words ripple through the air like a stone thrown into still water. My skin prickles as the syllables slide over me, wrapping me in the fluid movement of their sound, rich and melodic, every word falling from their mouths so heavy with meaning. Under the command of the Language, the two aspens begin to shake, tipping the space between them into a pitch-black blur. The view of the snow-covered forest behind them vanishes, and in its place a swelling darkness remains, twisting and turning until it transforms into something new. Something star-covered and brilliant. Something familiar yet still completely unknowable.

"It's a portal," I whisper to myself. "A portal to the Dream-scape."

The Elders offer Lillian a nod and a smile before taking Atticus by the arm and pulling him through the portal first, his shoulders tensing as he disappears. A murmur of excitement runs through the crowd.

Suddenly, there's a dull ache in my head that pulses like the beating of a drum. It beats in time with the rhythm of my name.

Oliver, Oliver.

My feet move an inch. Then another. And another.

Lillian widens her stance and closes her eyes, holding out her hands with a deep exhale. She stands there looking tall and proud but a little shaken too, as if feeling all this magic has overwhelmed her. "I am ready to Claim what is mine," she repeats.

Oliver, Oliver, the beat calls to me again.

Without thinking, I follow the sound of the pulse, and before I know it, I'm standing next to Lillian in the center of the circle.

"Oliver," she hisses as I shove past her. "What are you—"

Thin silver threads unwind from the portal where the Thread-ers had disappeared. They snake their way through the gleaming snow until they reach Lillian's feet. She stiffens in fear but holds perfectly still as the threads engulf her in their iridescent gleam. Slowly, they wind around her ankles and up the rest of her body, sliding down her arms before coming to rest in her hands. There's a flash of light so blinding, a few members of the circle stumble back in alarm. Once my eyes adjust and the afterglow finally fades away, I see that Lillian's face is shining even brighter than the silver threads—she's beaming.

"A Threader," she whispers. "I am Claimed as the next Threader."

"Tied and bound, I seal your fate." The words of the Threaders echo up from the portal of the Dreamscape, through space and time and whatever other magic makes any of this possible.

For a moment, the circle is dead quiet. The only sounds are the swaying of the trees and the shuffling of boots against the snow.

Then the circle erupts with a tumultuous roar of rowdy cheers and thunderous applause as Lillian spins around in a slow circle. It's started to snow again, but now nobody seems to mind the cold.

Lillian's gaze immediately lands on Cora, whose mouth is hanging open in disbelief. Lillian offers her a hesitant smile and shrugs one shoulder, holding out her hands full of the silver threads to show her sister.

I don't miss the look of disappointment that crosses over Cora's face. She tries to smile back at Lillian, but it seems forced. Their father frowns and places a hand on her shoulder, gently pulling her away from the rest of the group, their heads dipping low in conversation.

Lillian watches all of this take place without a word, but her hands, still full of starlight and magic, droop down at her sides.

Oliver, Oliver.

Again, I feel that strange pounding in my head. It reverberates through my skull, setting my teeth on edge. I trip over my feet in my hurry to follow the sound. A flash of color near the entrance to the portal catches my eye. It's another thread, this one blacker than the night. Slowly, so slowly, it unwinds from the expanse of the Dreamscape.

Oliver, Oliver.

"Oliver, stop—" Lillian groans in frustration and points to the surrounding forest that has begun to shake. The snow flurries in violent gusts as her grasp on her memory starts to slacken. The circle of faces stays frozen in time, totally immune to the swirl of snow or the tremor of the earth beneath their feet. "You promised me you would not deviate!" she calls out, her face growing pale at the sight of the black thread. "Wait!"

"I'm sorry, I just... There's something I need to see." My voice is barely audible above the howl of the wind as the memory continues to crash down around us. I'm halfway to the portal with no idea what I'm doing, but I can't shake this sudden compulsion. I can't ignore that glaring part of me that just *knows* I need to do this.

My hand reaches out to touch it, and Gemma's words to me all those nights ago enter my mind in a whisper soft and sweet: *magic calls to magic, there's no other way to explain it.*

"Oliver, do not—" Lillian's warning comes a moment too late, just as my fingers wrap around the thin black thread, so dark against the whiteness of the snow.

The thread tugs me forward, and everything slips into a blur of sound and color. Voices blend together until I can't distinguish a word; pictures fly past at a speed that's impossible to focus on. I'm drowning in memories again, and this time, I'm too overwhelmed to even properly panic.

With another painful tug, the black thread tries to hurl me into a new memory, but I can't fall completely into this new scene—whatever it is—because something is holding me back. It yanks on my other hand until I feel like I'm tearing in half from the pressure of being pulled in two different directions.

In the chaos, the black thread wraps around my arm, and when it does, I hear a quiet voice, a girl's voice, her cadence unfamiliar and strange.

We heard the tales when we were young. Of a power that made the sun rise and fall, that made a tree blossom after a harsh winter, or a baby cry as it took its first breath.

A power that meant new life.

But the stories never mentioned that if there is a power that brings life, there must also be one that brings death.

We heard the tales when we were young, sitting around the fire and nestled onto our parents' laps. These were the stories of my childhood.

I used to close my eyes and imagine holding such life in my hands. When I was very young, I would ask my mother where the power came from. Her answer was always the same. "From the earth itself, little one. From its very heart."

I gasp for breath as a hand jerks me back, the girl's voice fading away once the black thread slips from my grip. I stumble into Lillian at the same moment she shoves her midnight blue thread back into my hand. "Do not let go this time," she urges, her voice sharper than glass. "Stay inside my memory."

I don't have the ability to argue even though I want to. I can barely breathe as it is. Jumping between memories felt like stepping into a space that was far too small, too uncomfortably tight and suffocating. My hands rove over my clothes and body, absently checking to make sure I'm still in one piece.

As the darkness squeezes around me, I long for the peaceful halls of my imaginary library, for its order and its books and its floors that don't fall out from under me. But I couldn't form a clear visual of that place right now even if my life depended on it, which, at the moment, I guess it sort of does.

After another staggered breath, Lillian's thread tugs me forward, and suddenly I'm flat on my back on the familiar floor of the Dreamscape, the stars shining brightly overhead. I breathe in the warm air of the cavern, flexing my stiff fingers as they finally defrost from the cold.

Lillian watches me get to my feet, her mouth pinched into a tight line as she glares at me in disapproval. She doesn't even have to say the words; it's obvious from the look on her face that she's screaming at me inside her head: *do not deviate.* She closes her eyes and rolls her neck, turning away from me to focus on her memory of the two Elders and Atticus tying her Claiming.

I feel a slippery sense of déjà vu being back inside the Dreamscape. It's so strange to watch the man holding onto the ends of the silver threads that belong to Lillian. To watch as he finishes tying the knot and eases it back into the weaving. To see the woman placing her hands on the glistening walls, mumbling words of magic and bracing herself against the pulsing of the cavern.

The two Threaders work seamlessly together in a beautiful dance—the push and pull of magic. There's an energy about their work, a sense of joy and wholeness. There's no confusion or fear, no crippling disappointment.

I watch them, and I can't help but think that this is how it should've been for me and Gemma. This is how it could've been if our history hadn't been lost. But as I stand next to Lillian and Atticus and marvel at the wonder unfolding around me, another thought crosses my mind, something that Lillian said to me in the library before we entered the memory of her Claiming.

"But there is so much more to the story. Just like your books. It's as if you are reading a story with most of the pages torn out. You only have the ending. I had the middle. What we need is the beginning."

I lean over to Lillian and tug on her arm. She ignores me, keeping her focus fixed on the Threaders. "Lillian," I whisper as quietly as I can. "Did you hear that girl's voice when I touched that black thread? *'We heard the tales when we were young...'*" I repeat, imitating the gentle lilt of her speech. "Did you hear that memory? What was that?"

Again, Lillian ignores me.

"Come on," I hiss between my teeth. "Let's go back to the library or your garden, or whatever. Let's get out of here, I need to talk to you."

This time when I tug on her sleeve, she hardly moves at all. Her dark eyes have glazed over, the shimmer of the stars reflecting in them. Her shoulders are relaxed, and her feet are firmly planted as if she's settled inside this memory. As if she's finally realized that she's home.

"Lillian?" I ask again.

It's like I'm not even here.

"Lillian," I say, my voice catching in my throat.

No response. Zero recognition.
Time is an easy place to lose yourself.

CHAPTER TWENTY-SIX

GEMMA

T HE DINER IS as greasy as I'd imagined it would be.

Without discussing it, the three of us pick a booth at the back of the restaurant even though we're obviously the only customers. I wince when my jeans stick to the vinyl seat.

"Scoot over," Milo mumbles, nudging me on the shoulder.

"What do you think I'm trying to do?" I mutter back. The plastic squeals as I peel myself off the seat and inch over to the far side of the booth.

Zoe easily slides onto her bench on the other side, carefully setting her leather satchel down on her lap.

Milo stares at it apprehensively, drumming his still-glowing fingers on the surface of the checkered table in agitation. "Well?" he says. "Are you going to give me the antidote or what?"

Zoe eyes him back just as skeptically. "And if I give it to you, are you going to run out of here without listening to what I have to say?" Her hand reflexively tightens on the strap of her bag.

Milo snorts and opens his mouth to respond, but I interrupt him before he can say anything to make the situation worse. "Look, we're here, okay? We're not going anywhere. You don't need to spell Milo to make us stay."

Just then, a tired-looking waitress around my mom's age wanders over to our table with a coffee pot in hand, the plastic tag pinned to her shirt announcing that her name is Lisa. "What can I get you three to drink?" she asks in a bored voice, using her free hand to wipe a smear of ketchup off the corner of our booth with a rag. Milo tucks the bright light of his hands out of sight under the table.

"Just water, please," I answer back, my gaze still fixated on Zoe's bag.

"Same," she says.

"And I'll have a strawberry milkshake, Lisa, please, and thank you." Milo grins at her, and she straightens her posture, reaching up to adjust the messy bun tilting on her head.

"Sure thing." Lisa smiles back shyly and tucks the dirty rag into the pocket of her apron. She pours three cups of coffee even though none of us asked for any. The woman is clearly flustered.

Once Lisa and her coffee pot make it back to the kitchen, I turn to Milo and smack him on the shoulder. "*Why* must you flirt with every waitress you come in contact with? She could be your mom; it's embarrassing. And a milkshake? At 6 a.m.?"

He points to the brightly colored sign hanging over the long counter across from us, advertising that the diner is "world famous" for its shakes. "Can't miss an opportunity like that," he says with a shrug and another flash of his smile. "And please, that wasn't flirting. I was being polite."

Zoe makes a noise that sounds suspiciously like a snort of disbelief.

Milo raises one eyebrow. "Trust me. You'd know if I was flirting."

"Now please just give him the antidote," I say, breaking up their staring contest before it can turn into anything else.

Zoe sighs and digs through her bag, pulling out one of the thin vials swirling with purple liquid. She tosses it to Milo. "Bottoms up."

He squints at it under the glare of the cheap lighting. "How do I know this is the right one? You didn't even look at it, and you've got a lot of bottles in that bag of yours."

She blinks at him. "Trust me. You'd know if I was trying to poison you."

"Fair enough." Milo uncaps the mixing and swallows the contents in one gulp, then shivers and tips his head back against the booth, closing his eyes.

"Are you okay?" I ask, grabbing the bottle as it slips from his hand.

He shivers again. "Gross. Super bad aftertaste."

I set the empty vial on the table and swat him on the shoulder, rolling my eyes.

He sits up and watches the amber light slowly fade from his hands before extinguishing completely. "There. Much better," he says, exhaling in relief. "So what exactly was that mixing you gave me? And when did you do it?" He spins the Jeep keys around his fingers, trying to appear nonchalant, but I know it must be killing him that he was duped by a pretty girl.

"Your lemonade at the Claiming," Zoe says tersely. "After Gemma dumped her drink on your shirt to put out that fire you started, all I could do was pour the mixing in your cup and hope for the best."

Milo glares at her.

"It was simple enough. You were distracted." She flicks her ponytail and bats her eyelashes, a perfect imitation of herself at the dinner last night.

His cheeks redden, and he suddenly becomes very interested in the surface of the table. I sink deeper into my seat, chewing on my lip to hold back any potential laughter that might try to sneak out. I can't decide whether to feel annoyed on behalf of my brother or delighted by his embarrassment—it's a rare occurrence. A blink-and-you-might-miss-it kind of moment.

Just then, Lisa rounds the corner with our drinks in hand. She gently sets them on the table, sliding Milo's giant milkshake over to him.

"Perfect timing, Lisa. Thank you," he says, tapping his straw on the table and peeling the wrapper off, his face still as red as the cherry sitting on the mountain of whipped cream piled on the top of his shake

Lisa gives him another warm smile before nudging mine and

Zoe's water across the table without looking at us. "Let me know when you're ready to order."

The moment she walks away, Zoe leans across the table to continue. "It was a combination of a few mixings, actually. One for tracking, another for influence."

"Influence?" Milo repeats, his voice rising.

I elbow him sharply, looking over my shoulder to make sure Lisa isn't hovering near our table.

He ignores me and scowls at Zoe. "You weren't *influencing* me. You were controlling me. I had no choice but to drive here, exactly as you commanded. It was like I could hear another voice inside my head, sending my thoughts in a different direction." He shudders and looks down at his hands. "I didn't like it."

Zoe shrugs as if the difference is unimportant. "I did what needed to be done. I couldn't lose you." She leans back in her seat, an inescapable tiredness lining her face. "When I went to Sylvia's Claiming, I had no idea what I was walking into. But there you were, sitting right in front of me." She shifts her attention to me, her expression turning curious.

I try not to fidget under her examination. "What does that mean? You were trying to track us down?"

"Well, not exactly. But Charlotte gave me these and told me to keep an eye out." She reaches back into her bag and carefully pulls out something worn and yellowed.

But before she can hand the papers over, Milo motions around the diner exasperatedly. "Did you ever think about, I don't know, pulling us to the side to have a conversation before going through all this?"

"There really wasn't any time, now, was there?" Zoe replies, crossing her arms and lifting her chin. "Once I recognized Gemma and heard you mention Oliver's name, the Claiming completely collapsed, and I had to get out of there to call Charlotte. I didn't know what your next move would be, so I figured I'd follow you and find out."

Milo slurps his shake, his brow still furrowed. "Not sure how you overheard us saying any of that—"

"You two are really not as quiet as you think you are." Zoe's mouth twitches.

My heart thumps erratically, making it nearly impossible to sit still. "So, start explaining how you know Charlotte." I hold out my hand to accept the papers still held in her grasp, but she hesitates.

"First, I just need to know for certain: Oliver—is he really gone?" She arches one blonde eyebrow at me.

"Yes." I quickly spit the answer out as his absence presses down on my lungs. "He's trapped in the Dreamscape." I take a deep breath, preparing myself to explain what on earth the Dreamscape is, but Zoe's already nodding.

"That's what Charlotte thought," she says, her mouth tipping into a frown. "But I think she was still hoping that maybe she was wrong." She finally slides the tattered pieces of paper across the table to us. Strange sketches and scattered words flash before me, familiar somehow.

I grab the papers and stare at them in silence. The first thing I'm greeted with is a picture of my eyes. The sketch is rough and slightly smeared, like it's been held too many times, but they're my eyes all the same. I lay the pages out on the table, and Milo leans over to examine them with me.

"This is so creepy," he mutters. "It's *you*." He points to the illustration of my black hair, fanned out around my face like I've been captured mid-turn.

"And Ollie," I murmur back. "See?" I trace the outline of Ollie's profile caught in the shadows. The shape of his hands. The back of his neck, each picture fractured and incomplete. Pieces of us, but never the whole. Everything about it feels wrong and strangely intimate. I feel too seen, like I'm standing in front of everyone completely exposed, but in a dark room. Like I'm seen but not understood.

"James had pictures like these." I slide the papers back to Zoe, my stare accusatory. I'm such an idiot. And I think I'm going to be sick. "Remember? In his notebook? He showed them to us at the bonfire," I say, turning to Milo. "This was a mistake. He could be using her to track us." I glance out the window, half expecting to see a swarm of cars surrounding the diner. A trap set and bated by Zoe.

"No, you don't understand," she insists, but I'm not listening because it's getting harder to breathe.

The room starts to sway as I lean around Milo, ready to lunge out of the booth, but once again my jeans are practically glued to the sticky, grime-covered vinyl.

Milo grabs me by my shoulders and turns me to look at him. "You're safe, Gemma. We're safe. We're okay. Breathe."

I blink blankly at him a few times before the meaning of his words sinks in. Finally, I nod and close my eyes. Inhale through the nose, exhale through the mouth. Repeat.

I can do that.

After a minute or so, I open my eyes and smile weakly at Milo. "Thanks." He squeezes my arm and shrugs like it's not a big deal even though it's the biggest deal there is.

Zoe clears her throat and reaches for her bag. "I have something that helps with panic attacks if you want to try it." Her bag plinks noisily as she sets it on the table.

"I'm *fine*," I say, still struggling for breath as I shove Milo out of the booth. "Let's go."

He yanks on my arm, effectively unsticking me from my seat. "Yep. We're out of here."

"Wait." Zoe fiddles with her bag, but when she tries to open it, nothing happens. She tugs on the zipper again with a frustrated noise. "What did you do?" she spits at Milo, holding up her bag, which seems to be sealed shut.

He smirks and calls over his shoulder, "Good luck unwinding that casting. I made it extra complicated for you to remember me by. I doubt you'll ever see the contents of that bag again."

We turn the corner, nearly running into a frazzled Lisa, who's standing in front of the chrome doors blocking our exit. "Excuse me, but you didn't pay." Her bottom lip juts out. She glowers at Milo as if he's personally offended her.

He glances back at Zoe as he fumbles for his wallet. "Sorry about that, Lisa," he says, offering her a smile, but this time she's not buying it.

He slaps a five-dollar bill in her outstretched hand and Lisa pockets the money, stepping out of the way with a muttered, "Kids these days."

Zoe slings her bag over her shoulder and calls out, "1877 East Edgewood Lane, Bakersfield." Milo and I both stiffen as she recites Charlotte's address from memory. "That's where you're going, right? That's where I'm headed too. Please, just listen. She's desperate to find him."

She's desperate to find him.

Her words hit me harder than any slap ever could.

"You've got it all wrong. I got these drawings from Charlotte, not James." She holds up the carefully folded papers still clutched in her hand. "That's how I recognized you, Gemma. She told me to show them to you. Please." She sounds out of breath even though she hasn't started running after us yet. "Five minutes, that's all I'm asking for. Five minutes, and if you don't believe me, then you can leave, and I swear I won't follow you."

Milo waits for me to answer. My entire body is too tense and ready to bolt, but I take a deep breath and force myself to walk back to where Zoe's still waiting by our booth. I hold out my hand for the pages and she hands them to me without hesitating.

I open them and stare at the rough sketching of Ollie's eyes and wish for the millionth time he was here. What would he say to Zoe? What would he do? Would he trust her?

The words on the pages are cramped and hurried, and when I squint at them, I realize I can't make out what they say. "Are these written in the Language?" I ask Milo who's staring at the paper over my shoulder.

He looks up to see if Lisa is eavesdropping, but apparently, after Milo tried to dine and dash, she washed her hands of us. The diner is vacant and quiet except for the tinny sound of the radio playing an oldies station. Milo peers down at the page. "Yeah, but don't ask me what it says…" He scratches his head. "It's more of a feeling than actual words. This is going to take me a long time to sort through. Whoever wrote that doesn't understand the Language. It's like if I tried to write something in Latin right now when I have no clue how to do it. It's the Language, but it's not translated correctly."

I trace the letters, feeling the memory of their bitter weight on my tongue.

"Charlotte took those pages from the journal before she left home," Zoe says, sliding back into her seat. "Before she left James and her father. Back when she—"

"Left Ollie," I finish for her, sitting back down in the booth with Milo following behind me. "Why did she leave? Where was she going?"

"That's not my story to tell," she says with a small shrug, like that's the most obvious thing in the world.

"Seriously? You're not going to tell us?" I fire back, gripping the pages tightly in my hands. "I thought you were trying to convince us to trust you."

"Memories are a form of magic," she says in that curt way of hers. "And Charlotte's memories are not mine to share."

Grandma would like her. Grandma would trust her.

The thought marches into my brain, totally surprising and completely unwelcome. I grimace and push it away. "Well, how did you find Charlotte?"

She clears her throat and looks down. "I'll try my best to explain. I'm not used to sharing with people. I've been on my own for a while, and it's hard for me… it's hard for me to trust." She straightens her already impeccable ponytail and sighs. "I'm from a town not far from here," she says, pointing out the dirty window that looks into the still-empty parking lot. "It wasn't much, but it was home. It was just me and my parents. My dad was an Elemental, and he had a small ranch that he took care of. He was really good with animals. Mom was convinced he could actually talk to them." She smiles sadly, her mouth only lifting slightly before falling back down. "He was always happiest when he was outside."

Was. As in past tense. How can such a small word be so heavy with meaning? I brace myself for the inevitable tragedy that always follows a word like "was." My hands grip the sticky plastic of the booth seat as my mind flashes back to my grandma.

Was. I'm really starting to hate that word.

"My mom's a Mixer," Zoe continues, "and she used to let me watch her when she was mixing..." When she trails off, her expression shifts, making her appear younger, more vulnerable. She couldn't be more than a year or two older than us, but she has an edge to her that makes her seem even older, like maybe she's endured more. "One day, I got into her bottles when she wasn't home. I started shaking them up, pouring them into each other. It was a mess. My dad's the one who came in and found me."

I can picture it. A small but tidy kitchen, comfortable and homey. I can see a younger Zoe, her blonde hair swishing in her ponytail, her eyes bright with curiosity, the bottles strewn all around her.

Zoe shakes her head and clears her throat. "My dad found me. He tried to move the mixings out of my hands, but he..." In her pause, the story changes. It's the kind of pause that alters a life, the kind that swallows a childhood whole. She doesn't look at us; instead, she stares at the salt and pepper shakers shaped like race cars sitting in the middle of the table. "There was an accident."

She says it so matter-of-factly that I wonder if I misunderstood. She's detached from the story, so removed from it that it doesn't seem real. I can't imagine sharing the details of my grandma's death so succinctly, so clinically.

I can't decide if I would even want to.

Milo sets his milkshake down and waits for Zoe to meet his gaze. "I'm sorry," is all he says. But that's the only thing left to say. Nothing else makes up for the awful, groaning ache of losing someone.

Zoe straightens in her seat, her expression impossible to read. "Anyway, Mom was never the same afterward. She said she didn't blame me, but, you know." A shadow crosses her face, the first flicker of real emotion. "Things were different after that. We lost the ranch. We had to move into this tiny apartment that both of us hated. Mom stopped mixing. She hardly ever got out of bed, so eventually, I had to drop out of school to work two jobs."

I look at Zoe, so meticulously poised in her spotless white t-shirt and black jeans. It's hard to imagine her working at a fast-food restaurant or cleaning bathrooms somewhere.

"Things were... difficult. And it only got worse after I was Claimed."

No one states the obvious; how hard it must've been for Zoe to be Claimed as a Mixer when that was exactly how she'd lost her father. Milo's hand twitches toward Zoe's where it rests on the table, almost as if he's about to reach out and grab it. Like he wants to give her something to hold onto.

But she slides her hands off the table and rests them in her lap. "A few months after I was Claimed, my mom disappeared for a few days." Her voice hardens unexpectedly. "She was just *gone* for days, and when she came home, she didn't apologize for up and leaving without so much as a note. No. When she came home, she was changed. She was excited. Alive. She told me she'd met some-one." Her eyes sharpen to match the hardness of her tone. "She told me she'd met someone who had all the answers. For weeks, she spouted on and on about this place that held all of magic, a place where time itself was wrapped up in a knot, just waiting to be unraveled."

My breath catches as my heart threatens to burst through my ribcage.

"A place where fate could be changed," Zoe says, looking at me.

My back stiffens against the plastic seat of the booth. Milo must've noticed because he nudges me with his shoulder just slightly as if to remind me that he's still there.

James. Her mother had met James. And she'd fallen into his web spun of half-truths and madness.

"That's when Charlotte found me," Zoe says, fiddling with the strap of her bag. "My mom was living with James and his friends, or, should I say, his *cult,* at his house. I stayed at our apartment because I wanted nothing to do with those people. And then his father died."

"Hayden," I whisper. The sound of his name sends a shiver down my spine. I can hear James on the night of the bonfire, his face lit only by the glowing embers. *"Hayden Lowell, direct descendent of Cora."*

The father of Charlotte and James, and the last holder of the broken piece of red thread passed down through Cora's line. The man who had fueled his son with anger and hate. The man who had torn his family apart in the search for something he thought was better.

"My father was born without magic," James had said. *"But he had the piece of the red thread his grandmother had passed on to him. And this record."* He'd held up the worn-out notebook filled with scribbles and sketches, its cover too faded to reveal its true color. *"The record of our family and the truth of the Dreamscape. My father made me read this every single day of my life. I swore to him when he died that I would see this through. That no one would have to live without magic ever again."*

"My mom made me go to his funeral," Zoe says with a grimace, "even though I barely knew the man. In the handful of times I'd been over to their house, he'd been locked up in his room. James said his father was sick and unable to care for himself, but I think the truth was that he'd gone mad. And James blamed his sister, Charlotte, for everything that happened. He talked about it constantly—how she'd betrayed him and their family." She shakes her head. "The things that man would say.

"To keep the peace with my mom, I went to the funeral, but

I stayed on the edge of the crowd so I wouldn't have to talk to anyone. There was a woman standing in the back near me. Everyone ignored her. She had this weird misty look about her, like she wasn't all the way there."

"A cloaking spell," Milo says. "She must've been hiding behind a casting."

Zoe nods. "Charlotte approached me and told me who she was. She said she'd been keeping track of her brother, and she knew about my mom and our situation. She asked if I wanted to help my mom get out of this mess. To free her." Zoe tugs on the end of her ponytail and looks down. "Obviously I said yes, but the truth is that I don't just want to help my mom. I want to ruin James like he ruined her."

She flicks her hair over her shoulder as if to signal that her story has come to a close. Something tells me there's more she's not telling us, more layers of hurt and sadness. But isn't that true of everyone and every story?

I don't even have to use our twin telepathy to ask my brother what he thinks. All I have to do is take one look at his hand still stretched out and waiting on the tabletop to know that he believes her and wants to help.

"Okay," I say to Zoe.

"Okay?" she says back, her light eyebrows raised high.

I peel myself off the booth seat for what I hope is the last time. "Let's go see Charlotte."

Zoe releases a heavy breath and rises from the table, her bag in hand.

"But we didn't even eat," Milo grumbles, tipping the end of his shake into his mouth. But after another dirty look from Lisa at the kitchen window, he says, "Or maybe we'd be safer finding a drive-thru far away from here."

Zoe ignores his comment, stepping in front of him and blocking his exit from the booth. "Now, seeing as I no longer need your casting to remember you by, could you please undo it?" She shakes her still-closed leather satchel in his face, the contents rattling inside.

"Only because you asked so nicely." Milo smirks and whispers a stream of words under his breath, his hands golden and glowing.

Zoe flinches when her bag twitches. Then she quickly checks the zipper, her shoulders sagging in relief when she doesn't meet any resistance. "Don't ever do that to me again," she says in a low voice, holding her bag of mixings tightly to her chest.

"Don't ever give me another reason to."

Zoe huffs and stalks away from the booth, not pausing to see if we're following behind her.

"What?" Milo says all too innocently when he catches the look on my face. "Why are you staring at me?"

I shake my head with my lips pinched together, saying nothing. He's way out of his league here, but I don't need to be the one to tell him that. He'll figure it out eventually.

Just before we exit the diner, Milo pulls on my elbow and quietly says, "I didn't want to say anything in front of Zoe, but…"

"But what?"

He holds out his empty hands. "Just now, when I undid my casting on her bag… my magic felt off. It felt weird and distant again; I almost couldn't find the right words." He closes his eyes, clenching his hands into fists. "Do you think I'm losing my magic, Gem?"

"Do you have to use ketchup so early in the morning? The smell is killing me."

Keeping one hand on the wheel, I roll down my window and breathe in the fresher scents of warm asphalt and morning air as I nudge the crinkly fast-food bags off the center console with my elbow. True to his word, Milo made us stop at a drive-thru before getting back on the freeway, and now I'm the one dealing with the greasy aftermath.

"Hey, watch the fries," he says through his mouthful. "And yes, ketchup is always a necessity. I don't care what time it is." He flips through the Caster Chronicles with one hand while shoving french fries into his mouth with the other. Every so often his head snaps up to look for the navy blue Volvo.

"Yes, Milo, I'm still following Zoe. You can relax."

"I don't know what you're talking about," he says as he crumples up the wrapper from his hamburger. "I'm just being attentive to the road."

"Sure sure. You know, Aunt Libby's going to kill you if you get so much as one greasy fingerprint on those books."

"Well, it's a good thing I know how to do magic then, isn't it?" His mouth snaps shut after his unthinking words tumble out, his brow wrinkling as he ducks his head over the page. *For now*, his hunched shoulders seem to say.

I want to reassure him, but I don't know how, so I turn back to the road and try to ignore the sharp stinging feeling I get whenever he mentions his magic. It used to feel like jealousy, only lately it's tiptoed into fear. This morning I don't know what to call it, I just know that I don't like it.

The desert outside the windows flies by in depressing shades of beige, far too fast for me to see any color or life in the scrawny bushes or the rolling hills covered in yellowing dead grass. This desert looks nothing like mine, and staring at it makes me feel about a million miles away from home.

"So, how's it going?" I ask hesitantly, nodding at the book in his lap. "Are you still able to read the Chronicles?"

"Yep," he replies, his eyes fixed on the page. "It's fine. I'm fine."

"Everything is fine," I finish for him. I can't quit thinking about the fear on his face when he told me that his magic was acting strange. As much as I wish I did, I don't have any answers for him. I only have more questions. But the memory of the shattered floor of the Dreamscape and the stars winking out one by one has my foot pressing harder on the gas, the speedometer inching higher.

Why does it always feel like we're running out of time?

Milo pulls out two old pieces of paper, holding them flat against the Chronicles. In a show of good faith, Zoe let him hold onto the journal pages Charlotte had given her. He runs his fingers over the worn-out paper, pausing to puzzle over each word he comes across as he compares them against the Chronicles. "Whoever wrote this seriously butchered it. They've got it all wrong," he says, thumbing through the book.

Zoe signals for the exit, and my pulse thrums loudly in my ears.

This is it. I flick on my turn signal and follow her to the off-ramp.

Milo scratches his head and holds the paper up to his nose as he tries to read. "It almost looks like... like they were trying to spell your name. Remember how James said it took a long time for him to find you and Ollie? Well, this is probably why. He only had a handful of clues to go off of," he says, pointing to the cramped drawings of my eyes, my hands, my hair. "And your name, which is basically spelled incorrectly. That's not much."

"So if it's not written down right, how do you know it's my name?"

"I know this is going to seem weird, but it *sounds* like you. I can just tell. After all, I know you better than anyone," he says, sticking his chin out. "Well, almost better than anyone." He gives me a shrug and a half-smile.

I return his smile and accept his offering for what it is: yet another piece of Ollie to hold onto and claim as mine.

"And when I look at these words written down here," he continues, "I can tell that they're trying—and failing—to describe you."

My stomach jolts, but I try to keep my expression even. "Hmm. And how did they describe me?"

He squints down at the words. "Stubborn, smart, and a little brash at times," he says with a smirk. "But good-hearted, too." He looks back at the page and exhales until all the humor is gone from his face. "And extremely powerful."

I'm frozen in my seat; the only thing that moves is my hair whipping around me from the wind through the open window. And like the flash of a film reel that's stuck on the same scene, I see the vision of myself holding all three branches of magic, my eyes glowing and red. "They... they forgot to mention how good-looking I am," I say, stumbling over the words to my bad joke.

Milo's only reaction is to raise his eyebrows. "Seriously, Gem. Most of this is about how powerful you are, what you're capable of." He pauses, looking unsure how to continue. "Do you think—"

"How does only a handful of words say all that?" I blurt out, cutting him off. I don't want him to ask me what it means. I don't want to hear about how powerful or capable I supposedly am. That's the last thing I want to be reminded of.

"It's hard to explain," Milo says as he carefully folds the page back up, sliding his finger down the well-worn crease. "But I can feel it. I just know that's what they were trying to say. They were trying to capture you." He holds up the other sheet of paper and a pair of blue eyes, bright and piercing stare back at me. "And Ollie," he says looking down at the two papers side by side. "The two of you together."

I sink back into my seat, bracing myself for an awkward silence to settle between us, to suck all the air out of the car until we're both suffocating from a lack of communication rather than oxygen.

But instead, Milo asks, "When did you know? That you loved him?"

The Jeep swerves in response to my surprise. I grip the steering wheel more tightly in my hands and steal a glance at my brother. He's relaxed with his legs stretched out, idly thumbing through the Chronicles as he waits for my answer.

"I didn't know until last summer," I say, tipping my head back against the seat with a sigh. "But I think I've always loved him. I just didn't know what that meant until suddenly I did."

I rub my forehead and try to think of a way to explain it. But how do you put something into words you barely understand yourself? Something so big and real and undeniable? "It's like breathing, you know? Like how you don't ever have to think about it, it just happens on its own. Your lungs fill, your heart beats, and every second of it means you're alive. But then sometimes you notice it. You feel your breath in your chest. You count your inhales and your exhales and suddenly it doesn't seem very ordinary anymore. Suddenly, it's *everything*."

I bite my lip, feeling self-conscious after giving such a transparently honest answer like that; it's the kind of thing that only Ollie would ever say out loud.

Milo closes the book and looks at me for what feels like a long time. "I get it." He reaches down to yet another one of his fast-food bags, the paper rustling as he digs around. "It was as easy as it was inevitable—even I knew that." He pops a french fry into his mouth.

"You did?"

"Of course I did. And I can only drag my feet for so long." He holds his hand out, offering me a fry and I shake my head. "Even I can't fight fate, you know?" He grins and takes a sip of his soda.

"I know what you mean," I say quietly. "I know better than anyone."

I stare out at the road, not really seeing what's in front of me, and for a brief moment, my vision blurs red.

Fate.

Inevitable.

We drive in silence for a few minutes, following Zoe as she zips through the outskirts of town, past a couple of grocery stores and the post office, an elementary school, and a beauty salon. All the ordinary things in an ordinary town. A place that appears to be totally devoid of magic.

But magic is always hiding in plain sight.

Zoe pulls into a small rundown neighborhood on the very edge of town. The houses are crammed together in a single line, everything from their dried-up lawns to their sagging roofs screaming neglect.

I'm mentally rehearsing how I'm going to introduce myself to Ollie's birth mom when the GPS announces that we've reached our destination. Milo and I both peer out the window at the small house. All the blinds are shut and there's no car in the driveway. What if we drove all this way and Charlotte's not even here?

But Zoe's already parked her car in front of the house and climbed out. She holds tightly to her bag as she walks to the front door and enters without knocking. She doesn't wait or even look back at us, almost as if she knew we'd need a minute.

"I'll text Mom and tell her that we made it safely," Milo says as he taps out a message on his phone. He slides it back into his pocket and looks at me. "Shall we?"

My hand hesitates on the door handle. Part of me wants to wait, to flip down the sun visor and check my appearance in the mirror, but what's the point? I already know what it will show me: a tired girl with questions in her eyes who smells like stale fast food. And even though I want to make a good first impression, I know that even if I'd had the luxury of a good night's sleep and a long hot shower, I'd still feel nervous.

Ollie barely spoke about his birth mother. In fact, after he'd found out he was adopted, he avoided the subject at all costs. But I could still see it on his face sometimes. All the things he was too afraid to ask, the fragile hope that he carried around with him.

I think more than anything he wanted to feel wanted.

I suck in a deep breath and shove open my door. We both climb out of the car, walking side by side up the short walkway, the concrete aged and cracked. When we reach the front door, we follow Zoe's lead and don't bother knocking.

Milo's hands glow in his pocket as he slowly takes in the narrow entryway with a calculated look. He whispers a handful of words under his breath, their cadence sounding like a series of questions, almost as if he's asking the house if it's safe to enter.

"There aren't any castings you need to worry about," a soft voice says from across the hall.

We turn the corner to see a blonde woman and a flash of blue eyes.

I'd know those eyes anywhere.

Charlotte—Oliver's mother.

CHAPTER TWENTY-SEVEN

GEMMA

"HELLO, GEMMA, MILO. Zoe's told me a lot about you. I'm glad you came."

Charlotte sits next to Zoe on the single couch in a sparsely furnished living room. She gives Milo and me a once-over before flicking her gaze past our shoulders as if looking for someone else. "I'm Charlotte," she says, fidgeting in her seat, "but I guess you already knew that. You're friends of Oliver's?" She stumbles over his name like she isn't used to saying it out loud.

I chew on the inside of my cheek and suppress the urge to tell her that *friends* isn't nearly a big enough word for what Ollie and I are. Taking a few steps closer, I shove my hands into the pocket of my hoodie and pull out the wrinkled slip of paper with her address on it, placing it on the coffee table in front of her. "His best friends."

Again, she glances over my shoulder like she's still waiting for Ollie to amble into the room behind us. But after a moment, she looks down at the floor, unable to hide the last remains of her hope, vanishing like the final colors of a sunset—a sky tinged with fire before slowly fading to black. "He's gone, isn't he. He's stuck in the Dreamscape."

It's a statement, not a question.

"How did you know?" I ask.

"Because this is exactly what I've always been afraid of." She leans over and picks up the address with the ghost of a smile. "So Teresa did keep this. I was wondering," she says faintly before gesturing for us to sit in the only other seats available, a pair of hideously poofy pinstriped armchairs.

Milo looks at me out of the corner of his eyes, and I know he's thinking the same thing as me: Grandma would love these chairs; they're awful.

The house looks like it's barely lived in. There are no photographs in frames, no artwork hung on the stark white walls. Everything about it feels stiff and impersonal. The only unique thing about the room is the small bookcase off to the side packed full of worn leather volumes.

Unsurprisingly, Milo's the one to break the awkward silence. "Are those your Caster Chronicles?" he asks, pointing to the bookcase as he sinks into his armchair. "Wow, that's a major collection."

Charlotte nods, brightening. "It's taken me years to gather them, but yes. That's what I've been able to find from my bloodline so far." A stilted silence follows her response.

"Zoe." Milo acknowledges her with a curt nod.

"Milo," she says back in greeting, her face smooth.

More silence.

"I'm not home much," Charlotte says quickly, tucking a strand of her loosely curled hair behind her ear. "I travel a lot, so I haven't done much with the place."

"It's nice," I lie stupidly, just for something to say.

Charlotte raises one eyebrow, just like Ollie always does. I can't quit staring at her, searching for similarities, hungrily snatching up any missing pieces of him I can find.

Zoe clears her throat loudly. "So, should we get down to business, or do we want to continue discussing interior design?"

Charlotte deflates onto the couch, throwing her a rueful look. "I'm already failing at this, aren't I?"

Zoe snorts, and Milo bites his lip like he's trying to hold back a laugh himself.

Charlotte shakes her head and releases a breath. "Let me start over. Why don't you tell me about yourselves?"

Milo tugs the journal pages out of his pocket and holds them up between his fingers. "I think you know a bit more about us than we know about you, wouldn't you say?"

"Fair enough," she replies, rubbing her hands across her dark jeans. "I've spent the past seventeen years preparing for a day like this, but for you two, this must all be brand new."

"Not just for us," I say. "For Ollie, too."

Charlotte softens at the sound of his nickname. I expect her to start crying, but her eyes remain dry and unblinking.

"You cast a Shadow spell on Ollie and left him and his parents without any memory of you or magic." My voice rises as I remember all their hurt and confusion. "You were just *gone*."

"I didn't want to leave him, you know. The last thing I wanted to do was leave my son." Charlotte scans my face with those familiar blue eyes as if she's looking for answers that I don't know how to give. "But after what I saw, I didn't think I had any other choice."

I want to look away from her stare, but I don't. "What you saw? What does that mean?"

"I guess before I tell you that, I need to explain where I come from and why things turned out the way they did." She fiddles with her hands, nervously fussing with the hem of her shirt just like Ollie does when he's stressed.

Is everything she does going to remind me of him?

"I think it would be easier to show you," Charlotte says, rising to her feet.

Milo sits up straighter in his seat, which is an impressive feat considering that these overly plush chairs are trying to eat us alive. "Are you going to cast your memories?" He turns to me and says, "Like how Libby did when she showed us what was inside Ollie's parents—" He glances at Charlotte and scratches his chin. "I mean, his *other* parents... You know what I mean."

It's a weird situation, to say the least.

I remember Milo and Libby placing their hands on Ollie's forehead as she transferred the foggy, complicated, incomplete memories from Teresa's and Matthew's minds over to Ollie's. I remember his eyes widening in surprise, then closing in resignation when he saw the rain-soaked day that Charlotte gave him up.

"Okay," I say, shoving myself out of my chair. "Show us." I hold my hands out to her and wonder if she'll notice the way they're slightly shaking or the way my heart is pounding underneath my shirt. I stand there, trying to harness the kind of bravery that Ollie has, the quiet but insistent kind. The kind that I desperately want to belong to.

Milo stands behind me and places a hand on my shoulder. "Show us," he repeats to Charlotte. "Please," he adds as an after-thought.

"Please hold hands," Charlotte says, motioning for Zoe to join us, and the four of us form a tight circle.

Milo offers his hand a little too enthusiastically to Zoe, who raises her eyebrows. "What? It was Charlotte's idea, not mine," he mumbles with a shrug, trying to look nonchalant and utterly fail-ing.

Zoe sighs and takes his hand, with Charlotte on her opposite side. I grab onto my brother's other hand, hesitating for the slight-est second before taking Charlotte's.

"It's okay," she says softly. "I'm not going inside your mind. I'm just going to offer you a glimpse of what's inside mine." For the first time since we walked into the room, she sounds confident, her hands glowing a rich amber color as she wraps one around mine, squeezing slightly.

The depressingly sparse room begins to fade from view, the edges of my vision blurring into darkness. My heart climbs up my throat as a tingling burst of energy shocks my entire body with a jolt. I plant my feet firmly on the thin carpet, barely resisting the urge to yank my hands back and break the casting. Charlotte's magic crawls up my spine and into my mind, but it's different than when Milo used his magic to see the gray place. This time, instead of letting someone in, I have to be willing to let go, to venture out. To accept and allow memories that don't belong to me and let them take over what I'm thinking. It feels uncomfortably like spying on someone—intrusive and overly personal.

But with Charlotte's casting, she weaves in words that make it easier for me to let my guard down. She offers her memories willingly; nothing is being forced upon me. So as the first picture begins to brighten inside my mind, I take a steadying breath and let go, trusting that I'll be able to find my way out again.

She starts at the beginning.

Dusky light shines through the window of a small bedroom, highlighting two twin beds with matching quilts and a small basket of toys tipped over on the floor. A petite little girl with tight golden curls is playing with a strawberry blonde boy, the two of them sprawled on the carpet. He has a sprinkling of freckles across his small nose.

I flinch when I hear a door slamming down the hall, followed by a rush of shouting that filters in from under the closed door of the children's bedroom. The small girl and boy drop their toys and huddle together in the corner behind one of the beds.

"It's okay," Charlotte whispers to her brother James. "They'll stop soon, I promise."

She starts loudly humming a song, and after a moment James joins in, his round eyes fixed on his sister's, their knees bumping together as they shrink into the safety of the shadows. But even with the noise of their humming, I can still hear the shouting, each word tossed out like a poisoned dart of accusation.

A man and a woman fighting.

"When is this going to stop?" the woman cries, her voice taut, like it's about to break. "You've been acting crazy for months, years even. All this talk about magic—"

There's the loud sound of a slap, the ringing, stinging crack of a hand hitting skin. "Don't call me crazy," the man's low voice says in a rumble. "You want to leave? Go ahead, I don't care. We don't need you."

"But the kids—"

"Are staying with me. They're the end of my family line. You can't take them from me."

The woman chokes on a sob. After a weighted moment, she says, "I'm coming back for them." But even I can hear the anguish in her voice, the lack of confidence in her statement.

Then, the sound of feet running down the stairs and the front door flying open; a car roaring to life and peeling out of the driveway.

That must've been the sound of their mother leaving their father, Hayden.

Somehow the silence that follows is even more terrifying than the shouting.

The house is quiet, and James begins to cry.

The memory dissolves, sliding from my mind like rain dripping down a windowpane. Like the tears of a scared little boy. All the colors in the room bleed into each other until they swirl into something new—another memory of Charlotte's.

This time she's older, her blonde hair tumbling down her back in waves. She's a teenager—tall and gangly, probably close to my age. I watch her creep down a dark hallway, stepping carefully like she's avoiding the floorboards that squeak.

But halfway down the hall, a door flies open, and a pre-teen version of James pokes his head out. He has the still-round face of a young boy but all the awkward height of a recent growth spurt, and when he catches his sister heading toward the stairs he calls out, "Dad, she's right here!" He smirks, opening the door wider for her to walk through.

Charlotte glares at him. "Traitor," she hisses as she slides past him into the dimly lit room.

He tugs on her sleeve and pulls her to a stop. "I didn't want to be in here alone," he whispers so quietly I can barely hear him.

Charlotte softens but still shakes herself loose from his grip.

"What's up, Dad?" Her voice is calm, but her shoulders are stiff when she addresses a man with dark hair in the corner of the room seated at a large desk. He doesn't look up but continues to scribble on something stretched across the surface of the dark wood.

"Sit down," he commands, pointing with his spare hand to the two hardback chairs in front of the desk.

James and Charlotte sigh but take their seats without arguing. Hayden frantically scrawls for another minute, the pen scratching loudly in the silence. When he finally looks up, he startles at the sight of his children sitting across from him, almost as if he'd forgotten they were there. His hand clutches at his forearm, tugging agitatedly on his shirt sleeve. He cracks his neck twice before getting up from his seat and shoving the chair back into the desk with a crash. Charlotte and James both cringe away, but Hayden doesn't seem to notice.

Or he doesn't care.

Hayden is a large man—tall and broad in the shoulders, burly and fierce. His face would be handsome if he didn't have what appears to be a permanent scowl across it, dark and slashing. James looks down, fiddling with something in his pocket, but Charlotte holds her father's stare without blinking.

"Were you trying to skip your morning lesson?" he asks, leaning against the front of the desk and crossing his arms over his chest. He massages his forearm again, the muscles in his neck tightening.

Charlotte shrugs and says, "One morning off won't hurt anybody, Dad. I've read it a million times. I know it by heart."

Her father smiles, but it isn't a kind one. It's a warning. "Do you? Recite it to me."

She straightens in her chair, her head held high. "Fine." She closes her eyes and begins. "There is a place where... a place where..." She pauses and frowns, rubbing the space between her eyebrows with the knuckle of her thumb. "I know this," she mumbles. "I swear, I know this."

Hayden's smile widens as he leans in closer, leering like a cat over a cornered mouse. "I can't hear you, Charlotte. I said, recite it to me."

Her eyes stay closed. She clears her throat before trying again. "There is a place where all magic—where all..." She bites her lip. "I... I can't remember the rest," she finally admits after another drawn-out pause. She ducks her head, looking abashed.

"Of course you can't remember." Hayden slams one large hand on the desk beneath him. "That's the whole point! It's a secret that wants to stay in the shadows, but it can't stay hidden forever." His face darkens like a storm cloud about to break.

The memory flickers as if Charlotte herself doesn't want to watch what happens next. But then the picture grows clearer, all the details of the gloomy paneled room sharpening as Hayden hurls a book at the wall. "You have one purpose in this life, and one purpose only. And what is that, James?"

"To break the Claimings," he parrots back automatically, not looking at his sister.

"To break the Claimings," Hayden repeats slowly, enunciating every word. "That's right, my boy. And how do we do that?"

Neither of his children answers.

Hayden grabs a handful of papers off his desk and throws them up in the air. Charlotte and James both hold perfectly still as the snowstorm of loose papers flurries around them. I peer at the pages littering the floor. They're covered in symbols and pictures, each more confusing than the last. It looks like the rantings of a madman.

"When my Claiming was Skipped, my grandmother entrusted me with this task: to find the place where all magic resides, and to find the one who holds all magic in her hands." The pitch of his voice rises higher with every word. "*That* is the only way we can fix this. *That* is the only way to make it right. It has all been foretold. Fate itself has whispered it in my ears." He takes a breath, and mumbles something to himself, fussing at the sleeve of his button-down again and clutching at his arm. "Now read and remember. And learn your place."

"But what if we're Claimed?" Charlotte asks, standing from her seat in a rush, an air of confidence filling her once again. She points at her brother, and he shrinks back in his chair. "James and I could be, you know. It's a possibility. Just because you were Skipped doesn't mean that—"

Her words are cut off as Hayden rolls back his sleeve, slowly folding the cuff of his shirt until the skin of his forearm is revealed along with the stark red line running up the length of his arm.

I lurch back, fumbling through the magic and the memory as my fingers slacken their grip on Milo's and Charlotte's hands.

"Hold still Gemma," Charlotte's voice whispers in my ear. I feel her hand tighten around mine reassuringly even though I can't see her. *"Just hold on a little longer."*

Even in its broken state, the red thread is still brighter than I could've ever remembered on my own. A bleeding, brilliant crimson, it winds up his arm like the branches of a tree, like artificial veins pumping blood and pulsing sickly.

I want to close my eyes, but I can't look away. And I swear, even in this memory that does not belong to me, in a time and place that I had no part in, I can hear it whispering my name.

Gemma.

Hayden shoves his arm in his daughter's face. "You should be so lucky to bear the thread. Anyone can be Claimed. But only the chosen few have the honor of carrying the red mark, of knowing the future."

Charlotte scoffs. "Then why do *you* want magic so badly? Why are *you* so obsessed with breaking the Claimings if it's such an honor to have that *thing* leeching your life out of you?" Her voice thickens with emotion. "You already lost Mom. Why can't you just let it go?"

Hayden yanks his sleeve down in a quick and angry burst. "Because some things are meant to be broken."

Charlotte deflates, looking utterly defeated as she sinks back down into her chair. James squirms in his seat, half-heartedly paying attention. He keeps looking out the window at the bright sunny day with a longing expression. This sounds like a worn-out argument between Charlotte and Hayden; a conversation he's had to hear over and over.

Hayden cracks his neck again and sighs. "For the last time: read and remember. And do not question me again." He hands them two worn notebooks, identical in size and shape.

James opens to the first page, clears his throat, and after another glance at his father, he begins to read. "There is a place where all magic resides..."

Charlotte swallows roughly, blinking back her tears. "A place where fate itself lies sleeping, its red heart always beating. A place of waking dreams..."

The memory flickers and fades once again, the scene melting into a confusing mix of sound and color until I can't tell which way is up and which way is down. Charlotte's memories shift around me haphazardly. It's like being lost inside a kaleidoscope of sensations.

Then I'm in a backyard, once again with Charlotte. This time she's alone, standing still under the light of a full moon. She peers nervously behind her shoulder into the house where James and Hayden are fighting in the kitchen. Empty bottles line the counter and litter the table. Hayden throws one, and it shatters against the wall. Angry shouts fill the night as Charlotte's hands begin to glow a warm golden amber, the same color as the afternoon sun. She turns away from the house and the fighting, looking down at her palms with the first true smile I've seen from her.

"A Caster," she whispers to herself, her face lit by the soft light. "I'm a Caster." Her hands clench into fists as if she's trying to stop the magic from spreading. Like she's trying to hold onto a secret.

Hayden must've finally seen her out the window because the backdoor swings open in a sudden burst, and he comes racing across the dead lawn, straight to Charlotte. "You've been Claimed," he gasps in between heavy breaths. There's nothing celebratory about the way he says it, but his eyes shine with a blood-shot greed.

She extends her glowing hands, aiming them at her father, her voice unyielding. "Don't come any closer."

Hayden freezes a few feet away from her, his gaze transfixed. "Magic," he says, his voice full of childlike wonder. But then his face hardens, and he shakes his head as if trying to clear it. "Magic," he says again, but this time it's laced with anger and the barest hint of shame. "This doesn't change anything, you know. We still have work to do."

Charlotte doesn't answer or lower her hands. After another heartbeat, Hayden ends their standoff and marches back into the house, slamming the door shut behind him. James stays staring out the window until his father grabs him by the scruff of his neck and pulls him away.

Standing all alone in the dark yard, Charlotte's hands start to dim, a trail of tears carving down her cheeks.

I've never seen a Claiming so lonely.

The memory stutters before immediately giving way to a new one. I blink against the bright sun, watching as Charlotte waves her glowing hands next to a pile of boxes, each of them floating into the open trunk of a waiting, beat-up old car. Teenage James is already tucked inside, sitting in the backseat, his forehead leaning against the window mournfully.

"I don't get why we have to move," he mumbles through the glass. "And why so suddenly."

"I know, me neither," Charlotte says just as Hayden marches out the front door and down the driveway.

"Aren't you finished yet?" he asks Charlotte brusquely while glaring at her glowing hands.

Her magic flickers, and the last box tumbles to a stop, drop-ping from its point in midair. She rushes to grab it, dipping her head so her father doesn't see her red cheeks or her scowl. After loading the last box, she climbs inside the car to sit next to her brother.

No one says a word as the family rolls down the driveway. And no one turns to look back.

Everything tilts on its side until the memory shifts into a new landscape, this one with swaying palm trees and the blue crash of ocean waves—bright and vibrant after the dull and depressing scene on the driveway.

Charlotte walks along the shore, avoiding the busy pier packed full of tourists and smiling at her bare feet squelching in the sand. James follows a little way behind her, waving his hands over the sand, forming peaks and patterns as he walks. The sight of his hands, glowing and green, makes me feel sick.

"You're not supposed to do magic out here. Anyone could see you," Charlotte says, her tone disapproving.

"Who cares," James replies in a bored voice, not looking up from the walls of his sandcastle. "This is the only place I can think."

Charlotte watches him for another moment before turning away and leaving him be. Her face is sad and worn; she looks far older than her age, which couldn't be more than her early twenties. Down the beach, a man approaches. And when he finally comes into view, I have to swallow my gasp.

He's tall and loping, his pace quickening at the sight of Charlotte. The wind blows his dark hair across his forehead, and when he brushes it back with an easy smile, it makes me want to drop to the ground right then and there. He looks just like Oliver, except for the eyes. Ollie has his mother's eyes.

This must be Ben.

"You came!" he says, jogging eagerly to Charlotte.

She nods shyly, fidgeting with the pockets of her cutoff shorts as he approaches.

"I wasn't sure if you'd make it." He grins and tucks one of her loose curls behind her ears.

"Dad was out, so..." She bites her lip, looking like she wants to say more, but when her gaze flicks over to her brother, she sighs. "Ben, this is James. He wanted to meet you."

"Hey, James, it's nice to finally put a face to the name," Ben says, crouching down.

James merely grunts a hello, refusing to look up from his towering sand creation.

Ben watches him curiously for a minute before Charlotte steers them away, their hands brushing as they walk along the shoreline. As soon as their backs are to him, James snaps his head up and watches them go, his features twisted and cold.

The memory doesn't last long enough for me to get to see Charlotte and Ben laughing together on the beach or chasing each other through the rising tide. A stiff salty breeze rushes around me in a sudden gust, pushing me into the next scene.

A small and cramped kitchen. Peeling wallpaper, mismatched chairs. Multiple holes punched in the wall. Charlotte walks through the door, her face slightly sunburned and beaming. She looks younger when she's like this, looser and happier. But her smile slips into a frown when she sees the scattered papers on the table, her father and brother seated at opposite ends, the pages filling the space between them.

She snatches one of the papers closest to her and quickly scans the page. "What—what is this? Is this new? I've never seen these before."

Hayden crosses his arms and says nothing.

She squints at the page, her mouth forming the shapes of the words. "Wait, what does this mean? Why does this have Ben's name on it?" She spins to face her brother, shaking the paper in his face. I catch a brief glimpse of a sketch of Ben's profile, his jaw strong and his angles sharp. "You told him about Ben, didn't you?" Charlotte cries, clutching the paper as she seethes. "You promised me you wouldn't."

James sneers and leans back in his chair, swatting her hand and the paper away. "I didn't have to tell him anything, he already knew. Don't you get it, Charlotte? The *thread* told him. Dad can see the *future*. He was right about everything."

Charlotte's face drains of all its color, her golden-tanned skin going pale. "Is this... is he... is Ben the reason you moved us here?" She stares down at the messy scrawls. "You manipulated this whole thing so he could find me? Because you saw us together in one of your 'visions?'" Her fingers punctuate the air in angry, mocking quotes. "Why? Because he's one of your precious Threaders?"

Hayden glowers, his hand clenching into a fist. "The reason is always the same: to break the Claimings."

James flies out of his seat, his cheeks stained red. "Of course it's because he's a Threader! Did you really think you could keep that a secret from us? From me?" A shadow of hurt flickers across his face, leaving his expression even harder after it passes. "You're forgetting our purpose, everything Dad's taught us. You've completely lost focus—"

"You're both insane!" Charlotte groans into her hands, clutching at her hair. "I'm not losing focus; I never had any to begin with! I don't care about any of this, I don't *want* to break the Claimings, I just want both of you to leave me alone. I'm done." In one sharp movement, she tears the page with Ben's face on it in half, and then in half again. She grabs another fistful of papers from off the table and whispers a string of words, her anger burning hotter than a flame as the papers dissolve like ash in the wind.

Hayden leaps from his chair. "What have you done?" he yells, grabbing her by the arms and shaking her. "You stupid girl."

At his insult, Charlotte's hands glow brighter, but when her father shoves her down into a chair, they sputter before flickering out entirely. Fear spreads across her face, tainting every inch of this memory with a panicky, pressing urgency. I want to run; I want to hide. I want to grab Charlotte and get her out of here, to take her from this place and these people.

Apparently, I'm not the only one who's thinking that because the next second, the front door bursts open, and Ben barrels into the kitchen. His eyes flash when he sees Hayden's large hands squeezing Charlotte's arms, pinning her down onto the chair.

Ben's jaw clenches as he reaches out his own hand and gently offers it to Charlotte, her frightened face smoothing the moment she sees him. Her breathing slows, and she sits up straighter, shrugging her father's hands off as she rises to her feet. Without another word, Ben and Charlotte turn and head straight for the front door.

"It doesn't matter if you stay or if you leave," Hayden calls after them. "Fate is already unfolding. You're just the means to an end."

They ignore him. But just before Ben shuts the door behind them, Hayden's voice rings out, cold and quiet. "I know you go there. I know you go there every night and hold the threads. I know it. And someday I will see it." His fingers pick at the skin of his forearm, right where the red thread wraps around him.

Ben stops in his tracks, his gaze unflinching. "Then you should know that magic always has consequences."

"And fate always has its way," Hayden replies, his voice soft for once.

Charlotte tugs Ben's hand, pulling him to her side. "Don't follow us," she says with finality to her brother and father. And with a wave of her glowing hand, the door slams shut.

The memory suddenly goes dark, like a TV flipping off. I gulp for air, stumbling over my feet and landing on the cushy pin-striped chair in Charlotte's empty living room. Closing my eyes in relief, I try to relax my body and breathe. I can't stop shaking.

Zoe and Milo don't look like they feel much better than I do. Zoe fumbles for her bag and accidentally tips into Milo, nearly sending them both crashing to the floor. He grabs her by the elbow, righting her before she falls. He doesn't appear to have the energy to be annoyed with her or even to flirt, and she doesn't seem to have the strength to glare back.

And lying on the floor behind them is Charlotte, her eyes rolling back in her head. She's gone completely still, the light of her glowing hands pulsing, pulsing, pulsing—

Until it goes out.

CHAPTER TWENTY-EIGHT

OLLIE

"*GOING INSIDE A memory that is not your own is complicated and dangerous. You could very easily become stuck in a time and place that does not belong to you, losing all sense of self and purpose. If you do not maintain your mind and manage your own memories, you will be lost to the magic.*"

Lillian's warning runs through my mind on repeat like a siren.

Complicated and dangerous.

Easily stuck.

Lost sense of self and purpose.

"Lillian!" I can barely get her name out; my heart is lodged in my throat, making it hard to breathe. "Lillian," I say again, getting right in her face.

She doesn't respond. She looks right through me, her dark eyes bright as she wanders through the Dreamscape, listening to the Elders and Atticus describe the duties of the Threaders and the caretaking of magic.

I'm half listening, half spiraling as I watch the male Elder wave his hands overhead to show how the stars line up to reveal a complicated and intricate weaving, while the woman places her hand on one of the cavern walls and every silver thread glows like captured starlight. They demonstrate how it's all connected—not just their roles, but each part of the Dreamscape, too. A perfect mechanism.

Normally, I'd be into eavesdropping on a conversation like this. Magic 101? Sign me up. I've been desperate for a course like this for months. But now that Lillian has gone AWOL and basically abandoned me inside her memory, I'm more than a little distracted and most definitely starting to panic. "This can't be happening," I say, dropping my head into my hands with a groan.

I try to shake her by the shoulders, but my hands slip through her as if she were a ghost. Immediately, I try again, willing myself to grab hold of her, but still, nothing happens. Just an icy cold sensation as my hands drift right through her.

Looking down, I squint at the sheen of my skin underneath the pale light of the stars. I turn my hands back and forth, examining them from every possible angle, hoping that it's just a trick of the dimness and my overactive imagination. But sure enough, I'm a shade lighter than I was before I came into this memory. Not so much in color, but in *solidness*, like I'm less here than I used to be.

"I'm... fading." The realization comes out thinner than a whisper as if even my voice isn't substantial enough to have an impact.

Lillian's not the ghost—I am.

"I am a barely-there version of myself, merely a collage of recollections." That's how she described herself when she told me she was fading away.

Lost.

Stuck.

The longer I stay here, the quicker I'll vanish because no one here remembers me. How could they? Technically, I don't exist in this time. So even if there are people out in the universe right now—my parents, Gemma, Milo, my neighbors, or even some random kid I took biology with in the seventh grade—thinking about me, or missing me, it doesn't matter because they aren't *here*.

It's something I've taken for granted my whole life—being known. But I'm not known in this time or place, not in someone else's memories. Not when the only person who remembers me and my existence is currently caught in the snare of her own mind. Lillian was the one in the driver's seat, but now she's taken her hands off the wheel. And I'm the idiot riding shotgun in the car that's veering off the road with no idea what to do next.

And despite my crisis, the memory just keeps marching on.

Whenever the Elders address her, Lillian responds as the seventeen-year-old version of herself, not the woman who knows me or what's to come. This Lillian isn't the one who took a thread of memory in her hands and invited me to follow. Nothing I do or say manages to catch her attention. It's as if I'm not even here, like she never knew me in the first place. And the more insubstantial I become, the more solid she appears. Her muscles look loose and relaxed, her smile soft and decided. After all, she's the one who's known here, cared for and mentored. This is a place where she doesn't have to be the one with all the answers. In this memory of hers, everyone she loves is safe and accounted for.

After years and years of wandering alone, of wading through the sea of her memories and barely keeping her head above water, she's finally let her guard down and succumbed to the past.

And the worst part is, I don't think I can blame her. Aren't we all just trying to make it home?

I rub my hands across my forehead and close my eyes. It's getting harder to think coherently. Sorting through my thoughts feels like trudging through mud, sloppy and slow. I feel lethargic and clumsy as I stumble through the memory, following after Lillian and the others. I trip over my barely there feet and try to think.

Try to think...

To... think.

My steps falter as all the fight slowly seeps out of my body until I'm motionless beside the four Threaders, their profiles lit by the shine of the silver threads gleaming on the walls. I blink up at the countless stars shining in a sky the color of half-remembered dreams, a deep and unspeakably dark purple, wondering why I was in such a rush. Wouldn't it just be easier to sit down and rest? To finally let this fuzzy feeling of fading take me over completely?

Maybe surrendering would feel like falling asleep, a peaceful drifting off, and then—nothing.

The darkness of oblivion tugs at the periphery of my every thought, urging me to just let go. But my subconscious bristles, refusing to back down. My nails dig into the skin of my palms, sharp and shocking as something at the back of my mind nudges me to keep going, a nagging notion I can't quite remember or seem to forget.

I startle when Atticus sidles up next to Lillian and grins. He pulls her to a stop while the Elders continue on ahead. "What do you think?" he asks, holding his arms out wide. I stagger back, forgetting for a moment that he isn't actually talking to me.

"It is... indescribable," Lillian says with a soft laugh. "How is this real?" She spins in a slow circle with her head thrown back. "My whole life I have heard the stories, but this is more than I could have ever imagined."

Atticus's smile shifts slightly. "Did Cora say anything after you were Claimed?"

Lillian's own smile slips at the mention of her sister. "She did not seem as pleased as you are. She was almost angry with me."

"But she will get used to it," he says, his black eyebrows rising higher. "Right? After all, to have a Threader in the family is nothing but an honor. And two from the same settlement? It is unheard of. We are a marvel, Lilli. Cora will get used to it," he says again as if to reassure himself.

"Perhaps," she replies, but her face still looks uncertain.

The two Elders walk over, their black cloaks trailing on the ground behind them. The woman tucks her arm through Lillian's and pulls her to the center of the Dreamscape while the man ushers Atticus to follow.

"You must have thousands of questions. He certainly did when he was Claimed a few months ago," the woman says, pointing to Atticus with a wink.

He smiles sheepishly and shrugs.

My form wavers, threatening to gutter out as I try to follow the conversation. *Focus*, I remind myself, *hold on just a little bit longer.*

"Of course I have questions!" Lillian laughs. "How does this work? Where do the threads come from? And when can I start?"

"How about one question at a time," the man chuckles.

"Okay, okay," she concedes, her cheeks turning pink. "I wanted to ask about the ceremony, about the portal and the spell you used to enter: *'laws that govern, threads that bind...'*" She trails off and looks up at the weaving, her eyes full of stars. "How does that work? How do we enter the Dreamscape?"

"That spell," the woman answers, "along with the threads of magic we gathered from the Claimed, is what allows us to open the portal. As you will see," she holds up her hand and a silver thread floats free from the cavern wall, drifting lazily until it lands in the center of her palm, "we may leave the Dreamscape whenever we wish, but we may only enter when we borrow the magic necessary to weave an entrance, to begin a Claiming."

"We have to *borrow* magic?" Lillian cries in disbelief. "But why?"

"Because we have none of our own in the outside world," the man says. "Our magic is tied to the Dreamscape; the Dreamscape is our magic."

Lillian stares at them open-mouthed while Atticus scowls down at the pearlescent floor.

The woman smiles at them understandingly. "I know that may feel like a shock right now, but it is a sacred duty and privilege to work with the magic as closely as we do. There is no other way to describe it. Without us, there would be no Claimings."

Lillian's forehead scrunches as she thinks. "So, in a way, everyone else is borrowing magic from us."

The Elders both laugh as they start to walk again. "In a way," the man says. "Without one, there could not be the other. We need them and they need us—a balancing act."

"Without us," the woman adds, "magic would have no release. And there must be a release."

"Why must there be a release?" Lillian asks. She crosses her arms impatiently, almost agitatedly.

I can see the questions in her eyes, her hunger to understand. Her expression reminds me of someone. Again, something nudges at the back of my mind, begging me to remember: a swish of black hair and hands on hips; a flash of lightning and a shower of rain. *Why do we even have Claimings?"* the girl yells, tipping her face toward the sky before looking back at me, drenched and beseeching.

"Gemma," I whisper to myself, "Gemma." I can see the questions in her eyes, her hunger to understand. I cling to the idea of her, letting her face ground me back in the moment so that I don't lose track of who I am again. I say her name over and over again like a mantra, like a desperate prayer.

Gemma—don't let me fade.

Gemma—don't let me forget.

"Why must there be a release?" the male Elder repeats. "Because magic wants to find a way out. And this is only the gate," he says, gesturing at the expanse of the Dreamscape.

Lillian looks up, appraising the cavern. I can practically see her cataloging her questions for later. She pinches her lips together and nods, but her eyebrows quirk with skepticism. "And the rest of the spell, *our fates tied together in a single line,"* she quotes reverently, looking around expectantly. "Is it true what the legends say about the thread of fate?"

"Yes, it is true," the man says hesitantly. He shares a look with the woman who shakes her head. "But we do not touch the red thread of fate. That is a magic that is not to be meddled with."

"Can I see it?" Lillian asks in a small voice.

Atticus looks to the Elders, and they both give him a nod. Then, he points up.

Fate.

A deep sense of dread slowly creeps through my body until I'm completely submerged in the feeling.

Lillian frowns and follows his gaze. I can't help it—I look too. "I see the stars in the weaving, just as you showed me."

"Look again," Atticus says quietly.

She searches for a moment before pointing up, her mouth parted in wonder. "I see it!"

And there it is. The red thread of fate, circling the stars around the perimeter of the Dreamscape, always on the edge and barely visible. It's a bit anticlimactic, almost unimpressive. It's different than when I saw it last. There is no gash, no snag in the weaving. This was before it was broken, before it was changed. Back when fate had every single one of its possibilities and they didn't all revolve around Gemma and me.

I stare up at the thread, and I can't help but notice the sense of stillness about it, something immovable in the way it circles around, the beginning always feeding into the end. But there's something about it that whispers of *more*. And it makes me wonder: if this thread wasn't here, would any of the others even exist?

Lillian shakes her head and blinks a few times. "Strange," she murmurs. "When I look at it, it is almost as if... as if I can *hear* it."

"I hear it too," Atticus answers back just as softly.

I shudder and close my eyes, no longer interested in seeing. Because the longer I look at it, the harder it is to look away.

"Let fate unfold as it will, and there will be no trouble," the woman says with a tone of finality. "Leave the thread alone. That is a magic few can comprehend."

Her words jog something in my memory. An urgent warning, a frustrated sigh. I stare absently at my nearly transparent hands, lost in the jumble of my thoughts until all at once, I remember.

"The thread," I mumble to myself, suddenly aware of the midnight blue thread still wrapped around my hand. I almost forgot it was there. It's so insubstantial, it's almost like holding onto thin air. I trail behind Lillian, following the end of the thread until I find where it's laced around her pointer finger. Easing my hand over hers, I try to loosen her hold on the memory, but my ineffectual grip proves useless once again.

Clenching my jaw, my breath hisses through my teeth as I finally admit the truth to myself: if I want to make it out of this memory alive, I'll have to go alone.

I can take control. If I hurry, I can leave this memory before it's too late.

I take one last look at Lillian, who's still talking to the Elders. She points up at something in the weaving, another question on her lips. I look at the settled shape of her shoulders, the assurance in her tone, and feel a sudden pang of loss that makes my fingers tighten around her thread once again.

I don't want to leave her behind. I don't want to try to find my way home alone. I'm terrified to let go of her thread, to fall back into the sea of memories on my own, but what other choice do I have? My only other option is to stay here and fade away, no more than a blip in a time and place that was never meant for me.

"Thank you," I whisper near her ear, wishing she could hear me, "for helping me Remember."

Squaring my shoulders and summoning the last dregs of courage I have left, I slowly peel my fingers away from the thread of her memory, thinking desperately about my library and trying to organize all my memories back onto those tidy shelves.

But the more I try to Remember, the harder it becomes. I can't picture it clearly; the details are out of focus and far away. Even the sea of memories feels out of reach like something I dreamed up, impossibly ludicrous and totally inaccessible.

"Come on," I groan, "take me away from here." But my hand is still caught in the tangle of Lillian's memory. I try to shake it off, but it clings to me as if it doesn't want to let me go. "Magic wants to find a way out, right?" I repeat the Elder's word softly, weaving Lillian's thread in between my fingers. *So show me.*

The words of the Language fall from my mouth unexpectedly, the shape of the letters sharp against my tongue. Then, everything slows down, almost as if the sands tumbling from the hourglass of time have taken a momentary pause. The movements of the Elders and Lillian and Atticus are labored and sluggish, like the memory has switched into slow motion.

I turn away as the colors of the Dreamscape flare brightly, and when I look up, they're all looking at me—Lillian, Atticus, and the Elders. The man's eyes flash as they bore into mine. *"You have blown the gate wide open,"* he says, his voice low and deep and rich from the Language. He doesn't sound anything like he did only moments before.

I reel back, stumbling from the shock of it.

"You have blown the gate wide open," he repeats, this time with the woman joining in, their voices twining together like an eerie two-part harmony that reverberates off the cavern walls.

Atticus and Lillian add their voices to the chant, their faces eerily blank. *"You have blown the gate wide open."*

The hairs on the back of my neck stand on end. This isn't from the memory; this is something else. Something that snuck in, or maybe something I invited in myself.

"What... what do you mean? Who's there?" I stand up straight even while my voice wobbles unsteadily.

The four Threaders move as one to the far side of the cavern, their movements stiff and disjointed, like they aren't in control of their own bodies. They form a line and each of them places their hands on the shimmering threads of the walls.

"We heard the tales when we were young," they say in unison.

Out of the silver threads comes a single black one. I shiver at the sight of it. The Threaders unwind it carefully, spooling it into their upturned palms before slowly walking it over to me. Their stares are vacant and unseeing as they hold out their hands and offer me the thread.

I lean away from them, unsure of what I should do and wondering if I even have a choice in the matter. But I'd asked the magic to show me a way out, so how could I ignore it now?

When my fingers hover over the thread, I hear a young girl's voice ringing through the silence, humming through the cavern, the melody like a whispered secret long forgotten.

Oliver, Oliver.

Like the beating of a drum. Like the beating of my heart.

I grab the black thread in my other hand before I can talk myself out of it.

We heard the tales when we were young. Every story started the same.

At the beginning.

Back when the sky was so heavy and full of stars that one night, it split. It spilled, it cracked, it broke in two—

it poured out until it became something new.

But first, a darkness so profound you could feel it in your very bones. Then, a quiet so hushed it was as if sound itself had never existed at all.

This part of the story always scared me when I was small. I would sink deeper into my mother's lap, tracing the freckles on her skin as her arms tightened around me. "Carmen," she would whisper. "The light is coming soon, just wait."

She was the best storyteller in our village. I would close my eyes and listen to her voice as it lilted and danced across the words until I was convinced that when I opened my eyes again, I would no longer be seated around the fire or nestled against her. No, I would be twirling among the stars, watching them fall as they grew so heavy, they had to change into something else.

The sky split, the stars fell, and the darkness that followed seemed like the end.

Until out of that very darkness came a light brighter than the stars they once had been. Threads spun from silver, all tangled together, crisscrossing in a dance just like the words of the story my mother loved to tell so much.

"What did the stars become, little one?" she would ask me, tracing the lines of my face.

"Life." I whispered, my voice caught in my throat.

"Magic," she would say back. "That was the day the sun rose for the first time and life became something worth living."

As I grew older, I thought about the old tales less and less. But sometimes it was still the last thing I thought about before I drifted off to sleep.

Stars so heavy with light, silver threads trailing behind them as they fell.

Life.

Magic.

The beginning.

I'm halfway between memories, a place in between.

The pitch-black thread wraps around my arm, pulling me deeper into the unknown memory of stories and stars, while Lillian's thread from the Dreamscape anchors me to her and her memory.

But I can smell the woodsmoke from the fire; I can almost see its plumes rising higher into a dusky sky. A village. A desert. A girl with black hair sitting on her mother's lap. She plays with the end of her braid, wrapping it around her fingers as she listens to the story.

Her dark eyes land on mine.

Oliver, Oliver.

I can hear it. I can see it.

And I know I need to let go of Lillian's thread and follow. But before I let myself fall, I look down at my hands, gripping both threads. I'm even more translucent than I was before, a barely-there version of myself, merely a collage of recollections.

Nearly forgotten.

"I can't," I whisper to the girl and the tugging of her memory. "I don't know how to let go. Not yet."

The only thing I know how to do is Remember.

I'm not ready to fade away. Not before I see Gemma again. I need to be somewhere where I am known.

So I close my eyes and loosen my grip, dropping both the threads. I fold my arms around myself as I tumble into yet another unknown made of shadows and unfamiliar voices and the ever-present feeling that maybe I've made the wrong choice. I'm falling

falling

falling

again.

"The library," I say to myself with more conviction than I've ever possessed in my entire life. "I'm in the library, walking the aisles with the sun streaming through the windows. I can see the dust motes circling in the air every time I pull a book off the shelf. I'm in the library of my memories. Please." A thin cream-colored thread wraps around my hand, yanking me forward through the darkness.

I open my eyes to see the dust motes circling.

A startled laugh bursts free from my chest as I collapse against the closest shelf, burying my face in the spines of the yellowed paperbacks, a section with titles like *Walking to School, Part 256,* and *Fourth of July Fireworks, Volume III.*

When I glance down at my hands, I see they look more solid; not quite normal, but better than they did back in those other memories. Here in *my* memories, I'm more real than I was before. I'm in a place where I can be remembered.

It's quieter here without Lillian. I restlessly pace the aisles, looking through the titles and wishing she was here to help me. In between bouts of worry, I wonder about the black thread—the memory of that girl sitting by the fire with her mother, listening to old stories of starlight and sunrises.

"The beginning," I say to myself, feeling like a moron. That's what Lillian was searching for. That's what I need to find so I can fix what has been broken, and then maybe, just maybe, I might be able to find my way back home.

And I let it go because I got scared.

"That should be the title of my autobiography," I mumble, banging my head against the imaginary bookshelves containing every moment of my life so far.

How do I get her memory back? And if I do, how will I search through more memories before fading away? I pull out the ugly orange plastic chair that seems to be available in every aisle I explore, sinking down into it and trying to think.

"Carmen?" I say the girl's name out loud, feeling stupid. "Are... are you there?"

Nothing.

I sigh and lean back in the chair, tipping my head back to stare at the blinking fluorescents, wishing I wasn't alone and that I knew what to do for once. Suddenly, the silence of the library feels deafening. Totally and completely suffocating. "I'm sorry, Lillian," I whisper to myself in the vain hope that somewhere out there in the midnight blue of her memories, she can hear me.

I bolt out of my chair and over to the nearest shelf, scanning the titles of the books in a frantic search for a memory I can get lost in, even just for a moment.

My gaze catches on a title stitched in silver that seems to glow brighter than the rest, almost as if I'd willed it into existence with my desperation. "That'll work," I say with a small smile as I pull the book off the shelf with gentle hands. I crack it open, and a silver thread emerges, as bright as the threads described in Carmen's story.

"Magic," I whisper. I take hold of the thread and close my eyes. "Life."

And I Remember.

CHAPTER TWENTY-NINE

GEMMA

I CAN'T QUIT staring at Charlotte.

Zoe's the first to react, grabbing her leather bag off the couch while Milo and I just stand there, frozen in confusion. She elbows us out of the way, crouching down on the floor next to Charlotte, who's lying perfectly still, her eyes rolled back and her mouth popped open like even she's surprised that her memories ended this way.

Milo squats down next to her and picks up Charlotte's limp hand, which just moments ago had been pulsing with magic and light. "What's happening to her?" he asks in a hushed tone.

Zoe doesn't answer. She's too busy frantically digging through her bag, its contents rattling as her gaze flits back to Charlotte every few seconds. She pulls out bottle after bottle of mixings, her frustration mounting as she searches for the right one.

"Here, let me help—" Milo reaches for the strap of her bag, and she tenses. "Just tell me the name of the mixing, and I can find it, or we'll be here all night while you sort through that bottomless pit of yours."

She chews on the inside of her cheek before dropping the strap of the bag in consent. "It's a small bottle labeled *Charlotte*."

Milo holds onto the bag with one glowing hand while whispering his casting. A second later, a skinny stoppered bottle flies out of the depths of the bag and straight into his other hand. He gives it to Zoe along with her bag, then scoots back on the floor to get out of the way. I quietly sit down next to him, my pulse still racing.

"Thanks," Zoe says to Milo, her shoulders dipping slightly in relief.

She pours a few drops of an orange-colored liquid with a consistency similar to oil onto Charlotte's stiff hands, massaging it onto her fingers in quick fluid motions. The moment the mixing touches her skin, Charlotte visibly relaxes. For the next several minutes, Zoe continues to press gently on Charlotte's tense fingers, helping her to slowly unlock her stiff grip.

What seems like ages later, Charlotte finally opens her eyes. She sits up slowly, leaning back against the couch with her legs stretched out in front of her on the floor. "Thank you," she whispers hoarsely to Zoe, her breath coming out in sharp bursts.

Milo watches all of this unfold with a frown. "Was your magic... stuck?" he asks Charlotte, his brow puckered. "No, that's not the right word. But I don't know how else to describe it." He rubs his jaw, looking puzzled. "When I held your hand just now, I could hardly sense any magic in you. It felt staticky, like a radio signal experiencing interference." He taps his chin. "I mean, one second your magic was here, and you were showing us your memories, and the next—nothing. Almost as if you'd... run out." His mouth presses into a hard line as he quickly looks down at his own hands before shoving them into his pockets.

Charlotte sits up straighter and tips her head in Milo's direction, her face looking drawn out and wiped of all its color. "That's actually a pretty accurate description of what happened," she says, using her sleeve to dab at the sweat beading along her hairline. She turns to look at me, her gaze blue and unblinking. "There's one more memory I need to show you. But my magic..." She waves a hand at herself and sighs. "It's temperamental, to say the least. It will have to wait until tomorrow."

"*Tomorrow?*" I blurt out. "But we have all day! It's not even noon."

Milo coughs and nudges me with his elbow, pointing to the

front window. Even with the blinds closed, I can see the steady darkness of night, the soft orange glow of the streetlights. "It's almost nine," he says, holding up his phone for me to see. "At night, I mean."

We spent over half the day in Charlotte's memories.

I open my mouth to ask the dozens of questions I have lined up, ready and waiting. Questions about what she showed us and what it means. But before I can get a word out, Charlotte squeezes her eyes shut again.

Just after I've resignedly closed my mouth, Milo opens his. He crosses the room over to Charlotte's small bookcase, his hands twitching toward the stack of Chronicles. "Do you mind?"

Charlotte doesn't even look up. "Be my guest. Some of the Claimed like to keep their secrets close, but I, for one, am sick and tired of all that. What's mine is yours."

He grabs the closest one to him and reverently opens it, sighing as he reads through the first page. "It's incredible," he says in an awed voice. "This is so old."

"The Chronicles have so much history in them, but it's often overlooked by other Casters in the search for more spells." Charlotte's arms shake as she pulls herself up onto the couch, sinking against its sagging cushions in relief. "Sometimes we get too caught up in the riddle of it all, we forget to look at what's right in front of us."

I smile to myself as Grandma's voice floats through my mind. *"Such a fickle branch of magic,"* she'd said about casting, and she wasn't wrong. "So, what have you been looking for?" I ask, rising from the floor to flop back into the overstuffed armchair across from Charlotte.

"As you know, my family—" she clears her throat, looking uncomfortable, "my family history is... complicated. My father couldn't read these books because he didn't have the ability to, but he had enough of our history to fill in the gaps."

I know what she's picturing. Hayden's dark paneled office and the mandatory lessons; his fervor and intensity and total lack of care for anything else.

"My family line comes from one of the Claimed named Cora," she continues.

My stomach drops at the mention of her name. Instantly, my mind fills with the image of Cora grasping for the red thread, her hands clawing through the air. But then the picture shifts, transforming to one of her kneeling on the floor of the Dreamscape with tears running down her face as she whispers to her sister, *"Lilli, we can bring him back. We can change his fate."*

A girl who was scared. A girl who was missing her father.

A girl who just wanted things to be different.

Charlotte watches my face carefully. "You've heard her name before, haven't you?"

I bite my lip before answering. "Yes. In the Dreamscape."

She winces at the word, her mouth tugging down. "Tell me what you know."

I lean back in my chair and stare at a small stain in the carpet, talking as fast as I can to get through it. I tell her about the visions I saw in the Dreamscape, about the red thread and the madness it brought with it. Finally, after a shaky breath, I meet Charlotte's gaze and tell her about James. How he tracked me down and ordered me to break the Claimings. How he lost his temper, and my grandma lost her life. Nobody moves while I share my stories, the murmur of my words cloaking the room in a hushed silence.

"Oh, Gemma," is all Charlotte can say once I've finished, looking even paler than she did a few minutes ago.

Zoe sinks against the side of the couch from her spot on the floor, pulling her phone out of her bag and gripping it tightly in her hands. She looks down at the blank screen, probably thinking about her mom and James and all the other things she wishes she could change.

Milo looks over at me with a solemn expression, but I don't miss the hint of pride on his face. Because somehow I managed to tell our story. Somehow I found the words, and I'm still here.

"Break the Claimings," Charlotte says bitterly. "How many more people are going to get hurt because of those three little words? Those words took my family from me, and now they took yours. It's got to stop—*he's* got to stop. This magic," she says with a mournful shake of her head. "Sometimes I wonder if it's worth the price."

Nobody has an answer for her because the truth is, we all want magic. Everyone does. And I think we're afraid to find out who we are without it.

I know I am.

Charlotte motions for Milo to bring a stack of the Chronicles to her. "Ben told me those same stories; he saw those same memories in the Dreamscape," she says softly, her eyes somewhere far away. "Lillian and Atticus, Cora and the red thread. I always wrote them down after he finished so I wouldn't forget. It was probably my years of training ingrained in me." She scoffs and runs a hand over the worn pages of the Chronicles. "My father may have been cruel, but he always knew the stories were true," she admits, her tone sharpening into a hard edge. "But our story didn't begin with Cora."

Slowly, she opens the Chronicles one by one, handing them to Milo with instructions to line them up together on the floor side by side. "When you know what to look for," she says, leaning back on the couch to examine their work, "patterns emerge."

"Whoa," Milo exhales, his fingers lightly running over the pages. "They're all connected. That's so cool."

I squint at the books, trying to see what he sees, but it just looks like a bunch of weird shapes and unending black lines stretching from one page to the other, then looping back around and starting again. It makes my head start to spin if I look at it for too long.

"Is that your family line? I've never seen one go back this far before," Milo says, crouching down to get a better look.

Charlotte nods. "We're trying to find the beginning."

"And we're not anywhere close," Zoe mumbles, dropping her bag onto the couch and walking over to look at the books.

"We're making progress," Charlotte insists. "And that's something,"

"But why? Why does any of this matter? How does it help us get Ollie back?" I ask, trying to keep my voice even.

Charlotte eases herself up to look at me. "Because, Gemma, maybe if we find the beginning, we find the opening. We find the portal."

"We find the... what?" Milo asks, his eyebrows rising.

"The portal," I repeat slowly, testing the word on my tongue. I remember watching the memory of Lillian and Atticus run through the Dreamscape, their ghostly forms hazy and half-formed. *"Open the portal,"* he called out to her. And her anxious reply: *"It will not open! It will not respond to me!"*

"You think there's an actual entrance somewhere?" I ask skeptically.

Zoe pulls a small square of paper out of her bag. She opens it at a well-worn crease, unfolding the edges until a map brimming with numbers and scribbles is revealed.

Milo peers over it. "Wow," he says appreciatively.

One side of Zoe's mouth twitches like she wants to smile. "When I first met Charlotte, she showed me this." She points to a map of the United States covered in different tiny colored dots. "We've been tracking the location of every family, every group of the Claimed we could find. Charlotte and I would split up and go to different Claimings. That's how I found you."

"So you *were* tracking us," Milo says, sounding almost flattered.

"No," she says firmly, "but we figured we'd come across your family eventually." She reaches down and picks up the papers from Hayden's old journals, the ones covered in sketches of Ollie and me. "Charlotte always said it was only a matter of time." She hands the papers back to Charlotte, who folds them gently, tenderly even.

It's sad to think that those are the only pictures she has of him.

Zoe turns her attention back to the map. "Notice anything?"

While the dots are spread far and wide, the vast majority of them are lumped together in the western half of the map. I trace the shape of the circle with my finger. "Why are most of them here?"

"We think they're congregating around the portal without knowing it."

My heart stutters in my chest. "But that could be anywhere."

Charlotte sits up straighter in her seat. "There's an old saying among the Claimed, I'm sure you've heard it before: magic calls to magic."

Milo looks at me and we share a grim smile. Grandma used to say that all the time.

"For the past seventeen years, I've been traveling around, looking for anomalies among the Claimed *and* Nons. We might be missing pieces of our history, but that doesn't mean the rest of the world is. There are legends and myths, most of them dismissed as folklore—people and places that can't really be explained, at least to anyone who doesn't know about magic. The Nons who study these discrepancies in history usually blame money or greed, pandemics or natural disasters, but when you know what to look for, you can find it. Magic always leaves a trace."

Milo claps his hands once before rubbing them together. "This is awesome. Our Aunt Libby was telling me about this. Castings leave a mark behind, right?"

I raise my eyebrows. This is the first time I've heard him mention anything about a magical mark.

Charlotte appraises him, looking impressed. "I'm going to need to meet this Aunt Libby of yours. But yes, the Language leaves an echo of sorts. It's very hard to detect, but it does leave behind a trace. So do Elemental and Mixing magic. Each branch has its own signature, its own—"

"Thread," I finish for her, finally understanding. "Each branch has its own thread. That's what you can detect. You just can't see it." I stare at Charlotte, and she looks back at me with eyes as blue as her son's. "You really think we can find the actual portal to the Dreamscape? You think it's just hanging out, waiting for someone to fall in?" I cross my arms, disbelieving even while my heart races. It thunders on and on, each beat willing me to hope, to hope, to hope.

"Now that you're here? Yes, I do believe that," she says with conviction.

My arms fall limp, my shoulders curling in on themselves. I want to ask Zoe to bottle up Charlotte's belief and give some to me. This all just seems so impossible.

"If we want to find them, this is the only chance we've got," Charlotte says, stretching out across the length of the couch and resting her head against its arm.

Them? As I watch Charlotte settling into the couch, looking small and tired and a little bit broken, I realize that she isn't just searching for Ollie. She's still looking for Ben, too. My throat aches at the thought. Seventeen years of missing; seventeen years of wishing.

I just don't know if I could survive years of this. I already feel small, tired, and a little bit broken.

Milo pulls his chair closer to Charlotte and the two of them trade the Chronicles back and forth, talking about the different castings and what they mean. Zoe sits nearby on the floor, sorting through her leather bag of mixings and halfway listening.

"Aunt Libby would love to get her hands on these." Milo's voice cracks with sentimentality, and his eyes catch mine. We still haven't heard from her since last night. Even if she got her hands on these Chronicles, would she be able to read them? "She's kind of a nerd about this stuff," he says.

A pang of homesickness hits me so hard it knocks my breath out.

I wonder what my aunt would think about Charlotte and all her books, her quietness and her partially unraveled magic.

I think she would like her. I think Mom would like her too.

My mind wanders to the place I don't usually like to let it go:

the future, where everything is safe and normal and whole. I can see us in the backyard, where the table is set with a feast, the paper lanterns swaying, the cicadas buzzing noisily along with the conversation. I allow myself a moment to imagine Ollie seated next to me—whispers shared and glances given, our hands held under the table. Even with everyone there, it still feels like it's just the two of us.

And his parents are on his other side, laughing at some ridiculous story that Milo's telling across the table. I even picture Zoe sitting next to my brother, her mouth tightly pressed together like she's trying not to laugh.

There's Mom, creating a soft breeze that floats through the backyard, her face turned up and beaming because she's the most like herself when she's outside. She sits next to an empty chair that's painted bright purple and covered in lilies.

But next to that chair is a new setting. Charlotte sits there, her blue eyes trained on her son's face, watching him talk and laugh with his family, finally a part of what she gave up so many years ago. I imagine her smiling, but it's a little sad too, knowing that she's here now but missed so much along the way.

The image fades before it's fully formed, almost as if my mind won't allow something that seems so out of reach to occupy too much space inside me. Not until it's real.

Not until he's home.

Charlotte's head tips back against the couch. "Tomorrow, Gemma. I'll have more for you tomorrow, I promise," she says through her yawn, her eyes already closing.

"I think that's enough for tonight. Everyone's exhausted. Let's get some sleep." Zoe drops the small bottle of orange oil back into her bag where it lands with a loud *clink*. She points us down the hallway. "There's a guest bedroom over there, but it isn't furnished, so—"

"I'll grab the sleeping bags out of the Jeep." Milo hops to his feet. "I'm like a boy scout," he says in response to our surprised faces. "Always prepared. Try not to be too impressed."

Zoe rolls her eyes, and Milo gives her one of his best and brightest grins, whistling and tossing his keys from hand to hand as he heads out the front door.

As I turn down the hallway, I glance back to see Zoe spreading a blanket over Charlotte, who's already fast asleep.

"Is she going to be okay?" I whisper.

"I think so." Zoe sighs. "I've seen this happen to her a handful of times, but it always leaves me feeling... shaken, I guess. It's strange to see magic behave that way. I don't like it." I stand there waiting for her to explain, but of course, she doesn't. "That's not my story to share—" she starts to say, just like she did back at the diner.

"I know, I know," I mumble back, unable to hide the exasperation in my voice. "Memories are magic. Got it." I walk down the hallway to the guest room, which is just as stark and bare as the rest of the house, if not more so. I don't even know if Charlotte's ever stepped foot inside this room.

I sit in the middle of the floor on the worn and faded carpet, bringing my knees to my chest. I should feel tired, but instead I feel completely wired, totally wide awake. My skin is buzzing and my head won't stop spinning as it tries to make sense of everything I saw in Charlotte's memories. Witnessing her childhood like that has left me feeling hollowed out, and I'm not sure what to replace that emptiness with yet.

It was startling to see Hayden's cruelty, the way his manic obsession with magic and the red thread destroyed him and twisted every relationship he had. My shoulders hunch as I recall the frantic way in which James tried to prove himself to the father who would never be satisfied. I drop my face onto my knees, exhaling deeply; it's uncomfortable to feel pity for a man that I hate.

I wonder if Charlotte's mother ever came back. I wonder if that's why she never knew how to go back to Ollie.

My thoughts are interrupted by a sleeping bag to the face.

"Hungry?" Milo asks, holding up a grease-stained brown paper bag.

"Starved." I wrinkle my nose at the smell of his stale fries. "But I don't know if I can choke that down."

"Suit yourself," he says, ripping open the bag. "But good luck finding food in that kitchen." He rolls out his sleeping bag and sprawls on it before digging into his leftovers. "I'm so hungry, I could literally eat anything right now," he says, faceplanting into his fries. "And I'm so tired, I feel like I'm going to pass out." He yawns widely. "Unless you need to talk? Because that was..." He pops another fry into his mouth and chews on it as he tries to find the right words. "A lot."

I set up my sleeping bag next to his, pausing to ruffle his hair before heading for the door. "No, I'm okay. Get some sleep."

He smiles sleepily and snuggles into his sleeping bag with his soggy paper bag cradled in his arms. "Night, Gem. I'm here if you need me," he whispers, his words slurring together as he finally succumbs to his caffeine crash.

I wander down the dark hallway toward a banging noise in the kitchen. Peering around the corner, I find Zoe standing over the stove. She yanks a large wooden spoon through a pot of something bubbling and phosphorescent as it spills over onto the burner, sending smoke spiraling into the cramped space. She coughs and mumbles something, waving her hand in front of her, trying to clear the air.

It's weird to see her like this, so... unkempt. Strands of light blonde hair have escaped her slicked-back ponytail, curling around her face chaotically. There's even a small, bright purple stain on her formerly spotless white t-shirt.

"Need a hand?"

She whirls around, her eyes round. But she recovers quickly, her face smoothing back into its usual calm mask. "No, I'm fine. You should go back to bed."

"I can't sleep."

"Can't? Or won't?"

"Both? Plus, I'm starving."

She grabs a lone towel and mops up the bright green liquid. It smells like a spring morning, but now with the sharp note of burned grass clippings. "Well, there's cereal or cereal. Or tea. Take your pick."

"Cereal it is, I guess, with a second course of tea."

Zoe points to the small pantry closet off to the side, where sure enough there are only two boxes of cereal and a small container of chamomile tea. I grab the cereal with mini marshmallows in it followed by the tea tin, while Zoe slides a bowl and spoon across the counter to me.

"Why don't you want to sleep?" she asks, pulling out the half-gallon of milk.

I find a chipped pink mug in one of the cupboards, then pour the cereal into my bowl. "Because it scares me," I say, sinking into one of the mismatched kitchen chairs. The honest answer tumbles out of me unexpectedly. Maybe it's the shock of seeing Charlotte's memories, or maybe I just want to say it out loud and have someone hear me.

"Nightmares?" she asks.

"No, more like the absence of them, the absence of everything. I don't sleep, not really. I go to this gray place, and..." I shudder, unable to find the words. "I don't like it."

Zoe doesn't press me for details. She fills a tea kettle and sets it on the stove next to her crusted-over pot before reaching for her leather bag. "Where's that brother of yours when I actually need him," she mumbles as she begins to dig. "I've got to figure out a better sorting system than this." Finally, she pulls a vial out of one of the many pockets, the glass winking under the glow of the kitchen lights. "Drink this," she says, tossing it to me.

I catch the bottle lightly in my hands. "No. I don't think you understand, I don't need a sleeping mixing. I don't need help falling asleep—"

"That's not what it's for." The tea kettle starts to whistle. Zoe pulls it off the burner and fills my mug with the tea bag in it.

"Remember at the diner when I told you I had something to help with anxiety?" She points at the bottle held in my grip. "You've been having panic attacks, right?"

She says it so matter-of-factly, like of course I'd be having panic attacks.

I swallow and try to ignore the heat spreading across my cheeks as shame sinks its claws into me, squeezing my stomach. "Kind of. Only a few times."

"'Only a few times' is a few times too many. They're awful."

"*You* have panic attacks?"

She frowns at me. "Why do you say it like that?"

"I don't know," I mumble. "You just seem so put together. On top of things. Fearless, even."

She snorts. "Trust me, I'm far from fearless, and I'm not quite as put together as you think I am. Yes, I have the occasional panic attack. Enough times that I had to make a mixing to help with them." She nods toward the small glass vial in my hand. "Go ahead."

I give her one last skeptical look, and she puts her hands on her hips. "Listen, if I were trying to poison you, I would've done it already, and don't you think I might've been a little more subtle about it? Come on, give me a little credit."

"Fair point," I say with a laugh. I take another look at the contents swirling in the bottle, the liquid a bright clear blue the color of a cloudless sky at noon. *What would it be like*, I think to myself, *to not feel so afraid?* I uncork it with my thumb and swallow it down in one gulp.

The liquid is cool and sweet, but with a tangy aftertaste that's sour like a lemon. I drop the bottle on the table.

I know I'm sitting here in the kitchen with Zoe, but I'm also far away, lying on my stomach at the end of Oliver's bed. He's sitting up on the other end with a book in his lap as he reads out loud to me. I couldn't tell you the color of his shirt or the angle of the sun as it filters through the window. I can't even pick out the words he's saying as he reads, just the tenor of his voice and the way he stops and laughs, sometimes nudging me with his foot when he gets to his favorite part.

I could only describe it as the feeling of perfect contentment, of home. My chest heaves as I breathe in deeply for the first time all night, all week, all month.

After a moment, the sound of Ollie's voice fades away and the kitchen comes back into focus. Zoe's hunched over the stove again, carefully stirring the steaming pot.

I rub my stinging eyes with the back of my hand and sniff, grateful for the relative privacy she's given me to collect myself. "What was that stuff?" My throat is so tight, I can barely get the words out.

She doesn't turn around, but answers, "It's a mixing to help calm your body down. It helps you remember a place or a time when you felt safe."

"Thank you," I say quietly. "It's lucky you had that."

Zoe turns around and gives me a pointed look. She fiddles with the spoon in her hands. "It's not luck. I always carry that with me. I don't just struggle with panic attacks; I struggle with my magic sometimes." She sighs and gently sets the spoon down. "When I was Claimed as a Mixer, it felt like a sick joke from the universe. Almost like a punishment after what had happened to my dad. I was afraid to use my magic for a while, afraid I would hurt someone like I did before." She clears her throat. "Anyway, I've noticed how you act around magic. You're tense, like you don't trust it. It reminds me of the way I feel sometimes. So, I thought it might help."

You're tense, like you don't trust it.

Suddenly, I do feel tired. A bone-aching tiredness that I'm unconvinced a good night's sleep will help with. "Well, thank you."

"You're welcome. But you don't always need a mixing to access those memories, you know. Sometimes all you need to do is remember."

As if remembering is that easy.

I wolf down my cereal and rinse my bowl out in the sink. "Has Charlotte ever shown you those memories, the ones she showed us tonight?" I ask before picking up my mug of tea to take with me back to my room.

"No, she hasn't, she's just told me about some of them. That was a big act of magic. She doesn't normally use her casting that way."

Again, I want to ask. Again, Zoe offers me nothing but a small smile. She turns back to her pot on the stove. "Goodnight, Gemma."

"Night."

That calm feeling from the mixing is still sliding through me, clinging to my thoughts and keeping my breathing slow and even. But as I sit on my sleeping bag and slowly sip my hot tea and listen to Milo snore, I still don't have it in me to face the gray place yet.

So I wait until I hear Zoe clean up the kitchen and turn the light off, listening for the pad of her footsteps as she takes the other room at the end of the hall.

I open my door and walk back into the kitchen, facing the back door. The glass sliding door looks out onto a tiny backyard walled off with a cement block fence. There's a small patio and one crooked-looking folding chair.

It's not much, but it's outside, and that's exactly what I need right now.

CHAPTER THIRTY

GEMMA

I LEAN BACK in the plastic patio chair and close my hands around the warm mug, letting its heat seep into my skin. Sliding my phone out of my pocket, I call my mom. Even though it's late, she answers on the first ring.

"Gem?" A sigh of relief. "Are you guys okay?"

"Yeah, Mom, we're fine."

"You don't sound fine."

I breathe into the phone, pressing it hard against my cheek. "Today's just been different than I expected. I'm tired, that's all."

"How's Charlotte? Do you want to talk about it?" Her voice tiptoes around the question, curious and hesitant.

"I do. But not right now. Raincheck?"

"Always." She does a good job of hiding her disappointment. I almost believe her.

"I guess I just wanted to hear the sound of your voice." I press my palm against my eyes as the stinging feeling of trying not to cry clings to my nose and throat.

"Oh, Gemma girl," she says, sounding too far away and right next to me all at once. "I miss you too."

I tell her I'll call back tomorrow, and she reminds me to stay safe. After we hang up, the quiet of the backyard feels heavy and thick. There's not even the sound of crickets or the breeze stirring the solitary tree on the other side of Charlotte's fence, just the sound of my own thoughts. I can't decide if calling my mom made me feel better or worse.

Looking up at the handful of visible stars, I breathe into the stillness of the moment, trying not to let my mind wander to its darkest corners, the places where my fear likes to hide.

I can tell when Zoe's calming mixing has officially worn off, because the fears come out, as they always do, pressing and demanding and far louder than any of my best intentions. It happens slowly at first, one thought at a time, until soon enough it's all I can think about.

What if we never get him out?

What if I never see him again?

What if I fail?

what

if

I rub my face with one hand and tighten my grip on my mug with the other, willing myself to stop, to change the channel and think of something other than my past failures or future worries. Zoe's parting words to me echo through my mind: *"You don't always need a mixing to access those memories, you know. Sometimes all you need to do is remember."*

I try to think about Ollie reading to me, to capture that feeling of safety in the sound of his voice once again, but it's harder on my own; the details are too fuzzy for me to hold on to. I straighten in my seat, take another sip of tea, and try again, but this time my visualization is interrupted by a sudden question. It pokes and prods at my memory until the sunlit picture of Ollie and me deflates like a sorry balloon on its last legs.

When was the last time I was happy? Like truly and unabashedly happy. Content. Enamored. Thrilled to be here on this earth just so I could live in that one moment.

My back stiffens against the patio chair. *Won't it hurt?* I ask myself. *To remember such a feeling? To let myself be that happy again?*

I grit my teeth against my loud and annoying internal argument, feeling tired of myself and my inability to get past this fear and move on. I clutch the warm mug between my fingers and think about what Ollie would say. I imagine his brow furrowed over his glasses, his mouth puckered as he thinks. In less than a second, I have my answer. Because Oliver—careful, methodical, wonderful Oliver—would say, *"But isn't happiness always a risk? Isn't it a risk worth taking?"*

Even in my imagination, I have to grudgingly admit that he's right. Of course he's right. So with a sigh, I close my eyes and search for that moment of happiness, the last time I felt free.

It doesn't take me long.

I think back to my last kiss with Ollie. It was at the bonfire, right before Milo caught us and James showed up. The final seconds before everything changed. For the briefest moment, it was just the two of us tucked into the shadows of the desert, under the light of a silvery half-moon.

I was uncertain about so many things that night. Basically, about everything except Ollie. And in between moments of magic that confused me and all the other feelings I didn't understand, I could be with him and feel like myself—even *more* than myself.

It was happiness. True, unabashedly contented happiness. I was enamored, not just with Ollie, but with who he saw when he looked at me. In a moment like that, it was easier to believe in her, that girl that he loved.

In me.

I was happy to be on this earth just so I could live in that one moment.

I inhale deeply as the memory grows clearer. *One, two, three...* I hear the muffled sounds of the wood crackling in the bonfire and the muted tones of our friends talking in the background as I search for him. *Four, five, six...* I see a flash of blue eyes and an answering grin; I see every glittering star in the sky. *Seven, eight, nine...* I feel my heart pounding unevenly as I hide behind the tallest cluster of saguaros, their shadows looming overhead as I bounce up and down on the heels of my feet in anticipation, waiting for him.

Ten. I exhale.

The moment I see his dark silhouette lit by the fire behind him, I reach for him. His hand is warm, both foreign and familiar, the feel of his skin on mine sending a shock through my fingers. I run my hands up the length of his arms to the solid feel of his shoulders, tracing the lines of his neck and winding my fingers in his hair.

Ollie smiles at me, one side of his mouth tipping higher than the other. His hands grip my waist as he leans in, his eyes closing at the last possible second as if he still can't believe I'm real and this is really happening. And at the moment just before his lips touch mine, I feel it—that spark searing through my chest, warm and wild and true.

Happiness.

It's so real I can taste it. I can feel his breath against my cheek. I can smell the clean scent of his soap, like sunshine and citrus. My shoulders droop as the image grows sharper because with that surge of happiness comes the other side—the regret and the sorrow, the missing and the wishing.

I wish I would've known it was our last kiss. I wish I would've stopped and appreciated the moment for what it was, right then and there. I wish I would've never let it end.

I wish.

Tears roll down my cheeks and onto my t-shirt, dampening the fabric. I give a shuddering breath, one of those hiccupping, staggering things that always reveal how much you've been crying, and as I struggle to breathe, there's a sudden tugging sensation right in the middle of my chest. My eyes fly open.

When I see what it is, my breath catches. My heart completely stops. I drop my mug in surprise, and it shatters on the patio.

There's a single silver thread, trailing out of my chest in a straight line, through the yard and out beyond, farther than I can see. I nearly fall out of the weather-worn lawn chair at the sight of the glistening strand, which looks like it was spun from starlight itself.

Familiar and foreign, just like Ollie.

The small yard is quiet as I sit there and stare at this small piece of magic, this strange gift that appeared out of midair. My hand hovers over it, pausing just before my fingers graze it. I want to take hold of it, to see where it will take me, but I'm so terrified I don't know if I can summon the courage to move the necessary inch.

But isn't happiness always a risk? Isn't it a risk worth taking?

I release a breath and let my hand fall, carefully wrapping my fingers around the silver thread.

The moment I touch it, shadows darken on my right and left, tall and smokey as they grow, then solid as they settle into their shapes. The saguaros. I stare up at them, my mouth hanging open. My feet land on the scattered gravel, my sneakers slipping as they come to rest on the ground. Every second the picture grows clearer until even the moon is bright in the sky, the stars like scattered diamonds. My lungs fill with the smell of smoke and the surrounding creosote bushes, their scent like the desert after rain.

I gasp as I turn in a circle in disbelief, my hands gripping the cotton fabric of my white sundress, which flutters around my knees. Charlotte's tiny patio with its rickety chair and sliding glass door is gone, and there's no house behind it for me to return to. I'm in the desert, in my mountains, and it's just like I remembered, but somehow shinier and more vivid than it could ever be in real life. The sky flickers at the edge of the bonfire, where smoke spirals into the air, clouding the view of the valley's twinkling city lights. And when I turn around—

He's there, smiling at me.

"Ollie!" I cry out, throwing my arms around him and squeezing him tightly to me. My face burrows into his chest as his arms wrap around me, holding me close. I breathe him in, choking down another sob that's rising up my throat. "Ollie."

"Shh," he says near my ear, glancing quickly over his shoulder, like he's checking to make sure he wasn't followed.

"What's wrong?" I ask, peering behind him to see who he's

looking for. Then my awareness flickers on like a lightbulb over-head. Milo. If this is the night of the bonfire, Ollie was worried about Milo finding us. He'd wanted to tell my brother the truth, but I'd wanted to keep Ollie to myself for just a little longer. Guilt sours my stomach; I'd dragged Ollie out here under the false promise of "maybe tomorrow."

But when Ollie looks down at me, he relaxes. His eyes aren't worried anymore. They melt into mine, burning a trail down the entire length of my body. I shiver against the feeling, and his arms tighten around me. I don't know what kind of magic this is, but I can barely bring myself to ask a single question, not when he's looking at me like that.

"I can't believe you're here. Is this actually happening, or have I completely lost it?" I murmur, too relieved to see him, to touch him, to feel his solid realness that I'm not even sure if I want to hear his answer. "Or maybe I fell asleep. Maybe I'm finally dream-ing again." I place my hands on either side of his face, turning him this way and that. "This is a very good dream," I say with a grin, letting the sudden euphoria wash over me. I even giggle for what feels like the first time in years.

Ollie smiles back as he leans in, but just before our lips touch, he pauses, his brow puckering in that way it always does when he's confused. "Wait, that's not what you said last time," he says, step-ping back to examine me. "In fact, you didn't say much at all, we just—"

"We just what?" I ask innocently, tracing the shape of his lips with my finger. It feels strange and wonderful and so unbelievably normal to tease him. "Did *this*?" I try to kiss him again, but he continues to hold me at arm's length, frowning down at me.

"This doesn't make sense," he mumbles, more to himself than to me. "I must be creating a new version of the memory or some-thing. But how... Carmen? Are you there?" he asks skeptically, his frown deepening as he tugs on a silver thread caught in his hand, shimmering just as brightly as the one that led me here. He tugs, and I feel the movement in my chest.

I reach out and catch his hand, looking more closely at his thread. Suddenly my dream theory doesn't seem quite so believable. "Ollie, what is that? Wait, and who's Carmen? Where are you?"

He doesn't answer. He peers around, squinting out at the surrounding desert as if he's looking for something, but his gaze keeps darting over to mine like he can't bear to look away from me for more than a second.

"Oliver!"

"You didn't say any of this last time," he says, still eyeing me curiously. "And the memories never go off script, I'm the one who usually changes something—"

I put a finger over his mouth, and he stills. "Oliver Cade, I need you to tell me something. Is this real?" Hope blossoms in my chest, tender and fragile like an early spring bloom searching for the sunlight. "Or have I gone completely crazy and started hallucinating? Please tell me this is real." My fingers dig into the faded blue t-shirt on his back as I pull him closer to me. "You feel real." I lean my head against his chest and close my eyes, listening to the steady rhythm of his heartbeat. "You sound real."

Ollie makes a noise of disbelief. "But... how?" He raises a hand to my face and traces the outline of my cheekbone, his hand shaking. He traces my eyelids, my nose, and finally my lips. "There's no way my memories are this good."

"I'm *not* a memory, Ollie. It's really me. Here, I'll prove it to you." I step back and take his hands in mine. He willingly complies, his fingers intertwining with mine, his face in a daze like someone who's sleepwalking their way through a dream. "Do you remember the last thing you said to me that night in the Dreamscape?" He nods, still mesmerized. "You told me you love me. Remember?" My voice breaks on the word. "Well, you didn't give me much of a chance to respond after that, so I have something to say to you." My heart stutters, and for the slightest second, I wonder if I'll chicken out.

Ollie's focus sharpens. He stares at me, one of his dark eyebrows rising like a question mark. I smile and squeeze his hands, feeling every ounce of my nervousness disappear, and in its place a steadiness that I haven't felt in a very long time. "What I wanted to say, and what I should've said a long time ago was this: I love you too, Ollie. Always have—"

He cuts me off before I can finish, his lips warm and pressing as they crash into mine. It feels like a first and last kiss all wrapped into one. It's the kind of kiss that's made of worry and relief and wanting—so much wanting.

My pulse races as I breathe him in and hold him tightly to me, willing him to please, *please*, just stay with me. His hands circle my waist, his fingers flexing as he tugs me closer. I can feel his heart pounding against mine, the silver thread held between us thrumming along with every beat. It sounds like a song, like the best thing I've ever heard.

And finally, finally...

I feel like I am home.

CHAPTER THIRTY-ONE

OLLIE

I HAVE NO clue what's happening right now and about a million questions running through my mind, but for once I'm not going to stop and ask for answers.

Gemma's hands tug on my hair, her lips urgent against mine. Part of me doesn't want this kiss to end—ever. Part of me just wants to exist in this moment and watch it slowly unfold for the rest of my life. But the other part of me—the bigger and hopefully wiser part of me—knows that a single moment with Gemma will never be enough. The bigger and wiser and greedier part of me wants *more* moments like this. A lifetime of them.

My hands splay across her back, my fingers caught in the fabric of the white dress she wore on the last night I saw her. My lips move against hers in a desperate attempt to communicate, to show her even the tiniest glimpse of how much she means to me and how much I've missed her.

Gemma must understand my unspoken words because she wraps her arms around me even tighter, making it impossible for me to back away. As if I'd want to.

I might never want this kiss to end, but I'm still having a hard time believing that it's actually real—that *she's* real—and that she's here with me. Finally, I pull back and take her face in my hands, memorizing the light smattering of freckles across her cheeks. "How is this even possible?"

And how much time do we have left?

"I don't know," Gemma says, her voice coming out more than a little breathless, her gaze still trained on my mouth.

"Is this all happening inside my head? Do I just have an exceptionally creative imagination?"

She tilts her face up, laughing into the sliver of space between us. "I've missed you so much," she whispers, tipping her forehead against mine. "But you're not *that* creative, Ollie."

Even though we've gone off script, the memory hasn't started to shift or dissolve around us quite yet. Instead, everything around me glows even brighter—the stars shining overhead, the flash of the bonfire in the distance, the big brown eyes that I love so much.

But all of it feels temporary like it's made of glass, fragile and fleeting. Like even the slightest misstep will shatter the illusion and send us tumbling. In the quiet of the desert night, caught in the middle of a moment from our past, there's a sense of urgency coloring every detail that wasn't there the first time we lived through it.

I can almost hear the ticking of a clock counting down the seconds.

Even when I hold time in my hands, it's always in short supply.

"Can't I just, I don't know, bring you back with me? Right now?" she asks halfheartedly, like she's too scared to get her hopes up any higher. But even still, she pulls on my hand, tugging me toward her as if she could just pull me right through time and space and into her arms.

But I feel the impossibility of it, this slapped-together plan of hers. Even while I'm here in this memory with her, I can feel myself elsewhere too, with magical constraints wrapped around me like invisible shackles. I run my fingers through her hair, pulling it back from her face. "As much as I wish it would, I don't think that's going to work."

Gemma scowls and shakes her head, "But where *are* you? I saw the Dreamscape break, you fell through the floor, and then you were just... gone."

I release a deep breath, kneading my forehead with my knuckles. I don't even know where to begin. "You know Alice in Wonderland?"

"Well, yeah."

"It's been a lot like that. You know, down the rabbit hole and everything."

She shivers, tucking herself more firmly against my chest. "But are you safe?" she asks, tilting her head up to look at me more closely. I feel her whole body tensing up as if she's just waiting to hear the worst.

I look away, letting the ends of her hair trail across my fingertips. "As safe as anyone who's trapped inside a magical time warp with no beginning or end could ever be." I try to smile, but my mouth only quirks briefly before falling flat. I don't want to tell her how afraid I've been, or that at any possible moment, I could get lost at sea, set adrift inside my own memories. My arms tighten around her, my hands tracing the shape of her waist. "But really, I'm okay." Because for the first time since I let her go, that statement finally feels like it has the potential to be true.

How can I let fear win when she's standing right here in front of me, making the impossible seem possible?

"Good," she chokes out as she turns away, her breathing hitching; I can feel the moisture from her tears soaking through my t-shirt. "To say I've been worried doesn't even begin to cover it."

My thumb trails across Gemma's cheek. She tips her head, kissing my palm. There's something different about her, something a little quieter. Even though she looks the same as she did before, she seems older now. She's less fidgety and more grounded in the moment. Or maybe it's the set of her mouth or the slight wariness in her eyes, as if she's realized the world isn't quite as bright and shiny as she'd once thought it was. But it feels like too much too soon, like a highly concentrated dose of growing up.

It's not a bad sort of different, but it's different all the same. I hate that there are things I wasn't there for. I hate that I had to miss anything at all.

"Gem, are you okay?"

She swallows and glances down, but I reach out and tip her chin up with my knuckle until she looks back up at me. "I think so," she murmurs. I take her hand and squeeze it in mine, giving her the space to say more if she wants to. She closes her eyes and releases a heavy breath, her fingers tight around mine. "For a while there, I wasn't sure if I'd ever be okay again."

"And now?"

She opens her eyes to look directly at me. A soft smile, like the remnants of one of her old grins, stretches across her face. "And now I'm starting to think that maybe I will be okay. That maybe I'll be even better than okay. Someday, at least." She kisses the tips of my fingers. "You know, something about you seems different," she says, placing her hands on my shoulders and turning me from side to side as she examines me. "You seem... older somehow."

I laugh and pull her to me, resting my cheek against the top of her head. "I was just thinking that exact same thing about you."

We're quiet for a moment as we listen to each other breathing into the silence. The wood from the bonfire cracks nearby, the cloud of smoke obscuring the stars overhead, the distant chatter of people around the fire acting as our soundtrack. I look over the top of Gemma's head, still half-expecting the memory to start collapsing at any possible moment, to have her slip through my fingers like the smoke of the fire, hazy and out of reach.

There's just too much to say. I want to plan; I want to scheme. I want to figure out exactly how to bring me home, but I know we don't have enough time left. We've already stolen too much. "How did you find me, Gem?" I ask, my voice taking on a despairing edge. "What brought you here?"

"Well, it wasn't exactly on purpose," she admits. She trails her hand up and down the length of my forearm and tells me how she was sitting outside and thinking about our last kiss. "I finally let myself think about it even though it hurt."

I know that feeling all too well. It's a question I've asked myself too many times to count—what's more painful, remembering or forgetting?

"And when I thought about you and me out in the desert that night," she steps back, looking down and gesturing to the delicate thread trailing out of her chest, glimmering gossamer under the light of the half-moon, "*this* appeared out of nowhere."

I hold up the silver thread still laced between my fingers. "It's a memory," I say softly, showing how her thread connects to mine. "It's the memory of our last kiss."

"So we were both thinking about the exact same moment at the exact same time?" Gemma whispers, hesitantly looping the thread around her hand, her voice tinged with awe. "That's how we found each other?"

I nod and kiss her again quickly, just because I can. "We were Remembering, Gemma. It's a type of magic."

I can't help but think of Lillian's explanation to me. *"All memories are magic, Oliver. Every word said, every touch given, every sunrise and sunset. Every single moment is magic manifested, we just refuse to see it."*

"Remembering?" She tries and fails to raise one eyebrow. I chuckle and trace the shape of it with my finger. "I guess memories really *are* magic," she says, looking mystified. "Zoe was right."

"Who's Zoe?"

"She's—" Gemma pauses, suddenly unsure. "She's a friend of your mom's, Ollie. She's a friend of Charlotte's." My heart stutters and stops. "That's actually where Milo and I are right now. We're at Charlotte's house in California. And your mom—" She stumbles over her wording, shaking her head bemusedly. "I mean, your mom, as in Teresa, is the one who helped us find her."

My mouth opens and closes uselessly a few times. I don't know how to respond. It's just too much to process. "Are my parents okay?"

"As okay as any mom and dad with a son who's trapped inside a magical time warp with no beginning or end could ever be," she says, running her nose along the length of my jaw. "But they're surviving."

My mind ping-pongs back and forth. I have so many questions that I can't ask a single one.

Tick-tock, tick-tock.

"I know," Gemma says quickly, scanning my face. "It's a lot to take in. But I think you'll like Charlotte." She gives me a small smile. "Actually, you're going to love her. And we're all doing everything we can to bring you back home."

This. This is what I've been missing. The familiarity of someone who knows me and knows exactly what to say. Gemma's reassurance is comforting; it's like being held but with words rather than arms.

"I can't wait to meet her," I finally manage to say. "I can't wait to come home."

If we say it enough times, will that make it real? If we wish hard enough, will that create a magic all of its own?

"And you will."

"How's Milo?" I feel a twinge of guilt for not remembering to ask sooner.

"He misses you, of course. And he's a little different too," Gemma says, one corner of her mouth dipping into a frown. "But somehow still the same." She starts to say something else but then catches her bottom lip between her teeth before the words can get out.

"What is it?" I ask, my heart thudding unevenly.

"There's something wrong with his magic," she blurts out. "Libby's too. The Claimings are broken, Ollie. No one's getting Claimed, but the magic is still trying to release. And everybody else..."

Closing my eyes, I picture the stars of the Dreamscape flickering out one by one. I force myself to say the words. "Everybody is losing their magic?"

"We don't know yet. We're trying to figure that out. But tell me more about where you are. What can we do to—"

The silver thread stretches tightly between us, vibrating like a guitar string that's just been strummed. Gemma looks down at it and grimaces, rubbing a hand over her chest. "I feel... I feel weird." She clutches her head. "Ugh, do you hear that ringing sound?"

The silver thread hums a single piercing note like the sound of an alarm ringing out. A warning bell. Everything about the scene that was once so crisp and clear has started to blur like an unfinished watercolor painting dripping down a canvas. Soon all that will remain are splotches of color and leftover feelings—a memory dissolved and quickly abandoned.

The pit in my stomach intensifies as Gemma's outline grows dimmer, her form wavering; she's vanishing right in front of me. "No," I breathe out, clutching her to me, "please don't leave." The thread tugs on my hand, jerking my arm back as it tries to pull me out of the memory.

A stick cracks behind me, and we both jump.

"Wait, *Milo?*" Gemma's voice rings with incredulity at the sight of her brother walking toward us, his back illuminated by the flames of the fire, his shadowed face hard and angry. "How did *you* get here?"

He ignores her question and instead asks one of his own. "How long?"

Gemma's nose scrunches. "How long—oh. The bonfire," she whispers out of the side of her mouth. "This is when Milo caught us."

"The memory is trying to get us back on track," I murmur in her ear. "Just play along."

The silver thread pulls on my hand again as the memory pulses around us, squeezing tightly against my skin like it wants to shape me to fit inside it. I'm like an insect about to be trapped in amber as the magic threatens to engulf me, to hold me here forever, undisturbed and properly preserved.

"How long?" Milo asks again, still glowering at the two of us. I wonder if he'll repeat the question until I give in and let the memory continue how it's supposed to.

"Since the Claiming." The words come uninvited into my

mouth like I'm being force-fed dialogue from my past. "But I've had feelings for Gemma for a long time."

"So you think that means you can just *lie* to me?" he says harshly, his face a mask of quiet fury.

Gemma elbows me out of the way. "Milo, *stop*," she says, holding her hands out in front of her. The memory shakes, the ground trembling under our feet. "You're right. I should've told you. You're my brother and I never should have kept a secret like this, knowing how much it would hurt you." She places a hand on his shoulder. "I'm so sorry."

My mouth pops open—that was not what she said last time. The last time she fought with Milo she was angry and defensive and scared. But not now. This time she's quietly determined, apologetic, and sincere. She's somehow managed to go completely off-script, and yet we're still here.

She grips the silver thread tightly in her hand, anchoring herself to me and the memory as she looks up at her brother. "But the truth is, I love Ollie and he loves me. Can't that be reason enough for us to act just a little bit stupid? Don't you think that's worth forgiving?" The thread flares brightly, a flash of silver against the night sky as the moment stretches on, taut, and on the verge of unraveling.

Finally, Milo sighs, his shoulders drooping in defeat as he folds his arms over his chest. He looks between the two of us, his mouth a grim line. "Yeah, I guess. I mean, I figured this would happen eventually. It was inevitable. And I can only drag my feet for so long." The memory flickers and his face fades in and out of view, his voice distorted like the sound of it's coming from somewhere far away.

Gemma gasps, turning to me. "That's exactly what he said to me in the car earlier today."

The memory shifts again, shuddering almost uncomfortably, like it isn't sure what to do with us now. Then, the silver thread splits in two.

We both scramble back as the thread diverges between us,

its ends crisscrossing delicately as it frays. Everything else in the memory has frozen, staying untouched and unchanged—Milo, the noise of our friends gathered around the fire, even the light breeze moving through the trees. It's like everything's holding its breath, waiting to see what will happen next.

It's a memory divided.

My hands twitch like they want to take hold of this new thread, this alternate memory in the making, with Gemma on one side and me on the other. If we let the thread continue to split like this, who knows where we'll end up?

I meet her eyes, and she bites her lip, unsure. But after a moment that couldn't have lasted longer than a second, she lifts her chin and gives me a stiff nod, because what other choice do we have?

I can't lose her again.

The new thread shocks my hand when I touch it. I hold onto the two separate ends and wonder *what now?* But even as I hesitate, my magic stirs in my chest, sending my hands into motion. I cross the two threads as I weave the silver strands together, each movement unexpectedly confident even though I really have no idea what I'm doing.

Lillian's voice rings in my ear like a whispered warning. Something she told me the first time I tried to change one of my memories. *"You cannot alter the past, Oliver. You cannot add to a memory that has already written itself. That will weave something different, something new. That is a magic few can comprehend."*

I tie another knot to finish it off, and the moment I do, the fraying ends start to change color. Slowly, it grows darker and darker until the woven thread is no longer silver but a stark and bleeding red.

Magic always has consequences.

Gemma jerks back. "Is that—no. I... I can't—" Gemma shakes her head back and forth, her hands scrambling as they tug at the thread trailing out of her chest. "Ollie," she says frantically, "drop the thread."

I stare down at the thread and fight the urge to let it go. "I can't," I plead. "What if I lose you again?" I think about the sea of memories waiting to drown me. I think about all its threads so unbelievably full of magic that I don't understand and probably never will.

Gemma doesn't say anything because, like me, she has no answers, but her wide eyes stay trained on mine, her chest rising and falling rapidly. The thread in my hands stretches from my fingers onto the desert floor, running through the gravel like a snake on the hunt for its prey. The back of my neck prickles as the new strands of the red thread wind through our memory, coloring everything in its wake a blinding shade of crimson.

The horizon has lightened from the inky black of night to the fiery red of a sudden sunrise—the dawning of a new day that never actually happened, a sky full of dangerous possibilities. We stumble back, both of us tripping over our feet and each other as we watch the thread paint the desert red, circling closer.

Tick-tock, tick-tock.

"Wait," I say, gripping Gemma's arm tightly. "What if we do it again? Meet in a different memory?"

Her shaking hand finds mine, her gaze fixed on the bloody sky. "Do you think that will work again?"

"Might as well try. I don't think we should stick around here." I try to make my voice sound more confident than I feel.

Gemma forces herself to look away from the tumult of red surrounding us, her mouth puckering as she thinks. "Do you remember that time we went running last summer, the night before our seventeenth birthday? I ran past your house and you followed me out to the trail. We raced up the mountain to watch the sunset—"

"Of course I remember."

"Meet me on the mountain," she says, her hand flexing around mine. "Right when I gave you an earbud to listen to music with me, just as the sun started to set." Her fingers start to loosen their hold. "I'll find you there."

My plan suddenly seems very, very stupid. "But what if it doesn't—"

"It *has* to work." She drops my hand and closes her eyes, turning her back on the red thread only inches away.

And then she's gone.

Immediately, I drop my end of the thread too. The blood-red sky and the desert beneath it vanish in a blink, and then I'm falling through the darkness and into my memories. I don't have time to think of my library, to imagine the shelves lined with books. No time to organize the threads into anything but their natural chaos.

The sea is worse than I remembered. With its churning shadows and roaring waves, it's completely uninhabitable. I try to stay calm, counting my breaths as the silvery threads swell, rising above me in a solid wave. In a blink, the wave breaks, and the threads crash into me, latching onto my clothes and my hair, tugging me down, down, down.

"I need a memory!" I call out just before the darkness swallows me, throwing my words out like an SOS signal; like I'm a ship about to sink into the depths of the sea. The waves rise up over my head, inundating me with broken pieces of sound and fragments of color. "July 22nd, sunset run with Gemma!" I shout out the memory because thinking it just doesn't seem like it will be enough. "The moment she handed me her headphones and—" My words cut off as the threads slam into me again.

Too many thoughts. Too many feelings.

Everything all at once.

I claw my way to the surface, concentrating on that single memory with everything I have. I think about the way the sun painted the sky in such fierce shades of yellow and orange—a golden hour so intense the afterimage of it stayed burned inside my mind with no chance of fading away. I picture Gemma sitting next to me on the outcropping of rocks, our feet dangling over the edge. Our arms brush against each other, gritty from the dust and dried sweat of our run. She slides her earbud in, handing the other one to me, her dark eyes locking onto mine.

I'll never forget how badly I wanted to kiss her at that moment.

I let the ache of that memory overwhelm me until it's all I can think about. Until a single thread rises up from the waves, an orange thread as fiery as the sky that night.

I grab onto it, and I Remember.

The first thing I notice is the solid feel of the rock under me, rough as it scrapes against my legs. The second thing is the music blasting from an earbud jammed into one of my ears. The guitars wail as I squint into the setting sun.

There's a movement on my right. I hold perfectly still with my heart jumping out of my throat, bracing myself for the crippling disappointment that will come once I realize that my plan has failed.

Gemma's sitting next to me, staring off at the sunset as she hums along to the song until suddenly she turns to me and says, "Ollie? Is that you?"

My sigh of relief nearly knocks me off the boulder and flat on the ground. I throw my arms around her, the skin of her shoulders brown and warm from too many hours spent swimming and running in the heat. "We did it. You found me."

She breathes me in, burrowing her face into my neck. "After I let the other memory go, I started thinking about this one. I just closed my eyes and imagined being here with you, every detail crystal clear, and when I opened my eyes—" She stops and points down to her chest, where another thread has emerged, glistening and orange; it looks as if it came straight out of her heart. "I was here. With you."

We stare at each other as the magic of two people thinking about the exact same moment at the exact same time washes over us once again. But within another breath, the moment breaks. The sunset shivers in the sky, the valley tilting on its side as it shakes, the brightness of the golden hour fading as the memory begins to fall apart.

Everything's unraveling. Again.

"Already?" Gemma asks, yanking her earbud out and leaning into me, the curve of her shoulder pressing against my chest. "But we just got here."

"Memories don't like to be messed with," I say, scrambling to my feet as the orange thread wraps around my hand, tying me to the moment with the open invitation to stay awhile.

When Gemma and I both arrived in the memory of our last kiss, it was like we'd caught the magic of the moment off guard. It wasn't prepared to have the two of us in there together like that, changing things, shaping reality to what we wanted it to be.

But now it's on to us. It's ready to shake us out of the memory unless we comply with what already came before: two friends on a sunset run, listening to music and pining unrequitedly.

"Where to next?" Gemma asks, pulling on the hem of my running tank as the ground shakes the gravel under our trail shoes.

My mind buzzes as it prepares to jump into another memory. But as I look at Gemma, her body tight with panic once again, I realize that we're just prolonging the inevitable. Sure, maybe we could hop into another memory and steal a few snatches of time together, but then what?

I don't want to only relive memories with Gemma, I want to make new ones.

"Gem, we have to let go."

Her gaze narrows, her hand tightening onto our thread. "Wait, what do you mean?"

"I mean, as much as I don't want to, we have to let go if we want to move forward." I grab hold of her arms and lean down so that my face is level with hers. "I *know* we can find a way out of this." As I say the words out loud, I feel the truth in them for the first time. "It's not just the threads that connect us, it's all of this." I point out to the memory collapsing around us, the hum of the threads growing louder with every passing second. "It's every moment we've ever spent together. It's our history. It's you and me. That's the kind of magic I can believe in."

A sob shakes loose from her chest, low and hopeless. She stands on her toes, leaning her forehead against mine, and says, "But I don't have any magic, Ollie. It's gone."

I smile at her, at the way she's practically radiating warmth and light and power. "I'm not so sure about that anymore. How could that possibly be true if you're standing here with me right now?"

The orange thread tugs on my hand again, an insistent reminder that our time is almost out. Gemma's face flickers, her features distorted.

"I have some things to figure out down here," I say. "There are things I need to fix, things that only I can do. We need to find the beginning. But here—" On a sudden impulse, I place my hand over my chest and close my eyes.

I need her to know. I need her to Remember with me.

I exhale and imagine a handful of threads, multi-colored and shimmering, falling into my hands, and when I open my eyes, that's exactly what I see. A collection of my memories ready to be Remembered. "Take these. Maybe this will help."

Gemma shakes her head, her eyes shining with unshed tears. "I can't take those Ollie, I don't know what to do with them—"

I lean in and kiss her as hard as I can, refusing to believe for a single second that this is our last one. No, this is just another moment to add to our history, a past as well as a future. I have to believe that. I shove the fistful of threads into her hands at the very moment the memory scatters completely.

I let go of the thread, but this time as I watch her fade away, her face frozen in fear, her lips pink from our kiss, it doesn't feel like a goodbye. I don't shout out any last words or immediately slip into regret the moment my hand comes up empty. Instead, I let go of our memory and picture my library with its endless halls and rows of books. Instead, I choose to believe.

It *is* magic, after all. And it's as real as I wish it to be.

"Okay, Carmen," I whisper, hoping her memory can hear me. "I'm ready. Take me back to the beginning."

CHAPTER THIRTY-TWO

GEMMA

"**O**LLIE!" WITH A gasp, I open my eyes to Charlotte's backyard, still as small and empty as it was before, only with one noticeable difference. This time, the early morning sun is shining, the sky a shocking shade of rose. I scoot the plastic patio chair back, the legs squeaking noisily as I jump to my feet. "Ollie," I say again, this time more softly.

I squeeze my eyes shut tight and try to imagine the sunset on the mountains again, the headphones dangling between us and our breath heavy from running. I picture it as vividly as I can, but when I crack one eye open, my shoulders droop in disappointment. I'm not back on the mountaintop with Ollie, I'm still standing here alone in Charlotte's backyard. "Come on, Ollie. Where are you?"

I clench my hands into fists, and that's when I realize they aren't empty—thin handfuls of threads trail through my fingers and wrap around my wrists. They're nearly translucent, like they've lost some of their color now that they're no longer a part of Ollie. They gently wave back and forth in an almost patient way, as if they had all the time in the world for me to notice them. I flinch, holding my arms out stiffly, unsure what to do.

The back patio door rolls open with a metallic scrape. "Hey, Gem, did you sleep out here?" Milo steps onto the patio with a yawn, still rubbing the sleep out of his eyes. "Man, you were right to skip those fries because, let me tell you, they did not sit well with me."

"Milo! I just saw Ollie."

He immediately snaps to attention, his head whipping back and forth as he scans the yard like he's expecting Ollie to pop out from behind the single scrawny tree. "Where?"

"This is going to sound crazy, but..." I hold out my hands, revealing the wriggling pile of threads still clutched in my grip. "I saw him inside a memory."

He stares at me blankly. "A memory... inside your empty hands?" he asks skeptically.

"*No*, look closer."

"Gemma, there's nothing—wait, what are *those*?"

I tell him about meeting Ollie inside the memory at the bonfire, about the magic that slowly unwound from inside my chest, leading me straight to him. I describe what it was like to see Ollie again, to know that he's okay, but I skip the parts about how it felt to have him holding me in his arms and the way I pressed my lips to his. No brother needs those kinds of gory details.

"Milo, it was the weirdest thing. Everything was exactly the way it was before, a perfect recollection. But it was *more* than just a memory. When we first found each other, we could talk about anything, not just what we'd said before—"

"But how?"

I chew on the inside of my cheek while I think. "It was almost like we'd found a secret passage, like an unmarked hallway on a map where we could do and say whatever we wanted. But then the map changed and the hallway opened up to the rest of the house, and we had to go back to the way things were—the same walls and structure as before." It's hard to find the words to describe what that felt like, how the memory kept pulling us back and insisting we be who we once were rather than who we are right now. "But then, the memory *changed*."

"And how exactly do you change a memory?" Milo asks, his brows knit together.

I pace back and forth on the patio with the threads still gripped tightly in my hands. "I don't know. But it was right at the moment when you showed up at the bonfire. You know, when you found Ollie and me together."

He clears his throat and looks down, the pain of that memory still evident like the yellowish hue of a partially healed bruise.

"But instead of letting it all play out again," I continue, "I just said what I wanted to say, what I *should've* said to begin with. I apologized to you."

Milo reels back. "That is *so* weird."

"What, that I said sorry?"

"No. It's weird because I had that exact same dream last night. I dreamt about the bonfire and seeing you and Ollie together," he says, holding my gaze. "But then you told me you were sorry, and that you and Ollie were acting like idiots because you love each other."

"But I didn't say we were idiots—"

"I'm embellishing a little," he says, his mouth lifting in a small smile. "Apology accepted, by the way."

I release a long-held breath; it's a lot easier to breathe without the heaviness of regret relentlessly pressing down on me. "That *is* weird."

"What, that I accepted your apology?"

I roll my eyes. "No. That somehow you were actually there, in the memory with us."

We both stare down at the handful of threads. Milo sighs. "Just when I think I'm starting to understand magic, something like this happens, and it makes me realize all over again that I obviously know nothing."

"Tell me about it."

"So, what happened after you changed the memory? Because that's where things get fuzzy for me. I don't remember anything else."

"Well, the thread—the memory—it split in two." I tell him how once the thread started to divide, Ollie took both ends in his hands and tied them together. But the next part is harder for me to say. I shuffle my feet and clear my throat while the sharp edge of panic grazes against the back of my neck, making me shiver. "And then the thread turned red."

I don't have to say anything else. Milo straightens and looks at me, his mouth set in a firm line. "Where's Ollie now?"

"I don't know," I say, my heart constricting painfully. "He let go of that thread—" Milo's shoulders sink in relief, "—and he said he had to fix something." I hold out my fistful of threads, their opaline sheen glistening in the early morning sun. "And then he gave me these. Any suggestions?"

The back slider door squeals open again, and Charlotte steps out with one of the leather-bound Caster Chronicles tucked under her arm. She looks much better than the last time I saw her; the color is back in her cheeks and her eyes are calm and bright. "Good morning. Are you two hungry, or—" Her question is cut off by the sound of rustling pages as the book starts to vibrate. She frowns, holding it out in front of her. "What on earth..."

The threads in my hands begin to vibrate along with the book, the motion pulling me toward Charlotte. As I take a step closer, their glowing intensifies, their light shining through the spaces in between my fingers. Without a word, she holds the Chronicles out to me. The book springs open, its pages fanning like the rippling of a wave before landing on a blank one in the middle.

Charlotte stiffens, looking bewildered. "I've read through this book hundreds of times, but I've never seen this page before."

"Whoa," Milo says softly. "Magic calls to magic. Just like Grandma always said." He nudges me closer and the threads flash brightly. "Go ahead. See what happens."

My heart pounds as I unwind one of the threads from my hand, its pulsing intensifying the closer I get to the book. I carefully place it on the empty page. Immediately, it spirals across the paper, twisting and turning into strange shapes and patterns until it slows down, and words appear like cursive slanting across the page. The three of us peer down at the book in wonder as the thread continues to scrawl out words as if an invisible hand is writing them out. The handwriting is achingly familiar.

"*Ollie*," Milo and I say at the same time.

Charlotte lifts a hand, hesitating over the page as if she wants to gently trace a finger along the curve of one of the letters, her expression a mix of wonder and profound sadness. "Looks like we have some reading to do."

She turns back into the house with Milo and I following behind her. Zoe's in the kitchen, standing over the stove once again. Next to her, the counter is piled high with various herbs and bottles full of neon-colored liquids. Charlotte carefully places the book in the middle of the small table, and the three of us huddle around it.

"What's going on?" Zoe asks, dropping her wooden spoon with a clatter onto the counter. She turns off the stove burner and walks over to us. "Oh. Wow."

Milo reaches a hand out to pick up the book, but Charlotte stops him. "Wait. I think it should be Gemma."

I quickly glance at Milo to gauge his reaction, but all he does is nod. "Sure, I just thought since—"

Charlotte shakes her head and nudges the book closer to me. "Gemma?"

I tuck the rest of Ollie's threads into one hand, taking a step back from the table and the three pairs of eyes scrutinizing me. "But I don't know how. My magic... It's gone..." I trail off, feeling uncertain.

I *saw* Ollie remove my magic that night in the Dreamscape. I *saw* him reverse the knot of my Claiming and felt my magic slowly drain from me, leaving me feeling empty and alone.

I saw it happen.

And yet...

I take a step back toward the table, my hand hovering over the page, the words shimmering under the shadow of my fingertips. Whenever I think about having any kind of connection to magic again, my breath snags in my throat. Every time I imagine it, all I see is a girl with red eyes, so consumed with magic that she lost herself.

I was that girl.

And yet...

As I waver over the page, wrestling with what to do, Ollie's words enter my mind, drowning out all my other thoughts. *"It's every moment we've ever spent together. It's our history. It's you and me. That's the kind of magic I can believe in."*

The room is quiet as I slowly let my fingers trail across the glimmering words. "It's you and me. I can believe in that too." I press my palm against the looping cursive and feel a sharp electric shock. There's a pulse under the page, just like the beating of his heart. "Show me," I say, closing my eyes, because the moment I pressed my hand to the page, I knew this was more than just a story to be read.

In the space between breaths, Charlotte's kitchen fades away, and I'm pulled into a different world, one made of Ollie's memories.

It starts under the stars of the Dreamscape.

He paces back and forth, muttering Scrabble words to himself as he circles the cavern, his quiet footsteps the only sound. Somehow, I know this is right after I vanished and Ollie was left alone in the Dreamscape. It's a strange feeling, eavesdropping on his memories like this. It's like I'm hovering right over him, watching it all unfold. I can see him, but more than anything, I can *feel* him. He's anxious and overwhelmed, his pulse racing and his palms sweating. He's nervous that he's made the wrong choice, and he's angry that he even had to make the choice to begin with.

But mostly he's scared to be alone. And he misses me.

All of his emotions come crashing into me at full speed; it's like going from zero to sixty in less than a second. The weight of his memories combined with my own thoughts and feelings makes me want to fold under the pressure, to curl up in bed and never pick my head off the pillow again—it's just too much.

But Ollie gave me these memories—these small pieces of magic, these big parts of who he is—for a reason. So I square my shoulders and steady my breathing, holding onto the knowledge that he already made it through this, and so can I.

I watch as Ollie struggles against not only his magic but mine too. How it latches onto him, pinning him down like a fly in a spider's web. I watch as he battles his demons, the ones that hiss in his ears, *"She wanted the magic more than she wanted you."*

The guilt that washes over me is so intense I'm practically choking on it. "That's not true," I whisper at the same time Ollie does. "It's not."

And then I watch as all the fight seeps out of him, how he finally gives in and lets the magic—mine and his—completely take him over. He rises into the air, suspended by the silver threads that bind him. His eyes are white and his face is blank, and the only time he speaks is when he repeats the words, *"Tied and bound, I seal your fate,"* as he marks the threads with his blood to tie off the Claimings.

I've never seen anyone look so lost. It's haunting. It's everything I'd been imagining and worse.

It's hard to tell how much time passes, but, eventually, there's a flash of color off to the side. A streak of purple across the starry sky followed by the scent of lavender and sage and something sweet. "Chocolate," I say to myself. "It's Grandma."

Ollie's fingers wrap around her thread, and when they do, his eyes flash blue. He gasps like someone who's been holding his breath for too long and shakes his head like he's trying to clear it. And that's when he remembers. Who he is, what he's doing, and who he's missing. He remembers me.

He looks down at all the threads surrounding him, at the purple thread caught in his grasp. *"Ollie, let them go,"* he hears her voice inside his mind. *"Let them all go."*

So he does.

He drops the threads and lands on his feet, and the Dreamscape shakes like it's on the verge of collapsing. "I'm done," he says firmly. "Find someone else."

Then the memory goes dark.

When I open my eyes, I'm greeted by the sight of light pouring through Charlotte's kitchen windows and Zoe, Milo, and Charlotte all staring at me. "How long was I gone?" I ask, squinting back at them.

"Like, maybe 45 seconds?" Milo says with a little laugh.

"That's it?" It felt like I was wrapped in Ollie's memory for hours, days even. "That was... that was incredible." I sink down into the kitchen chair next to me. "And awful and strange and overwhelming and just so... Oliver." I look down at the other threads of memories in my hand, these little gifts so unexpected and rare. I'm already anxious to start the next one, but first I slide the book over to Milo. "See for yourself."

He eagerly places his hand on the page and closes his eyes. Less than a minute later, he's blinking at us in amazement. "He's okay. He's really okay." Milo looses a shaky breath as he slumps into the chair next to mine and puts his arm around my shoulders. "And no offense, Gemma, but your Dreamscape letter really did not do that place justice. Your descriptions were average at best. It's just so—so... I mean, it's—wow."

"There really aren't words, are there?" I say, remembering how it felt the first time I saw the endless stars and the countless threads spilling out of them.

"I guess not." Milo pushes the book across the table toward Charlotte and Zoe. They look at us and then at each other before each putting a hand on the worn page. A single tear rolls down Charlotte's cheek, but by the time the memory has finished and she opens her eyes, it's gone.

"So that's Oliver," she says quietly, her hand still pressed against the Chronicles. And I realize right then and there that that's the first time she's seen her son in seventeen years. "Is he..."

"Really that neurotic? Most definitely," Milo cuts in.

We all laugh, and Charlotte wipes her nose on her sleeve. She glances at me, and I give her an encouraging smile. I pull out another thread, placing it gently on the following page, and another memory writes itself out, the words quick and urgent.

This time, we all put our hands on the page at the same time. And we Remember.

We go through all of Ollie's memories like this, one at a time. We watch as he refuses to tie the Claimings, how he falls through the center of the Dreamscape and ends up on the other side, swimming through a terrifying sea made of fierce and flowing threads. And I don't have to imagine how scary it was for Ollie; I get to experience that firsthand. I feel his frustration, his bafflement, his never-ending sense of wonder. Even when he's afraid, he never stops marveling at it all.

It's exhausting. I never feel like I have a chance to catch my breath.

We watch as he falls through memory after memory until he's completely tangled in them. When Lillian is the one to pull him back out, I'm surprised to see her again, just as Ollie is, but I feel an immense sense of relief at the sight of her familiar face: he's not alone anymore.

She tells him about the magic of memories and how she needs him to help her repair what's been broken. How they need to search for the beginning.

My heart thrums as I watch Lillian's Claiming unfold, my eyes widening when the Threaders take magic from each of the Claimed in the circle, using it to open a portal to the Dreamscape. It's something I've wondered about for such a long time. It's strange to watch how things used to be, to see how the Threaders worked seamlessly together, everyone celebrating the myth of their magic. It leaves the bitter taste of jealousy in my mouth.

Curses and Claimings and all the other lost things of magic—it's a lot to take in.

But even while all this is happening, Ollie's attention is divided. There's another thread—a black one, stark against the fallen snow—calling to him. *Oliver, Oliver,* the unfamiliar voice chants. The pulse of it reverberates through him, through me. Something about it is ancient and raw, but fragile too, like a story that's been told so many times the words have lost their meaning.

Ollie's gaze is dark and transfixed under the pale light of the moon. When he catches hold of the black thread, I hear a voice saying, *"We heard the tales when we were young. Of a power that made the sun rise and fall, that made a tree blossom after a harsh winter, or a baby cry as it took its first breath. A power that meant new life. But the stories never mentioned that if there is a power that brings life, there must also be one that brings death."*

I shudder against the memory of it, wishing I could close my eyes or cover my ears.

Whatever this is, I don't feel ready for it.

But then that memory fades, and I'm wandering the halls of Ollie's library with him, searching through the spines for something familiar and comfortable. He's reeling from the loss of Lillian and the fear of fading away, and he's distracted by the leftover smell of woodsmoke and the sounds of old magic—the memories of a girl named Carmen.

Ollie grabs a book off the shelf and a silver thread unwinds from inside it. And when he opens his eyes, he sees me out in the desert under a star-filled sky—the memory of our last kiss.

It's surreal to feel everything he's experiencing layered on top of what I'm feeling too—his elation at finding me, his dread that he'll have to let me go again. But it's his all-encompassing love that I'm not prepared for. The magnitude and depth of it leave me feeling overwhelmed and more than a little confused.

But why? I keep asking myself. *Why does he love me this much?*

It would be easy to question the validity of it all. To sink into self-pity disguised as self-deprecation and say, *who am I to deserve something as good as this*?

It would be easy, but I have the magical advantage of knowing both Ollie and myself—every thought and emotion. And while I struggle with feeling worthy of something as spectacular as being loved by someone like him, he's currently wrestling with the exact same worries as me.

Who am I to deserve something as good as this? he asks himself as his hand cups my cheek.

So maybe that's all love is: a lucky shot in the dark—a hope and a wish and a little bit of magic. Two people choosing to make the impossible become true; two people deciding to deserve each other.

We watch as Ollie fades away along with the memory of our sunset run in the mountains, the desert shifting until it becomes Charlotte's dingy kitchen once again. The four of us blink in the bright light, blinding after the rosy glow of a sun nearly gone. We all startle when the book flutters its pages once again, flying through the rest of the spells and the history until it lands on another blank page.

I look at my empty hands. "There aren't any threads left," I say to Charlotte, Zoe, and Milo, but also to the waiting book. "That was the last of the memories he gave me." The page ripples like the undercurrent of a river, looking more alive than any piece of paper ought to.

"You see that too, right?" I ask, elbowing Milo. "The page is—"

"Moving," he finishes. "Like there's something underneath, something *inside* that's trying to get out."

I remember saying the same thing back in the library of our house when I was looking at the Caster Chronicles with Aunt Libby and Milo. I remember when Ollie and I touched the book, silver threads unwound from its center. They danced across the page as if they were trying to write us a message, the words appearing in an instant before vanishing just as quickly.

"Maybe this is part of what Ollie needs to fix," I say, my fingers hovering over the page as I watch it move. "A memory that still needs to be found." With a held breath, my hand lightly presses against the book. But nothing happens. I grit my teeth against the sudden and grating sensation of disappointment.

"These Chronicles have always had a life of their own," Charlotte says, closing the book and resting her hand on the worn cover. "It's just that we get in the way sometimes." Her face looks shadowed and far away, her chair creaking as she flops down into it. "I'm beat."

"Me too," I say, tipping wearily onto my own seat. Watching all of Ollie's memories like that couldn't have taken more than ten minutes, but I feel as tired as if I've just pulled another energy drink-fueled all-nighter. Milo blinks at me blankly, looking just as exhausted as I feel.

Zoe leans over to grab four mismatched glasses from the cupboard. "Here," she says, pouring a bottle of bright clear liquid into each one and sliding them over to us.

"What is it?" Milo asks, mustering what little energy he has to scowl at her. "Spiking our drinks again?"

She tries to snort but it sounds more like a sigh. "Just shut up and drink it. And you're welcome."

After watching Charlotte obediently drink her own cup, I tip the contents of the glass into my mouth. Instantly, the fizzing, floral-tasting liquid makes me feel more alert than I have in days. A steady stream of energy flows through me like I've just slept for two days straight and eaten nothing but green vegetables. A relieved laugh bubbles out of me as I look down into my empty glass. "I need a shot of this every morning. Wow."

Zoe sets her own glass on the table and shakes her head, her blonde hair swaying. "Too bad the more you drink it, the less effective it becomes. There's no substitute for the real thing, you know."

"No substitute for what?" Milo asks, shaking the last drops of his glass into his mouth.

"Oh, you know, *health*."

He waves her off with a flippant hand and turns to me. "So what now?"

My back stiffens as they look at me expectantly, but it's Charlotte who clears her throat. "Now I'll show you one last memory," she says. "The night my magic broke. The night I lost everything."

CHAPTER THIRTY-THREE
OLLIE

M Y FEET LAND on the gray-speckled industrial carpet of the library. I inhale the musty smell of old paper and ink, shoving the book containing the memory of my last kiss with Gemma back onto the shelf. I try not to notice how the spine is cracked with a jagged red line running down the length of it like a fresh wound, but it's pretty impossible to ignore. Just the sight of it sends my pulse racing.

Tick-tock.

I grip the cream-colored thread of my library tightly in my fist as I turn away from the shelf and start jogging down the aisle. "Carmen?" I call out. "Um, if you're listening, I'd like to see the memory you were trying to show me earlier. Please?"

It never fails to be polite, especially when you're dealing with unknown entities.

But there's no reply. The library is quiet except for the muffled sounds of my feet running down the length of the aisle. I pass title after title of my own memories, which offer no help to me other than the promise of the past. The rows upon rows of tidy books, all carefully cataloged and arranged make the urgency of my situation all the more glaring.

If I'm ever going to make new memories, I need to get out of here.

And if I'm ever going to get out of here, I need to fix what needs fixing.

I scan the never-ending shelves, searching for anything that looks out of the ordinary. "A little help would be nice," I mumble to myself and the threads, unable to keep the annoyance out of my voice. "Feel free to chime in anytime."

I think back to when Gemma and I were in the Dreamscape and how she would speak to the threads, accidentally asking for help when we needed it. Back then, it seemed like an impossible game, a never-ending riddle that we didn't have the right answers to. But now I know a little more about magic—*very* little, I should add—and if this insane experience has taught me anything, it's that I have a lot more say than I originally thought. I used to feel like a chess piece being played by magic, but now I'm wondering if maybe I could be the hand that's making the moves.

So I stop running and close my eyes, leaning my back against the closest shelf as I focus on what I'm looking for and how I'm willing to do anything to get it. *The beginning,* I think to myself. *I need to understand the beginning.*

"We heard the tales when we were young." The words of the Language pour from my mouth, dripping and sweet like honey. I don't know how I remember the exact words from Carmen's memory, but they tumble out like they've been waiting on the tip of my tongue.

I open my eyes and look down the end of the hallway. There's a glowing green exit sign that wasn't there only a moment before, and behind it, a door—beige and unassuming. My stomach flips. I'm worried that the moment I make my move, the image will scatter and fade like a mirage made of wish fulfillment and delirium. I take a step toward it, and when it doesn't immediately vanish, I start to run.

Checkmate.

I slam into the door, pushing it open with both hands and nearly plummet headfirst into the darkness. "Whoa." My arms swing wildly as I attempt to right myself. Clinging to the doorframe, I look down over the abrupt dropoff and into what appears to be endless nothingness. But the tingling sensation running down my spine tells me I just need to look harder.

"We heard the tales when we were young," I whisper into the gloom. *"Of a power that made the sun rise and fall, that made a tree blossom after a harsh winter, or a baby cry as it took its first breath."* The black expanse ripples at the sound of my voice.

I exhale heavily and rub my face with my hands. I know what I need to do, but that doesn't make it any less terrifying. Raising my foot over the looming darkness, I let it hover for another heartbeat. "This better work," I mutter under my breath, and then I take a step.

Dark-colored threads wind under my feet, forming a solid-feeling staircase that glistens even with the lack of light. *"A power,"* I say, as I watch in amazement, *"that meant new life."*

The shadows melt around me, churning the air until the darkness is transformed into an echoey stairwell that spirals down. My hand rests on a metal railing, rusted over from age and disuse. Nothing about this scene is familiar; there isn't even a staircase at my library back at home—the whole building is a single story. Something tells me that I've left the library and the sea of memories behind. I've gone somewhere else entirely.

Into uncharted territory.

I swallow and take another step down, the staircase creaking under my weight. *"But the stories never mentioned that if there is a power that brings life, there must also be one that brings death."*

Death, death, death.

The word reverberates off the walls and back to me. I shudder and glance over my shoulder only to see that the door I came through has vanished along with the glowing green exit sign. Even though I wasn't planning on turning back, the fact that I no longer can is enough to make anyone feel the heaviness of trepidation. Gripping the railing tightly, I race down the stairs, taking two at a time because half of me is still worried the steps will vanish at any second.

But they don't. The staircase winds downward in a close spiral, and the further I go the weirder things get. Threads spill from the walls like waterfalls, cascading in shocking shades of color—bright pinks and bursting oranges; cool blues and calming greens. They slither and slide against each other, tangling without any sort of pattern. I keep my distance from the threads as I make my way down the stairs, not wanting to call attention to myself. But while they do nothing to stop me, they whisper things. The sound of it makes all the little hairs on my arms stand on end.

The air is warm and humid, my neck beading with sweat the further down I go. I start to feel dizzy and claustrophobic, like the walls are shifting and slowly inching closer with every step I take. There's a humming sound up ahead. It pulses through me, pounding in my skull. It's that same rhythm, like the steady beating of a drum, that I heard when Carmen's thread first called out to me.

Oliver, Oliver.

I have no choice but to follow.

Just when I think the staircase is never going to end, the steps suddenly cut off in front of a weather-worn door. The threads from the stairwell feed into the doorway with a reverent sort of intensity, their movements soft and slow like a murmur. The dark wood is old and stained and pockmarked with age, its polished silver handle shining in sharp contrast.

I close my eyes and think of Gemma. I think of home. And then I wrap my fingers around the silver handle and give the door a gentle push.

Sunlight glares through my eyelids. I look up into a sky so bright it seems closer to white than blue. The smell of woodsmoke and the dry dust of the desert fills my lungs. Turning in a slow circle, I look for some sort of clue for what I'm supposed to do next, but all I see are miles and miles of flat desert, the land scorched and cracked. Blue sky, red earth.

"When I was very young, I used to ask my mother where the power came from."

I jump at the sound of an old woman's voice and clamp my jaw shut so I don't scream. When I turn back around, she's standing next to me, her shoulders stooped with age, her skin brown and leathery like she's spent too much time in the sun. Her eyes are dark and piercing, her long gray hair braided down her back. But her form is partially translucent—a memory already half-gone.

"Her answer was always the same," the woman says quietly. "'From the earth itself, little one. From its very heart.'" She taps her hand once over her chest and a long black thread unwinds into her withered hand. She holds it out to me.

"Carmen?" I ask uncertainly.

She nods and offers me the thread again.

I take a breath and hold out my own hand, trying not to panic when I see that I'm not quite as solid as I was only moments before. "Show me."

She places the black thread in my palm, and my fingers close around it.

Remember me, Gemma, I think to myself, flinging the words out and up like a last-minute prayer.

Remember.

CHAPTER THIRTY-FOUR
OLLIE

BLUE SKY, RED earth.

The memory lurches forward, sending me sprawling to the ground. I land on my hands and knees, my palms digging into the soft clay. When I look up, I'm startled for two reasons. First, Carmen has vanished. Second, I wasn't expecting to see such a familiar scene.

A mountain range with sharp ridges and rust-colored cracks, full of shadows that slice and craggy peaks that tower. My breathing stutters as I clamber to my feet. All I can do is stare.

The Superstition Mountains.

Home.

I wipe my hands on my jeans and exhale. The irony isn't lost on me. Of course this is where the story begins—a full circle.

These are the mountains of my home, and yet they're not the same. There's a certain lushness here, the kind of fresh quality that only comes from a land free from development, untouched and unclaimed, raw in its natural form.

Brighter, bolder, younger. These are my mountains a very long time ago.

Through the twilight, I see a swirling tower of smoke, thin and curling as it spirals into the sparse clouds dotting the sky. "Carmen?" I call out to the open desert. No response. All I hear is the sound of the slight breeze rustling the branches of an ocotillo shrub nearby, its tiny leaves rattling with a quivered sigh. I can't decide if the absolute quiet is peaceful or unnerving.

As I stand there deciding what to do, the smoke continues its lazy ascent. Since it's the only sign of life and soon it's about to be pitch-black out here, I follow it. I jog through the overgrown desert, dodging cacti and snake holes and all the other dangers that seemingly pop out of nowhere when you're out in the wild. Even though I'm at the base of the mountains I've lived under my whole life, it's hard to gauge where I am. Everything looks so different.

The smoke is coming from a large fire in the center of an open stretch of land just where the mountain begins to climb steeper. At first, I don't see anything else, just the abandoned rock-rimmed fire pit with its golden flames. But then I notice the homes surrounding it. The adobe structures are small and compact, built into the edge of the mountain itself. They blend in with the beige rocks, so earth-toned and natural that I nearly missed them.

It's a village, quiet and calm and as much a part of the desert as the mountains and the saguaros.

Then, I hear the sounds of children shrieking. Two grinning girls run past me with their heads tucked and their arms pumping as they disappear behind the home closest to me, their black braids swishing around the corner. A group of boys follows behind them with sticks held high over their heads and laughter on their lips. I hear them scuffling—their war cries and their banter.

It's the universal signs of play, of brothers and sisters and childhood.

My throat twinges with a nostalgic ache that makes it hard for me to swallow. How is it that no matter the time or the place, there will always be kids chasing each other until the sun goes down and it's too dark to play? If I squint hard enough, I can pretend it's Milo, Gemma, and me racing through our backyards like a pack of feral wolves.

I look down at my hands, which are more translucent than ever. Closing my eyes, I think of Gemma and the handful of threads I gave her—all my memories of magic—and hope my desperate plan works. I hope my memories give her a visual and something to hold onto as she Remembers me here, so I won't disappear completely.

"Who are you?" a small voice asks with a tug on the hem of my t-shirt, startling me out of my reverie. It's one of the young girls with the long black braids, her tan cheeks rosy from running.

"Carmen?" I ask cautiously, searching the child's face for any sign of the older woman who'd brought me into her memories.

"Who are *you*?" she repeats, taking a step back, her dark eyes wary.

I hold my hands up in an effort to show that I mean her no harm. "I'm visiting. You invited me here. My name is Oliver, but you can call me Ollie."

"Oliver," she repeats slowly, her accent curling around the syllables of my name. "Ollie." Her expression brightens. "I know that name, I have heard it before. Come with me. I need to show you something." She leans forward and takes me by the hand, tugging me with surprising strength; she can't be more than six years old.

The moment she pulls on my hand, we travel the whole distance to the center of the village in the span of a blink. I drop her hand and look back over my shoulder. "How did you—" I start to ask, but Carmen has already turned away from me.

She runs over to a tall woman with an identical long black braid running down her back. Carmen takes a flying leap and jumps into the woman's arms, who drops her basket full of soft-looking threads, each bundle dyed a different bright color. "Carmen!" the woman exclaims, looking down at the sprawling mess.

"Sorry, Mama," Carmen says nuzzling into her neck. "Will you sing me the old stories?"

Her mother sighs and looks out at the other kids still playing in the distance. She shakes her head with a rueful smile. "Only if you help me, little one."

She sets Carmen back on the ground and they pick up the tangled mess of threads. Then they pull out the wooden frame of a loom, and the two of them sit on low carved stools near the fire where they begin to work. Her mother's hands are busy and quick as they move through the motions of weaving—in and out and in and out—while Carmen cradles the bundles of threads carefully in her arms.

True to her word, her mother begins to sing. She tells the story of the stars that fell from the sky and how the earth formed around them, her voice sweet and clear as she hits the high notes.

"Listen," Carmen says, turning to me. "You need to hear this."

It's strange the way she's able to speak to me without disrupting the memory. The moment just shapes around her, like she's some kind of anomaly that not even the magic understands.

I lean forward, trying to soak in every word her mother sings, but it's just the same thing I've heard before, an old folktale about magic. "I know, you've told me this part, I heard it when I touched the thread—"

"But you are not listening," Carmen says, her gaze still trained on the weaving. "*Listen.*" She tips her head onto her mother's lap, watching her confident hands slide the threads through the loom.

Her mother's face changes when she arrives at the next verse, her voice shifting to a heavier tone, still just as melodic but more melancholy in mood. With her words, she weaves together the next part of the story. She sings of a valley where nothing ever grows.

In between the cliffs of stone,
in the jagged spaces you feel most alone,
lies the Valley where nothing lasts—
no, nothing stays.
In the darkest places where fates are frayed.

Her voice fades into a hum, the melody as dark as the black thread still clasped in my grip. I shiver and edge away from the fire, letting Carmen's thread trail over the back of my hand, wishing I could let go and leave this moment while still understanding that I have no choice but to stay.

"The stories all start the same, and they end the same way too," Carmen whispers. "Always with death." She tilts her head up to look at the stars just beginning to shine.

Her mother doesn't react to any of this, she just continues weaving, her hum a low rumble in her chest.

"Because if that much life fell from the sky..." Carmen says, waving her hands above her, sweeping her fingers through the air to mimic a falling star. "Would it not bring the other side too?" She slowly moves each of her hands up and down, like a weighted scale tipping to find its balance.

Life and death; death and life.

The beginning and the end.

Anxiety creeps through me like a slow and steady drip. "What's that supposed to mean? Why are you telling me this?" It's not just her mother's song that's giving me the creeps, something about Carmen has me on edge too. Maybe it's because she says things like she's far older than the child she appears to be, or maybe it's the way she stares off, her eyes unfocused and unseeing as she gently rocks back and forth by her mother's side. All of it's unsettling.

"You will see." She hums along to the song, her focus back on her mother, who's completely unaware of me and the side conversation we've been having. "I always hate to leave her," Carmen says sadly as she unwinds another thread from her chest, holding it out to me. "But now we must go."

The second black thread wraps around my hand, tugging me forward. My stomach swoops, then drops, just like I'm on a roller coaster right at the edge of the free fall. Another blink and night has fallen. The fire at the center of the village has gone out, its embers glowing red in the distance.

"Watch carefully," Carmen says from right next to me. I glance down, expecting to see the little girl from before, but I'm startled to see a young woman close to my height, wearing a simple dark dress with tiny wildflowers embroidered on it. She's lean and graceful, her limbs like the branches of a willow tree. She's lost the roundness in her cheeks, but she has the same dark eyes and long black braid.

Carmen looks up at the mountains looming overhead. "Our village was struggling. This was a harsh place to settle. Some had already given up and moved on, seeking fertile land that was more forgiving. But not my family. Papa was proud of these mountains. He said this was where he was born, and this was where he would die." She shakes her head. "Sometimes I thought he was a fool, but on nights like this?" She stops and breathes in the fresh air tinged with a hint of leftover smoke. "I think I understand…"

She trails off, and we stand in silence, both of us watching the shadows deepen across the purple mountain range. But after a minute, I grow impatient. "So, what are we waiting—" But the rest of my question is cut off by the sound of approaching footsteps, rough against the gritty gravel. A boy about my age appears out of the darkness.

"Carmen," he says with a sigh. "I am glad to see you."

She punches him lightly on the arm and offers him a grin. "Of course you are, you absent-minded fool. When are you going to pull that head of yours out of the clouds?" She reaches a hand up to ruffle his dark hair, but he dodges her easily.

"It was an accident, I swear—"

"It always is with you."

"I know, I know. But if we do not find them tonight, my father will…" He shudders, unable to finish the sentence.

"He will lock you inside for the rest of your life," she finishes with a laugh. "Calm down, Mateo. We will find them."

They tease each other with the familiarity of old friends. Even while only observing a single moment of their relationship, I can feel that they *know* each other. My chest aches as I listen to their banter. I wish Gemma was here with me.

Mateo hangs his head and mutters, "At least ten got out."

"*Ten* of the cattle?" Carmen scoffs. "How is it even possible to lose ten cows," she mumbles to herself.

His face falls, and he wrings his hands.

"What?" she asks, looking serious for the first time. "Is there something else?"

"I tracked them as far as the Valley." He says the words in a rush like he's anxious to get them out.

Her mouth falls open. "But you didn't—"

"Cross over? *No*. You know it is not allowed."

Carmen's face shifts from fear to excitement in less than a second. "Then we should go before the sun comes up. Before your father notices." She looks around to make sure they're still alone, then adjusts her leather satchel securely against her side before spinning on her heel and heading in the direction of the mountains. "What would you do without me," she says, looking back at Mateo with another grin.

He smiles back but says nothing. He just follows behind her with a look of relief. It's obvious he's glad he doesn't have to search for the cattle alone.

Carmen gestures to me with another black thread held in her hands. She wraps it around my wrist while saying, "We followed their tracks for hours, and Mateo was right: they led straight to the Valley."

The thread tugs me forward through time, past their hours of searching, and into the next part of Carmen's story.

"We had been told never to venture into the Valley ever since we were little children," she says to me, pointing up at the narrow space between the mountains. "In song, in story, in warning upon warning."

I peer over Mateo's shoulder to get a better look at the Valley. From where we stand about fifty yards away, it doesn't look quite so terrible, it's just a flat stretch of red rock extending in the space between mountain ridges, tucked away and nearly out of sight. I grew up in the shadow of these mountains; I've been up and down these trails more times than I could count, but I've never seen this strip of land before.

"I once heard my father and some of the other men huddled together, talking about the Valley," Carmen says softly. "I hid behind the stables nearby and listened in on their whispers, the rise and fall of their worries. One of their sons had traveled across the border and had not returned. They never found him, and, eventually, everyone stopped looking."

She hums her mother's song again as she watches the first glimpse of sunrise kissing the tips of the mountain. "Every year on the day of his birth, his parents light a candle in his window, and they leave it burning for the whole night. The sight of it always makes Mama cry." Carmen's gaze hasn't wavered from the Valley since the moment she laid eyes on it. "But he was not the first to be lost, nor was he the last."

The sky is a gentle shade of morning, like it hasn't decided yet what color it'll be. Looking at the Valley under the pale light of the sunrise, it's hard to imagine this rock as a place of loss, a place to be feared. But ever since I was a kid, even before I knew magic existed, I'd heard the legends surrounding these mountains—the mysteries and the myths. Some people even believe that it's the gateway to hell itself.

"I always thought our village was foolish and far too superstitious," she says, shaking her head. "But the warnings were true. More true than anyone ever believed."

"It wasn't just a story?" I ask.

"You of all people should know the weight a story carries."

I try not to squirm under her sharp stare. "But how can you say that? How do you *know* me, Carmen?"

She doesn't answer, she just continues our staring contest. I'm the first to look away.

The three of us walk the last few yards to the edge of the mountain trail, and the closer we get, the stranger I feel. There's an electric current in the air that leaves me feeling agitated and itchy, like I'm suddenly too big for my skin.

We stop right at the border of the Valley where the gravel of the mountain gives way to a smooth-looking sandstone. Crouching down, Mateo points to the dirt still smudged with hoof prints. "This is as far as they go," he whispers. He swivels his head from side to side as if still half-hoping to find his cows hiding in a nearby bush.

But the mountain is quiet, and they are alone.

"Why are you whispering?" Carmen asks.

Mateo shrugs and the tips of his ears turn red. It's clear that he's much more scared than Carmen is.

She wipes her hands on the front of the thin apron pinned to the rough fabric of her dress. "The only place they could have gone was *in*, Teo. We have to cross," she insists with a quirk of her lips, revealing a slight hint of rebellion. Her posture tightens with anticipation.

"No, I could just tell my father the truth: I lost them."

Carmen edges closer to the red sandstone, stark against the brown rock of the rest of the mountain. "Are you not just a little curious?"

Mateo shuffles his feet. "Not as curious as you. Look, the tales are true. *Nothing* grows here." He points to the bare rock. He's right; the rest of the mountain is teeming with life—trees and cacti and desert shrubs with colorful blooms—but the sandstone is completely bare. A shockingly blank slate. I want to reach out my hand and touch it. I wonder if it feels as smooth as it looks.

"And I feel... I feel strange," Mateo says. "Do you feel it too?"

Carmen has turned away, the toe of her worn sandals just barely grazing the red rock. "I don't just feel it, Teo. I *hear* it. Something calls to me." She blinks rapidly as if she's just coming out of a trance. "It sounds like the dinner bell that Mama rings to call me home, how the noise fills up my ears until the sound has nowhere to go but back out..."

He frowns and crosses his arms, looking annoyed. "You are always trying to get me into trouble, Carmen. I want to leave. This is—"

But right at that moment, she drops her satchel to the ground where it lands with a thud and a small cloud of dust. She looks back at me and says, "I know you hear it too."

And I do. It's that same overwhelming pulsing sound that I

heard before. Like the mountain itself has a heartbeat thundering under our feet.

Oliver, Oliver.

Carmen takes a breath, steps onto the rock, and...

She vanishes.

Mateo stumbles back, clutching his own bag to his chest. "Carmen?" he calls out, his voice cracking at the end. "Carmen, come out. Quit playing." He paces back and forth at the edge, still too afraid to cross over himself.

But she doesn't answer. The sandstone is as blank and empty as it was before—no signs of life. Just when I'm starting to feel nearly as freaked out as Mateo, the black thread on my wrist pulls me forward, and before I know what's happening, I'm tumbling onto the sandstone and into the Valley, running straight into Carmen.

I squint at her under the harsh sun, which is suddenly directly overhead like it's midday. Mateo and the rest of the mountain have vanished. It's that same stretch of blue sky and red earth that I'd seen before, right when I came through the door at the end of the library stairwell.

"Where's Mateo? Where are we?" I ask, my breath coming out in sharp bursts.

"When I was very young, I used to ask my mother where the power came from," Carmen says again, just as she did when I found her inside her memories. "Her answer was always the same. 'From the earth itself, little one. From its beating heart.'" She holds the dark folds of her dress in her hands as she starts to walk, the rock slanting slightly from the incline.

Before I follow behind her, I reach down and touch the sandstone, the grainy surface coating my hands in a fine layer of pink sand. I rub my fingers together, testing its silty texture. All I can see for miles around is an endless sea of sand and stone, red and carved up from too many years in the sun and the wind. My hand brushes against the thin white stripes that cut across the stone in a pattern like a rolling wave.

We walk in silence for a few minutes, the sound of the pulse growing louder with every step. "When I crossed over into the Valley, Mateo disappeared, and I could not find my way out again. All I could do was follow the sound." Carmen chuckles softly to herself, toying with the end of her braid. "Part of me believed it would lead me to the cattle, that I would come out on the other side a hero." She puffs out her cheeks and sighs. "Me, a hero."

"Did you ever find the cows?"

"Oliver, look."

I follow her gaze to where she's pointing up ahead. The carcasses are scattered across the stone, their lifeless forms already to the point of decomposition as if they'd been out here for days, not merely hours. I cover my nose with my hand, trying not to gag. Their glassy eyes glare back at me, blank and milky white.

How? How did this much destruction happen so quickly?

Carmen begins to sing as tears trail down her cheeks, her dress rustling around her ankles in the breeze.

"In between the cliffs of stone,
in the jagged spaces you feel most alone,
lies the Valley where nothing lasts—
no, nothing stays.
In the darkest places where fates are frayed."

"But I don't understand," I say, frustration flaring through me. "Magic doesn't just do things like this." I can't stop looking at the bodies of the cows lying there, my eyes stinging from the smell.

"Life and death," she says as if it's that simple.

"I *know*," I say, even though I really don't.

Carmen raises a finger to her lips, motioning for me to be quiet. "Death." She points to the cattle. "And life." She turns in the opposite direction, pointing to something up ahead. She starts to walk again, leaving me and the cows behind. I quickly skirt the remains of the cattle to catch up with her.

"After I found them, I was sick. I emptied the contents of my stomach, and I could not stop shaking." She wraps her thin arms around herself as she shivers. "But I still could not find a way out. And I could not ignore that sound." She pauses and we both turn our heads toward the steady beat, the pulse that pulls us onward.

"But I grew weak. There was a heaviness inside my bones, and it frightened me." Carmen stumbles over her feet, her breathing labored. "It became hard to catch my breath. I feared that I would end up the same as the cattle—dead and forgotten with no one brave enough to recover my body." She drops to her hands and knees and begins to crawl, her fingers grasping at the sandstone.

Even though I wasn't the one who lived through this, even though this isn't my own memory, I can still feel the effects of the Valley creeping through time and space and layers upon layers of magic. I sway on my feet, feeling light-headed; the sky won't stop spinning. "And then... and then what happened?" I choke out.

Carmen's nails dig into the red sandstone, fumbling for something to hold onto. "And then I found this." She grasps one of the thin white lines that run through the sandstone, pulling at it until it spools into her hand.

A silver thread.

Her arms shake uncontrollably, and she falls face forward onto the smooth stone. She rolls over and stares up at me, a fine coating of sand dusting her skin. "I thought I was losing my mind because it looked like the stone was *moving*," she says breathlessly, pointing to the silver threads writhing against the rock. "It flowed like a river, pulling me along with it. But you and I both know what this is." She looks at the thread flashing like a handful of stars under the bright glare of the sun, heaving herself up and brushing off her dress. "As I said, we already saw death. Now it is time for new life."

The sandstone grows steeper and harder to climb, but the silvery threads embedded in the rock drag us forward until we reach the crest of the hill. My knees buckle beneath me as I stumble at the top, looking down into the most incredible and impossible forest I've ever seen.

This place is the embodiment of the color green. Everything's unspeakably lush and spilling over with a vitality that seems to bubble up from the ground itself, a ground covered in a carpet of moss and other plants I don't know the names of.

As I stand there staring with my mouth hanging open, I can actually *see* the cycles of growth continuing right in front of me like everything is stuck in fast forward. I watch as clusters of flower buds open their petals in a pale pink burst, turning their fresh faces toward the sun. The leaves on the trees sprout from their branches, bright green and translucent before fading to yellow, orange, and red.

Rain falls in a gentle mist, covering my skin in a sheen of moisture and filling up brightly colored pools in the weather-worn holes on the rock. I still see the signs of desert life—ordinary plants and shrubs jutting out from the sandstone, but so much of it is *new*. It's an intoxicating mixture of familiar and foreign, the ordinary and the ethereal, all of it connected with the shining silver threads of magic, each one feeding into the other in an unending web of color and life like the most extraordinary tapestry. Even the air is shimmering. I reach out a hand, convinced that when I pull it back, it'll be covered with luminous specks of light.

It feels like a true beginning, a fresh start, somewhere I could imagine that time began.

But nothing about this makes sense. A place like this shouldn't exist. The abnormality of it all fills me with the urge to run away and never come back, but at the same time, I'm already mourning the moment I'll have to leave.

While we stand there watching, the forest acknowledges us by slowly stretching out, each plant deliberately creeping forward like it wants to absorb Carmen and me, to make us a part of its endless cycle. The branches of the trees extend over our heads, their quivering leaves slipping through my hair like fingers. I jerk back, feeling afraid over how much I want to stay, to belong here.

But the further the branches stretch, the more brittle they become, their limbs snapping with a loud crack as they break, their vibrant leaves turning brown and crumbling away to nothing. Right before my eyes, the flowers that had been blooming only seconds before wither and die, their shriveled petals falling to the ground. The pools of water run dry, leaving behind empty earth, barren and waiting.

All this life can only extend so far. It can't escape its inevitable demise. Everything before us is in one stage of life or another: the early beginning, the steady stretching middle, or the final last breaths. And then it begins again. And again.

And again.

I felt that same feeling whenever I tied a Claiming. I could see the beginning and the end all at once, everything tied together through the threads, through our memories and our magic. It's an aching sort of feeling. It's not purely joyful or entirely made of sorrow, but a marriage of the two. The ultimate balancing act—two sides of the same coin.

Carmen's eyes brim with tears as if she's seeing it all for the first time again. "You feel it too, don't you?"

"Yes, I do. I feel it too," I whisper, my throat tight.

"The threads led me here, and I do not know why. Were they calling to me or were they warning me to flee?" She shrugs one shoulder. "I will never know. But once I saw this," she says, motioning to the forest, to the wondrous cycle of life, "I did not know if I could ever go back to my mundane life of black and white."

She takes a few steps into the forest, the dappled sun creating patterns of shadow and light across her face as she looks back at me. "How could I go back to sleep now that I was wide awake?" She runs her hand along the trails of threads, following them further into the forest.

The pulsing grows louder as I run to catch up; it's pounding nearly as loud as my heart. The threads grow thicker here, piling on top of each other and slithering like snakes around my ankles as I carefully pick my way through them.

Suddenly, Carmen stops. "I needed to know," she says, pointing to a long narrow opening carved into the rock in front of her, where a warm wind blows and countless threads spill from its center. "I needed to know if it was true." She leans forward on her toes, parting the threads that cover the entrance like a silver curtain. The rhythm of the pulse quickens until it's an incessant ringing in my ears. A tingling sensation starts in my hands and climbs up my arms, sending chills through my whole body.

"All I could think about were the old stories, the ones Mama used to sing me before I fell asleep." She hums the opening notes of the song, but then her voice breaks and her smooth face slips into an expression of true terror. "Tell me, would you have turned back?" Without waiting for my response, she pushes through the threads and vanishes with nothing but darkness in her wake.

"You've got to be kidding me," I mumble to myself, hesitantly reaching out to part the curtain of threads. I poke my head through and glance down to see a black expanse with no end in sight. Another literal leap of faith.

Gemma's always been the one to jump first.

I close my eyes and shove my way through with a whispered wish, like my own version of a spell. "*Please* let me get out of this alive."

And then I fall.

The inside of the cave is like a night with a new moon—pitiless and blacker than ink. I'm suspended in the air, but I'm no longer falling. My heart climbs up my throat as I hover in the darkness, waiting for what comes next.

It's too dark to see, but at least I can hear. "Oliver," Carmen breathes from somewhere nearby. "I cannot simply show you what happened next. I need you to *understand*. I need you to Remember with me."

I swallow my yelp when I feel the shock of her cold fingers against my wrist. She presses another thread into my palm, then places her hand on my forehead. "*Remember,*" she says again, this time in the Language, her voice clear and full.

I wrap the thread around my fingers and give it a tug, willing it to show me more than I could see on my own. Instantly, Carmen's voice fills my head, the memory of her thoughts layering onto my own in a confusing stream of consciousness. It's hard to distinguish between her thoughts and mine, and the immediate loss of mental clarity sends me scrambling back in a panic. My grip on the thread loosens as the discomfort of having her voice inside my head intensifies.

"Do not resist, Oliver," Carmen says, wrapping her hand around mine and refusing to let me go. "You will not be harmed. You just need to *listen.*"

I exhale and try to relax my body even though it's the last thing I feel like doing. Carmen's thoughts slowly creep back in, the thread stretching thinly between us, a tenuous connection between two separate minds from two very different times.

"I had never felt so alone," Carmen's voice whispers in my mind. *"The darkness felt heavy and permanent, like a physical reminder that I had finally gone too far. I do not know how long I stayed like that, but it felt like an eternity. Me, suspended in nothingness."*

The memory shifts around us until all I can see is Carmen floating alone in the empty space, her dark dress rippling behind her, nearly indistinguishable from the blackness.

"I had never imagined my life ending like this—so small and meaningless. So insignificant. I could not stop thinking about that boy who had crossed over into the Valley, the one who never came home. And how after he disappeared, his parents would light a candle for him every year on the day of his birth, leaving it burning all through the night. Would my parents light one for me?"

The intensity of her emotions overpowers mine in one fell

swoop. I feel her absolute fear, the crippling panic shaking her body in waves.

"Then I felt something brush against my hand, unassuming and feather-light." Carmen startles, her dark eyes twin pools of light in the all-encompassing gloom. *"Two threads wind around my fingers, glowing faintly. One was a deep red color, steady and sure like the last breath of a sunset, the other a shade of silver I had only seen in my dreams. I grabbed onto them because I needed something—anything—to hold on to."*

The two threads spiral around Carmen, wrapping her in their gossamer strands like a caterpillar in a cocoon. She doesn't resist; she stays frozen in place. I feel her fear dissipating as the moment expands, and in its place a spark of curiosity, that familiar yearning from her childhood reawakened.

"As the threads envelop me, words fill my mind, rising from my chest and up through my mouth, escaping my lips and popping like bubbles."

"I want to see," she says, in the Language, her face lit by the glow of the threads.

"My voice sounded strange in my ears. Lyrical and clear and heavier than I ever imagined it could be, as if each word had weight to it—a price and a purpose. Those words shone like the flames of a fire, offering warmth and light."

The moment Carmen speaks the words, the darkness evaporates, and a soft golden glow fills the cavernous space, leaving me feeling like I'm floating in the middle of a hot summer day when the sun is at its highest in the sky. I turn my head to see her drifting next to me, her arms extended, and her palms turned up like she's ready and waiting to receive.

The two threads continue to twist around her body until only her head is left free, but Carmen hardly seems to notice that the magic is about to consume her. *"I want to stand,"* she exclaims.

"Those words tasted like soil and rain, like the loose crumble of dirt whenever Papa checked the harvest, his fingers raking, his brow furrowed under his hat. Those words sounded like the earth."

Our feet land on solid ground, copper and smooth like the sandstone of the Valley. It shifts under my feet with more silver threads running through it in bold, waving stripes.

Blue sky, red earth, as far as the eye can see. The space is so expansive—

"*—that I could not see the end from the beginning.*"

Carmen's thoughts tangle with mine, leaving me feeling out of breath and confused. My head feels like it will split right down the middle from the pain of sharing brain space with her. It's getting harder to hold onto who I am.

"*The two threads wrap around me tightly, tugging at the back of my mind like an insistent question.*" Silver and red, red and silver, the threads wind around her neck and up across her face. Carmen takes a deep breath as if she's plunging underwater. "*I feel the pulsing once again in my chest. I feel them asking if I want to become something new.*"

Now only her eyes are visible; a momentary flash of fear before the threads cover her completely. "*I do not remember saying 'yes—*'" Her body goes still as once again she's surrounded by darkness, the threads obscuring her vision entirely. "*—but I did not let go. I did not want to. I did not know how.*"

I feel rather than see the threads wrapping around her hand tightly in a single loop, slicing delicately across her skin until a single bead of blood rises up from the center of her palm. She flinches, clenching her hand into a fist. "*Tell me,*" she says, her voice cracking in the quiet. "*Tell me if the stories are true.*"

In a sudden burst, the threads spring free in a dazzling display of color, leaving Carmen standing back on the sandstone, her legs shaking underneath her.

"*Countless threads respond to my question. They unravel from every surface, pouring from the sky and the ground like a roaring river, like the crashing of the sea. They wrap around me in a single blink, encompassing me in so much feeling and sensation I am sure I will die from it.*"

I'm caught up in the tumult of silver threads along with her, struggling against the current as it threatens to pull us under, the red thread at the center of it all.

"I saw every moment of my life so far and every moment left to come. I saw everything as it began and everything as it will end. But if you asked me to put it into words, I could not have uttered a single one. Even now, I cannot describe it or conjure a picture that would satisfy me."

The sky explodes with a blinding flash of light, and Carmen's body goes limp, falling to the ground in a heap. I stumble over to her, wading through the threads in a blind panic, forgetting for a moment that this is a memory that happened long before my time. Fate's already had its say—I'm powerless here.

Carmen's eyes fly open, and for a moment they're a blinding crimson, as red as the blood drying on the palm of her hand. An ominous sign.

"I cannot see, for my eyes have become fire itself. I cannot hear, for my ears are full of the rushing of water. I cannot speak, for my mouth is full of words that bellow and crash. I am no longer Carmen, a girl who lives at the edge of the mountain. I am the sun and the moon and the stars in the sky."

I am everywhere.

I am everything.

Carmen hums her mother's song. She sings of the stars that broke in two; of a sky that split in half, its edges fraying as it poured out until it became something new.

Life.

Magic.

The beginning.

CHAPTER THIRTY-FIVE

GEMMA

I BRACE MYSELF to fall into another memory.

Charlotte motions for the four of us to hold hands around the table. She takes a breath and dips her head, her blonde waves tumbling over her shoulder as her hands begin to glow.

"Wait," Milo says, dropping my hand and Zoe's.

Charlotte's eyebrows pinch together. "What's wrong?"

"Are you sure you should be casting your memories again? Last night—"

"Last night my memories were more extensive and further back, which makes the casting more complicated and much harder to dredge up." Charlotte leans back in her chair, her blue eyes pale in the morning sun shining thinly through the kitchen windows. "Reopening old wounds and processing trauma is not for the faint of heart," she says, trying to keep her voice light, but she blinks a few times before clearing her throat. "Today I only have one memory to show you, and even though it was eighteen years ago, it feels like it was just yesterday. Casting will be simpler." She sits up and smiles, but it comes off a little stiff. "I feel fine. I've rested, and thanks to Zoe's mixing, I can use what magic I have. Okay?"

"Okay," Milo says hesitantly, still looking unconvinced.

"Would it be easier if you show us your memories in the Chronicles like Ollie did?" I ask, nudging the book toward her.

She smiles. "I wish I could, Gemma. But I don't know anything about that kind of magic. I don't know anything about the threads." I sink back into my seat, feeling stupid. "But you might?" she says hopefully.

"No," I say, my cheeks reddening. "I really don't. I barely know more than you." Milo, Zoe, and Charlotte all look at each other and then at me. "What?" I blurt out.

Milo's the one to break the awkward silence, as usual. "It's just that, we think you *do* know more about this magic," he says, pointing to Ollie's threads still shimmering on the pages of the book. "You just don't *want* to."

I sit up straighter, the back of the wooden chair digging into my spine. "What's that supposed to mean?" I ask, my pulse quickening.

"It means that I don't think you're as disconnected from your magic as you think you are," he says matter-of-factly, even a little smug, like he's solved some kind of riddle or something.

"But I don't have any magic," I protest. "At least I thought..." My chest hums with a feeling I don't understand. I turn away from them and stare down at my hands. Everything looks the same; I see no markings and my skin doesn't glow with any magic waiting to be released, but still—

I feel *something*.

"Milo, when you look at me, can you sense my magic? Do you see... anything?"

He tips back in his chair and crosses his arms over his chest. "Yep. Definitely. You're practically shimmering."

I can't keep the disbelief out of my voice. "I'm what?"

"Your brother's being a tad dramatic," Zoe cuts in with a slight eye roll. "You're not exactly 'shimmering.' It's more of a vibration you're giving off. Right?" she says, turning to Milo and Charlotte. They both nod. "You've been that way since I met you." She pushes back from the table and walks across the kitchen, clicking the stove burner back on.

"Since Grandma's funeral," Milo adds. He reaches out and squeezes me once on the shoulder. "Ever since then, you've had this kind of gleam about you." Zoe looks over her shoulder from where she's adding a handful of finely chopped herbs to her pot on the stove and raises her eyebrows. "Or vibration, whatever you want to call it," he concedes.

The funeral. When I first saw the threads during the Remembrance. A shiver runs down the length of my body. "Why didn't you say anything?"

"I thought it might be better to wait until you asked. You've been pretty jumpy around the subject."

I frown and watch Zoe stirring her mixture vigorously, the steam clouding her face from view as the sharp scent of something acidic fills the kitchen, burning my eyes. She plucks a bright orange petal off what looks like a poppy and tosses it into her mixture before switching the direction of her stirring, her movements quick and agitated. I turn back to my brother, wanting to argue with him, but I know he's right. If he would've told me I was "glimmering with magic" a few days ago, I don't know how I would've reacted.

Actually, I do. It would've been bad. I would've been too scared to acknowledge any sort of truth in what he said. But now? I look down at my empty hands again. Now I don't know what to feel. "But I saw Ollie take my magic," I say more than a little obstinately.

"Did he, though?" Milo asks.

I purse my lips and shrug. I didn't *actually* see what he was doing. I just felt the absence of my magic the moment I woke up in my backyard, lying in the grass, the rain softer than a whisper against my skin. "I feel separate from it." I place my hand on my chest and feel the beat of my heart. "It just feels so far away."

"I think there's a part of you that's still holding onto your potential for magic," Charlotte says with a kind smile.

"The possibility of it." I remember Aunt Libby talking about that very same thing when we found out Ollie had magic. She said that even before we're Claimed, we have the potential for magic and that it grows in strength every year until we turn seventeen.

"Exactly," Charlotte says. "You're born with the potential for magic, and then your Claiming decides how your magic will manifest."

I stare out the kitchen window, looking at Charlotte's scant backyard but not really seeing it. She's right. A Claiming anchors a person's magic to them, giving them the ability to use it. But before the Claiming, the potential was always there.

"So what now?" I ask. "What am I supposed to do?"

We all flinch at the sound of glass shattering on the tile floor. Zoe mumbles something under her breath as she bends down to pick up the scattered pieces of her broken bottle, her burnt orange mixing splattered across her jeans and shoes and oozing across the kitchen floor.

She sighs, staring down at the mess and looking frazzled. "It's not just your magic that feels far away, Gemma," she says, gesturing to her failed mixing. "There's something wrong with my magic too."

I think back to the smell of Zoe's mixing burning in the kitchen last night, her disheveled appearance and the hint of frustration hiding beneath her calm exterior.

After a beat, Milo holds up his hands. "Mine too," he says despondently. He whispers a word of casting, and his hands flicker once, twice, three times before staying fully lit. His forehead creases in concentration as he waves toward the mess on the floor. Nothing happens. He closes his eyes and mumbles another word, his hands glowing brighter. Finally, Zoe's shattered bottle reforms in her hand where her off-colored mixing is now safely contained. The kitchen is spotless once again.

Milo leans back in his chair and shoves his hands into his pockets. "That's a simple cleaning spell. I shouldn't even have to think about it, but the words... they just aren't coming as quickly as they used to." He looks at me, his face shifting from hopeless to determined in the space between blinks. "If we don't find Ollie, if we don't fix this, I think the words might stop coming altogether. I think we'll all lose our magic."

"I know what it feels like to lose that connection," Charlotte says, her hands glowing amber. She gestures for the four of us to gather around the table once again. "One step at a time, right? That's all we can do."

This time as she begins her casting, nobody interrupts.

The memory softly floats into my mind as if it's been here all along.

I'm standing in the middle of a dark and nearly empty parking lot where the only light offered comes from the sporadic streetlights giving off an orange muted glow. I wrap my arms around myself, shuddering against the sudden crisp feel of the air.

Part of me still feels the chair I'm seated in at the small table in Charlotte's kitchen. It's an uncomfortable sensation being in two places at once. It's distracting and disorienting, like multitasking but worse. Milo squeezes my hand to remind me that he's here too even though I can't see him.

A younger version of Charlotte climbs out of a small black car and strides purposefully across the asphalt over to the only other vehicle waiting in the parking lot. She's wearing an overly large coat that drowns most of her movements, but it's obvious that she's tense. She glances at her watch at least ten times before approaching the old truck and rapping once on the window. The door squeals open with a rusty groan.

"I wasn't sure if you'd come," says a gruff voice from inside the dark cab. Hayden steps out of the truck and slams the door. He's older and heavier, a little grayer too, but with that same piercing stare.

Charlotte hangs back in the shadows, refusing to step into the light pooling around her father from the streetlight. "You didn't give us much of a choice, did you?" Her voice is colder than the wind nipping at my cheeks.

Hayden cracks his neck twice and rubs his arm roughly where

the red thread is fused to his skin. "It'll be worth it, you'll see. This is what it wants," he says, grasping his forearm and tugging the sleeve of his jacket down. "It's what *I* want, and it's what we need."

Charlotte doesn't answer, she just chews on her bottom lip and checks her watch again before adjusting her coat and crossing her arms tightly over her chest. The two of them wait in silence, avoiding each other's gazes, only the sound of Hayden's incessant arm scratching breaking the tense quiet.

"Where's James?" she asks after another long minute. "Did he grow tired of you and your scheming? Did he finally leave?" There's an impossible-to-miss hint of hope in her words.

Hayden scowls, clenching his meaty hands into fists. "He doesn't know I'm here."

She scoffs. "And why is that?"

Hayden turns away from his daughter and leans against the side of his truck. "He doesn't understand. He doesn't think this will work."

"Well, you are asking for the impossible. You're asking for magic when it doesn't belong to you. For once James is right: this probably won't work. But you promised that if I arranged the meeting, you'd finally leave me and Ben *alone*."

Hayden's mouth flattens into an angry slash across his face, but before he can say anything, another shadow moves through the night, solidifying through the gloom to stand before them. I jerk back when I see his face, my entire body tensing.

"Well, we finally meet," Noah's voice drawls. "Ben's Charlotte, in the flesh. I've heard a lot about you. Ben talks about you all the time."

It's weird to see my dad again and even stranger still to see him outside the Dreamscape and inside another memory. He's taller and broader than I remembered, his dark hair swooping across his forehead in the same way Milo's does; they have matching unmanageable cowlicks. My stomach twists when I realize that he's wearing the same jeans and flannel shirt I saw him in last time.

I remember standing with Ollie and watching that memory

unfold like a bad dream. Noah and Ben—two Threaders, two soon-to-be fathers, trapped in an unending argument about fate.

This is probably that same night. The night my dad lost himself to the magic and never made it back out again. I look around the empty parking lot, at the rows of discarded shopping carts and discount stores with neon signs screaming about late spring sales. It's depressing to think that this was my dad's last view of the real world. It should've been home. It should've been my mom and Grandma and Libby.

It should've been Milo. It should've been me.

He smiles at Charlotte, but it's a distracted sort of expression, half-hearted and uninterested. But when he turns to Hayden, his smile widens, his white teeth gleaming under the dim light. "And the man of the hour, Hayden Lowell," Noah says, extending his hand.

Hayden scowls, ignoring the gesture. "Who are you? Where's Ben?"

Noah tucks his hands into the pockets of his jeans, a perfect picture of casual calm. But even though I've never actually met my dad, I can still see through his facade to read his obvious signs of stress: the way he chews on the inside of his cheek like Grandma used to when she was thinking about something serious, or the way he sways on his feet like he's ready to run, just like me.

"I'm the one who's going to give you what you've always wanted. I'm the one who's going to change your fate," he says, sounding confident, but I don't miss how his voice slightly wavers at the end.

Hayden's shoulders stiffen, and he clutches at his arm once again. Charlotte frowns, stepping between them. "Where's Ben? I thought he was meeting us here?"

"Someone has to stay and hold down the fort. That's Ben's specialty. He ties the Claimings, after all. We need him *there* in order to bring the magic *here*. So, shall we?" Noah gestures for Hayden to move closer, his eyes shadowed and dark.

Hayden drops the rest of his doubt in a hurry and eagerly steps forward, shouldering Charlotte out of the way.

"Just give me your hand," Noah says, "and I'll take care of the rest."

Charlotte stands off to the side and pulls her coat around herself snugly, the space between her eyebrows creasing as she watches the two men. They reach for each other at the same time, their hands clasping tightly. Hayden's jaw clenches as Noah's hand begins to shine with a golden glow, the same color as the band around his wrist.

"Wait, what's that?" Charlotte asks, leaning forward to get a closer look at my dad. She points at the golden thread around his wrist. "What kind of casting are you—"

"Don't worry about it," Noah says in a strained voice, a brief flash of panic crossing his face.

I understand his fear. I remember how it felt to hold onto magic that didn't belong to me. How the power surged through my skin only to stutter and stop, changing directions at a speed I couldn't keep up with. And I'll never forget the consequences that followed.

Hayden turns his back on his daughter, trying to block her view. "Go home, Charlotte. We don't need you anymore."

But she pushes back, tumbling forward until her hand connects with theirs. There's a burst of light, like the color of a blood-red sun just before it tips beyond the horizon. It sears across my eyes even after I close them. Hayden lets out a strangled yell followed by the sound of Charlotte's cries, the two mixing together into something horribly guttural, a noise full of loss and hurt.

I take a deep breath and force myself to open my eyes. All three of their hands are tangled in the red thread as it slowly unwinds from Hayden's forearm. It lashes around, whipping wildly as if unsure where to land. It's thin and frail, its ends splitting into countless directions.

Hayden tries to grab onto it with his free hand. "No, wait, don't leave me," he mutters, his eyes rolling back in his head.

But Charlotte's eyes are wide open, round and icy blue, completely frozen in pain. "Not him. No, please. Not him. They will take him, they will take him. No, please!" She yanks her arm back, but the thread remains wrapped around her fingers, tying her to Hayden and Noah and this moment that feels like it will never end.

Through it all, my father remains motionless, his face impassive as whispered words fly from his mouth in a steady stream. His hands glow brighter as he gently tugs the missing piece of the red thread until it's free from Hayden's and Charlotte's grasp and safely held in his.

Then everything goes still. After the chaos from only seconds ago, the sudden quiet is startling. Now it's just three people huddled together in a dark and vacant parking lot—there's nothing magical about it.

Charlotte falls to her knees and sobs into her hands. "No, please. Not him too. Don't take my son from me."

Hayden stumbles back in a daze, unsteady on his feet. He stares down at Charlotte. "Your *son?*" he says, gawking at the shape of her belly under her baggy coat.

She pulls it tighter around herself. "This has nothing to do with you."

"It's just as fate foretold," he says, his face lit with an eerie kind of wonder. But there's no excitement about his future grandson or any concern at all for his daughter. Hayden rolls up the sleeve of his shirt, looking for the fragment of red thread out of habit. He cocks his head to the side like he's waiting for it to whisper things to him, but instead, he's left staring at an empty stretch of normal-looking skin.

He blinks. "It's really gone," he murmurs. "It's so... quiet." Then he shakes his head and yanks his sleeve down. "Where's the magic I was promised?"

Noah's fist closes around the piece of the red thread. "Yeah, about that. I can't actually *give* you magic, you know. You weren't fated to have it," he says with a shrug. "I guess you could say it wasn't written in the stars." He gives them a quick smile like it's an inside joke. "Now, if you'll excuse me." My dad turns on his heel, his black boots slapping on the asphalt.

"But you took the thread from me. If I can't have any magic, I *need* that! It's mine—my grandmother passed it on to me, and her father before that, all the way back to Cora herself! Give it back, I have to break the Claimings." Hayden lunges, his hands grasping wildly through the air. But Noah steps to the side smoothly to avoid Hayden's thrashing grasp, the red thread clutched tightly against his chest.

Hayden falls to the ground, his breath coming in sharp gasps. "No—I—I need it. I can't see without it." He tips over on his side and stares off blankly, slowly rocking back and forth. "I need it."

It's strange to see this big burly man, this cruel and manipulative father brought down like this. But even after everything he's done, I still don't have the stomach to watch him falling apart.

"Wait," Charlotte calls out to my dad. "Please, tell Ben I need to see him. Tell him to come home. It's about our son."

Noah hesitates. "You know that's not possible. Ben comes home when the magic releases him, only when the Dreamscape is done with him."

"But *you're* here."

My dad's face tightens. "That's because I've done things Ben doesn't have the nerve to. I've seen things he doesn't understand." He rubs the back of his head with his hand. "I just need to fix this, and then everything will be okay," he says, looking down at his closed fist.

"Then take me with you." Charlotte climbs shakily to her feet, her hand clasped against her swelling stomach. "Take me to Ben."

"I can't do that."

"You're doing magic that doesn't make sense, performing castings I've never seen before. *Please*, just try," Charlotte presses.

Noah's shoulders stiffen, but he doesn't walk away. "Just go home, Charlotte, you—"

"Do you know what I saw when I touched that thing?" She

points to Noah's closed fist, her voice rising to talk over him. "I saw my son in the Dreamscape, trapped and alone. And do you know what else I saw? My son, taken by my own father and brother—my own *blood*—so they could continue on with their insane quest. They want to collect a Threader, you see, so they can enter the Dreamscape." She wraps her arms around herself, tears sliding down her cheeks. "That thread didn't show me a single glimpse of a future where my son was safe and protected away from all of *this*. Those can't be my only options."

Noah's eyes flash. "Your son will be a Threader? Did you see who was with him?" he asks, his voice taking on an anxious edge.

Charlotte shakes her head. "It only showed me pieces, broken like shards of glass. Possibilities frozen in a future that hasn't happened yet." She shivers. "I could hear things," she says, looking down at her father who's still practically catatonic on the ground. "Strange things. Has it shown you your future?" she asks warily.

My dad clenches his hand around the piece of red thread. "It shows me what it needs to." I watch as he struggles over what to do; it's like I can hear the internal battle raging inside himself. I can hear it because I've heard it all before too.

Take more power.

Change your fate.

Break the Claimings.

He closes his eyes and rolls his shoulders because the battle is already over, and he didn't win. There's no reasoning with him. The red thread is already wrapped around him too tightly, whispering secrets and promises it will never keep. "I can fix it. I can fix it," he mutters to himself as he turns away from Charlotte, who deflates with disappointment.

Noah reaches out in front of him, grabbing through the air until his hand lands on a thin golden thread—the one containing the casting power he stole. It's the one that led him here, and it's the one that will lead him back to the Dreamscape.

For the first time, I feel a true surge of empathy for my father. He was just another pawn controlled by a power he didn't understand. I know what it feels like to want more than you can handle. I can still hear the lingering whispers now: *You just have to take it.*

Charlotte glares at Noah's retreating form, holding up her glowing hands. She breathes out a casting, but it never reaches him. Her hands flicker once, twice, three times, and then they extinguish completely. "What did you do to my magic?" she cries, shaking out her hands and trying to cast again.

Noah glances back over his shoulder with a twinge of guilt. "I can't always control this magic," he says. "It has a mind of its own. And magic always has consequences. I'm sorry you had to bear the brunt of the bargain." For a moment, he really does seem sorry, but then his features harden, and he grabs the golden thread before disappearing.

Then, it's just Charlotte and Hayden left in the deserted parking lot, the two of them lost in their own wildernesses of grief. Charlotte wipes her tears and slowly walks over to where her father is seated against the tire of his truck. His mouth is slack, and his eyes are out of focus. She opens the truck door and pulls out Hayden's worn-out notebook, the one with all the scrawled pictures and random dates and names. The one that hopelessly tries to piece together an incomplete future about me and Ollie and magic.

Charlotte flips through the pages until she finds what she's looking for, tearing them out with a final-sounding rip. She slams the truck door and reaches down to pull her dad's phone out of his pocket. She opens it and presses a number. "You need to come get Dad," she says quickly. She listens for a moment, then says, "No, of course it didn't work." Another pause. She closes her eyes, her lashes wet from tears, and swallows. "He's... he's not doing well. Please, just come get him," she says again before reciting an address and ending the call. She tosses the phone back onto her dad's lap.

"James will be here soon." She takes a shaky breath, releasing it through her teeth. "I'm sorry you wasted your entire life chasing something you couldn't have, but don't try to contact me again.

Ever." She races to her own car and throws the door open, then sits and waits until another car pulls into the lot and parks next to Hayden's truck.

My heart thumps in my chest when James climbs out, flicking his blond hair out of his face. First, he looks at his dad all scrunched up on the ground like a wrinkled heap of a man, and then at Charlotte, who's still waiting in her car and watching them both. James opens his mouth like he wants to say something, like he's about to call out to her, but what do you say after all the years and all the hurt? After another moment, Charlotte pulls out of the parking lot and doesn't look back.

The memory lurches me forward, pulling me inside the car with her. The overworked heater rattles noisily, smelling overwhelmingly like melted crayons. After driving a couple of blocks away, she makes a sharp turn, pulling over on the side of the road. She sniffs and wipes her face with her hands, then mutters under her breath until her hands begin to glow on the steering wheel. But a moment later, they flicker out, the words of her casting dying on her lips—her magic is too weak.

"Come on," she mumbles, her eyes shining with panic. "I need you to work right now." She relaxes her grip on the steering wheel and tries again. This time, whatever she's casting seems to work because her hands stay lit with a warm golden glow. She quickly turns the radio on, scanning the stations until she finds one that's filled with static, then closes her eyes and continues to whisper her casting.

I nearly jump out of my skin when Hayden's voice fills the car, coming through the radio speakers as loudly and clearly as if he were speaking right next to me.

"She's pregnant," he rumbles. "With a boy."

"Just like you predicted. Just like the thread told you." James's voice carries the reverent fervor of someone completely in over their head. "And he will be one of the next Threaders?"

"Eventually," Hayden says through labored breaths. "If fate has its way, which it always does."

"So the end is near, it's finally happening. They'll break the Claimings."

"*She* will, the other Threader. *It will end with the one who holds all magic in her hands,*" he chants softly.

"Then we need to go after Charlotte, we can't lose them. We've been waiting for years—"

Hayden starts laughing, but it comes out high-pitched and sour. I shudder against the backseat of Charlotte's car; it sounds like a laugh past its expiration date. I can imagine the crazed look in his eyes and the manic grin stretching his lips into the false shape of a smile. "There is a place where all magic resides," he says in a breathy sing-song voice. "A place where fate itself lies sleeping, its red heart always beating. A place of waking dreams." He laughs again, this time weakly. "A place..." he says vaguely, "a place of... I can't remember."

"Here," James says over the rustling of paper. "Read this. Wait, what happened to these pages?" There's a muttered curse followed by the sound of Hayden's notebook slapping against the asphalt. "She took them, Dad. Charlotte stole some of the pages."

But Hayden's not listening. He's still mumbling to himself in between broken-up peals of laughter.

"*Dad*, did you hear me? What are we going to do? What's next?" James asks, his voice rising.

"What's next," Hayden repeats slowly, dragging out each word. "It's just so quiet, James."

"Come on, sit up. Let's get you home." There's a scuffling sound as if James is lifting his father off the ground, half dragging, half carrying him back into the truck.

"It will end..." Hayden mumbles, "it will end with... there is a place... a place..." He laughs again but this time it sounds more like a sigh. "I can't remember."

His miserable admission makes me wonder how much he depended on that piece of red thread. It makes me wonder if there was anything left of him after it was taken.

Charlotte clutches the torn-out pages in her hands and looks down at them. I peer over her shoulder to see the scrawled draw-ings of Ollie and me; the scattered pieces of us, never the whole picture. Fractures of time, glimpses of the future—the broken piece of red thread wasn't capable of giving any more than that.

She runs her finger over the paper, tracing the shape of Ollie's dark eyebrow. "I'm sorry, Oliver," she whispers. When she says his name out loud, the whole memory shakes, flaring brightly around its edges as if the moment she decided to give him a name, every-thing changed.

And then, like fog rolling out over the ocean, dark and deep, the memory fades away, and I open my eyes to the stark white walls of Charlotte's kitchen in her California home where the sun has shifted in the sky, hinting at early afternoon.

Her face is wet with tears as she drops our hands and turns away. Zoe, Milo, and I share a brief look. What do you say after witnessing a memory like that?

"That night, I lost some of my magic to the red thread," Char-lotte says quietly. "And I lost Oliver, too. I lost a future where I could have him. I saw myself losing him, over and over again, in countless different ways." She stares out the window, her posture stiff. "I saw so many possibilities, but all of them ended with him trapped in that place. Alone. Just like his father.

"The next morning, Ben didn't come home. I waited for him for days, rereading his letters about the Dreamscape to keep my memory clear, but after a few weeks, I knew he wasn't coming back. His magic had never kept him from me for that long before." She presses a hand to her forehead, looking beyond tired. "I knew then that the only chance I had of getting either of them home was to give Oliver up. I needed to keep him away from my family and away from any magic. Including mine."

I think about that rainy night seventeen years ago when Char-lotte brought her newborn son to her cousin's house in Chicago. I can imagine how it looked, how it sounded as she pleaded with Teresa and Matthew to raise Ollie, to give him what she couldn't. I can picture it all, her hands shaking as she let him go, her heart breaking as she said goodbye. But just because I can picture it doesn't mean I'll ever understand how it really felt. The loss, the doubt, the never-ending questions.

That night, Charlotte gave him up, casting a Shadow spell so strong that Ollie couldn't even dream at night. She tried to keep the magic away from him, but it was a battle she couldn't win. Because Hayden was right: fate does always have its way. Despite Charlotte's best efforts to protect him, Ollie still moved across the street from us, Claimed his magic, and fell in love.

Inevitable—that's how Milo had described Ollie and me.

The Threaders of magic, two ripped at the seams.

The feeling of unfairness catches me in its claws, digging in just below my ribcage. *Don't we get any say at all?* I want to ask the question out loud, but I'm afraid I already know the answer.

"You make your own fate, Gemma girl." Those were my grandma's last words. Now I just have to decide if I believe them or not.

I hesitantly reach out, placing my hand lightly on Charlotte's arm. "You tried to give him a chance. That was incredibly brave of you."

"And I failed."

"*You* didn't. It's just that the magic was stronger."

Even though I meant the words for Charlotte, they hit me hard, like a ringing slap to the face. My breathing staggers as I sink back into my chair.

"Gemma, are you okay?" Milo asks.

I didn't fail. It's just that the magic was stronger.

I try the sentiment on. It feels a little uncomfortable, slightly snug like a sweater that's too tight. But it also feels much softer than the guilt I've been wrapping myself in. More breathable, too.

There's a humming in my chest, steady but quiet, like if I don't pay close attention, I'll miss it. *Maybe,* the humming says, *you'll be okay this time. Maybe you can trust yourself to try again.*

Charlotte watches my silent wrestle, and her eyes soften. "Maybe," she says, as if she could hear my thoughts, "that's what

Oliver did for you. Maybe he cast his own version of a Shadow spell over you to keep you safe, to take you home."

My hands flex against the table. "But how? He doesn't have that kind of power."

"You'd be surprised what the heart is capable of when it really wants something. That's a magic beyond anyone's understanding."

I let her words slowly unwind, carefully holding onto each one as they settle deep inside me.

"Will you tell me about him? About Oliver?" Her question tumbles out like she's been waiting to ask it since the moment we walked into her house. Like she's been waiting seventeen years to hear the answer.

A smile stretches across my face. "Ollie is the best person I know."

And I tell her why. I start with my earliest memories of him, ones that are so faded I don't remember if they're actually mine or just stolen from old photographs and things our mothers told us.

I tell her about how I learned to ride a bike a full year before he did. I tell her about sun-soaked summers and family road trips, all the movie marathons, and the inside jokes. I tell her about the years he won the spelling bee (every year) and how he talked the librarians into increasing his book limit when he was eleven. Milo jumps in with his own anecdotes and well-worn memories, his love for his best friend evident with every word he shares.

The longer we talk about him, the clearer he is in my mind. It's like he's sitting next to me, his shoulder brushing against mine as we laugh about how when we were in first grade, he wore his ninja costume to school for two whole months after Halloween because he loved it so much. How the summer I broke my arm on the trampoline, he waited on the side of the pool with me because he felt bad that I couldn't swim with everyone else.

I imagine the weight of his hand resting on my knee, how he'd draw circles on my skin like he was trying to memorize me. Chills run up my arms as I picture the way he'd glance at me out of the corner of his eyes when he thought nobody was watching.

"You love him," Charlotte says quietly.

I hold her gaze and lift my chin. "I really, really do."

"Gemma, look," Milo murmurs with wonder in his voice.

Charlotte gasps, looking down in astonishment. But I don't even have to look; I already know what I'm going to see.

A sparkling silver thread hums from the center of my chest and into my hands. It vibrates gently, filling my whole body with a single, clear note.

It sounds like a sunrise, like the morning of a brand-new day. It sounds just like Ollie.

I wrap my fingers around it and close my eyes.

CHAPTER THIRTY-SIX

OLLIE

S UNLIGHT.

Wind.

The ground pressed against my cheek.

There's a noise overhead, loud and irritating. It sounds like someone's yelling, but the words are muffled and incomprehensible as if I'm underwater.

Keeping my eyes closed, I try to sit up, but I can't move. My whole body aches as if I've been hit by a truck.

"Carmen! Carmen! Wake up!" The voice is frantic now, low and persistent as he repeats the words. "Wake up, Carmen, please. Wake up."

I slowly blink my eyes open to find myself sprawled in the dirt just outside the border of the Valley. The sun has barely risen over the tip of the mountain, the desert quiet and still in the early hush of morning. I turn my head to see Carmen lying face up on the ground next to me. Her eyes are closed, and she's barely breathing.

I sit up with a jolt, adrenaline coursing through me. "Carmen."

Mateo crouches over her body, shaking her arms and running his hands over her face. He smooths back her hair, which has come loose from its braid, and sprinkles water over her from his waterskin. "Please wake up," he pleads again. "I never should have brought you here. I am so sorry."

Carmen gasps and pulls herself up in a sudden movement, her dark eyes flying open in a flash. Mateo startles and drops the waterskin to the ground where it spills and sinks into the dry earth in a matter of seconds.

"Mateo," she breathes, her chest rising and falling rapidly. "What—what happened? Where am I?"

"You scared me," he says as he collapses next to her in relief, the two of them lying side by side in the dirt. "We are right outside the Valley, of course. You crossed over and hid from me—"

"I did not."

"Well, where did you go?"

Carmen doesn't answer, but her face has a hollowed-out quality to it that it didn't have before. "How long was I gone?" she asks in a low voice.

"Only a few minutes," he answers, nudging her with his boot and giving her a scowl. "And then you stumbled back over the line and fell flat on your back." He shudders, turning his face into her shoulder. "I thought you were dead."

"I was only gone a few minutes? But how..." she rasps, trying to clear her throat. "How is that possible? It felt like I was gone for days..." She folds her arms around herself and shivers violently.

I sit up and shake Carmen by her shoulder. "What happened back there, and how did we end up out here?"

But she ignores me like I'm not even there. I look down at my hands only to see how transparent I've become, all the color draining out of me in a slow and steady leak. I clench my hands into fists; I don't have much time left.

Mateo jumps to his feet and looks over his shoulder at the Valley stretching out behind them. "Forget the cattle, we should go. You might be ill, or—"

Carmen sits up and rolls her neck, wincing. "Teo, I'm fine."

He raises an eyebrow and stretches out a hand to help her up. "Are you going to tell me what happened now?"

She hesitates before taking his hand. "You would not believe me if I did."

The moment she wraps her hand around his, magic pours out

from her fingertips, unwinding like spools of thread, silver and gleaming in the pink glow of the sunrise.

I scramble behind Carmen, watching Mateo trip over his feet as he tries to get away from the threads, but they're faster than he is. They wrap around his arms and legs, pinning him to the spot. "Carmen, what—" He throws his head back and lets out a scream.

"Teo!" she stumbles over on trembling legs, her mouth falling open when she sees even more threads swelling behind them, trailing out of the Valley and into the mountain range. *"Stop!"* she commands in the Language, her black hair flying around her shoulders.

In one fluid motion, the threads slide off his body, falling to the ground in a graceful arc. Mateo sways on his feet, looking like he's about to be sick. He hunches over, grabs onto his knees, and heaves.

When he slowly straightens, all Carmen can do is blink at him, her arms hanging limply at her sides. "You... you have changed, Teo."

Changed is an understatement. Mateo looks as if he's aged about a decade in the span of a few seconds. His beard has grown in full and thick, and he's about a foot taller than he was before, his shoulders broader, too. He has laugh lines from smiles he never gave, and his eyes are creased with the start of wrinkles that didn't exist only moments ago. In a single breath, he went from being a boy to a man.

He looks at his hands, then touches his face in disbelief. "What happened to me?" Even his voice is deeper and more gravelly. "And what was that word you said? What language did you speak?" He points to the threads swirling around Carmen's feet, and when he does, sparks fly from his fingers, landing on the hem of her dress.

I jump back, but Carmen barely reacts, she's too busy staring at Mateo. "The Valley, Teo—the threads—a cave—I—" she chokes out with a sob, unable to form a complete sentence.

He grabs the fabric of her dress and suffocates the flames.

"How did I *do* that?" he says coughing from the smoke and shoving his hands behind his back.

She takes a shaky breath and tries again. "All the tales are true, Mateo. The stars, the power, the *magic.*" She looks down at her hands in wonder and disgust. "What have I done?" she whispers.

In a sudden burst like a dam collapsing, threads of every color break free from the Valley in a massive tangling wave. It looms over us, tall and towering before crashing to the desert floor and shattering the red rock below it.

The threads stretch languidly like they're just waking up from a long nap as they wind through the surrounding desert in a torrential rush of raw power. The ground rattles beneath me, cracking with a loud groan as the quiet morning transforms into something else, something new—something it was completely unprepared for.

I watch in amazement as a nearby ironwood tree triples in size, its thorns turning into daggers as its branches groan from the new and unexpected weight. A small yellow bird that was safely nestled inside its boughs falls to the ground and lands with a soft plume of dust, its body going limp from the onslaught of magic.

"The village," Carmen says urgently, grabbing onto Mateo's arm as she stares at the lifeless bird. "We need to go home."

They take off in a sprint back in the direction they came from, back when the stars were still out and the biggest worry on their minds was whether or not they'd find some missing cows. Carmen's gaze drifts over to Mateo as they run, her shock over his sudden change written all over her face; it's as if a stranger has taken the place of her friend.

I'm running after them when suddenly Carmen turns to me with another black thread held in her grasp. "Are you paying attention?" she asks, her mouth pinched into a tight line as she sprints across the desert floor, chasing after the threads in their downward spiral.

"Of course," I say in between breaths. "What was that? What happened—"

She shoves the black thread into my hand, plunging me into the next phase of the memory, and less than a second later, we land on the outskirts of her village with Mateo breathing heavily beside us.

"I let it out," Carmen says to me bitterly as she watches the villagers—her family and friends—going about their morning chores, the seemingly monotonous routines that make up a life. "All that magic, too much magic. I let it out." She closes her eyes, her lips quivering. "And it needed somewhere to go."

With her eyes still squeezed shut, she turns and points behind us where a tidal wave of threads has risen up, cresting over Carmen's village and glistening under the light of the sun. It would be beautiful if I didn't know what was going to happen next.

"*No*," I say under my breath. "No, no, no." As if saying it will change anything.

With a rumble like thunder and a blinding explosion of light, the wave breaks over our heads and crashes down on the village, completely encompassing everything in its path and transforming the once tranquil morning into a day of destruction. As the sound of terrified screaming rips through the air, Carmen and Mateo run toward the chaos, with me following behind in their wake.

I feel like I'm going to be sick.

We pass a group of villagers sprinting away from the outpouring of threads, the rush of magic licking at their heels like a rapidly rising high tide. Carmen and Mateo run beside them, scooping up crying children and handing them to their parents as everyone runs west, away from the mountains and the threads spilling out from its heart. I follow behind Carmen, wishing I could do something besides tripping after her ineffectually in the background, but my hands are utterly useless here, translucent and fading fast.

"How do we control it, Carmen?" Mateo shouts over the heads of the villagers running for cover. "What do we do?"

In a blind panic, she raises her hands and cries out in the Language—coaxing words, deliberate and forceful—trying to make the threads stop, but it's no use—there are far too many for her to control at once. She's just one girl, and she has no idea what she's doing.

At her words, a flash of dark threads spread out quickly, freezing the earth beneath our feet until it's shockingly blue and icy cold, like a pond in the dead of winter. Carmen's mouth pops open as she slips and falls on its slick surface, her arms flailing.

Mateo attempts to call out his own casting, but his words are caught in his throat as another wave of threads cascades across his path, dragging him by his feet and pulling him under its fierce current before spitting him back out a hundred yards away from us where he lands on his hands and knees, choking for breath.

"Teo!" Carmen runs in his direction, but she doesn't make it far before the frozen ground starts to shake, splitting right down the middle and creating an impossibly wide crevasse with Mateo on one side and Carmen and me on the other. Spindly trees rapidly sprout up on either side, piercing the flat roofs of the adobe homes as their branches stretch wildly toward the sky, their sprawling roots shooting out across the center of the village, upending the stables and demolishing the crude wooden fence that held the animals back.

Carmen dives out of the way as a herd of horses stampede past her in a tremendous roar of hooves, but only a moment later the threads cover them too. Some of the horses grow in size and some of them grow in age, but most of them fall to the ground in a quiet lifeless heap when they're unable to bear the weight of the magic snapping out of the threads like whips cracking overhead.

The villagers try to shield the children as they run, but nothing can stop the relentless momentum of the threads. One by one, they latch onto each villager, either gifting them with power or completely draining them of it, taking their lives in the process.

The young and the elderly are hit the hardest, their youthful or aging bodies unable to handle the strain of the magic as it wraps around them. My stomach clenches as we pass the still forms of men, women, and children, the threads sweeping over them in an unforgiving swell.

Those who are strong enough to hold onto the magic don't know what to do with it. Power flies from their hands, only making things worse as they try to help the others. Their cries of confusion turn into accidental castings, their racing footsteps sending unintentional tremors across the ground. My heart pounds as I watch a small child, no older than four, hold out her gleaming hands and cry. When her mother reaches down to help, she's hit with an unharnessed jolt of power that sends her flat on her back with her arms outstretched and empty, her face blank and her last words still trapped in her mouth.

I've never seen magic like this, unbound with no restraints.

It's absolutely terrifying.

Black billowing clouds block out the morning sun as a sudden downpour soaks the mountain. I'm squinting through the rain, trying to keep my eyes on Carmen when the first flash of lightning strikes, hitting one of the towering trees nearby. It bursts into flames with a strange greenish glow, like a fire made with driftwood. It consumes the tree with unnatural swiftness, its progress completely unhindered by the pouring rain. Lightning strikes again and again until every tree is ablaze, sending acrid spirals of smoke into the air.

I spin in a slow circle, staring out at the wreckage. The village has become a battleground riddled with the cruel casualties of war. It doesn't look like we're winning.

After making her way around the crevasse, Carmen finally reaches the slumped-over Mateo, but he brushes off her helping hand and says, "Go—find your family."

She hesitates for a moment, then nods rigidly. They quickly grasp hands before running in opposite directions, not pausing to look back.

I follow behind Carmen, watching as she searches through the ruins and swarms of people, dodging stray threads and keeping her hands safely inside the folds of her dress. "Mama!" she screams through the smoke and the rain and the cries of the injured.

"Papa!" She runs inside the half-standing remains of one of the adobe homes at the edge of the village.

She cautiously peers around the corner of one of the crumbling walls. "Mama?" she whispers, her voice cracking into a thousand pieces. Carmen's mother has fallen to the ground near their small table. She reaches out a withered hand toward her daughter, her skin papery thin and nearly as translucent as mine, her once black braid now a stark and startling white. Her rasping last breaths rattle in her chest.

"No," Carmen howls, throwing herself to the floor. She wraps her arms around her mother's stooped and frail shoulders and cries. "Please stay, do not leave me."

Her mother offers a weak smile and touches a strand of Carmen's dark hair. "What did the stars become, little one?" Carmen just shakes her head, refusing to answer. "Magic," her mother sighs. "Life. You always knew the stories were true, did you not?" She softly hums the final notes of her song, letting the tips of her thin fingers trail through her daughter's hair before falling limp.

Then the music goes quiet, and Carmen is alone.

"*Why?*" she cries, yelling up at the piece of stormy sky that's visible through the torn open roof, at the threads still covering their house, dripping down its sides like silver rain. "Why did you do this to me?"

But the magic doesn't stop to answer. It doesn't even pause. It consumes and devours, changing or destroying everything it touches.

"Carmen?" a rough voice calls out through the wreckage. A tall man with salt and pepper hair tied at the nape of his neck rushes through what was once the doorway of their home. "Carmen," he says, this time in relief when he sees her sitting on the floor, but his shoulders stiffen when he takes in the full scene. "No, Maya," he moans, falling to his knees and taking his wife's pale hand in his.

"Papa," Carmen cries, reaching for her father. "I did not mean—" But the moment her hands touch his, more silver threads burst free from her fingers, shining brightly in the gloom of the small house. She groans through her teeth and hides her hands behind her back, but it's too late.

"What curse is this," he hisses vehemently, jerking away before the threads can catch hold of him. He clambers to his feet, pressing his back against the wall and staring at his daughter in fear. The threads writhe on the dirt floor, inching closer.

"No! Leave him alone!" Carmen commands in the Language, her voice ringing with authority. The threads slow their approach before changing direction and charging out the door, leaving Carmen and her father alone and staring at each other in silence.

"It was you? You did this?" he asks, his voice barely loud enough to be called a whisper.

She doesn't answer. She just buries her face into her hands and sobs.

I slowly back out of the house, not wanting to intrude on such a personal and devastating moment. I wish I could unsee it all. Pictures of my own parents' faces flash before my eyes as I turn and run out the remains of the door. The second I'm out of the house, I lean forward and dry heave, my whole body shaking uncontrollably.

I just wish I actually had something in my stomach to vomit.

I thought I understood magic because I tied a few Claimings and swam through some memories. I thought I had a tentative grasp on power when I held onto the threads—life and death, death and life—as if such things could be so easily summarized in a sentence or two.

But I knew nothing. Magic isn't just spells or tricks. It isn't just wishes spent or memories made.

It's a hunger that will never be satisfied.

And I don't want to witness another second of it.

I'm tucking myself into the nearby shadows to wait out the rest of the memory when someone tugs on my hand, and I nearly start dry heaving again out of sheer panic.

"Ollie!" Gemma exclaims, throwing her arms around me and

nuzzling her face into my neck. "You're here," she breathes against my skin.

My hands tighten against her back as my head sinks onto her shoulder. "Gemma?" I say in disbelief, my voice hoarse. "How did you get here? How did you find me?"

"It's a long story. I'll explain later." She leans back, peering around at the aftermath of the destruction; at the threads still slowly rolling over the village in rippling waves; at the smoke still rising overhead and the ash falling like snow. "What happened here?" she asks, her mouth tucked into an apprehensive frown.

"It's a long story. I'll explain later." I wrap my arm around her waist. "I'm just so glad you're here."

We hold onto each other, watching Mateo lead a group of villagers across the charred and pockmarked land, their expressions wary of any stray threads as they search for a safe place to hide. Gemma folds her arms across her chest, her face solemn. My heart rate slows as I lean into her side, feeling the kind of steady stillness that only comes from being next to her.

"Hey," I say, my brow furrowing. "You're wearing that white dress again." My gaze lands on the tear on the hem, the grass stains skirting its edges. There's even a sprinkling of blood on it, dried and dark.

Her dress looks exactly like it did on the night I lost her.

My neck prickles in warning. "Gem, what's going on? How did you get here?"

She squeezes her arms more tightly around herself. "I told you, it's a long story."

"I've got time," I say, gripping Carmen's black thread of memory tightly in my hand.

Except I don't. I'm growing less and less solid by the second. I'm the barest slip of a memory at this point. But if she's here, right now, Remembering me, why am I still fading away?

I take Gemma by the shoulders and look her up and down. I touch her cheek, my fingers trailing across her jaw. She doesn't react. She barely moves at all. I trace the outline of her lips with my thumb and lean in closer, hesitating right on the edge of a kiss. She sighs a resigned sort of noise and closes her eyes, but I leave mine wide open. And finally, I can see.

The second before our lips touch, I push her back with a shove. "Who are you? You're not Gemma." I scramble back as my spiking fear catches up with me.

"Ollie, what are you talking—"

There's a loud cracking sound as what's left of Carmen's front door is blasted away. Carmen emerges from the rubble, her face caked in dirt and tears. She freezes when she sees us standing nearby.

"What are *you* doing here?" she seethes, looking at Gemma.

Gemma shakes her head with a light little laugh that's flat and off-key, the sound of it sending a deep ache running through me. The moment her laughter leaves her mouth, the last of the illusion is shattered. When she turns to the side, her silhouette is a dark blur against the mountains, only partially there and melting into the background like she was only ever a figment of my imagination this entire time.

"Well, you caught on a little sooner than I thought you would," the strange, specter version of Gemma says. "Sometimes you can be a bit dense." Her voice has an odd ringing quality to it, a sharpness that rubs me the wrong way, like nails against a chalkboard. Her face flickers as she smiles at me. "Like the dress? I thought it suited the occasion."

And when her eyes land on mine, they flash a burning, glinting red.

No. It's every thought I've been avoiding. It's my worst nightmare come to life. Gemma, possessed and gone. Gemma, completely consumed. Just an empty shell of the girl I love, entirely taken over by the red thread of fate.

"Where is she?" I can barely get the words out. "What have you done with her?"

"Calm down," she says, petulantly, "I'm sure she's just fine. She's probably off scheming with that idiot brother of hers, trying to figure out a way to get you out of here." She pauses and her grin widens, her lips a shocking shade of crimson. "Or maybe she's trying to figure out a way back *in*."

"But why are you here? How did—"

"How?" She snorts and rolls her eyes. "*You*, of course. You did this."

A sinking sensation fills the pit of my stomach as she watches me, her head tilted casually to the side, like a cat watching a bird that's fluttered too close. A predator and its prey.

"Oliver, do not speak to that thing," Carmen warns. She turns her back on Gemma and pulls another black thread out of her chest. "Come with me."

I take a few steps toward Carmen, wanting to follow and leave this facade behind, but part of me knows it won't be that easy.

The red version of Gemma trails behind me. "Must I spell this out for you?"

Just hearing her voice makes me feel off-balanced. It sounds like Gemma, but at the same time, it doesn't. It's like her voice has tangled with hundreds of others, blending into something that's supposed to sound familiar but utterly fails. It doesn't have her warmth; it doesn't have her humor. It's cold and inhuman—the sound of fate, demanding to be heard.

"You just couldn't help yourself, could you? You had to go back and find her in your memories," she says with mock disappointment. "And then you tried to alter what's already been." She tugs on my sleeve, pulling me to a stop. I yank my arm out of her grip. "You damaged the memories, *Oliver.* You fractured them."

A vision of the silver thread held between mine and Gemma's hands comes into my mind—when we met in the memory of our last kiss. I think about how it split right down the middle, how it changed into something new, something red.

A memory divided.

"You know what happens when you break something? Hmm? It makes it easier for things to slip in through the cracks." Her hands blur in front of her face, smokey and shapeless as she waves her fingers back and forth through the air. "So you see, you invited me here." She laughs again and shakes her head like she just can't believe how stupid I am. "When are you going to learn? Magic always has consequences."

"But I wasn't doing any magic." The lie tastes bitter on my tongue.

"We both know that isn't true. You altered the memories, you messed with the magic of fate," she says, gesturing to herself with a wink. She flicks her hand, and a piece of red thread unravels in the center of her palm. She tosses it lightly back and forth. "And then, like a fool, you tied a new knot, creating new possibilities for me to see, and opening a path for me to follow you here."

I shuffle back a few steps on unsteady legs as the realization slams into me: this is my fault. When I tied that new knot, I all but handed over my memories of Gemma, letting them get twisted and warped in the hands of fate. It's like the red thread took different parts of her—her eyes, her mouth, her hair, her legs—and stitched it all together in a haphazard way that's supposed to make sense but doesn't. It's missing everything that matters.

An imitation always pales in comparison to the real thing.

This haunting version of Gemma glances around at the torn-up village, her expression unaffected. "I remember this day," she says, looking at Carmen. "After all, how could I forget?"

"Just ignore her, Oliver. You need to see what happens next," Carmen says with a grimace, offering me her outstretched hand again.

"Ignore me?" Gemma's ghostly form bristles with rage that simmers just below the surface. "Oh, Carmen," she says, her voice low and patronizing, "you know how impossible I am to ignore. Isn't that what you're going to prove with this next part of your little story? And just what are you hoping to accomplish by telling *him* anyway?"

The trailing ends of Gemma's red thread spring forward, wrapping around my feet and rooting me to the spot. The moment the thread touches me, my skin sears with a hot flare of pain followed by a flurry of brightly colored pictures parading through my mind. It's me and Gemma on an endless loop, going faster and faster. It's like watching a time-lapse of our history, every memory that led us to this point. "He's not the one we need, *she* is," Gemma says with a hiss, lightly trailing her finger down my cheek.

I swallow down the revulsion that's crawling up my throat. "You don't know anything about her," I retort.

"Now that's the biggest lie you've said yet. I know *everything* about her. Every hidden secret. Everything she's never told you. The reason she chose me… over you."

I don't want to deflate; I don't want to let my shoulders droop or my face fall. But they do, and Gemma sees it. She grins with gleaming too-white teeth and leans in closer.

"She is mine," the red thread Gemma whispers near my ear. "She will come back and finish the binding spell. And then I will be free." She gestures to her shape-shifting appearance, to the white dress splattered with Gemma's blood. "This is just a little preview of what's to come. You can't fight fate forever, you know."

The smug look on her face, the absolute fervor in her voice, all of it sends a blinding flash of anger through me. I kick off the remainder of the red thread winding its way around my legs as I reach for Carmen's hand and her black thread of memory.

"I wish she was wrong," Carmen says sadly, looking back over the destruction of her home as her thread tugs us forward, leaving the glowering shadow of Gemma behind. "But she's not. I could not fight fate any more than you can."

We land back at the entrance to the cave inside the Valley where this all began. "I could not fight fate," she says again, her dark eyes flashing against the bright and sudden sunlight. "So I bound it."

CHAPTER THIRTY-SEVEN

GEMMA

"OLLIE—"

I expect to see him standing there in front of me with a crooked grin and his arms ready to wrap around me, but when I open my eyes, all I see is Milo, Zoe, and Charlotte sitting around the table, their faces expectant and waiting.

"I thought... I thought I was going to see him," I say, holding up the silver thread still dangling between my fingers. My disappointment feels like being shoved off a cliff. *That's what happens when you get your hopes up too high*, the free fall reminds me. *You crash.*

"Did you see anything when you touched the thread?" Milo asks, moving closer to examine it. "Like another vision or something?"

"No. I didn't see anything." I try to shake the thread loose from my hand, but it just wraps around me tighter, its humming intensifying as it tugs me closer to the Chronicles lying on the table.

"All right, here we go," Milo says eagerly, clapping his hands together. "Maybe it's another memory like the ones Ollie gave you."

The four of us stand waiting with bated breath as the old book flies open, its pages fanning in a delicate arc of whirling paper and faded ink until it lands on the very first page. We each lean in closer, trying to get a better look. Charlotte peers down with a frown, her brow puckered.

"What is it?" I ask.

Milo looks over her shoulder, squinting as he reads. "It's the first casting ever recorded for Charlotte's family line by a man named..." He pauses as he mouths the word. "Mateo? Yeah, I think it says the name Mateo."

My heart thrums along with the thread. "So, what does it say?" I can feel my hope taking me back up the cliff, painstakingly making me climb higher and higher just so disappointment can push me off again. "Anything about a portal or the Dreamscape?"

They both shake their heads. "It's a casting," Charlotte says, her frown deepening, "for boiling water. It's a rudimentary spell that—"

"What?" I exclaim, my voice tinged with dismay. "Why is the thread showing us *that?*"

Charlotte runs her hand over the page and shrugs. "I have no idea," she murmurs.

The thread shakes in my hand again, jerking toward the page in agitation. With a sigh, I tentatively reach out and lay my palm flat against the page. We all wait.

And nothing happens.

"I don't understand." Frustration burns through my body, hot and buzzing. But the thread won't stop tugging on me, pulling me by my wrist to the worn inside cover of the book. When I touch the warm leather, it shocks my skin with a jolt.

I take the thread and place it on the hinge of the spine, right where the first piece of paper meets leather, where the book is stitched and bound. "Tied and bound, but only in dreams, the Threaders of magic, two ripped at the seams," I whisper into the stillness. "I think there's supposed to be more pages here," I say, looking up with a start.

Everyone stands on their feet to hover over the book, watching the thread shudder along the hinge. "Well, how do we get it to show us?" Milo asks, poking the Chronicles with his finger. "Should we try to cast—"

"No," I say, cutting him off. For some reason, I just know deep in my gut that any other magic won't work. If anything, it might scare the thread off.

You're acting crazy, I think to myself, *these threads aren't alive.*

But the longer I watch it waving slowly back and forth like an open invitation, the more I realize that these threads really *are* full of life. They're more alive than I am, even with my heart beating in my chest.

I close my eyes and try to clear my mind, to connect with that feeling stirring inside me—the one that's connected to my magic, no matter how impossibly far away it seems. I imagine approaching it slowly, tiptoeing around it carefully, in the hope that I don't send it running.

I'm here, I whisper to myself. *And I'm ready to try again.*

Immediately, my mouth opens on its own, and words come tumbling out. *"We heard the tales when we were young. Of a power that made the sun rise and fall, that made a tree blossom after a harsh winter, or a baby cry as it took its first breath."*

I open my eyes to see Milo, Charlotte, and Zoe staring at me. "What did she say?" Zoe asks, nudging Milo with her elbow. "I couldn't understand her."

"You were speaking the Language, Gemma," he says in amazement.

"Look." Charlotte points down at the book. "The thread, it's—"

"Weaving," I finish. My sweaty hands are rigid on the table as we watch the thread looping in and out through the spine of the book, stitching together a brand-new page, blank and waiting.

A chill races down my spine as another flurry of words fills up my mouth. *"A power that meant new life,"* I recite, the words heavy and rich with a fullness I don't understand. The thread glows brighter as it curls across the page and releases a stream of words in ink that looks as if it came from the stars. *"But the stories never mentioned that if there is a power that brings life, there must also be one that brings death."*

I let the last of the words fall from my lips, surprised to feel tears rimming my eyes. "It's the beginning," I say with a steady assurance that makes no sense. "Ollie said we needed to find the beginning."

The thread finishes its weaving, growing brighter still before shuddering one last time and sinking into the page. I catch Milo's eye. "Are you ready?"

He nods and looks at Zoe, who glances at Charlotte. All three of them square their shoulders and stretch their hands over the page to join with mine.

The story is told in a second, like a blink that lasts a moment too long. Like how your eyes slowly tip over into sleep, and then...

Dreams.

There's a girl with long black hair tucked into a braid, her gaze fierce and dark and so like mine. She sits on her mother's lap, listening to her stories. But it's more than just simply listening, she's *absorbing* the words—she's making them a part of her.

Because to her, they aren't just stories about the stars that fell from the sky. No, it's more than that.

It's magic, and she believes in it.

I watch as she grows into a young woman, taller and slightly awkward, but still just as fierce. She tugs a dark-haired boy up a familiar mountain, sheer and looming, bringing him to a stretch of rust-colored sandstone, a place where nothing grows.

She takes a breath and crosses over, her leather sandals scuffing the stone as she leaves the boy behind in her search for something *more*.

I feel her terror just as I feel her wanting; it's like a deep surging pit within her, ready to consume. She follows a pulsing sound that beats to the rhythm of her name:

Carmen, Carmen.

She passes the scattered carcasses of dead cattle and crawls weakly across the sandstone until her arms and legs give out. She lies there on her back, blinking at the bright sun until the white stripes of the sandstone curl around her, soft and welcoming.

The threads pull her along until she reaches the end, and the sandstone shifts, transforming into a forest, green and lush and completely unexpected. She watches in wonder as the plants bloom and grow in one breath, then wilt and die in the next. Over and over again the cycle continues.

And still, the pulse calls to her.

Carmen, Carmen.

She follows the silver threads to a narrow opening in the rock, just wide enough for her to slip into. A cave covered in gossamer strands like a spiderweb dripping with dew.

She doesn't hesitate. She closes her eyes, and she jumps.

I watch as she tumbles headfirst into the darkness where two threads twine around her—one silver and the other red. I flinch at the sight of the red thread gleaming across her skin as it surrounds her, but Carmen isn't afraid. It doesn't whisper and it doesn't shout. Instead, it's a quiet question; it asks her if she wants to become something new.

She grips the threads tightly, accidentally slicing her palm, and they drag through the blood on her hand, flaring brightly through the gloom. There's an indescribable surge of power as countless threads wrap around her until she's completely enveloped in the magic.

A quiet question, a transformative answer.

She wakes up outside the sandstone, her body weak and tired—so very tired. The boy shakes her; he's afraid that she's dead. And that's when everything changes.

Magic pours from every inch of her, unstable and out of control, and then it pours from the mountain itself like an unstoppable wave.

Like a flood, free and raging.

It crashes through her village, through her home. It steals and it sweeps, it swallows and it takes. The magic is even hungrier than she is.

There's loss—so much loss—and the emptiness that follows.

It's too much, it's too much, it's too much.

And then, it's over and the threads slowly wind their way back home.

Once the smoke clears, Carmen climbs the mountain again, but this time she's alone. She crosses the sandstone and stands before the cave with tears on her cheeks and dried blood on her dress, the hem of it burned and blackened. "Never again," she whispers to the magic as she climbs through the opening.

This time she doesn't jump. This time her eyes are wide open.

She purposefully strides through the expanse, taking handfuls of silver threads and humming a mournful tune, unfamiliar and haunting. She separates the threads slowly, methodically unwinding them until her fingers land on the red one. "You could have shown me what would happen," she says, her voice tired, so very tired. "I could have saved them. I could have saved them all."

The red thread glows brightly against her hand. She hums the next notes in the song as she winds it around her fist, her face grim and determined. "So show me how to fix this."

CHAPTER THIRTY-EIGHT

OLLIE

"**W**HAT DO YOU mean you 'bound fate?'" I ask, pulling on Carmen's arm just before she steps through the silver curtain of threads at the entrance to the cave. "Wait, just hold on a minute." My heart is still racing after seeing Gemma like that; a crude depiction, a mockery in the red hands of fate. It's left me feeling shaken and unsure.

I look over my shoulder to see the once beautiful and lush forest at the edge of the Valley slowly withering behind me as the silver threads ooze out from the cave's opening in a steady unstoppable gush. They cover the trees and break their branches. They overwhelm the flowers in the middle of their blooming.

Death and more death—it's just too much magic spilling out all at once.

And the threads don't look like they'll be stopping anytime soon.

"Everything's dying," I murmur.

Carmen swiftly turns back to the opening in the rock. "Which is why I came back. Come." This time when we enter the cave—the dark beating heart where the magic resides—Carmen isn't wonderstruck, and she isn't lost. Each of her movements is precise and purposeful.

She tugs me along with her black thread of memory through the glistening threads and into the cave's center. Every time she shoves another handful of threads aside, she flinches, her voice hitching as she softly hums her mother's song.

"Carmen," I say into the darkness, "I'm so sorry."

"About what?" she asks absentmindedly as she shifts through the silver threads, her focus occupied and somewhere else.

"About everything. Your village, your mom—"

"It never should have happened," she replies curtly. "So I made sure it would never happen again." Her eyes shine through the liquid gloom. "Watch. Listen. Pay attention."

With a wave of her hand, she shapes the darkness around her, transforming the sky into the sun-kissed red of twilight. She steps determinedly onto the ground below her. This time, instead of sandstone, it's a wide field of long yellow desert grass.

"Where are you?" she calls out. "I know you are here."

The grass whispers in the breeze, rustling near our feet. Slowly, the red and silver threads wrap around Carmen's ankles, winding around her legs until she snatches them up. She pulls the two threads apart, holding them each in separate hands. "You could have shown me what would happen," she says, her voice sharp in accusation. "I could have saved them. I could have saved them all." A mournful cry bursts from her lips, but she swallows the rest of the noise before it turns into tears that will never stop.

The red and silver threads sway in her hands as if they're listening along with me, waiting for what will happen next. "Show me how to fix this," she says. The red thread glows brightly in her hand as she wraps it around her fist. "*Show me.*"

If I blinked, I would've missed it. Carmen's eyes burn red before rolling back in her head as she collapses motionless onto the ground at my feet. The red thread flashes once before unraveling from her grip and then...

Nothing.

Stillness. Silence.

"Carmen?" I say hesitantly, crouching down to shake her shoulder. "Are you—"

She rolls over and coughs like she was just dragged out of the ocean, her chest heaving as she sucks in lungfuls of air. Sitting up, she rubs her face tiredly. "Oliver?" she asks, searching my face.

"Yeah, it's me," I say, trying to pull her up to stand.

She jerks on my arm and forces me back down to her level. "I saw you."

"You saw me when?"

"Just now. When I asked the thread to show me how to fix this."

My stomach flips over itself. "What do you mean, I don't know how—"

"No. I *saw* you. And Gemma. I saw every Threader who would ever hold the threads. I saw everyone who would ever be Claimed. I saw myself forming the Dreamscape." She swallows and looks down. "And I saw what would happen if I didn't."

A feeling of trepidation creeps over me. "What did you see?"

She blinks back tears, and with a watery sigh, she climbs to her feet. "More chaos, more destruction. I saw a future where magic was out of control." She holds out her hand and shows me a thin silvery scar across her palm. "You see, when the magic bonded to me, I changed its fate."

"Whose fate? Magic's?" I ask, my voice incredulous. "But how does *magic* have a fate?"

"Everything has a fate, Oliver," she says, her mouth pulled into a frown like she's disappointed I don't understand. "You, me, magic—it is all the same. Before I came down here, magic was content to slowly seep into the world, natural and unnoticed. It just *was*. But after me?" She shivers. "It wanted more."

She points to the edge of the grassy field where the silver threads are winding like a river, like an unstoppable force, curving around the bend and trailing out of sight. I remember how the threads gushed from the opening of the cave like a bubbling spring, pouring into the forest and sliding down the sandstone.

She waves a hand above her and the sky fades from the red of a sunset to a night of midnight blue with countless stars glittering overhead. "It was not going to stop. Magic wanted *us*, it wanted people. I opened the door to a partnership I did not foresee or even want." She tips her head and stares up at the sky. "No," she whispers, "that is only half true. I wanted more too. I just had no idea what that really meant or how far the effects would ripple."

Carmen whispers a word, and with a burst, countless silvery threads fall from the stars. "I had no idea that after the magic changed me, it would change everyone else in my village too—it captured those who wanted it and those who didn't. I could not have known that my father would have magic forced upon him even though it was the very thing that killed his wife." She staggers on her feet, looking pale. "Over half my village was lost that day, and the other half was stuck learning how to wield the power they were afraid of," she says, tangling one of the loose threads around her fingers. "Well, most were afraid. Others were glad for the change, no matter the cost."

She falls to her knees, the long yellow grass closing in around her. "The magic was not malicious, though. No, I could feel its intentions. It was simply... curious. But I could not let that curiosity harm anyone else." She presses both hands to the ground and murmurs something under her breath. The grass vanishes and the true nature of the cave is revealed: a galaxy of swirling stars and thousands upon thousands of swaying threads—a rippling sea, wild and untamed, feeding into the river that flows out of the cavern.

"When I asked fate to show me how to fix this, I saw myself holding the threads of magic and whispering words in a foreign tongue. I saw myself creating a weaving so beautiful, it would have made Mama weep." Carmen's memory unfolds around me in a blur of movement and color. "It needed to be contained and slowly released," she says. "That is what I saw. Because we were *changed*—our bodies, our very natures. I saw that this magic would be passed down to our children, there was no escaping that fate. But..." She moves the silver threads through her hands, humming her mother's song. "With a little tweaking, I could change things for the better."

In a sudden surge of power, Carmen flings the weaving of the silver threads out from her grasp. I watch as the threads snap into place, cutting off the flow of the river and creating a sort of net to keep the magic from escaping. Glistening walls extend from the floor and up into the stars shining overhead, forming the shape of a cavern.

"The Dreamscape," I say with wonder.

"Yes," she says, her tired eyes still trained on the stars, "a place to hold onto magic and a place to let it go. But it was not enough, Oliver, I was too late. There was already too much magic released out into the world."

Carmen circles the cavern, her steps slow and heavy. "When I held the red thread, I saw babies being born with their magic, completely out of control and volatile. Can you imagine it? Little ones holding this kind of power, harnessing the magic of the earth before they could even walk on their own." She shudders and shakes her head. "I would not allow it."

She presses her hands to the cavern walls and whispers a stream of words, coaxing, pleading. "I promised the magic it could still come out if it had some patience and waited until the children were older."

"Until they were seventeen," I say as understanding dawns on me. "That's why you created the Claimings. And the three branches of magic—"

"To keep one person from being too overwhelmed with power. Because raw magic, all on its own with no guidance, no path to follow," she turns to me, her gaze imploring, "is too much."

I think back to the sea of memories, to the tempestuous ocean of threads swelling around me, always on the brink of engulfing me in its waves. Life and loss, heartache and love—all of it feeding into the memories of magic.

"*This place is not meant for us,*" Lillian had told me. And she was right.

It's too much to hold onto without sinking under the weight of it. It's like Carmen wanted to teach us to swim even though we were destined to drown.

"The magic needed direction." She runs her fingers along the threads dangling from the walls. "So I gave it one. Or three, I should say. One branch was controlled by words, too rich with meaning to be fully comprehended, but borrowed only. Because no person can hold the Language in their mouths and minds forever," she says with a sigh. "Not without going mad." With a wave of her hand and another stanza of her song, some of the threads change from silver to a glistening golden amber. "I gave this one to the soundest of mind, to the ones who would have the patience to spend their whole lives searching for the right words."

Casting.

"Another branch was controlled by the earth itself, by all the elements in their natural state. This one is the most physical, and the one that caused the most damage when it was left untethered; our bodies were not meant to hold that much energy at once. So I gave it to the strongest, to the ones most capable of holding fire in their hearts." She hums along to her song and the next wave of threads turns a dark and mossy green.

Elemental.

"And the last branch was a marriage of the two. One that required more time and creativity, but one whose possibilities are infinite. This magic took what was given and what was wished for and made it a reality. I gave this power to the ones who let their wisdom guide them, to those who know power need not be impulsive." With the final notes of her song, the last of the threads turn a deep purple.

Mixing.

The Dreamscape pulses as she scatters the threads back up into the waiting stars, the countless pinpricks of light that would either be Claimed or wouldn't. A tapestry of what was to come.

"Laws that govern, threads that bind, the knots that tether us to time." The words hiss from her mouth in a delicate stream, soft and fleeting and melting in the air like snowflakes as she ties the knots and binds the magic, bending it to her will and her rules.

It's a wonder to see it all laid out before me like this; every piece of magic, every branch bound and tied and waiting to be

Claimed. But there's this nagging question in the back of my mind that I just can't ignore. "I don't understand," I say slowly, watching as Carmen continues to wander around, tying knots on the silver threads that anchor the Dreamscape. "How did *you* decide what each branch would be? And how did you decide who would get it?"

She pauses, dropping her hands to her sides, her face full of shadows and things left unsaid.

"Well, *she* wasn't supposed to," a voice says from behind me. "Isn't that right, Carmen?"

The red thread version of Gemma walks out from the darkness in her torn white dress, her feet bare and lighter than smoke on the shining floor. Her eyes flash red when they land on me, and my stomach drops in warning. She crosses her arms and looks up at the stars, her mouth tucked into a pout. "Go ahead Carmen, finish your story. You're getting to the best part," she says, her voice laced with a ringing bitterness. "Tell him how you asked me to show you the way, to show you a future where you could have magic *and* peace, but how you got cold feet in the end."

I hate acknowledging this version of Gemma, this cheap imitation brought to life by fate, but the question bursts from my mouth before I can stop myself. "Cold feet?"

Carmen clutches the sides of her head and groans. "Every time you are here, it is so loud," she says, glaring at Gemma. "I cannot think."

Gemma smiles, but it's a cruel sort of thing that looks wrong on her face. "Well, that's what happens when you ask to *see*, to *know*. That's what happens when you look ahead. You humans are all the same. So demanding, so ungrateful."

Carmen crouches on the ground and wraps her arms around herself, rocking gently back and forth. "It is so loud," she mutters again. "I hear so many voices."

Gemma steps around her and circles me slowly. "So you see, Oliver, I showed Carmen how to weave the Dreamscape, how to divide the magic into three branches. I taught her everything she knows. And then she decided to take what didn't belong to her."

"What—what did she take?" I ask, my eyebrows raising. I try to step away from Gemma, but she yanks me forward by the hem of my t-shirt until she's pressed up against my chest.

"My job," she hisses, her voice magnified with the sound of thousands. "She took on the role of fate."

Fate.

The memory crashes around me as the word reverberates off the walls of the Dreamscape and into my skull with a dull aching throb.

Suddenly, Carmen's memory shifts, and there she is, tugging Mateo into the cavern by his hand, his face lit with fascination "What is this place, Carmen? Is this where you found the magic?" There's an eagerness to his voice that shocks me. I'm still reeling from the destruction of his home. Is he not? "It looks like a dream," he says under his breath.

Carmen has a hard time meeting his gaze like she's still uncomfortable with the suddenness of his aging, this physical reminder of how the magic affected him. "This is where we will keep the magic," she says, not quite answering his question.

"Keep? We?" he asks with a frown.

"I need your help, Teo." She walks over to the wall closest to her, and points to the silver threads trailing down across the floor. "I need you to help me tie the last of the knots."

"But what are you doing?" he asks. "No one has seen you for days. Your father is out of his mind with worry. You just vanished. And so soon after everything."

"I have been gone for days? It has only felt like minutes," she says softly. "How is everyone? How is Papa?"

Mateo looks down at his feet. "Everyone is... adjusting."

"He does not want to see me, not until I fix this."

"What are you talking about? Of course he does," Mateo says, trying to take her hand, but she pulls away, leaving his hand swinging limply by his side. "But Carmen, maybe we can find some good in this."

She takes another step away from him and closer to the threads, her features hardening at his words.

"Look," he says in a rush, "I know you are hurting. I am too. We all are. But our village could *thrive* with this magic."

Carmen's mouth flattens into a thin line. "I need you to help me tie the last of the knots," she repeats.

He walks closer, staring at the silvery threads that hang from the walls and the stars gleaming in the sky. Thick clouds billow in the distance followed by a flash of lightning. "What is this place?" he asks again.

"If you want our village to *thrive*, then you need to give me your hand," Carmen says.

"Are you watching?" Gemma asks me, leaning in closer, her red eyes boring into mine. "Because this is the moment when everything changed."

My heart hammers in my chest as Mateo slowly gives his hand to Carmen. The moment his fingers make contact, she loops the red thread around his wrist. "What are you doing?" he asks in alarm, trying to peel the thread off, but Carmen only tightens her grip.

"It will take two of us to close this gate." The red thread on his arm glows, eerie and bright. She adds a silver thread to the knot around his wrist. *"Tied and bound,"* she says, her dark eyes shining with tears.

Teo cries out again and tries to pull his hand free. "Wait, Carmen—"

"Enough, Mateo. Hold still, you're only making this more difficult." She quickly slices the thread across his skin until the silver is darkened by his blood. *"I seal your fate."*

She drops his silver thread and watches as it lazily drifts up into the stars.

The first Claiming.

Mateo looks down at the blood on his hands and shudders. "What did you do, Carmen? I feel strange, I feel..."

Tar-black clouds circle the cavern; a storm brewing. "I had to take your magic," she says in a small voice. "I had to give it to the Dreamscape. You and I—we will be Threaders, we will be the keepers of magic. We will control—"

"*Control?*" Mateo laughs flatly. "You think we can control anything?"

"But we can," Carmen insists. "We can fix it," she pleads.

Gemma snorts next to me and rolls her eyes. "Where have I heard that before," she mutters, elbowing me in the side. I cringe and step away, but she follows me like a shadow.

Carmen tugs the red thread loose from Mateo's arm and turns her back on him as she meticulously unwinds it from the rest of the silver threads in the cavern. It's slow and difficult work—fate seems to be wrapped up in nearly every strand of magic. Finally, she pulls it free until it's a solitary single thread, pulsing in her hand like a lonely heartbeat.

"Never again," Carmen whispers to it, "will you steal from me."

She clenches her jaw as she weaves the red thread around the perimeter of the Dreamscape, binding it to the weaving, but not allowing it to be a part of it, leaving fate untied from the magic it always belonged to. Somehow, I can feel the thread's sorrow permeating every inch of the Dreamscape; its grief is palpable. Gemma winces next to me as if watching this causes her actual physical pain.

Mateo vanishes from the memory in a cloud of smoke, scattered on the wind from the storm rolling in. It starts to rain, lightly at first, then shifts to a downpour. Carmen sinks to the floor and covers her face with her hands.

"Now do you understand?" Gemma says, putting her hands on her hips. "It wasn't Cora who broke everything, at least not at first. It was Carmen." She tuts and crosses in front of me. "She was the first to wake me up to human frailties. Cora just finished the job when she ripped me in two. Two different girls from two different times, each unwilling to let fate unfold as it should."

When Carmen finally looks up, she looks like an old woman once again, ancient and exhausted, just as she did when I first found her in her memories. "I did not understand the consequences," she says in a weary voice, her wrinkled face stricken. "I did not know."

"Know what, Carmen?" I ask.

Gemma shakes her head, her short black hair flying out around her face. "Time for the grand finale, Carmen. Show him what you did."

Carmen's black eyes find mine, the light of the stars reflecting in them. "I did not know," she says again. "Forgive me."

The utter anguish in her expression leaves my chest feeling so tight with fear that it's hard for me to breathe. "Why do you need to be forgiven, Carmen?" I ask, reaching down and taking her hand.

She squeezes mine gently. "Because you are Claimed."

I blink back, feeling confused. "I know I'm Claimed, but why—"

Gemma groans in frustration. "Oh, this is painful. Here, Ollie, let me clear things up for you since Carmen can't seem to get the words out." She pokes me hard in the chest, her hazy, red-tinged form wavering. "*You* are Claimed, Oliver. Your *soul* is Claimed. Each and every one of you humans that possess magic is *Claimed*," she says slowly, harshly enunciating every word. Her red eyes gleam as she throws her arms up and all the threads from the stars come tumbling down like the rain falling around us. "The souls of the Claimed," she hisses, her whisper swirling around me and mixing with the wind, sending chills down my neck. "Trapped in the weaving, unable to move on after death. Tied and bound, forever."

I look to Carmen, hoping that she'll tell me it isn't true, but she offers no reassurance. She just hunches her shoulders and sinks deeper in defeat.

Gemma fixes her attention on me, her red gaze cold and unblinking. "Now do you understand why I don't think humans are worthy to possess magic? Look what you did with it."

CHAPTER THIRTY-NINE

GEMMA

THE MEMORY ENDS abruptly, pushing us out with a shove. I land back in Charlotte's kitchen chair just as the Chronicles slam shut on the table, doing a double take when I look at the clock. We were only in Carmen's memories for a few minutes, but it felt so much longer.

It's hard not to feel disoriented by it all. Time feels oddly flexible these days, and I can't seem to wrap my mind around it; it's just too slippery of a concept to hold on to. It either stretches on for hours or flashes by in an instant, leaving me breathless and wondering.

"So Carmen was the first of the Claimed," I say slowly. "She was the first to have magic." The four of us sit in silence as we remember the destruction and chaos that saturated her village, how it swallowed it whole and spat it back out. A chill slides under my skin, giving me goosebumps. The magic had felt so *alive,* so eager. "She's the one who created the Dreamscape and the three branches of magic. Fate showed her how. She looked ahead to the future and saw how she did it, and that gave her the confidence to know that she could."

Every time the red thread flashed in her memory, I felt myself stiffen. When Carmen wrapped her hand around it, asking for its help, I wanted to scream—

Don't listen.

I can't stop thinking about how it felt when I held onto the red thread, that awful moment when my fingers wrapped around it, clutching it tightly. How my mind filled with countless convoluted pictures, all of them painted in dizzying shades of red. They flew past with an urgency that's still impossible for me to describe or even to fully understand. There was too much detail but never enough clarity.

How was I supposed to make sense of all that? How was Carmen?

Milo jumps out of his chair and grabs his backpack off the couch. "You know what this means, right?" he asks, slinging it over his shoulder.

My legs shake as I stand, but I steady myself by thinking of Ollie. "It's time to go home."

Zoe and Charlotte look at each other and then at the two of us, their mutual question evident on their faces.

"Those mountains we saw in Carmen's memory? That's basically our backyard," I tell them.

"Can I see that map you have?" Milo asks Zoe.

She reaches for her leather satchel and pulls out a folded piece of paper from an inside pocket. "Here."

"Thanks." He spreads it out on the table, carefully smoothing out its wrinkles. "See? Right there." He points to the center of the circle. "You were right. The Claimed are gathering around the portal, whether they know it or not."

"Magic calls to magic," Charlotte says wryly. "And that's where Oliver was raised?" She rests her fingers lightly on the map, right at the mountain's heart. "I can't believe it."

"I can," I say quietly. There truly is something spine-tingling about it, how we grew up under the shadow of the mountains where it all began. I'd always known there was magic between Ollie and me, I just never understood the depth of it, the far-reaching complexities.

"Are you ready?" Milo asks, looking at me, his eyebrows drawn.

"I'm ready to bring him home," I say, skirting his question.

And, for now, that could be enough.

The four of us spring into action.

Milo grabs our sleeping bags and throws them into the back of the Jeep while I toss in our hardly touched duffle bags after him. Zoe and Charlotte follow behind with their own sparse supplies.

"Any chance I could get more of that fantastic mixing of yours?" Milo asks Zoe, leaning against the side of her Volvo. "You know, the one with the super-power energy boost?" He stretches his arms overhead and groans. "I'm not getting my usual six meals a day or fourteen hours of sleep. It's a struggle."

Zoe looks at me, raising an eyebrow.

"Unfortunately, he's not exaggerating," I mumble, climbing into the passenger seat of the Jeep. "And he'll be useless to us if he's cranky."

"It takes a considerable amount of fuel and beauty sleep to be this charming, not to mention good-looking." Milo smirks at Zoe.

"Honestly, I could use some of that mixing too," Charlotte chimes in as she slumps into the passenger seat of Zoe's Volvo. She tips her head back against the headrest and closes her eyes, looking drained from all our morning memory hopping. "I don't want to be useless to you either."

Zoe purses her lips and tugs on the strap of her bag. "All right. I only have a little left, though, so it might not be as potent."

"I'll take what I can get," Milo says, his smile widening.

She dismisses him with a flick of her hand, sighing heavily as she turns toward the house. "I'll grab us some water."

"Wow, take it down a notch, Milo," I mutter as he slides into the driver's seat. "Keep the flirting to a minimum, please. Zoe seems annoyed with you; you're probably driving her crazy—"

"I certainly hope I am."

"Not in a good way."

He shushes me as Zoe approaches the Jeep with an armful of

plastic water bottles. "Here." She tosses us each a bottle before handing one to Charlotte as well. "I already poured the mixing in."

"How sweet. That reminds me of the night we met."

Zoe ignores Milo's comment, but her cheeks redden as she raises her own water to her lips. "To your beauty sleep."

"I'll drink to that." He chugs his entire bottle in one giant gulp.

I take a sip of my water, letting the slightly fizzy floral liquid bubble in my mouth. Zoe's right: it's not nearly as strong as it was last time.

Milo tosses his empty bottle into the backseat and pauses as if he's waiting for the effects of the mixing to take hold of him. But after a moment, he grips the steering wheel and shrugs, still looking worn around the edges. "Well, that was disappointing," he says under his breath so Zoe can't hear. "I wonder if she's stressing that she won't be able to make more since..." His jaw clenches as he looks out the window.

Since our magic is fading, he wants to say but can't.

Milo busies himself with adjusting his seat, and I hand him a granola bar before he has the chance to ask. He's going to need it. "Thanks," he grumbles, but he gives me a grateful look.

Zoe climbs into the driver's seat of her car. She checks her phone, then her watch. She's obviously had it with my brother's antics. "We'll follow you. Ready?"

Milo flashes her a thumbs up. "Let's hit the road." He grins, sliding on a pair of sunglasses.

A feeling of déjà vu washes over me. "Let's hit the road," I say back, leaning my head against his shoulder. "I'm glad you're here with me, Milo."

He ruffles my hair before pulling out of Charlotte's driveway. "You know I always have your back," he affirms, punching in our home address to his GPS.

"I know." After a minute of silence, I sit up and say, "I'm scared." I let my admission hover between us, fragile and small and so painfully true it hurts.

Milo chuckles and peers at me over his sunglasses. "Of course you are. I am too." He shrugs like that's the most obvious thing in the world. "We all are. But at least we can be scared together."

I settle into my seat and look out the window, watching as the town flashes by under the afternoon sun. Flipping on the radio, I proceed to skip through every station before Milo gets annoyed and tells me to just plug in my phone and pick a playlist, so I do.

"Perfect," he says, once the opening song starts to play. "This really sets the mood for the 'I'm about to dive through a magical portal to rescue my boyfriend' road trip we're taking." He elbows me and raises his eyebrows.

"Oh, shut up," I say, elbowing him back and holding in the start of a laugh.

"We'll figure it out, Gem. We always do." His tone is reassuring, but the hint of a shadow crosses his face, barely discernible behind his dark sunglasses, and it's just enough to make me wonder if maybe he's not quite as confident as he wants me to believe he is.

After driving for about an hour, I grab my phone and pause the music, my thumb hovering over the call button. "I better call Mom and update her. Maybe she and Libby can meet us there."

"Sounds good," Milo says with a yawn as he mumbles something about Zoe's lame mixing. "I'd be better off with an energy drink," he says to himself.

Mom picks up on the first ring like she's been waiting by her phone since last night. "Are you okay?" she asks by way of greeting.

"Yeah, Mom, we're fine. We're actually headed home—all of us."

She sighs into the phone; I can practically hear her smile. "We can't wait to see you."

"Same here. How's Aunt Libby?"

Mom shifts the phone and lowers her voice. "She's struggling. Her casting is all over the place." After a weighted pause, she adds, "And my magic is acting up too." Her voice shrinks until it's almost nothing. "I can hardly hear the trees, Gem. It's so quiet."

I close my eyes, resting my head on the seat. I hate hearing her like this. "It'll be okay, Mom," I say, trying to summon some of Milo's confidence, but mine comes out lukewarm and lacking. "I can fix it." I realize a moment too late that I sound just like my dad.

Milo yawns again and swerves, the tires squealing against the asphalt as he yanks the steering wheel back into position. "Whoops, sorry." He blinks blearily, his eyelids heavy, each blink lasting longer than the last.

"Hey, you okay?" I ask, pulling the phone away from my ear.

"I'm fine, I'm just—" His sentence breaks off as he yawns again, his hands going limp on the steering wheel. "—really tired."

"Mom, I'm sorry, but I need to go. I'll call you back." I don't wait for her response before hanging up. "Do you need me to drive?" I ask Milo, swatting his arm when he doesn't answer. "Hello? Did you hear me? I said I can drive."

He doesn't answer. He just blinks and blinks and blinks again, but this time his eyes stay closed.

"Milo, wake up!" My heart nearly stops as I yank on the steering wheel just before the Jeep veers into oncoming traffic. I jerk the wheel to the right, steering us onto the shoulder of the road. Milo's foot slides off the gas, and we slowly roll to a stop. After flipping on the hazards, I grab his arm and give him a shake. "Wake up!"

Milo's face droops as he cracks one eye open, searching for me. "Gem—" he chokes out in a strangled whisper. He sounds scared, but his face remains oddly still, his expression heavy and on the brink of sleep.

"I'm right here. Tell me what's wrong," I plead. My phone starts ringing on my lap. I glance down to see my mom calling me back, but I ignore it.

Milo closes his eyes and tips forward, his forehead slamming onto the steering wheel with a loud crack.

"Milo!" I try to lift him back up, but his body is heavy and unresponsive, his head lolling to the side as he slumps further in his seat.

Zoe's navy Volvo pulls up next to us, dust clouding the air as she comes to a stop. She climbs out and walks over to the Jeep, motioning for me to roll down the window. "You guys all right?"

"Milo just passed out," I say my voice tinged with panic. "Something's wrong with him."

She glances down at her watch, her lips pursed. "He'll be fine," she says, looking back up at me. "You both will."

"Wait, what?" Zoe doesn't say anything, she just checks her watch again. "Charlotte?" I call out, looking over Zoe's shoulder to the Volvo. Charlotte sits reclined in the passenger seat fast asleep, her head tilted against the window at a weird angle. Unease washes over me like a bucket of icy water, cold and clinging. "Zoe—what's—"

But I can't even finish my sentence, my tongue feels sloppy and slow. I can feel my mouth moving, trying to form the words, but I'm too tired to speak. Everything feels like it's spinning. I lean my hands against the dashboard, trying to steady myself against my sudden dizziness. "Please," I whisper to Zoe as her face blurs above me. "Help."

Her hand reaches out to catch my head before it slams against the side of the Jeep.

I blink and blink and blink again, and this time my eyes stay closed.

The last thing I hear is my phone ringing.

A door slams. A car roars to life. Music starts, then immediately cuts off with the sound of a hand slapping the volume button. The car rolls forward, and my head tips back, landing gently on something soft and warm.

And then...

darkness.

My consciousness fights against it, screaming at me to wake up, but I don't know how. It's like swimming through sludge—everything is murky and muddled. I can barely remember who or where I am. I struggle to maintain awareness, but it's like trying to hold on to the breeze as it floats by. The only thing I feel is the slow tick of time.

Until I open my eyes to the gray place. My stomach clenches at the sight of the fog swirling around me. "Ollie?" I call out through the gloom, not really expecting an answer. And there isn't one.

Why am I here? I don't remember falling asleep.

"Finally." A car door slams and a man's voice cuts through the silence. "What took you so long?" His voice is sharp and impatient. He sounds familiar, but I can't remember why. I spin through the shadows in a slow circle, looking for the source of the voice, but all I see is more emptiness, cold and gray—the quiet space between dreams.

"I came as quickly as I could." Another familiar voice, this one softer, the voice of a girl.

Then, in a sudden shock, I remember everything.

Zoe. The Jeep. Milo and Charlotte slumped in their seats. Zoe must've used another one of her mixings on us, slipping it into our water bottles. I remember how she kept checking her watch as if she was counting backward in her mind, waiting for the effects of the magic to take hold.

I try to focus on what's happening, but my awareness feels split, torn between two possibilities. I feel the soft leather of the Jeep's seat underneath me and the awkward angle of my neck from where my head's resting on Milo's shoulder; we must've been tossed in the backseat, and maybe Charlotte was too.

I can feel all of that happening to me, but at the same time, all I can see is the gray place and the cold nothingness that's seeping its way through my clothes and onto my skin. My whole body burns from the feeling of being in two places at once; it stings like I'm being ripped in half.

"You got what you wanted, now please, just let my mom go," Zoe says desperately, her voice filtering in through my ears and into the grayness. "You promised you'd let her go if I brought them to you." Her voice breaks at the end, turning into a hollow-sounding sob.

"You brought them to me, but now we need to finish what we started. I need the girl. Take me where she was going."

The man's voice grates against my every nerve as memories flash before me. Hands glowing and green, gripping my grand-mother's shoulders.

No.

It's James.

And he has Zoe's mom.

I start to run through the emptiness, searching for a way out.

"How did you know I was with Gemma?" Zoe asks. Her voice sounds muted and stuffy like she's been crying. "How did you find me?"

"When you didn't check in with your mom for a few days, she got worried," James says gruffly. "So she had a friend cast a locator spell on you. You know, if you don't want to be found, you shouldn't leave so many personal effects behind. It almost makes it too easy." He shifts in his seat and his voice grows louder and closer as if he's twisted his head around to look at the back-seat. "And it seems that fate was on my side because you not only had Gemma with you, but my long-lost sister too." He snorts. "There you were, gathered around a map, talking about portals and threads and the origin of magic—" His voice snags longingly on the word. "It seems my patience has finally paid off."

Zoe sniffs. "But if you don't have magic anymore—"

"Because she *stole* it from me," he hisses through clenched teeth. "She's going to give me my magic back, and then I'll use her to open the portal." His voice takes on a manic quality; he sounds just like his father. "Then I will finally break the Claimings, and everyone can have as much magic as they'd like."

"But the Claimings, they're—"

"Just shut up and drive."

I feel dizzy from trying to listen to their conversation while still being in the gray place, my mind aching from the effort of maintaining consciousness in both places. My whole body feels like it's being pulled in opposite directions, so much so that I'm pretty convinced I'll be ripped in half at any second. The pressure pounds in my skull and rattles my teeth.

And it *burns*.

I look down, half expecting to see my heart falling out of my chest in a gaping wound, a jagged tear trailing down the length of my entire body. But when I look down, all I see is a silver thread, brighter than moonlight and stronger than ever before. My breath hitches as I reach out to touch it. I slowly curl my fingers around the thread and give it a gentle tug. It wraps around my hand almost playfully, like it's glad to see me, shimmering as it slides over my skin, coiling around me with a soft hum.

"The Threaders of magic, when two become found," I whisper inside my mind, thinking of Ollie and the threads that stretch between us. My chest hums in response, a deep and resonating note that vibrates through my whole body. It sounds like a quiet reminder, like something I've known all along.

"What are you trying to show me?" I ask the thread, the words of the Language ready and waiting.

The gray space fills with a light so blinding, I have to shield my eyes. That same searing, stinging feeling of being ripped down the middle intensifies until I'm sure I must be screaming from the pain of it. But as my hands clutch at my chest and my stomach, I realize that I'm not splitting in half; I'm not being torn in two.

I'm mending.

The silver thread wraps down the length of my body, pulling me forward through the brightening light. My hands catch onto thread after thread; the entire gray place is full of them, so many that I lose count. And on the other side of the silvery threads, I see the faint flickering of stars, burning bright and familiar.

It makes me wonder if the threads were always here, patiently waiting for me to remember. Maybe this place only seemed gray because that's how it always felt to me—unbearably lonely and leached of all its color. A sigh escapes my mouth, an exhale so deep there must be nothing of me left at all. I reach out a hand, and then...

I'm drowning.

Water fills my lungs and sputters out my mouth, sending me into a coughing fit. My eyes fly open to a dark sky, dusky and indigo with a handful of scattered stars. But these aren't the stars of the Dreamscape. The Superstition Mountains loom over-head—a stark silhouette against the late evening sky.

I'm home.

I lower my outstretched hand and sit up, wiping the water off my face with my sleeve.

"Rise and shine, Gemma," James says, staring down at me coldly. He tosses an empty water bottle onto the ground and crouches down so his face is level with mine. I try not to flinch, but seeing him here like this brings every single bad memory of mine to the surface in a roaring rush. It's hard to stay steady under the weight of it. It feels almost impossible to hold my ground.

"I want my magic back," he says softly, menacingly, holding out his hand as if I could just hand it to him.

CHAPTER FORTY

OLLIE

I DON'T KNOW how I'd never noticed them before, the voices of the Claimed.

Their whispers sway alongside their threads, dangling from the stars that contain them, their voices rising and falling like waves lapping against the shore. I can't get over the fact that they'd been here this whole time, all the Claimed who came before me, lost in the blinking of the stars with their threads tumbling out on the other side, feeding into the white-capped sea of memories.

"Tied and bound, I seal your fate," Gemma recites as she saunters toward me, more phantom than substance, her red eyes glowing under the sheen of the threads. She swats a few out of her face. "Every fate sealed with a drop of Threader blood is sentenced to prison, tied and bound to their magic forever. Because where does magic always return, Ollie?"

Carmen's words come racing through my mind. *"When I was very young, I used to ask my mother where the power came from. Her answer was always the same. 'From the earth itself, little one. From its very heart.'"*

"It comes back here," I say softly. "To its home."

I think back to when I was trapped in the Dreamscape and lost in the magic, checked out and unaware, completely surrendered to the Claimings. It was a bright flash of purple that woke me up, followed by the scents of lavender and sage. It was Ellen's thread.

That was the moment her soul returned to the Dreamscape, never to move on.

"Ten points to Oliver!" Gemma exclaims with an emphatic slow clap. "It comes back *here*. And thanks to Carmen, so do the souls of the Claimed."

I back away from Gemma, my eyes fixed on the shimmering threads. I don't know how I ever could've assumed that tying a Claiming, that fusing a person with magic, was a temporary, fleeting thing that only lasted the span of a lifetime.

Gemma reaches out and grabs my arm, her touch both too hot and too cold at the same time, making me shudder. Her fingers trace over the barely-there scars across my arm, each line a pale slash of silver. "And now you've added your own blood to the problem." She pushes my arm away, her red lips curling. "You've joined the long list of Threaders who thought they were in control. Fools," she spits out, her scathing gaze flicking to Carmen.

"I did not know," Carmen croaks miserably from where she's still curled up on the floor, her shoulders hunched and her wrinkled face pinched in anguish. "I did not know that my spell would keep every soul here, that it would keep mine. I thought—"

"*You* thought you knew better than fate itself," Gemma sneers, her shadow growing taller and darker. "And that was your biggest mistake."

Carmen shrinks back, her spine stiffening in fear.

Gemma's form wavers, flickering back and forth like a TV that's flipping channels. She grits her teeth and turns to me, her burning eyes narrowed like a cat's. "I must say, I'm surprised you haven't asked me yet. Aren't you even a little curious?"

I try to ignore her since I have zero desire to be a pawn in whatever game she's playing. But after a minute, I find myself blurting, "Curious about what?"

"Where your father is in all this mess." She sighs and taps her chin. "Benjamin. Wouldn't you like to see him?"

I try to keep my face composed, not wanting to reveal how badly I want this. With an easy flick of her hand, Gemma summons a thread, this one steel gray, like the color of the ocean when a storm rolls in. "Go ahead," she says, her expression unreadable.

My eyes track the back-and-forth motion of the thread. "So that means he's really... he's actually—"

"Dead?" Gemma cocks her head to the side, studying me. "I thought that was obvious. He faded away, Oliver. You can't live on magic alone and expect to survive. Eventually, it catches up with you." She gives me a knowing look, and I turn away, shoving my nearly translucent hands into my pockets.

The thread continues to sway like a pendulum swinging.

Tick-tock, tick-tock.

"Last chance to see him," Gemma says in a bored voice.

I don't know if this is a trap, or how this plays into her schemes, but I just can't bring myself to say no to an opportunity like this. So I grab onto the thread and close my eyes, willing myself to *please* not fade away.

Not yet.

The scene opens on a long unoccupied stretch of shoreline. The ocean waves crash heavily on the sand, spraying seafoam and tiny slivers of bone-white shells flying across the beach. The sun has already gone down, and in its place is a lonely sky—a melancholy blue with only the barest hint of light. Off in the distance is the sharp outline of a pier jutting out into the sea, where a few solitary fishermen cast their lines out into the deep.

I stand there for a moment, watching the waves break as the moon rises higher in the navy sky. *This isn't the worst place to spend a prison sentence*, I think to myself as my feet sink into the sand.

It's peaceful, at least. Beautiful, too.

I turn my head from side to side, searching for Ben, squinting through the fog that's started to roll in over the water. Finally, I see him. He's walking toward me along the shore with his jeans rolled up, his bare feet sending graceful arcs of water through the air as he splashes.

There's a woman walking next to him. "Stop!" she cries, the salty breeze carrying her voice over to me. "You're getting me soaking wet!" But a wide grin splits across her face even as she complains.

Ben laughs and slings his arm around her waist, pulling her closer. "You'll live," he says, kissing her cheek.

Ben and Charlotte. My parents.

I start to run in their direction, my feet squelching in the wet sand, my gaze unblinking as I memorize every detail. Her blonde hair whips around them, tangling in the wind; his eyes crinkle when he smiles. Something about her laugh sounds familiar even though I've never heard it before, and when I watch his easy gait—his absolute assurance that all is right in the world just because he's standing next to her—it's like looking in a mirror. I forgot how much I look like him—my dark hair and the shape of my nose, even the angle of my jaw and the curve of my eyebrows. It's all him.

Charlotte and Ben stumble through the sand and into each other, the matching gold bands on their ring fingers glinting under the light of a full moon. It's the kind of moment that's packed full of so much happiness it's almost unbearable. It fills me with an instant ache, not just because I know how their story ends but because every star-kissed moment always comes to a close. A flicker and fade and then—

lights out.

By the time I reach them, Charlotte's taking Ben's hand and pressing it against her stomach.

"Really?" he says, his voice filled with wonder.

She nods and leans into his shoulder, her smile more expansive than the sea. "Really."

Ben wraps her in a fierce hug and lets out a loud whoop, spinning her around in a circle. She laughs and swats him, telling him to put her down.

I collapse onto the sand, letting them walk past me with their hands held tightly together, the night full of promises it can't keep. I rub my face with my hands and release a heavy breath. This is the memory Ben's trapped in. The moment he found out about me.

Then, like a broken film reel, the memory restarts and they're back down the beach where they started, trudging through the sand with Charlotte smiling like she's got a secret and Ben splashing his feet in the waves.

And that's how he'll live on, in this single moment, forever.

There's a pressure mounting in my chest and behind my eyes, a tugging, sinking sensation that begs me to give in as I watch them walking across the shoreline. It kills me that this is the moment Ben got stuck in because this memory is merely a beginning, just a brief blip of happiness before the actual living took place. And that blip is all he has of his family, of me and my mom.

There should've been more.

I close my eyes and drop my father's thread, a thread the same gray color as the moon shining on the surging waves, and when I open my eyes, I'm back in the Dreamscape with Carmen and Gemma. They look at me expectantly, but all I can do is shake my head.

"Ben flitted from memory to memory, revisiting this one most often until eventually, he caught himself in it. Depressingly sappy, isn't it?" Gemma says, picking at her nails. "You two have that in common."

Carmen's legs buckle as she tries to stand, the fabric of her black dress rustling as she struggles. "I tried to fix it," she says to me imploringly, her wrinkled hands worrying her long gray braid. "I tried to undo it, but no words would come to me, no magic could untie what had already been bound. So I thought if all the Claimed gathered together to Remember each soul after they departed, if we all shared our memories and offered them some of our magic, it would be enough to carry them Beyond all this, but..." She dips her head, her chin quivering. "It was not enough. Our memories, this magic, all of it holds us here, trapped in an endless loop of the people and places we miss. Never progressing, never moving on."

"A fine method for torture, Carmen," Gemma says with a smirk. "Well done."

Carmen's leathery face is anguished. "I tried to fix it," she says again, "but by the time I saw the first of the souls returning to the cavern, it was too late. Mine returned soon after." She grips her hands tightly together. "Now I cannot even find temporary peace in the repetition of my memories as many of the other Claimed do. For me, there is no rest. There is only the passage of time and my guilt, the warp and weft of who I am."

"Don't you just love the dramatic irony, Ollie?" Gemma says, tilting her head up at me, her face blending into the shadows.

I ignore her. "But why didn't you ask the thread to fix it?" I refuse to look at the specter of Gemma even though technically I am talking about it. "Fate showed you how to form the Dreamscape, couldn't it show you how to undo what you'd done?"

"What a novel idea," Gemma murmurs.

Carmen shakes her head, her eyes black with regret. "I was too afraid to see again. I was too scared to let go." She scuffs her worn sandal on the pearly cavern floor. "You saw what happened the last time I left it up to fate." She lifts her chin, and for a moment, I see the fierce girl she used to be shining in her face. "So I warned the new Threaders to never touch the red thread. They became the village Elders, and they passed down that warning for many years after, until—"

"Until your warning became the stuff of legend, and, oops, someone decided not to listen." Gemma rises to her full height, her white sundress growing darker by the second, deepening to a sickly shade of red.

I stoop down to look into Carmen's face. "But why hasn't anyone been able to help you or the others? Why doesn't anybody *know*?" I ask, trying and failing to keep the judgment out of my tone.

Carmen shifts on her feet. "Mine and Mateo's power had already passed onto the next generation of Threaders, and people were already forgetting. The younger ones reveled in their power, and the fame of the Claimed was spreading. Soon the memories of the chaos and destruction that magic had brought us had all but disappeared, and the Valley had become a thing of myth once again. And then once the red thread was broken—"

"Thanks for that pleasant reminder," Gemma inserts.

"—fate had finally been stretched too far, and no one could remember anything about the Dreamscape as punishment. I *tried* to show my memories to the other Threaders, to find one who was willing to go further than the rest, but none of them would follow. They'd lost the magic of Remembering."

"But—" I start to say.

"Don't you get it, Oliver?" Gemma interrupts with a frustrated noise. "People *want* magic, and they'll do whatever it takes to keep it, no matter the consequences."

"No, that's not true," I say. "They didn't understand—"

"Oh, but it is. And they did." She smiles widely at me, but everything about it is flat and cold. "To some extent, at least. Don't you remember how badly Gemma wanted more magic?" she says inching closer. "All the secrets she kept and the lies that she told? Gemma understands the price that must be paid. That's why when she comes back, she'll be the one to finally set me free, and she'll—"

"Break the Claimings," I say with a sigh, dropping down on the floor to sit next to Carmen.

"After all, it's been foretold," this version of Gemma says, her edges blurring red. "So I don't think you really want to gamble against me." She winks.

I look down at my hands, barely able to see myself. I've nearly faded away, lost to the memories that don't belong to me and the magic that I don't understand.

Suddenly, the cavern floor shakes, sending all the threads in a flurry of movement, the silvery walls trembling and threatening collapse. "What's going on?" I ask, my stomach sinking when I look at the two of them. Carmen looks defeated; Gemma is triumphant.

"Time's almost up," Gemma says in a sing-song voice, throwing her head back to look at the stars as they shoot across the sky in a riot of motion and color. "What did you think was going to happen when you left the Dreamscape? That the magic was just going to sit there and wait?" She crosses her arms, her once white dress skimming her knees, red and cutting. "Oh, Oliver."

Fear roots me to the spot. "But why is Carmen's memory falling apart?"

"Because it's all connected. All the memories, all the magic." She threads her fingers together to demonstrate. "And no one's there to let the magic out as it was promised. No one's there to Claim it." Gemma's hands spring apart as she mimes an explosion. "And, well, I think you can guess what's going to happen next."

It's impossible not to visualize the soaring wave of threads that nearly wiped out Carmen's village. The surging, roaring power that consumed everything it came in contact with.

Gemma's eyes flash, crimson and bright. She moves unnaturally fast, her red dress flickering in and out of sight amongst the threads. *"She's here,"* she says, her voice a gleeful hiss. "She's back. I can feel her. Gemma's on the mountain, and she's going to look for the portal." She tilts her head to the side as if she's listening, a smile tugging on her lips. "She's coming for you."

"No." I stumble on my feet when the cavern shakes again, watching as the threads that hold Carmen's memory together start to unravel, one by one, like stitches coming loose.

I feel like a child for thinking I could fix this, for believing that anything I did would make a difference. I took Gemma's magic and trapped myself here, essentially ensuring that she would come back and find me, walking straight into the arms of a future she can't escape. A vessel for fate, a container for magic. Every thread bound to her, filling her up with power until nothing of Gemma remains.

Has this all just been a pointless detour on the road to the inevitable?

When I look back at Carmen, she's a child once more. She sits on the floor of the Dreamscape with her thin arms wrapped around her knobby knees, fresh tears sliding down her face. Taking me by the hand, she whispers, "I am sorry. I did not mean for this to happen."

When I look at her, I can't help but see Gemma too, her dark eyes lit by the glow of our childhood campfires as she counts the stars in the sky, wondering what it would be like to hold them.

I can't blame them for wanting more. I've always wanted more, too, I just never knew how to ask for it. I've always been too scared, too uncertain. But now I know what I want.

I just have to reach out and take it.

Gemma wipes her hands on her dress and tucks her hair behind her ears, each gesture so familiar and practiced that I have to remind myself that she isn't real, that the apparition made of red thread and half-truths isn't really her.

"No hard feelings, Oliver," she says, her voice growing louder and more inhuman with every word. "It never would've worked out between us. It's not you, it's me." She laughs, clearly delighted with herself; it sounds like she's swallowed shards of glass. "You humans have the most ridiculous sayings, I swear." The Dreamscape rattles around us. "Well, it's been fun," she says, "but it's time for me to go and welcome Gemma home." She spins on her heel, her midnight hair flashing behind her.

I don't stop to think. I just reach out and grab her hand, pulling her roughly back to me. "Let's try things a little differently this time, what do you say?" I squeeze her hand tightly, and her eyes widen. For the first time, she looks afraid.

"What are you doing?" Her echoing voice tries to sneer, but it comes out like a quiver.

"I'm making a different choice." The feel of her sears my skin, but I don't let go. I pull her closer, tugging on her hand until the trailing end of the thread unwinds into her palm, gleaming and scarlet red. The longer I hold onto her, the less human she looks.

"*Wait!*" she calls out to me, her panic ringing out like the clamor of bells. "Don't—" The facade of Gemma vanishes in a sudden burst like it was never there at all.

Carmen stares at me, her small bare feet making no sound as

she runs over. "Oliver, what are you doing?" she asks, her face lit by the glow of the red thread.

The cavern continues to unravel around us as I take the thread between my fingers. The moment I touch it, I see...

everything.

I watch as possibility after possibility flashes before me, each one shakier than the last. Every image the thread shows me is disjointed and chaotic—crisp one moment before fading like a forgotten photograph, crumpled and worn and hardly worth keeping.

It's too much for one mind to hold on to. I can feel myself slipping away, fading into the background the longer I hold on to it. I inhale sharply as the thread twitches wildly in my hands, attempting to escape. But I don't let go, I only tighten my grip.

It's like tying the Claimings, but even more surreal. Everything's magnified. It's life and death, death and life, retold over and over again. It's the song that's supposed to never end but eventually it does.

It always ends with me and Gemma.

Fate can't see past the two of us, right at the point where it was fractured. Because even though fate has found its missing piece, even though it was supposedly repaired, it still isn't whole. It's been altered by all of us—tied and bound by humans who didn't understand, by the ones who refused to let go.

So now the thread doesn't want to let go either.

It whips back and forth in my hand, its whispers rising to a crescendo. *Stop,* it howls.

Unleash us unleash us unleash us.

My hands ache with the effort of holding on, my chest heaving as I search for the answer, the thin line between dreams and reality blurring. It would be so much easier to give in and give up. To close my eyes and surrender to the countless futures unfolding before me, to the magic that wants to eat me alive.

But even fate can't outrun itself, and there's one possibility it's trying to keep me from seeing. As everything flies past me in an unending blur, one option calls out to me like the sound of Gemma's voice in the wind.

It's an elegantly simple solution, one that depends entirely on Gemma knowing what to do.

I wrap the thread around my hand and whisper the words in the Language, *"Tied and bound, I Claim this fate."* I tie off the simple knot, but this time, I don't seal it with my blood.

The cavern shudders one last time before going completely still. "I trust you, Gem," I say into the quiet, my faith in her more powerful than any spell I could ever cast.

My vision starts to blur. The last thing I think of is her face—her lips forming a soft smile, her eyes locked on to mine.

Gemma, I sigh. And then I let go.

When I open my eyes, everything is red.

CHAPTER FORTY-ONE

GEMMA

"I DON'T HAVE your magic," I say to James, pushing to my feet, my sneakers sliding in the gravel. "And I wouldn't give it back to you even if I did. You don't deserve it." I try to keep my voice steady even though my legs are shaking.

Zoe lurks behind James, her head down and her ponytail disheveled. The Jeep is parked on the side of the road near one of the lesser-known trailheads close to our neighborhood, with Milo and Charlotte still slumped motionless in the backseat.

James's cheeks flush angrily as he takes a step closer, his hands clenching into fists. His dirty blond hair is matted and greasy, the stubble of his beard streaked with gray. He looks even more haggard than the last time I saw him, like all his sharpest edges have been worn down from the loss of his magic. His eyes flit back and forth as he watches me carefully, not saying a word because he knows I can outrun him and he doesn't have the magic to stop me this time.

Zoe emerges from his shadow with her hands raised in supplication. "Gemma, wait! Please just listen to me." Her face is red and splotchy from crying. "Please. James has my mom, and he won't let her go unless you help him find the portal."

James's jaw flexes at the accusation, his dark gaze still trained on me.

"You could've told us he was threatening you." My hand instinctively reaches for the phone in my pocket, but it's gone. Zoe must've taken it from me when I fell asleep. I vaguely remember the sound of it ringing; I never called my mom back, so she must be panicking. My eyes flick in the direction of my house on the outskirts of the mountains, somewhere out there in the darkness. A lump forms in my throat, making it difficult to swallow. "Maybe we could've helped. *This* didn't have to be the way."

Zoe presses a hand against her neck and releases a shuddering breath. "I know. I'm sorry. I didn't know what else to do."

The heavy feelings of betrayal and empathy battle against each other inside me, each with its own arguments of rightness and truth. But after a moment, my shoulders droop. I want to be furious with her, but I just can't. I know what it feels like to want to do things on your own, to not have the capacity to confide in others. Wouldn't I have done the same thing if it were my mom?

Zoe and I must've worn out James's already thin patience, because he grabs me by the arm and mutters, "You two can save your heart to heart for later. Take me to the portal *now*." He looks like a man who's barely holding himself together.

He looks just like his father.

"Let me go," I say forcefully, feeling sick at the sight of him. I jerk my arm out of his grasp as the bitter taste of bile floods my mouth. I lost my grandma because of his angry grip and his refusal to let go. Anger simmers deep in my stomach, threatening to boil over at any second.

But there's also a stirring in my chest, one with more purpose than my anger could ever give me. One that connects me to Ollie and my family, our history and our magic. This feeling wraps around me, warm and intentional as it secures me in place and reminds me that even when it feels like it, I am never truly alone.

I brace my feet against the rocks, looking out over the desert where the lights are flickering on in all the homes where normal people live their normal lives, totally oblivious about the things that happen when they go to sleep at night—the magic, the loss, the cycle that never ends. I close my eyes, willing myself to be braver than I feel. Trusting that I'll know what to do when the time comes.

My phone isn't in my pocket and my only reliable sources of magic are currently out cold, so my options are limited and narrowing by the second. When I open my eyes, I've made my decision. "I'll take you to the portal."

James doesn't smile or gloat. He just grabs a flashlight from the trunk of the Jeep and walks to the trailhead with Zoe following behind him, her sniffling growing quieter.

"Wait," I call out. "What about Milo and Charlotte?"

"My mixing will last all night long," Zoe says deliberately, not looking at me. "They'll be fine. They won't even know we're gone."

And that's the problem.

James shoves me to the front of the line. "Lead the way," he says gruffly. I try to ignore him as I breathe in the familiar air, the scent of dry earth mixed with the hint of rain. I glance up to see dark clouds gathering at the top of the mountain, obscuring its rugged peaks from view. "It's this way."

We walk in silence with only James's flashlight and a sliver of moon to guide us. Zoe rifles through her bag and pulls out a small jar, shaking it a few times until it shines brighter than any flashlight ever could—it's like a bottle of daylight. She holds it out to me with a wordless apology. With just one look, she's begging me to understand.

I take the light because what other choice do I have? I give her a single nod that isn't exactly forgiveness, but maybe it could be the start.

And we begin to climb.

The Superstition Mountains have always been surrounded by legends. Stories filled with obscurity and betrayal, tragic accidents and murder. Some people think these mountains are cursed. Others believe there's an abundance of gold tucked away inside its hidden caves, and many people have died trying to find it.

I never paid much attention to these stories because they didn't sound like *my* mountains; a place of jagged red rock and towering cliffs, swaying desert grass and ancient saguaros.

But what if those stories weren't just folklore? What if there was something far more valuable than gold hidden inside these caves?

I've run and hiked all over this mountain range, but I've never even come close to covering all of it. There are at least a hundred miles of unmarked trails weaving throughout. When I was inside Ollie's memories and watching Carmen climb these very peaks, I didn't recognize any familiar landmarks. The mountains were so different all those years ago, newer and less traveled.

Basically, I have no idea where to begin looking for the portal. I just haven't told James and Zoe that yet.

So we climb while the pounding in my chest grows stronger. And I wait, hoping the age-old saying will prove true once again.

Magic calls to magic.

After hiking in silence for what feels like hours, we arrive at a fork in the trail that I've never noticed before. I peer through the dark at the thin, winding route, unmarked and grown over with shrubs. A humming in the air intensifies as I toe the edge of the unknown path.

"Why'd you stop?" James asks brusquely, his face shadowed and out of reach of the beam of his flashlight.

"I've never seen this path before."

He makes an impatient noise. "Well, is that the way we need to go?"

I take another step closer, and the humming grows louder, picking up its steady pace until it matches the beat of my pulse.

Gemma, Gemma.

Like the beat of a drum.

"This is the way," I reply, just as curtly. I don't wait for either of them to follow as I take my first step off the trail.

We walk and we walk and we walk. My arms and hands are covered in scratches from clearing the path of the overgrown shrubbery and the sometimes unavoidable cacti. It's slow going. All three of us have to stop and pull out thorns and needles from our pants and shoes repeatedly. I'm exhausted and thirsty, but I don't say a word. I don't want to give James the satisfaction of knowing I feel weak.

The moon is high in the sky, and my feet are aching by the time we've reached the end of the curving path where a flat stretch of barren sandstone extends out in front of us, tucked between a crevice of the mountains. Even in the dim light, I can see its burnt orange coloring and silky-smooth texture with white winding stripes running through it. It looks so out of place in the middle of this rocky and rough mountain range.

The Valley.

The pulsing grows louder and louder.

Gemma, Gemma.

I pick up my pace, stumbling ahead of Zoe and James. In a surge of adrenaline and pure relief, I cross over the border of the Valley without waiting for them. The moment I do, something trickles over me, like the slow drip of an icy stream of water, and the stirring in my chest changes from a whisper to a roar.

I don't wait to see if they follow. I take off in a sprint, my legs like a loaded spring. I run, and for a minute, I forget why I'm out here, or that the air is humming with so much magic I can taste it—I run just to run. Just because it feels good.

I hear James and Zoe calling out from behind me, but they never catch up as I follow the call of the threads across the sandstone, sprinting as fast as my legs will take me. I keep waiting for the effects of the Valley to slow me down, to force me to crawl on hands and knees to the end of the stone, just as I saw Carmen do, but my pace never slows. The air pulses with energy, but something about it feels off, and it has me on edge.

My arms are covered with goosebumps by the time I reach the small cresting hill. I look down, expecting to see a forest teeming with life, but instead, I'm greeted by a graveyard.

I hold up my light to see what looks like the charred remains of a forest fire. Spindly broken trees lie tipped on their sides. They cover the scorched earth, their branches stiff and blackened like they froze mid-decay. There are no colorful pools of water, and the air doesn't shimmer. Nothing blooms, nothing changes. Everything's stuck in a state of ruin and rot.

Black clouds churn overhead as a flash of lightning strikes one of the already dying trees. I wrap my arms around myself and shiver when the thunder rumbles loudly in the aftermath, my throat clenching tightly. Even though I only saw the magic of this place through the eyes of Carmen and her memories, it's enough for me to know what a devastating loss this is.

I run past the remains of the forest, following the few silver threads that slide along the path. They point toward a small dark opening that's nearly completely covered with threads. I take a breath and shove my hands in, tearing through the strands and trying to find an opening. But I can't get through. There are too many threads sealing the opening shut. *The gateway is closed,* I think to myself, *just like Carmen wanted it to be.*

But that doesn't stop the magic from snaking out of any of the cracks it can find. Multicolored threads slip past my feet and into the trees, magic unbound and unsure where to go. Because without the Claimings, who does it belong to? They ravage the forest before spiraling out into the night, a flash of color against the darkness.

Someone grabs onto my arm, yanking me roughly and sending me tumbling onto the sandstone, ripping a hole in my jeans and skinning my knee. James sprawls next to me on the ground, his hands scrambling along the stone as he tries to grab onto the quicksilver threads.

"It's here. It's here. I know it's here; I can feel it. Bind it to me." He wraps the threads around himself, covering his arms and legs. "Give me my magic back!" he cries. It's a broken sound of longing.

I slowly crawl away, not wanting to get caught in his mess of threads, until a hand squeezes my arm and pulls me to my feet. I nearly scream when I see Zoe's face poking out from behind a fallen tree. She slaps a hand over my mouth and points over her shoulder. Milo's eyes find mine through the shadows, and I'm so glad to see him that I almost burst into tears.

Another figure steps out of the gloom. Charlotte. And behind her, Mom and Libby. My heart surges at the sight of them, their expressions fierce and their hands extended, ready to fight. They run to my side, Mom wrapping her arm around my shoulder. I breathe in her earthy scent. She smells like her garden; she smells like home. Libby takes my other hand and stares out at the charred remains of the forest and the threads spewing from the dark opening like a festering wound.

Charlotte lunges forward as her brother tangles himself further in the threads. "James, stop!" she calls out, hovering behind him. "You don't know what you're doing!"

But he ignores her. Soon the other threads are drawn to his commotion, and they all begin to pile on top of him, sliding over his body and tugging him down to the earth until he's flat on his back with his arms outstretched.

"Finally," he whispers reverently. But the colorful threads don't bind to him or give him any magic. Instead, they slowly leech the life out of him, just like the tree in Sylvia's backyard on the night of her failed Claiming. Too much magic with nowhere else to go.

James's blonde hair goes white, his skin tightening over his bones. Charlotte runs over to him with her hands aglow and tries to cast the threads off his arms and legs, but it's too late. They wind tighter and tighter, so full of life that the only thing left is death.

His breath rattles in his chest as his eyes finally focus on his sister. "Charlotte," he croaks.

She doesn't offer any words of comfort, but she does take his hand. Even after everything, he's still her brother.

"Dad was right," he says, choking on his words. "It *is* real. 'There is a place where all magic resides...'"

"'A place where fate itself lies sleeping, its red heart always beating. A place of waking dreams,'" Charlotte finishes with a shake of her head and a single tear down her cheek. "What a sad waste of two lives." She swallows a sob and drops his hand.

James's skin is gray and ashy by the time he turns his head to me. "'It will end with the one who holds all magic in her hands,'" he wheezes. "I just wish I could've seen it." I turn away in disgust, but he says, "Wait." He coughs, and a trickle of blood drips down his chin. "I can't sleep at night because I always see her face," he whispers. "Just before she died, how she looked at you." He coughs again, his chest heaving. "I can't sleep at night. Can't... sleep..."

I reel back, but my gaze stays locked on his.

Grandma. He can't sleep because he always sees my grandma's face.

He doesn't apologize because he knows it won't matter. "Zoe," he rasps, turning away from me. He recites an address in California and sighs. "That's where your mom is." Then he closes his eyes and takes his final breath.

And just like that, it's over. A cycle of abuse and madness ended in a blink.

We're all silent as we watch the glistening threads slide over James's body, some slithering past us and down the hill, others back toward the entrance of the cave. The dark clouds overhead finally break, and it begins to rain, a soft pattering sound on the sandstone.

Mom leans around me, addressing Charlotte. "May I?" she asks gingerly, gesturing down to James's body lying motionless on the ground. Charlotte wipes her tears and gives her a swift nod. Mom's hands glow a soft green as she waves them over the body. Moss from the forest slowly creeps over his decrepit frame until a small mound covers him completely. It looks as if the unmarked grave has been there for centuries, as much a part of the forest as the arching oaks or the timeworn stone.

Charlotte places a hand on the mound with a murmured, "Goodbye, brother. I hope you finally find peace."

Nobody else offers up a word or a memory. What else is left to say?

Charlotte straightens and looks over at me. "You okay?" she asks, her face unreadable.

"Yeah," I say with a grateful glance at my family surrounding me, "I'm okay." And I mean it. "How did you guys find us?"

"Oh, that was all Zoe," she says.

Zoe's standing away from the group, looking at her feet. "I used your phone to send a message to your mom, and then I made sure the mixing I gave Charlotte and Milo would wear off as soon as we started climbing the mountain, which wasn't hard since my mixings have been so weak lately. Also, I left markers behind for them to follow, hoping they would catch up quickly," she says quietly.

I stare at her, stunned.

"I'm so sorry, Gemma. I wish I could've explained more sooner," she implores, "but James had my mom, and I was so scared, I couldn't think—"

"I know." I lean into the irreplaceable weight of my own mom's arm around my shoulder. "I get it."

"Well, I'm fine, thanks for asking," Milo retorts with a glare at Zoe. "Even though you drugged me once again." He stretches his arms before folding them across his chest, trying to play it cool but still looking annoyed that he missed out on some of the action. "Actually, I just had the best nap of my life."

Zoe's mouth twitches like she wants to laugh, but instead, her chin trembles like she's still on the verge of crying.

It doesn't take more than two seconds for Milo's glare to soften into something tender that makes me feel like I should look away. He takes a step closer to Zoe, his fingers brushing against her elbow.

"So, where are we exactly?" Aunt Libby asks, speaking up for the first time. She looks over my shoulder to peer at the blackened forest, backing away when another small wave of threads trickles out the cave entrance.

"Just the portal to the Dreamscape, no big deal." Milo shrugs off his backpack and drops it to the ground with a thud.

"The... wait, what?" Libby's brow puckers. I can practically see her mind spinning. "How?"

"It's an extremely long and very exciting story," Milo says, pulling her and Mom to the side to stand with Charlotte and Zoe. "We'll tell you later, and I promise we won't skip any of the good parts."

Another flash of lightning strikes nearby, temporarily lighting up the sky a dazzling shade of purple. Thunder crashes as the rain starts to fall harder, forming a curtain of water between us.

Milo gives me a reassuring smile and calls through the rain, "You ready?"

Suddenly, I'm standing alone in front of the small cave. My face flushes with heat even through the downpour. "I tried to get in, but it's sealed shut."

Everyone starts talking at once, their voices a noisy mix of confusion, encouragement, and suggestions. But underneath their words and the pounding of the rain is that same rhythmic pulse I felt before:

Gemma, Gemma.

I close my eyes and breathe. *One, two, three...* My mind roves over every thread of memory Ollie gave to me, searching for clues. *Four, five, six...* I imagine each of his threads held in my hand, full of his heart and intuition. *Seven, eight, nine...* One memory flares brighter than all the rest. A snowy night in a forest of pine trees. *Ten.* Lillian's Claiming.

"I know how to open the portal," I say loudly, and everyone stops talking. "I need to borrow your magic."

CHAPTER FORTY-TWO

GEMMA

"**B**ORROW MAGIC?" LIBBY says, totally bewildered. "But how—"

"Aunt Lib." Milo slings his arm around her shoulders. "We've been over this. Everything you thought you knew about magic? Throw it out the window." He turns to me with a grin that requires no twin telepathy. "Trust Gem. She's got this."

He ushers everyone forward to form a tight circle around me, then gestures for them all to join hands. I plant my feet firmly on the sandstone and hold my own hands out, my palms facing up.

Here goes nothing.

I try to remember the Elders' exact phrasing when they borrowed magic to open the portal at Lillian's Claiming. "Who here will offer some magic so that I may Claim mine?" I ask, wincing at the formal wording.

That doesn't feel right, so I try again. I clear my throat and wipe my sweaty hands on my already-wet jeans, peering at my friends and family through the pouring rain. "I need your help," I call out over the deluge. "I need to borrow some magic so I can free Ollie from his. Will you help me?"

"I will," Milo says before I've even finished talking.

"So will I," Zoe adds with a small smile.

"Me too," Charlotte promises.

"You know I will, Gemma girl," Mom reassures.

Libby drops my mom's and Milo's hands, stepping away from the circle. "I want to help, Gem, but I don't think I have any magic left to give," she confesses, her face a mournful blur in the rain. "I can hardly feel it. The words are just... gone."

I reach out and grab her by the hand, pulling her back to the circle. "There's more than one way to offer magic, Libby. You being here is enough."

She wipes the rain out of her eyes, considering me before taking my mom and Milo by the hands once more and completing the circle. "You can take whatever I have left," she says, finishing the spell, her voice barely audible over the storm.

One by one, their hands start to glow as everyone adds a bit of their magic to the circle until the blackened forest is lit with an otherworldly gleam, like the softest sunrise. The circle is simple and lacking in pageantry, but I think it's the most beautiful thing I've ever seen.

They don't just believe in magic, they believe in me.

I start with Milo, taking his glowing hand in mine and watching in wonder as a delicate golden thread unravels from his palm. I don't hesitate before taking it between my fingers. I just keep breathing and try my hardest to believe as much as they do.

He offers me an encouraging smile as I move over to Zoe and take the purple thread held in her hand, weaving it together with Milo's. Charlotte and Mom each offer me their magic as well, adding their threads to the intricate braid of gold, purple, and green. Somehow, impossibly, my fingers know the exact pattern to follow. They dance across the threads, more certain than they have any right to be.

When I get to Libby her hand is empty except for a meager light caught in the center of her palm, flickering like a candle that's about to burn out. I take her hand in mine and give it a squeeze, taking the magic of her support—thread or no thread. She squeezes me back, her chin held high as the rain falls in sheets around us.

The braided threads glow through the gloom as I walk over to the entrance of the cave and stretch it over the opening. The words come easily; I don't even have to search through my memory for them.

"*Laws that govern,*" I whisper in the Language, "*threads that bind. The knots that tether us to time.*" I imagine Ollie saying the words with me, his voice mixing with mine, the words ancient and dripping with magic. "*Woven in starlight, written in the sky. Our fates tied together in a single line.*"

The braid of threads flashes with a surge of light, shaking underneath my grip, but I don't let go.

I'm coming, Ollie, I add to the spell. *I'm coming.*

The mouth of the cave widens as the silver threads that were once sealing it shut peel off the stone and slide out of the way, bowing in submission. Beyond the opening, there's only darkness, deep and all-encompassing. Everyone gathers behind me, peering into the cave. Mom and Milo each place a hand on my back.

"All right, let's go," he says, swinging his backpack over his shoulders.

I hold out a hand to stop him. "No. I have to go alone." The scared part of me wants them to argue—to demand that I let them come—but I know that listening to my fear won't save Ollie. "I have to do this. My magic belongs in there. Yours doesn't. Not anymore." I take a deep breath and release it. "I can do this."

I say it more for me than for them, but Milo throws his arms around me in a bone-crushing hug. "Tell him I say hi."

"You can tell him yourself when we get back."

Mom's the last one to let me go, her arms swinging limply by her side. I wonder if she's thinking about my dad and how he left and never came back. "Be safe, Gemma girl."

"Wait," Zoe calls out. She rushes to my side and slips me a small bottle with crystal-clear liquid inside. "It's another dose of my mixing that restores strength. You look exhausted, so I figured you could use a little boost." She chews on her lip and dips her head, her wet ponytail swinging. "It's the real thing this time, but if you don't want to drink it, that's fine, I—"

I grab the bottle and tip the fizzy liquid into my mouth.

Instantly, I feel as if I've just woken up from a very deep and satisfying sleep. My feet and head no longer ache, and a steady stream of energy flows through me. "I trust you, Zoe," I say, tossing her the empty bottle, "and thanks."

Her eyes are wide with surprise as she backs away to rejoin the circle. Milo slips his arm around her shoulders, and for once she doesn't shrug him off. This time, she leans in, her stiff posture finally relaxing.

"Bring him home, Gemma."

Charlotte's words are the last thing I hear as I step into the cave, my feet slipping on the slick stone and the leftover threads tangling in my hair and clothes. Darkness presses in all around me, leaving me feeling claustrophobic and out of breath. I turn around to take one last look behind me, just one more reassuring glimpse of the people I love, but there's no one there.

The cave has sealed itself shut once again.

Now all that's left to do is jump.

I feel it before I see it; the weight of the air, the electricity crawling through my skin. I run my hands over my arms and shiver, pausing before taking the next step, feeling like I'm toeing the edge of a cliff.

In my mind, a bright summer sun cuts across my face, its reflection blinding on the blue of the lake. I can see Milo treading water below me. He throws his head back and lifts his hands to his mouth, amplifying his voice and heckling me to jump.

Ollie floats next to him, his lips pinched together as he takes in the height of the cliff. But when his eyes catch mine, he smiles, one corner of his mouth flicking higher than the other. He might be afraid to jump, but he never wavers when he watches me. He knows I can do it. He gives me a nod, then tips his head back to watch me leap.

I feel it before I see it.

I step off the ledge, plummeting straight into a free fall that seems as if it will never end. But for the first time in what feels like a long time, I don't dread the fall. Instead, I keep my eyes open, letting them sting from the wild wind as I breathe in lungful after lungful of cold dry air that feels as if it's never been touched by another human before.

I breathe and I see and I let myself feel *alive*.

When my feet land soundlessly on the smooth stone floor, I look up through the curtains of my soaking-wet hair, still half-hoping to see a galaxy full of brilliant stars. But instead, I'm greeted with the black and billowing clouds of a storm that churns through the sky, tearing through the limp threads with a tremendous gust of wind, the Dreamscape shrouded in a darkness so vast, the sight of it knocks the air right out of me.

The cavern shakes as I step out into the open expanse. It's wider than I remembered. I see the large crack straight through its center where Ollie fell through, his hand reaching out to grasp mine. The darkness shapes itself around me, molding to my body as I run, my footsteps echoing with a hollow sound. But once I reach the edge of the massive crack splintering through the floor, I stop.

Because somehow I know that I can't go another step until I take care of my unfinished business first.

I look up to the barely there stars and watch the weaving continue to unravel, the silver threads that once held it all together snapping like sharp shocks of lightning across the sky. The cavern is full of the sound of whispers, a low and steady hum that rattles my teeth as the colorful threads fall from the stars, each one like a wish that came a moment too late.

Magic ricochets off the walls, breaking through the barriers that were once made to hold it in. Like a slow and steady leak, the pressure has built until there's nowhere else to go but out.

Any second now.

The threads hang loose and untamed, blowing back and forth in the wind, whipping around me in a frenzy of color and sound, everything an incomprehensible tangle, an all-consuming blur. My mind flashes back to Carmen's village and the tidal wave of magic that washed over it, transforming her home and her people and changing them into something new.

All for too high a price.

As I look at the threads swirling overhead, I hold my breath and wait for that all-too-familiar hunger to rise up inside me. My want, my *need*, for more, more, more. I brace myself for the battle, but the fight never comes.

I see all the magic, tumultuous and powerful, but I don't want it for my own. I feel steady and sure.

Well, if the hunger isn't coming, then surely the fear will, I think to myself. My gaze shifts to the crimson tear in the weaving, the old wound that never seems to heal. But there's no red thread waiting to taunt me with promises of power, to murmur or scream inside my ears.

I'm standing here like an idiot, waiting for my old ghosts to haunt me, digging my heels in and expecting things to stay the same. But I'm not the same person I was. I've been broken open and rearranged. I've seen all my bumps and bruises in the bright light of day, and I have changed.

Into something new.

Then, a single silver thread falls from a star so far up ahead, I can hardly see its dull light from here. The thread unfurls slowly, so slowly, as if it's giving me a chance to change my mind, to turn and run and never look back. But I hold my ground, waiting until it comes to rest right in front of my face, still and unwavering.

My heart starts to hum, like a song of recognition, and slowly, so slowly, a silver thread inside my chest begins to unwind. I cup my hands in front of me, giving the thread a soft place to land as the humming intensifies until it's all I can hear.

I stare at the two silver threads, each end patiently waving back and forth as if waiting for me to decide whether or not I want to make it whole again.

To make me whole again.

I just have to reach out and take it.

But I don't know how to tie the Claimings; that's not the magic that belongs to me. I close my eyes and imagine Ollie standing behind me, one hand on my shoulder, the other on my waist.

He nudges me forward, his whisper filling my ear. *"Tied and bound, you seal your fate."*

I take the silver thread from my chest and hold it out to its other half from the stars, my hands shaking as I close the gap between them. But just before the threads connect, I pause.

I know that if I touch this thread, I'll see things I've never seen, feel things I've never felt, and nothing will ever be the same. I've never held onto my own thread like this before. What if I don't like what I see?

The Dreamscape shakes in response, a few stars falling from the sky in a flash like a wink. I imagine Ollie pressing his lips against my hair, his sigh turning into a laugh. Since when is he the one to urge me on? Since when am I the one who hesitates?

You make your own fate, Gemma girl. My grandma's whisper mingles with the fading sound of Ollie's laughter.

I reach out my hand and take the two ends of my thread, tying them back together in a simple knot. There's a blinding burst of light before everything goes dark. And then I see...

me.

In the space between breaths, everything I've ever said and everything I've ever done flies through my mind in a sudden flash, too fast for me to drink in the details, yet painfully slow in its crushing nostalgia. I feel every drop of rain that's ever danced across my skin, every ray of morning light that's ever pulled me from sleep. I see my mother and my brother, my grandma, and Libby too. Ollie is a bright streak across the sky, every kiss from him standing out in vivid fluorescent colors, absolutely impossible to miss.

As I hold onto my thread, I see myself clearly for the first time ever, and it's horrible and wonderful and too much to even comprehend.

But still, I understand. I don't know how, I only know that I do.

It's a beginning that feels too short and an ending that always comes too soon. It's the span of my life in a single blink. And it takes my breath away.

Because it is *beautiful.*

I stumble back, gaping at my thread. No blood was required, no words from the Language came tumbling out of my mouth, nothing ancient and binding. I realize in that moment that Ollie never said a word when he removed my magic.

Except for this: *I love you, Gemma. Always have. Always will.*

A different kind of magic, but isn't it all the same?

So maybe Milo was right. Maybe my magic really was here all along and I just needed to learn to reach out and trust it. To trust myself again.

I think of the moment before I kissed Ollie for the first time, the fear and the thrill. The sudden realization that I could have everything I'd ever wanted. But when everything is within your grasp, you have the chance of losing it too. I'm only just beginning to learn that even with the risk, the wanting is still worth it.

I let my thread go and watch as it spirals up and out of sight, the dark clouds covering the Dreamscape beginning to scatter. The stars stutter to life, and the sky blushes a rosy pink, bleeding into a pale purple the color of beginnings. The cavern still looks wrecked and beaten down, but it's a start. It's half of the whole.

Collapsing onto the floor, my hands slam against the shimmering stone. A pulse of light shoots out of my fingertips and up the walls, lighting up each of the countless silver threads until the whole cavern sings, until every inch of the Dreamscape sighs with relief.

Welcome home, it seems to say. *Welcome home.*

CHAPTER FORTY-THREE

GEMMA

O NCE I FINALLY catch my breath, I rise to my feet on shaking legs and press my hands against my still-pounding heart, wondering if I'll feel any different now that I've fully reconnected with my magic. A reclaiming, of sorts.

But as I stand there in the cavern with a newfound energy buzzing beneath my skin, I realize I still feel exactly the same. I'm just Gemma. Only now, I have a better understanding of what that really means.

I approach the crack in the floor where thousands of threads are spilling out in a riot of color. "Okay," I whisper, the Dreamscape shuddering in response, *"take me to him."* The threads hum in recognition.

When I look over the edge, I see yet another dark unknown that I have to leap into. But this time I don't think, I just jump, and the last thing I see is the sky of the Dreamscape turning a gleaming, burning shade of red.

When I was seven years old, Ollie's grandpa died. And the day after the funeral, I woke up before the sun did. I just couldn't fall back asleep. So, I padded down the hall to my grandma's room like I always did when the darkness felt too heavy.

"Grandma, where do we go when we die?" I asked, crawling

443

into her bed and pulling her quilt over me, cocooning myself in the warmth.

Her graying hair was piled on top of her head, her usually sleek bun frizzy from sleep. She curled into me, yawning widely, then flinched. "Your toes are freezing, Gemma. Quit rubbing them all over my legs."

I giggled into her pillow and scooted closer so I was right next to her face. "You didn't answer my question," I said, poking her on the cheek.

With her eyes still closed, she swatted my hand away. "That's because it's early, and it's Sunday, and for some reason, you want to have an existential crisis before I've even had breakfast." She grunted and rolled over. "That's highly impolite, darling," she said, tugging the quilt more tightly around herself.

I leaned over her shoulder and nestled my face into her neck. "What's 'existential' mean?"

Grandma pulled me to her chest and laughed; I could hear the rumble of it under her soft fleece nightgown. "It means you want to talk about the Beyond." She sat up and fluffed her pillows before propping me against them. "Now, what's on your mind, sweetheart?"

I looked down and fiddled with the edge of her quilt, tugging on a loose thread. "Ollie was so sad yesterday, Grandma. The funeral was *awful* and weird and..." I leaned forward to whisper the last part, worried that someone would overhear. "And *so* boring."

Grandma bit her lip to stifle her laugh and slapped my hand away from the quilt where I'd been pulling multiple strings loose. "Well, of course he was sad, honey, he's going to miss his grandpa."

I clutched at her nightgown, worrying the worn fabric between my fingers. "But what if you die? What if Milo or Mom or—"

"Oh, Gemma girl, you can't live your life like that."

"But I'll miss you if you're gone!"

She brought my feet into her lap and gave them a squeeze. "I'm not going anywhere, Gem. Not for a good long while. But if and when I do go, whenever you miss me, you can think about me in the Beyond."

"Where's that?" I asked, pulling on her sleeve.

"Well, I have no idea. I just know that there's *more*."

"How do you know that?"

She leaned forward like she was going to tell me a secret, but then she pinched my nose and grinned. "Because I believe in magic. Don't you?"

I nodded my head up and down vigorously. "Yep, yep, of course I do! I see you and Mom use it all the time."

"I'm not just talking about your mom's garden or my pots on the stove, Gemma. I'm talking about every time I watch the sun rise over our mountains or when I hear you and your brother laugh." She tweaked my nose again, prompting me to giggle. "Every moment my heart beats, that's what I'm talking about. Everything else is just a bonus." She winked and pulled me into a hug. "So yes, my darling girl, we will die. But first, we get to live. And isn't that a marvelous thing?"

The memory fades just as quickly as it began. A lavender thread, the color of my grandmother's nightgown and softer than silk, unravels from my fingers and floats away. "Wait!" I cry out with tears in my eyes, desperate for just a few more moments with her. It went by too fast.

It always goes by too fast.

But the thread has vanished into a darkness so thick, it makes me question if I ever knew what light was in the first place. I breathe into the shadows, bracing myself for what I know is to come, for what I saw in Ollie's memories, but I don't think this is the kind of place you can prepare for.

The sea of memories.

My feet land on an unknown surface, smooth and slick. I feel unbalanced, like at any moment I could tip over and tumble into the darkness on either side of me. It's an unnerving feeling, and it forces me to stay unnaturally still. I know I need to keep my mind clear and not focus on any memory in particular or the threads will reach out and take me there, but it's basically impossible to empty your mind when you know that you have to.

And then I see it.

The steady rising of the swelling sea. My gasp stays caught in my mouth as I watch the threads roll back and forth, back and forth in a rhythmic dance, their colors glittering and luminous in the blackness. My heart thunders in my chest, and Lillian's warning to Ollie floats into my mind.

"Remain still, or they will overwhelm you."

But now I'm thinking about Ollie and Lillian, and it's too late to empty my mind again. The threads of memories come rolling toward me with a roar. The wave crests over my head, breaking with a massive crash, and then I'm swimming in memories.

My mind feels like a book that's been blown wide open, its pages flying by in a ferocious flurry, making it impossible to see a single word on the page. It's memory after memory, moment after moment, and suddenly I'm not swimming anymore.

I'm drowning.

No.

"No!" I say, gasping for air as I break the surface of the threads. They cling to my clothes and rip through my hair, each memory asking me to stay, to stop fighting, and just...

be.

Just breathe, Gemma girl. Just breathe through it, I imagine her saying. *It'll pass.* My mind focuses on the single memory of my Grandma teaching me to settle my body by steadying my breath. I think about us sitting on the back patio in the hazy orange light, my grandma's hands holding onto mine as she counted to ten.

One, two, three... All the threads whipping around me start to slow as they slide from my body like the tide going back out to sea.

Four, five, six... A shimmering peach thread appears before me, and I know even before I touch it that it will lead me back to my grandma. To a sun-soaked memory where I'd be safe and held as she taught me to breathe. *Seven, eight, nine...* My hand hesitates before grabbing on to it. I watch as the memory sways back and forth in the sudden stillness, waiting for me to climb inside and make myself comfortable.

Ten. I drop my hand back to my side.

I can't keep reliving old memories when what I really want are new ones. My chest burns with the realization that moving on without her, as painful as it is, feels better than staying stuck on repeat, day after day.

I exhale.

"Show me where he is," I say to the threads, to every single memory that brought me to this point. I feel a sudden surge of confidence that if these are *my* memories, then I can control them. They are as much a part of me as my feet or my hands; appendages available to do my bidding.

The sea stops its surging, the rolling waves settling as the threads lay flat, completely still like glass. I look down to see my reflection peering back at me on its gleaming silver surface. A single black thread emerges from the sea, leaving ripples in its wake and coiling around my ankles. I reach down and take it in my hands.

The moment I touch it, I smell woodsmoke and desert rain.

"Carmen," I whisper. *"Take me to him."*

The black thread tugs me forward, past my memories and into the blinding sunlight of Carmen's mountains, their peaks ragged and raw in the hash afternoon light. Heat radiates across my body as I'm pulled through her village and past the sandstone of the Valley, deeper and deeper into her memory until I reach the cave once again.

I swear I can hear his heartbeat across the miles and the memories, through all the time and space and magic between us—he knows I'm coming for him.

Another blink, and I'm in Carmen's Dreamscape, under the night sky where it all began. Threads spill from the stars in a confusing tangle of colors. They wave back and forth through a rain-scented breeze, like streamers that fell long after the party was over.

The closer I get, the more my skin crawls. There's a strange energy in this memory, and I can't shake the feeling that I'm being watched. Even the air hums as if it's full of whispers. It makes me feel as if I'm standing in front of a crowd of people or walking down a busy street.

I push past the countless threads, wading deeper into the Dreamscape.

And then I see him.

Oliver.

OLLIE

Oliver saw the girl he'd always loved even before he knew what love was. He saw her and he knew her, but it was like watching someone else. Like a scene from a movie or a play on a stage.

"Go to her!" he screamed. He wanted to slap the boy who used to be Oliver right across the face and tell him to wake up, grab his girl, and get out of there.

He could see the girl's mouth moving and the desperation in her eyes, but he couldn't hear a word she said. It was all just noise, useless and shapeless, the words falling around him like ash from a fire that had already burned out.

It was like watching a horror movie, the kind of movie he'd always hated. The one where the hero walks into the dark room, the old house creaking under his feet with lightning flashing in the background. It was one of those moments when the danger seemed painfully obvious to everyone on the outside, to the watchful observer.

But Oliver knew that he was somehow both the observer and the observed.

"Wake up!" he yelled.

The boy who used to be Oliver stayed still.

Then a single thought crashed into him, unbidden and painfully loud.

She's ours, the red thread hissed, wrapping around his mind until he could think of nothing else. *And you can only hold on to us for so long.*

Oliver tumbled further and further inside himself until he was no longer sure which way was up and which way was down. His grip started to loosen until he looked at his empty hands and wondered what he'd been holding on to so tightly in the first place.

He fell.

And he didn't get back up again.

GEMMA

Ollie stands there motionless, his feet rooted to the spot and his body completely covered by the red thread of fate. It slithers and slides, constricting around him. He looks like he's about to be devoured. His eyes dart to mine, and when I see how red they are, I feel like I'm going to be sick.

His mouth is slack, his expression unreadable, and he doesn't react whatsoever as I reach out and shake him by the shoulders. "No," I breathe out. "I didn't come this far just to lose you now. Come on, Ollie, wake up!" The red thread burns beneath my hands when I touch him.

Ollie doesn't respond. He just sways on his feet with the thread clutched tightly in his grip, lost inside his own mind—a place where even I can't follow.

"He tried to stop it," a child's voice says. There, in the shadows behind Ollie, is a small girl sitting on the floor, her spindly arms wrapped around her legs and her long black braid hanging down her back.

"Carmen?" I ask, crouching down to see her more clearly. The girl blends into the darkness, her slight form wavering in the dim light, hidden amongst the dangling threads.

"I was only trying to help," she says in between sniffles. "I thought he could fix it. I *saw* him fixing it."

My pulse starts to race. "What do you mean you saw him?"

"Fate showed me. I saw him, and I saw you." Her black gaze is fathomless as it takes me in. *"It ends with the one who holds all magic in her hands,"* she mutters, sending chills down my spine. "That is what I heard." She looks up at Ollie, her lower lip trembling. "Can you fix it? I did not mean to meddle." Her face flickers like she's on the verge of disappearing.

"I can try," I say, rising to my feet and pushing back against the crippling weight of expectations. "But I don't know what to do. I'm not holding all the branches in my hands. I don't have that kind of magic."

Carmen doesn't answer. She just sinks back further into the hanging threads, barely visible except for her dark eyes shining.

When I look at the glistening red thread wrapped around Ollie's body it's like looking into the broken future of what I would've become—a vessel for magic, lost to fate. And now Ollie's standing in my place.

I reach out and touch his face, running my fingers over his smooth skin, shuddering over how cold he feels. "Oliver, I'm here." My voice breaks as my tears begin to fall. "I'm here, it's okay. Ollie, wake up, please. Please wake up." I try to loosen his grip on the thread, but his fingers are stiff and immovable. "You can let go now. It's my turn to help you."

But Ollie stays motionless, his red eyes blank and staring. My frustration builds inside me, beating against my ribs with clenched fists. I don't know how to fix this. I don't know what to do. I barely remember how to take care of myself.

"Remember," I whisper, as the solution slams into me like a punch. "That's it. I need to Remember."

I think about how my memories once led me to Ollie, inside the magic of a last kiss Remembered. Then I think about what he said to me right before I lost him again. *It's not just the threads that connect us, it's all of this. It's every moment we've ever spent together. It's our history. It's you and me. That's the kind of magic I can believe in.*

"Do you know what my earliest memory of you is?" I say, keeping one hand on his face as my other moves to my chest, right over my heart. "I know I must have earlier memories than this, but those are more like the memory of a feeling, not an actual memory-memory. But I remember when we were four, maybe five, and you were at our house eating lunch. Grandma made us grilled cheese sandwiches, and you refused to eat yours."

I laugh and press my hand harder against my chest, where a yellow thread the color of afternoon starts to unwind. "Grandma asked you what was wrong with your lunch, and you told her that you couldn't eat a *girl* cheese sandwich, you wanted a *boy* cheese sandwich." Another laugh escapes my mouth—I can't help it.

"So Grandma made you a new sandwich with Colby-Jack and told you it was boy cheese." I snort as the yellow thread settles into my hand. "I'm sorry. You're probably annoyed that that's my first solid memory of you, but what can I say? It left an impression." I trace the shape of his dark eyebrow. "I think that was the day I knew you were irreplaceable, that I wanted you in my life for as long as you'd have me."

The yellow thread shines brightly as I slowly wrap it around his hands, intertwining it with the red thread. When I close my eyes, I smell the buttery bread and the melted cheese; I see Ollie's legs swinging from his bar stool, his little arms crossed over his chest; I hear my grandma's laugh and the sound of her indulgent sigh.

"Do you remember that party at Leslie's house in junior high? I think we were in seventh grade. We played spin the bottle in her basement, and I was sitting next to you. She liked you, you know.

I remember she wanted to sit next to you, but I scooted the other way so I was by your side instead of her. When it was her turn to spin the bottle, I held my breath. It was like everything was moving in slow-motion."

A dark burgundy thread, the color of the old carpet in Leslie's basement unravels from my chest and into my hand. I tug on the thread, pulling it over to Ollie's clasped hands, winding it slowly around his fingers. "The bottle landed on you, Ollie. It landed on you, but I nudged it with my foot so it tipped back to Milo. I told myself I was just looking out for my brother because he was thrilled when Leslie leaned across the circle and kissed him right on the mouth." I sigh and watch as the burgundy thread shimmers between us.

"But I think I didn't want anyone else to kiss you, which isn't fair, I know. I didn't want to share you. I wanted you then before I even knew what true wanting was." I smile at him through my tears, and I don't wipe them away, I just let them roll down my cheeks. "I'm sorry if I ruined your moment with Leslie, I really am. But mostly I'm sorry it took me so long to see what was right there in front of me." My hand slides down his face, tracing the hollow of his cheekbones and the curve of his upper lip. "You knew. You knew all along. And now I know it too."

The burgundy thread glows brightly as it joins the others wrapped around his hands. I see the flash of the glass bottle spinning; I feel my heart pounding and my palms sweating; I hear the gasps of all the seventh-grade girls in the basement.

"Do you remember when I was learning to drive and I got in that car accident? The Jeep was pretty banged up, and I got a minor concussion. Mom swore she would never let me drive again." My laugh scrapes against my throat as another memory unwinds into my hands. "I remember when you ran through the doors of the ER. You were red-faced and out of breath because you sprinted from the parking lot." The bright white thread slides through my fingers and onto his hands, intertwining the two of us. "Then you confessed to me that you got a speeding ticket on the way to the hospital." I hiccup through my tears. "And then *your* parents declared you would never drive again."

The white thread is the color of bandages and sterile exam rooms. As it wraps tightly around our hands, I see the bad lighting in the ER waiting room, the glow of the vending machine shining on Ollie's anxious face; the whole memory smells like disinfectant. "I think that was the first night I wanted to kiss you."

The white thread sinks into my chain of memories with a sigh, flashing brightly once again. Ollie stirs under my hands, his shoulders shifting and the muscles in his jaw twitching.

It's working.

I give him memory after memory, everything I can think of. From the time we were just little kids wrestling on the floor to when we were grown and falling in love. Each memory has its own shape and texture, its own smells and colors. Each one is so beautifully fragile and impossibly tender that it makes me wonder how we walk around with all this magic inside us every single day like it isn't the biggest deal in the world.

Memories are magic.

And I hold them all in my hands.

Soon the red thread is completely covered in the iridescent threads of my memories. They wrap around it, pulling the thread out of Ollie's grip, loosening his fingers and prying them gently apart.

The Dreamscape shakes and more threads tumble down from the stars, swaying between us. Carmen shrinks further into the shadows. I take the ends of every thread connecting me to Ollie—every memory shared and Remembered—looping them once around my wrist and once around his.

Ollie's eyes snap shut. He shudders once, and then his arms fall to his side, the red thread finally slipping free from his grip. But I'm there, ready and waiting to catch it. Because it ends with me, the girl who holds all magic in her hands.

The red thread of fate is hot against my skin, flaring brightly against the darkness of the Dreamscape as it coils in my hand.

Unleash us unleash us unleash us, it cries.

This time, its howls don't leave me feeling confused and shaken, because this time, I understand. "Okay," I say softly. "You've been bound for far too long." I let the thread slip in and out between my fingers, but I pointedly ignore the flashes of the future it tries to offer me. I'm not stubborn for nothing. "It's time to break the Claimings."

The red thread pauses, no longer struggling against me, all the fight seeping out of it at the sound of my unexpected admission. It goes still in my hand like a held breath waiting for what comes next.

"Gemma," Ollie croaks, his hand finding mine.

I look up with a start.

He smiles down at me, his eyes a crystal clear and wholly Oliver blue. "You found me."

CHAPTER FORTY-FOUR

OLLIE

GEMMA THROWS HER arms around me, the red thread held tightly in her fist. "Of course I did," she says, crying into my neck. "Did you ever doubt I would?"

I think back to the Dreamscape shaking and the stars falling, the red thread wrapped around me so tightly that I could hardly remember who I was. "I mean, things did get a little dicey there for a minute."

She makes a noise that lands somewhere between a laugh and a sob, and she clings to me, her body shaking as she cries. I hold her to my chest and breathe in the scent of her hair. My arms look solid around her; I'm no longer on the brink of fading away. I'm here, I'm Remembered.

Gemma leans back and wipes her face on her sleeve, her big brown eyes taking in every detail of my face. "Hi," she says with another laugh.

"Hi," I say back.

And then I kiss her. I take her face in between my hands and press my mouth to hers, her lips warm and immediately responsive. My fingers tighten on her hips as I deepen the kiss, holding on to her with a grip that doesn't want to loosen anytime soon. She wraps her arms around me, breathing me in like she can't believe that I'm really here and she's really here, and maybe we just might make it through this after all. My hands get lost in her damp hair that smells like rain, and I feel myself leaning into hope like I'm leaning into her.

Solid, tangible, undeniable hope.

A silver thread stretches between us, glistening brighter than any star overhead. It wraps around us, softer than our shared breath, before flashing once and vanishing into the air.

I lean back and rest my forehead against hers. "What was that?" I ask, my head so full of her I can hardly think.

"I think that was a new memory made."

I imagine that silver thread settling somewhere deep inside my chest where it will be available to me whenever I want to close my eyes and relive it.

If that's not magic, then I don't know what is.

Gemma looks down at the red thread still coiled in her hand. I try not to flinch and totally fail. It's surreal to see her holding it like that, carefully yet confidently. She gives me a reassuring smile. "It's okay, Ollie. I know what we need to do."

"I know you do. I saw it. The thread showed me. That's why I held on to it so tightly." I shudder at the memory of it inside my head. How it tried to drown me out and make me forget who I was. How it tried to convince me that Gemma would fail. "I needed to keep it here for you to find me."

She touches my cheek. "I hated seeing you like that."

"I know. But it worked," I say, placing my hand over hers.

There's a rustling behind us and a movement in the darkness. This time, instead of a small girl or an old woman emerging from the shadows, it's seventeen-year-old Carmen with her head held high and her black eyes piercing. "What will you do with that?" she asks, cringing away from the red thread in Gemma's hand.

"We're going to leave this memory and take it back to our Dreamscape," Gemma says, sounding sure. "And then we're going to weave it back into the magic where it belongs."

Carmen shifts on her feet, looking uneasy. "I did not understand the consequences," she says quietly, "of removing fate from magic. I thought I could control it. I could not bear it if others were hurt because of me—" She breaks off, silent tears streaming down her face. "But in trying to avoid pain, I created so much more." She gestures to the threads tumbling down from the stars.

Gemma looks up, her brow scrunched in confusion. "What's she talking about?"

I put my hands on her shoulders. "When Carmen created the Dreamscape and the branches, there were unintended consequences. *Tied and bound,*" I say, slipping Gemma's fingers in between mine and lacing them together, "our fates were sealed. Our souls were Claimed, Gemma."

She raises a hand to her lips. "So that means..."

"That even after we die, we return here with our magic because the two are inseparably connected." I point to the countless threads swaying between us. "And we exist in our memories, trapped in the past."

"But what about the Beyond? My grandma always said there was *more.*"

I shake my head, my stomach dropping at the bewildered expression on her face and the panic in her voice. "There isn't more for us. We stopped fate from unfolding the way it was supposed to when our blood was used to tie the Claimings. That was magic we didn't understand."

The red thread shivers in Gemma's hand, quiet and watchful. Listening. Carmen shrinks back into the shadows, her head hanging low. But I don't blame her; we've all had a part to play in this.

Gemma looks at all the threads hanging down around us. "So she's here? My grandma?"

I squeeze her hand. "Do you want to see her before we go?"

She glances down at the red thread still wrapped around her hand, biting her lip. "No. I don't need to. She's already here," she says, tapping once over her heart. "And seeing her one last time in her memories won't change that. But there is someone else I need to see."

GEMMA

The moment I think his name, his thread appears, drifting lazily back and forth in front of me, a dark burnt orange—the same color as the sun just before it sets. I let go of Ollie's hand, but keep the red thread safely enclosed in my other. Then I reach out and take the orange thread, wrapping it once around my wrist and closing my eyes.

The Dreamscape fades as everything distills into one single memory, a pinprick on the timeline of Noah Fitzgerald's life. I recognize the house as soon as the fog clears. I'm in my kitchen. Sure, it looks a little cleaner and newer, but it's still scattered and lived in like it's always been. Grandma's pots and glass bottles are everywhere, stacked on the stove and spilling out of every cupboard and drawer, each of them full of her mixings and musings.

A younger version of my mom is seated at the kitchen table with a gigantic pile of hot wings balanced on a full plate that Milo would surely envy. I look around with a pounding heart, waiting for the moment I'll see him.

He smiles and saunters, his loping walk the mirror image of his son's. I have to fight the urge to rub my eyes and make sure I'm seeing clearly, because even though I'm the one who looks like my dad—dark hair, dark eyes, black eyebrows slanting across our foreheads—everything else screams Milo.

He pulls out a chair next to where my mom is sitting. She doesn't stop feasting to say hi to her husband, she merely waves a wing with her mouth full and covered in sauce, and raises one eyebrow, gesturing at the plate in front of her.

Noah grimaces and laughs. "No, I don't want any, thank you. I don't think I'll be able to eat another hot wing ever again. I tap out." He taps his hand twice on the solid wood table to emphasize his surrender, and Mom smirks and shrugs as if to say, *more for me.*

That's when I see the enormous swell of her stomach, half-hidden under the table and her flowy blouse. I slide into the chair across from them as fresh tears threaten to spill over.

Now that I'm looking at him more closely, I see the tension in my dad's shoulders and the creases beneath his eyes. He looks exhausted. I glance down at his wrist, and sure enough, the gold band of casting is there, marking him with the magic he stole. This moment must've taken place right before he lost it all and never came home.

Maybe my dad is stuck in this memory because it's his last happy one. Maybe it's the closest he got to the future he'd always wanted, and now he doesn't know how to leave it.

I think back to when my head was full of the whispers of fate, of all the promises and pictures of what my life could be. They were incessant and demanding—totally consuming. As I look at my dad, for the first time ever, I realize that he carried those same voices around for a lot longer than I did. And the future he wanted so badly to fix was for *me*. He just didn't know how to fight the whispers long enough to save himself.

Another piece of my resentment crumbles at that thought. Empathy is funny like that. It's a lot harder to hold on to your walls when you see someone else clutching so tightly to theirs.

My dad leans over to my mom and wraps his arm around her shoulders. She sighs contentedly and melts into his side, her fingers still covered in buffalo sauce. He chuckles and hands her a napkin, then places his other hand right on her belly, where my brother and I are waiting.

I can see it now—what could've been. I can see it more clearly than I ever saw it when I held the red thread. There were too many possibilities then, all of them fractured and frayed, each of them revolving around me and what I wanted. What *I* could possess.

I didn't see the bigger picture then. I didn't understand that there were other players in the game, that everyone else was trying to win too, all of us scattered on a board so expansive you couldn't possibly see the end of it.

But I see it now. The players, the pieces, the chance to play the game at all.

We're all just trying our best.

I blink at my parents and stifle a sob.

Noah turns and stares out the window, but from this angle it seems as if he's looking directly at me, his eyes dark and searching. His mouth tugs up into a smile. It's soft at first, but then it turns into a wide-stretching grin, real and true.

It's the first time I've really seen him smile. And it looks like me.

When I see his face like that, the rest of my resentment and leftover hurt fall away, collapsing in a sudden burst as if those long-held feelings can't support the weight of themselves for another second.

He doesn't say anything—I don't even know if he can actually see me—but he doesn't have to say a word. It's a lifetime's worth of smiles all tucked into one, and he's giving it to me right here and now like he's been waiting for me to find him in this moment for the last seventeen years.

And it's absolute magic.

"Goodbye, Dad," I say faintly.

And then I let go.

OLLIE

Gemma watches as the dark orange thread drifts away, mixing with the other lost souls of the Claimed. She was only in her dad's memory for no more than a minute, but when she turns to look at me, she seems lighter. Changed. "We can fix this," she says, wiping her eyes.

"I know," I agree, truly believing it for the first time. "You ready?"

She takes my hand as I turn to Carmen. "Thank you." I give

her back the black thread of her memories that's carried me for so long and through so much.

Carmen blinks at me. "For what?"

"For showing me the beginning. I think you should stick around for the ending." Gemma offers me the other end of the glowing red thread, and I take it. "It's going to be a good one."

Carmen's face flickers as she gives us a small but hopeful smile before retreating back into the shadows, humming the final notes of her mother's favorite song. "I am ready to move on," she says, her whisper fading into the background along with her.

Gemma and I hold the red thread between us. It shivers with anticipation as we weave it between our fingers. "*Take us home*," she says.

And it does.

I open my eyes to the blushing sky of the Dreamscape of our time. The floor is still cracked roughly through the middle, but the silver threads gleam and hum the moment Gemma and I arrive. The red thread hums along with them, ready and waiting as it quivers in our hands.

"Time to break the Claimings," Gemma says. "The right way this time." She tucks her hair back behind her ears and smiles up at me. I lean down and give her a quick kiss, still marveling over the fact that I can.

I doubt I'll ever stop marveling.

"What do you think this will mean for magic now? Do you think this will be the end of the Claimed?" she asks me, her gaze fixed on the faintly glowing stars. They stutter and pulse like a heart trying to find its beat again. "Will everyone else lose their magic too?"

I wrap my arm around her waist, tugging on the hem of her shirt. "I don't know. It'll be out of our hands. We'll just have to wait and see."

She chews on the inside of her cheek and inhales sharply, her expression still determined. "I guess it's up to fate now, as scary as that sounds."

"So this is it? Our magic ends here?" I look around the Dreamscape, at the walls that once felt like a prison I would never be free from, at the magic that both confused and delighted me. "We have to use ours to fix the weaving. We have to give it back."

Gemma nods. She turns to one of the gleaming cavern walls, running one hand along the threads and placing the other on her chest. A silver thread unwinds, identical to the threads of the Dreamscape. Her magic, Claimed and bound.

I walk to her side and place my hand over my chest where my own thread of magic uncurls. Then I lift my other hand up toward the stars, waiting for the threads of the weaving to come tumbling down.

Gemma holds on to her silver threads from the walls—the warp.

I hold on to mine from the stars—the weft.

Contain and release.

Tied and bound.

Life and death.

Isn't it all the same?

We each take one end of the red thread and carefully weave it back in amongst the silver threads. Fate and magic once again united and whole. The result is a dazzling tapestry; the crimson thread a beautiful shock of color against the moon-spun silver. There's a certain sense of rightness seeing the two colors side by side, the threads intertwining as if they'd never been separated in the first place.

With each movement of our hands, the red thread of fate glows brighter. It doesn't whisper and it doesn't scream. Instead, it's quietly restful, and finally, finally at peace.

Ready to unfold as it will.

I don't know how long we stay like that, the two of us with handfuls of threads, fixing a weaving that didn't know just how broken it was. It feels like days, but it could've been minutes. Our hands slow as the ending draws nearer. We look at each other before letting the ends of the threads slice across our palms, leaving thin trails of blood in their wake.

"Untied and unbound, we release you from your fate," we whisper together, the words of the Language dipping low and sweet. The red thread flashes once before settling back into the weaving, now touching every single strand of magic in the Dreamscape, just as it always should've.

GEMMA

It's the last act of magic I'll ever do, and it's one that's needed to be done for centuries. Like a collective sigh that sends a shiver down my neck, I feel rather than hear the souls of the Claimed gracefully arcing out from the stars, finally free from their magic and their memories and ready to move Beyond. Their whispers slide across my skin as they float away through a scarlet sky the color of fresh starts before gently fading into a peaceful silence.

I don't look around to see if she's still here. I know she's not. My grandma isn't one to stay behind when there's adventure to be had and mischief to get up to.

She'll always be the first to jump.

I feel her leave the same way I feel my dad leave. And Ben and Lillian and Atticus along with them. All those who let the magic Claim them before they really knew what it meant, and every Threader who unknowingly bound them. It's a long history of enchantment and misunderstandings, a legacy of refusing to let go. It's the end of a vicious cycle of people trying to control what they couldn't—magic and fate.

Cora and Lillian didn't trust that they would recover from their father's death. Atticus didn't believe that he would ever be enough without more power. And Carmen never believed in magic again after it destroyed her home and took away the people she loved. So she looked ahead and tried to cut it off from what made it magic in the first place—the mystery and the wonder, the unknown of what's to come. Fate, slowly unfolding, for better or for worse.

Hayden and his children, my dad and Ben. Even Ollie and me. Cycles and circles, doomed to repeat until two Threaders decided to give it up and let it go.

Carmen's the last of the Claimed to leave, almost as if she's making sure everyone else made it out safely before her. And then with an exhale that sounds older than the earth itself, she goes too.

Beyond. And finally free.

I look at the red thread back in its rightful place, intertwined with every thread of magic, no longer a fractured piece unable to see the end from the beginning. And now when I look at it, I'm not afraid anymore. Because it's when we feel broken that the worst parts of us come spilling out; why would it be any different for something like fate, grabbed and controlled by humans who just refused to understand?

I'll never be able to stop tragedy in its tracks. I'll never be able to prevent the inevitable. But I can practice believing that I'll be okay, even when it feels like I won't.

I can break the claiming that fear has on me. I can loose the chains of regret. I can stop clinging to what was and rest in the knowledge that what is to come could be even better.

I look at the red thread, and I don't try to see the end. I'd rather not read the last chapter when I'm still only at my beginning.

I don't want to miss my best parts.

CHAPTER FORTY-FIVE

OLLIE

MY LUNGS FILL with the musty stagnant air of a cave long forgotten as I look up at the stars of the Dreamscape for the last time, the sky now a tranquil midnight blue—full, deep, and unknowable. The silver threads of the cavern gently ripple, flickering in our direction as if trying to shoo us out.

We don't belong here anymore.

I feel the empty space in my chest where my magic used to reside. There's no yearning when I look at the threads or the stars, no humming pull that moves my hands into motion. I feel nothing.

But when Gemma slips her hand into mine, I feel something else. Her skin is soft and warm against mine. It's the reminder that I needed.

This isn't the end.

"Let's get out of here," she says, tugging me forward. I'm about to ask how we do such a thing when the sharp scent of cool air, fresh and biting, stings my nose.

"Wait, where are we?" I don't let go of her hand—I don't know if I'll ever be able to let go of her again—but I pull her to a stop and look up. Instead of being greeted with a million shining stars or threads of every color, I see the same sky I grew up under, the predawn sun hidden behind the mountains, tucked under the leftover clouds of a storm come and gone.

"We're home," Gemma murmurs, her dark eyes shining in the hazy half-light.

"Home," I repeat slowly, testing out the word on my tongue. This isn't just another memory; this time, it's real. But there's this fear creeping along the edge of my happiness, trying to sneak its way in. Have I forgotten what it feels like to *live*? To not float from one memory to the next, but to actually move forward?

I'm scared I won't remember how.

We're just outside the entrance to the cave, inside the forest that shouldn't belong out here in the middle of the desert but somehow does. I shuffle back a few steps, trying to take it all in. Everything looks different from the last time I saw it in Carmen's memories. The trees are blackened and cracked, lying broken on their sides. Acrid smoke clings to the plants that remain, curling around the death and decay.

Gemma gingerly moves through the maze of the wreckage, her hands running along the rough bark of a pine. "Do you think it will ever grow back?" she asks, looking over her shoulder at me, crestfallen.

Before I can answer, something stirs near my feet. A handful of silver threads unwind from the mouth of the cave, sliding through the debris of the once lush forest. Gemma steps out of the way, her mouth popping open when one of the threads wraps around the fallen pine tree. The moment it connects with the charred bark, the tree shudders and stands, its roots stretching widely. Dark green needles spring out of its bare branches, and in a sudden burst, the tree is tall and thriving.

Gemma clutches my arm as the rest of the threads encompass the forest, a slow and steady stream of magic that isn't out to consume but to revitalize. I lean down to look at the tiny blossoms of wildflowers now carpeting the ground, watching as they stretch toward the morning's first rays before slowly shriveling into nothing and starting again in a never-ending cycle.

Life. Magic. The beginning and the end.

"It's beautiful," Gemma says with an ache in her voice because she knows we can't stay. Then she frowns and peers around me. "But where is everyone? Milo, Mom—they're not here."

"How long has it been?" I ask, squinting at the horizon as it slowly lightens and wishing I had my glasses; it's a lot harder to see without magically induced 20/20 vision. "How long have we been gone?"

"I have no idea," she says, leaning into my side. I tuck my arm around her. "It could've been hours; it could've been days." She doesn't say that it could've been years. I don't think either of us is ready to entertain that possibility. "Only one way to find out." She starts to follow the threads into the heart of the forest, her shoes squishing in the wet dirt, still damp from the rain.

"Wait," I say, tugging her to me, my heart pounding in my chest. "There's something I need to do first."

I pull her straight into a kiss, one hand resting on the back of her neck, the other trailing down the curve of her cheek. Her lips part and she pulls me closer, holding me tighter and kissing me harder. Every move she makes seems meant to remind me that this is real. She kisses me like she's got something to prove, like she wants to sear the memory of herself into my brain.

Doesn't she know that all I can think of is her? Doesn't she know she's the memory I never want to escape? She's both my daydream and reality—a juxtaposition I want to spend my whole life untangling.

I can feel her smiling, her lips pressing against mine. I lean back and grasp her by the waist, my breathing rough and ragged.

This is real, this is real.

"You have no idea how much I thought about this moment," I breathe into her hair. "No idea."

She laughs and throws her arms around my neck. "I'm pretty sure I do."

This. I will remember this moment for as long as I live. Maybe even longer. I lean back, expecting to see threads of every color dangling around us, my hands snagged in the ones I like best. But instead, my fingers are knotted in her hair and her lips are on mine with the feeling of home humming between us.

A new memory in the making.

Time passes strangely in the Valley. One moment we're leaving the green of the forest behind and stepping onto the dry red of the sandstone, and the next we're left standing in the gravel-filled dirt of the Superstitions. The Valley lies behind us, smooth and stark against the rough rock of the mountain surrounding it. We just traveled over the whole thing in less than a second.

"Whoa." I lean into Gemma feeling like I'm about to tip over, I'm so dizzy.

"Yeah, I don't think that's something anyone could get used to," she says a little breathlessly, swaying on her feet. Even as we watch, the desert shrubs near the border curl up and over the pathway leading to the Valley, hiding it from sight until it looks like a completely ordinary patch of desert, blending in with the rest of the scenery.

It looks like fate wants to keep the location of magic a secret, and I can't say I blame it.

Now it's just another legend caught amongst the peaks. Another myth to be heard and then forgotten.

We amble down the mountain trail, sometimes talking but oftentimes not, letting moments of peaceful silence settle over us. There's no sense of urgency, no race to catch up. We know we've got time. For now, it feels good to just be together. A luxury I never want to take for granted again. We keep stealing glances at each other, our grins stretched wide and reckless as the sun rises higher in the sky.

About halfway down the trail, I hear a loud *whoop* before someone hurdles into me at full speed.

"Ollie!" Milo tackles me in a giant hug, shaking me with his laughter. "You're back! I knew she could do it. I knew it, I knew it. And fast too—we didn't even make it down the mountain, and you're already back." But hidden inside his assurance is an obvious edge of anxiousness that tells of long days and sleepless nights.

"Milo," I say, unable to find the words to express how much I missed him. So I settle for, "It's so good to see you."

He shoves me back and gives me a once-over. "Did you grow taller? Change your hair? Something's different. And where are your glasses?"

I shake my head and laugh, but he's right—I *am* different. I think we all are. Even he looks older, a little more worn around the edges. But it suits him.

With a grin, he slaps me on the back. "All right, all right, get it together, man." He sniffs loudly and turns away from me, wiping his eyes with a great big shuddering breath.

Then he throws his arms around his sister, completely breaking down on her shoulder. "I'm so glad you're okay," he says through his hiccups.

Gemma ruffles his hair, which he promptly smooths back down. "All thanks to you, big brother."

"And don't you forget it. Those extra four minutes I've got on you really make a difference," he chokes out between shaky breaths.

She laughs and messes up his hair again. Vivian and Libby join them in their hug, the four of them laughing in pure relief as they lean into the feeling of family and togetherness.

There's a tall blonde girl standing off to the side, looking unsure of where to stand or what to do. She clutches at a leather bag slung across her chest and smiles shyly at me.

I raise an eyebrow at Milo, and he says, "Ollie, meet Zoe. Zoe, the famous Ollie."

Zoe's smile widens as she looks at me. "Welcome home, Ollie. I've heard a lot about you."

Milo hovers around her, fidgeting with his shirt and smoothing down his hair. He catches me watching him and gives me a grin and a shrug.

I know that look. Milo's got it bad.

I grin back at him before turning to Zoe. "And I'm sure I'll be hearing a lot about you."

She blushes and scoffs, elbowing past Milo to stand next to a blonde woman whose face is half hidden under the shade of a mesquite tree.

A face I've only seen in memories.

She lifts her chin like she's trying to prove she's not nervous, but I see the way her gaze darts to the side, the hesitation in her steps. "Oliver," she says, holding out a shaking hand. "I'm Charlotte."

I take her hand in mine and hold it for a moment. When her blue eyes meet mine, I feel a little piece of myself click into place.

"Hi," I offer lamely. Gemma's fingers brush against my forearm, just to remind me that she's there. I try to concentrate on the warmth of her touch rather than the sudden onset of awkwardness that's overtaking me. I desperately wish that everyone wasn't just standing here watching me meet my birth mother for the first time. "It's, um, nice to meet you."

Charlotte smiles at me, and this time it's full and genuine. She *knows* me. I drop her hand and wrap her in a hug, surprising us both. "Thanks," I say, "for giving me my best chance."

She clings to me and cries, shaking her head back and forth. "I don't know. I questioned every single day of the last seventeen years, wondering if I made the right choice. And when I found out you were *still* Claimed and *still* trapped, I wondered—"

"It had to happen the way it did," I say, pulling back to look into her familiar eyes. "Things needed to change."

Milo nudges me in the side. "So what does this mean for the Claimed?"

"You tell us," Gemma answers. She chews on her lip and looks away. "If your magic is gone, I'm sorry. We did the best we could, but we had to repair—"

"Gem, look," Milo interrupts. She jerks her head up to see his glowing hand waving in front of her face. "Everyone's magic is up and running. We're all good."

She spins around, her arms reaching for her Aunt Libby. "You too?"

Libby's beam is answer enough. She waves her amber-lit hands toward Gemma and with a whispered word, she finally dries out her rain-soaked clothes. "Like your brother said. We're all good."

Gemma stares at me in disbelief, her smile an exact match for mine. She shrugs, and her shoulders look lighter without the weight of the Dreamscape on them, but a little off-balanced all the same. It's going to take time to get used to our new reality.

"So, are you guys going to tell us your epic story or what?" Milo asks, stepping in between Gemma and me.

She pushes him out of the way and takes my hand in hers. "Yes, we'll tell you our story. And yes, it is most definitely epic, but can we please get something to eat first? I'm starving."

Everyone laughs in agreement and starts to descend the mountain once again, but I catch Milos's eye, my body tensing in preparation for his discomfort over the fact that Gemma's practically draping herself around me. After all, the last time he saw me touching his sister, he basically tried to electrocute me.

But all he does is slap me on the back in passing and mumble the words I'd only heard him say once in a memory. "It was inevitable, wasn't it?" He looks at me and Gemma and sighs. "And I can only drag my feet for so long. But still—the Golden Trio lives on." His gaze flicks to Zoe. "Things are always changing, aren't they? I guess that's not such a bad thing."

"Not bad at all." I loop my arm over Gemma's shoulder, tucking her into my chest. I think about my parents sitting at home waiting for me, and my bed, warm and inviting. Suddenly, I'm so exhausted, I don't know how I'll make it the rest of the way down the mountain. "Let's go home," I say, turning my back on what used to be.

And on we go. Another moment come and gone.

I stand on my front porch, feeling like a soldier returning home after the war.

"See you soon?" Gemma calls out from behind me where she's perched on her own front porch with her brother. I recognize the anxious look on her face; it mirrors my own. I don't really want to let her out of my sight so soon, but I need to do this alone.

The light is on in my room. I could see it as I walked up our narrow driveway. My curtains are thrown open and the blinds are open wide like my parents were trying to light the path to lead me home.

I turn the handle and push the door open. It squeaks the way it always does, and suddenly I'm choking up, blinking back tears over the sound of my front door opening. I quietly step inside and rub my face with my hands, leaning back against the door as it shuts.

Rounding the corner into the family room, I see my parents where they fell asleep watching TV on the couch, my mom's head resting on my dad's shoulder, the morning sun shining on the scene with perfect clarity. They look exactly as I remembered them. But memories never do it justice, do they?

There's no replacement for the moment while you're in it. The smell, the taste, the sound—I can almost feel the air crackling with magic, as if the threads are here right now, weaving around this moment in time to tie it back into the long chain of my life. A chain that I wasn't sure would ever move forward again.

I don't make a sound. I just watch them breathing together and feel my muscles relaxing, the kind of loosening up that only happens when you come home after a long day.

Mom sits up with a jerk and looks over her shoulder. "Oliver," she whispers. "I'm dreaming of you again."

I give her a lopsided grin even as I'm wiping my eyes. "I'm home, Mom."

She blinks at me a few times before frowning. "That's what you always say." She turns back around and nestles into my dad's shoulder again.

But then seconds later she jumps to her feet and screams, "Ollie!" She runs around the couch and slams into me with all the force of every hug she's ever given me for the past seventeen years. "It's you, you're here, you're home," she sobs into my shoulder. "Matthew! He's home!"

Dad is slower to respond; he's a deep sleeper. "Sure, sure, honey," he yawns, staring blankly at the TV. "Did you see the final score? I think—"

Finally, he registers what my mom said. Finally, he sees me standing in the kitchen. His glasses are askew as he jumps the back of the couch and runs toward us. He holds my face in his hands, claps me on the back, and cries with my mom.

It's a moment for sure. One that I'll never forget. Sandwiched between the two people who chose me when they didn't have to, who raised me when they didn't know how, and who loved me through it all like it was the easiest thing in the world.

I let the memory sink into me. I let it blaze across my mind.

Never forget this, I say to myself. *Always remember.*

It sounds like a spell.

It feels like one too.

CHAPTER FORTY-SIX

GEMMA

IT'S ONLY BEEN two days since we made it off the mountain, and those days have mostly been filled with sleeping—because it turns out that magical expeditions like ours really suck the life out of you—but they've also been full of storytelling.

The morning we got back, I gave Ollie an hour of solitude with his parents, but that was all I could handle before I was on his porch and swinging the front door wide open. As soon as I heard the sound of him in the kitchen with his family—their familiar back and forth, the noisy clattering of breakfast dishes, all of it just so wonderfully and unbelievably *normal*, I turned the corner and ran straight into his arms, causing him to drop a bowl of waffle batter, splattering it everywhere. Matthew and Teresa didn't look surprised to see me. In fact, there was already a place set for me at the table.

They wrapped me in a hug while Teresa cried onto my shoulder, thanking me over and over again for bringing their son home. I didn't want or need their thanks, but I accepted it nonetheless, along with their invitation to stay for breakfast.

"And lunch," Ollie added. "Plus dinner and dessert, and—"

"Oliver, we get it," his dad said in mock exasperation. "You love the girl, and you want to eat every meal with her until the end of time. Let's just start with breakfast, shall we?" He winked at me as he pulled out my chair.

Ollie blushed and busied himself with looking for something in the fridge while Matthew and I snorted into our orange juices.

So we told them our story over waffles and eggs with Ollie and I trading off and holding hands under the table. Matthew and Teresa's eyes widened every time we mentioned the Dreamscape and all its magic, but the longer we talked about it, the less real it seemed. It started to feel like a strange fever dream we'd shared, all the details melting into each other in a confusing mix of half-remembered colors and sounds, people and places that couldn't possibly be real.

And the longer we talked, the more exhausted we felt. Ollie was nearly lying face-first in a plate of leftover syrup by the time we'd finished. But still, we managed to finally break away from his parents to go make out in the backyard until we were both too tired to stand up straight.

I then went home, collapsed on my bed, and slept for a full sixteen hours.

I dreamt about the threads, but it wasn't like before. Nothing about it was tangible; it felt far away and out of focus, just like regular dreaming. Like my brain was trying to make sense of everything, trying to put meaning to something completely indescribable. When I woke up, I stared at my ceiling and held perfectly still as the pictures grew fainter and my room grew brighter, wondering if any of that magic would stay with me.

Over the past few days, we've told our story many times. We've told it in the library, with everyone huddled on different squashy armchairs or leaning against crooked bookcases. We've told it over the Scrabble board and riding in the Jeep with Milo.

Our story is even stitched onto the pages of the Caster Chronicles. The morning after we got back, Libby came racing into my room with a worn-out volume in her hand and about a million questions flying out of her mouth. "A friend in Colorado just called and told me that new pages were added to her family's Chronicles too!" she said in a rush, her words piling on top of each other. "Which means that soon all the Claimed will know your story, Gemma. You and Ollie are a part of *history*." She said the last word with reverence, her eyes shining.

Her obsession with the Chronicles has exploded overnight now that she sees it as a new source of magic—as a living, breathing thing that's connected to something far bigger than she understands. Milo's joined her in completely geeking out over it. They're rethinking how we record our spells, our histories, our family trees, all of it.

I thought Ollie would be pulling up a chair right there next to them, hunched over all the books and breathing in their leather scent. I thought for sure that it would take a serious amount of flirting for me to get him out of the library, but he hasn't shown any interest in their fascination.

He's completely indifferent. Or at least that's how he's trying to appear. But I know Ollie better than anyone, and I definitely know when he's putting on an act. I think I know what's really happening.

He's avoiding.

We've told and retold our story to everyone, except for Charlotte. We hadn't seen her since the morning we left the mountain. "She said she wanted to give me some space to adjust," Ollie told me, scratching the back of his head and giving me a shrug. "I don't know. I think she needed a little time too, after everything."

Time to discover who she is as a mother. Time to mourn her husband who never came home.

But tonight, Mom declared that we all needed to celebrate our homecoming, so she's throwing us a proper dinner party with Ollie's family, including Charlotte, and I couldn't agree more. I'm still catching up on decent sleep and meals—a girl can only survive on energy drinks and cereal for so long. I think it's safe to say we're all long overdue for a meal like this.

I'm searching through my closet, trying to find something to wear when I see the crumpled shopping bag shoved back in the dark dusty corner. I crouch down and pull the bag out, pausing for a moment before carefully opening it.

Two dresses. One white, one red.

I roughly shake each dress out before laying them flat on my bed, running my hands over their smooth fabric and remembering the times when I couldn't even stand to look at them; just the sight of them made me feel sick. The mistakes I made, the people I lost. These dresses felt like physical reminders of everything I'd wanted and couldn't have.

I take the white sundress and hold it up, looking at the torn hem, the grass and the blood stains. And then I fold it up—nicely this time—and place it back into the bag with considerate hands, because now I understand that this dress is a memory I need to handle gently and with extra care. The pain of that night still lingers and probably always will, but I can keep breathing through it.

Just like Grandma taught me.

I pick up the red dress and hold it over myself as I look in the mirror. The last time I wore this, I thought my Claiming had gone wrong. It was a time of confusion and disappointment, loneliness and frustration. But it was also the night that Ollie was Claimed too. A night full of starry skies and silver threads. It was the end of my life as I'd known it and the start of something new.

And it's the perfect dress for tonight.

I slip the fabric over my head in a flash of red, and when I look at myself in the mirror, I see the girl who holds all magic in her hands, even though now they look empty.

I race down the stairs, my heart climbing up my throat at the prospect of seeing Ollie soon, my mind already scheming with possibilities of how to sneak off alone with him. The kitchen is bright and messy and full of delicious scents that leave my mouth watering. Mom's bustling out the back door, her arms overladen with dishes and serving platters. Milo follows closely behind her with giant bowls of fruit and salads magicked to float in front of him so he can hold Zoe's hand.

She blushes when she sees me staring. "Oh, shut up," she says, trying not to smile.

"But I didn't say anything," I protest.

"You didn't have to. Your face said it all." Zoe pinches her lips together, dropping Milo's hand. He makes a noise of protest, but she pointedly ignores him.

When she tries to march past me, I grab her arm. "Wait. How's your mom doing?"

Zoe softens. "She's okay. We're staying nearby with an old friend for now, trying to get her back on her feet." She sighs and flicks her long blonde hair over her shoulder. "It's going to take time. Being with James for so long really did a number on her. I didn't want to leave her tonight, but she told me to go, and..." She looks back at Milo, blushing again. "And, well, I wanted to see you guys. And Charlotte," she adds quickly.

"You just couldn't stay away from me, could you?" Milo says, grinning like an idiot.

In response, she bumps his parade of floating salad dressings with her hip before sashaying away without looking back. I grab the last bottle before it falls since my brother is too busy gaping after her to correct his casting.

"Nice," I deadpan, shoving the bottle into his hands. "Mind the Italian. That's my favorite."

"Did you see that?" he asks waggling his eyebrows. "I *knew* I'd win her over." His voice is smug as he tosses my beloved salad dressing back and forth precariously between his hands.

"You did not. You've spent most of your time together arguing about how she keeps spiking your drinks with her mixings."

"Well, sure. But all the best relationships start with a few magical mishaps and misunderstandings, wouldn't you say? All it took was a little charm, plus my exceptional good looks, and—"

"Her betrayal and groveling apologies?" I ask, snagging a grape from one of his floating bowls of fruit.

He laughs, totally delighted. Like now that it's all over it's just a fantastic story. "Exactly. This is fairytale stuff for sure. I always knew I'd have an epic love story."

"*Love*?" I repeat, my mouth falling open.

"Only time will tell," he croons, and with a wink, he waltzes onto the patio in search of Zoe, his procession of bowls and dressings trailing after him.

"You're utterly ridiculous," I call after him. "And I give you a week before she calls it quits!"

"A week is generous," a voice says from behind me. Two hands wrap around my waist. Ollie leans in and presses his lips to mine, kissing me quickly. "He won't make it past the weekend. He's in way over his head."

I laugh and kiss him back, running my fingers through his hair until someone behind us clears their throat. I pull back to see Ollie's parents standing there, each holding a tray of food.

Matthew brushes past us with a mumbled, "Come on, kids, not in front of the parents."

But Ollie just pulls me closer and grins at his dad, who grins back just as hard.

Teresa smiles too, but it's a little stiff, her shoulders tense as she balances her tray of veggies and dip. "Hi, Gemma," she says distractedly with a quick glance at me. "You look lovely." She smiles at us again before following her husband outside.

"What's up with your mom?" I whisper.

"Well, she's right. You do look beautiful," he says, eyeing my red dress.

My cheeks turn pink under his gaze. "Thank you," I say, tugging on the sleeve of his collared shirt. "You don't look so bad yourself. And I'm glad you have your glasses on again. I missed them. But quit distracting me. Why is your mom being weird?"

Ollie exhales heavily. "She's nervous about seeing Charlotte again," he murmurs near my ear, sending a shiver down my spine. "Is she here yet?" His voice is low and filled with his trademarked Oliver Concern.

"She's over by the fire with Libby. Those two are already thick as thieves," I say, sliding my hands down his neck and tracing the shape of his shoulders. "But what's there to worry about? It's going to be fine. We've faced worse, haven't we?"

He takes my hand, pressing the inside of my wrist to his lips.

"I don't know. Having an awkward dinner with my newly found birth mother and adoptive parents sounds pretty bad."

I elbow him in the stomach and he huffs out a laugh. "Don't be such a chicken," I say, taking him by the hand and pulling him onto the patio and under the light of the swinging lanterns. "Now go talk to your moms." I nudge him in the direction of the fire pit where Teresa is slowly approaching Charlotte.

It feels as if the whole yard is holding its breath; even the breeze quit blowing. Everything pauses as the two women stare at each other.

Then Teresa and Charlotte throw their arms around each other, both of them bursting into tears. Ollie sinks into my side, blinking rapidly. It's like watching all the tension ooze out of him in slow motion, a steady trickle that leaves him wasted with relief. It's as if he's realized for the first time that he doesn't have to choose a family, and he doesn't have to let anyone go.

They can all belong to each other.

Ollie smiles down at me. It splits across his face like a firework in a hot July sky. Then he crushes me to his chest, his arms wrapping tightly around me.

"See? You were freaking out over nothing," I mumble into his shirt.

He laughs and shakes his head. "Engrave that on my tombstone."

I stand on my tiptoes to kiss him on the cheek, then leave him to get acquainted with his new family dynamic.

Mom's over by the table, waving her hands over her beautiful flower arrangements—bright pink peonies and peach-colored roses, tiny white daisies, and tall sprigs of lavender. I watch as she carefully sprinkles each petal with glistening drops of dew. She stops when she notices me, her glowing hands going out in an instant. She tucks them behind her back and says, "Oh, I'm sorry, Gemma. I didn't see you there."

"Mom, stop. You don't have to hide your magic from me." I tug her hands free from the tense knot she's wound them in. "It's a little too late to keep that secret from me."

She frowns and rubs her forehead. "I know, I know. It's just that... I see your face every time one of us uses magic, and I—I don't know what to make of it." She takes my empty hands in hers. "I don't like seeing you hurting."

"I'm fine, it doesn't bother me." Mom raises an eyebrow skeptically, tilting her head to the side. "Okay, fine. It does bother me a little," I admit. She squeezes my hands and I let out a laugh. "Okay, *more* than a little."

I sigh and sit down at the table, resting my head against my arms. "It's just that I spent the past seventeen years of my life thinking it was going to turn out differently than it did. I thought I'd have magic. I thought I'd be like you and Grandma." I look over at her empty seat, painted purple and covered in lilies. "It's just hard to imagine who I'll be now. Everything feels like it's been thrown wide open, which isn't all bad, it's just—"

"Different," she says, sitting across from me. "I understand what it's like to have your life turn out differently than you planned." My mind fills with the memory of her eating buffalo wings and smiling up at my dad. Her face softens as if she's seeing it too. "It's going to take time to sort through it all. And then, just when you think you've got it figured out, something else will change. That's how it goes for all of us, sweetheart, whether you have magic or not. That's the beauty of it."

I lean into my chair and breathe in the smell of her blooms and the food and that unidentifiable scent that just means *home*. "Thanks, Mom."

"You're welcome. Besides, *you* are enough magic all on your own."

I groan, tipping my face into my hands. "You're my *mother*, you're legally obligated to say that."

She laughs and pushes her chair back to stand. "That only makes it all the more true," she says tenderly.

The dinner is just how I'd imagined it would be, whenever I

dared to let myself hope. All of us gathered around the table, the paper lanterns swaying in the breeze, Ollie and I sitting next to each other, our elbows nudging and feet overlapping. Yes, there are empty chairs that should've been filled. Grandma, my dad, and Ben—we all feel their absences, pangs of hurt that quietly throb in the background.

But tonight, we don't talk about what happened, we just *talk* and laugh and share more memories.

It's just how I imagined it, but somehow even better.

A few nights later, I sneak out and run across the street to Ollie's house where the light is still on in his room, shining through the window. He's lying on his bed, still in his t-shirt and jeans from the day, like he was too tired to even change into pajamas. He's leaning back against the headboard, his hair mussed from staying in the same position for too long. He takes his glasses off and rubs his eyes, setting them lightly on the nightstand. There aren't any books out. He's just lying there, staring and quiet and sadder than I've ever seen him.

Ollie is careful and sensitive, and sometimes he holds back what he's really feeling because he's worried about upsetting someone or putting anyone out. Sometimes he takes his sadness and tucks it away until he's wound it up so tightly that it turns into something else, something not quite sad but not really happy either.

Seeing him like this with his guard completely down and his misery on full display knocks my breath out. He's hurting, and I don't know how to make it better.

I rap one knuckle on his window. He jumps at the sound, but when he sees me, his face rearranges into a smile. It's like watching a curtain swing shut over his eyes. He's happy to see me, I know that. But there's something underneath that happiness that he doesn't want to show me.

He climbs off his bed and pads over, pulling up the window in one swift motion. "What are you doing here?" he asks as he reaches out a hand to pull me through. As soon as I'm in his room, he folds me into his arms in a bone-crushing hug. "I missed you."

Earlier that night, I ate dinner at his house and played a rousing game of UNO with him and his parents. Technically, I saw him only hours ago, so there wasn't much time to miss me. But still. I know what he means. I don't know if I'll ever stop missing him now, too.

I can't get used to the shape of him, the way he fills up a doorway or flops in a chair. He's *here*—he's real and solid and no longer just alive in my mind.

And I'm not quite sure how to handle that.

I lean forward and press a quick kiss to his lips. "Do you feel like getting out of here?"

His arms tighten around me as his gaze darts to his door. His parents have kind of had him on lockdown mode after everything. I mean, I don't blame them. I want to lock him away too.

I tug on his hand and grin. "Come on, you know you want to."

He raises one eyebrow at me, and my heart skips a beat. A slow smile spreads across his face before he leans down and picks up his shoes. "I'm in."

We sneak down the hall to grab the keys to his dad's truck before dashing out the door and down the driveway. He opens my door for me, which makes me roll my eyes, but when he puts his hand on the small of my back, I'm blushing all the way to my hairline.

He pulls onto the road in between our homes. I huddle deeper into the seat, wishing I'd brought a sweater with me because here in Arizona it's hot until suddenly it's not. And tonight is one of those nights. Ollie notices me hunched down in my seat and scoffs, then flips the heater up a notch.

"You know it's not actually *cold* outside. It's like, 67 degrees."

"That *is* cold."

He laughs but then rubs his hand over his own goosebumps, pretending that he isn't just as big of a wimp as I am. "Where to?" he asks.

"Just drive."

We drive to the lookout point without either of us deciding to. It's like we've been drawn back by the same ancient pulse that called Carmen to the Valley all those years ago. I hold my breath to see if I can hear it, but everything is still and quiet.

Ollie unbuckles and reclines his seat all the way back, and so do I. We lie there, side by side with our elbows touching, and stare out the windshield at the mountain that has always been so much more than a mountain, we just never knew why.

"I don't know how to do this anymore." Ollie's whisper sounds loud in the silence of the car.

"Do what?"

"Be normal. Move on. Live like it never happened." He sighs. "I just don't know how to do that."

I think about the way he's been with his parents and how inclusive he is with Charlotte as they try to get to know each other after all this time. I think about him joking with Milo and spending time with Zoe, and the way he kisses me when we're alone. But I also think about how I just found him lying on his bed and staring up at the ceiling with that lost, far-off look in his eyes. "You seem to be managing."

He looks out the window, chewing on his lip and gazing up at the few stars we can see through the clouds. "*Seem* being the keyword here."

I roll over so I'm facing him. "You know, when I woke up the morning after I lost Grandma—" I pause and swallow the rising emotion welling up inside me. "And after I lost you, I didn't think I'd ever be okay again." I pick up his hand and lace my fingers through his. He squeezes me back tightly. "I ran and I ran and I ran. I ran so much I thought I was going to wear out the soles of my shoes." His lips twitch in a weak smile. "I thought if I ran hard enough, I wouldn't have to face anything. I thought I could leave it all behind, but it didn't work, Ollie."

"Of course it didn't," he mumbles. "You're just not very fast." His voice cracks with a laugh at the end; he can't even say it with a straight face. Soon he's laughing and I'm laughing, and we're leaning in together with our noses touching and tears blurring our eyes even though his joke wasn't that funny in the first place.

Ollie gasps for air as his laughter finally dies out. "I don't know how to move on. I saw too much. It's all I can think about now." He peers down into my face. "It's funny because when I was trapped down there, all I could think about was getting out and running back to you." His hand trails up and down my back. "All I wanted was to be together again. I would've given anything, and I did. And it was worth it. I would do it a million times over..."

"But..." I prompt, pinching him lightly on the arm. "It's okay. You can tell me."

He pulls back and stares at me. In the shadows, his blue eyes look just as dark as mine. "But I dream about it now. Every night. I dream about all the threads and the magic. And when I wake up—"

"You miss it."

He looks away, his face flushing with guilt. "Yeah, I do. I didn't think I would, but I do." He takes his glasses off and rubs his face with his hands. "I just feel so ungrateful, you know? I'm home, I have you, I have everything I need. But it just feels like there's this piece of me missing now," he confesses. "It's not just about the lack of magic. I miss being a part of something bigger than myself."

I place my hand on his cheek, turning him back to face me. His skin is warm and scratchy under my touch; he needs to shave. "I dream about it too. And every morning when I wake up, I miss it just like you do."

"Really?" he asks, his eyebrows shooting up. "But you seem fine after everything—"

"*Seem* being the keyword here." He laughs softly and kisses the knuckles on my hand. "Of course I miss it, Ollie."

"I guess I should've told you the truth after the first night we were back, after I had that first dream. Then at least we could've felt terrible together."

I smile and pat his cheek. "I'll feel anything with you. I'll go anywhere, I'll do anything."

His eyes light up, fierce and full like they did on the first night we kissed. "Anything?" he whispers, tugging me closer.

"Anything. I mean, I literally went to the ends of the earth to find you—"

His lips crash into mine, warm and soft and urgent. I take his face in my hands and kiss him back, tugging on his hair to pull him closer. Ollie wraps his arms around me, anchoring me to him and this moment until it feels as if we're the only people left on this planet, in the whole entire universe. Just the two of us and the stars.

I imagine a silver thread wrapped around us, a new memory frozen in time, preserved in glaringly perfect detail. I imagine that thread so vividly it's almost as if I can see its pale gleam through my eyelids. I can almost hear its humming, how it matches the rhythm of our heartbeats.

Ollie breaks off the kiss and pulls back in a sudden rush, shoving his glasses back onto his face. "What the—"

That thread I'd been imagining so clearly in my mind is actually twisted around me, softly pulsing and shimmering like a sliver of moonlight.

"How did that get here?" I exclaim, jerking back. In my shock and panic, I pull open the car door and jump out, slamming it shut behind me. But the thread still follows, wrapping around me more tightly.

"Gemma, hold still!" Ollie bolts out his door and jogs over to me. "Hold still," he says again, looking me up and down. "Do you hear that?"

I stop struggling and just breathe. The breeze blows through the palo verde trees, brisk and cool. But in between the breeze, there's a whisper. Like the earth itself has something to say to me.

Claim your magic, it seems to say. *Make your choice.*

Ollie takes my hand and looks at me. "You heard that, right? Or am I officially going crazy?"

"Make my choice? But what choice is there? We let our magic go, we gave it up. We broke the Claimings... didn't we?"

"Maybe this is something new."

We watch the silver thread wrap around my hand almost hesitantly, as if it's waiting for me to say yes. Maybe he's right. Maybe this is a new kind of Claiming. But how can we trust it after everything we've been through?

I can't keep the anxiousness out of my voice. "But the Claimed, they're finally unbound. What if we trap them again? What if—"

Ollie puts a finger on my lips. "What if it all works out in the end? Hmm? Did you ever imagine that?"

I knock his hand out of the way and snort. "That's hilarious coming from you, Mr. Worst-Case-Scenario."

He grins and tilts my chin up with his knuckle. "I already lived my worst-case scenario and survived to tell the tale. But it's up to you. It looks like you have a choice. Maybe fate is giving you another option."

I step back from Ollie and turn my hands facing palm up. An open invitation. "Okay," I whisper back to the thread, to the magic waiting for me to answer. "What's the deal here?"

The thread splits, spiraling into three: one purple, one green, and one golden.

Mixing, Elemental, and Casting.

Claim your magic, it repeats softly in my ear. It sounds like a freshly caught secret, like a song sung at sunrise. It sounds like the earth and the sky and memory and magic.

It sounds like the color red.

I don't have to deliberate for long. I wrap my hand around the one thread that's always called to me, volatile and wild, yet grounded and true—just like my mom.

"Elemental," I say into the quiet. "I Claim Elemental as my magic."

The ground below my feet pulses once, twice, and then there is silence. The golden and purple threads disappear, fading into the night sky. But the green thread—the one that glows the color of grass in the morning sun, of moss and pines and the looming saguaros—slowly wraps around my wrist in a single knot.

Uncomplicated. A loop, tied off and finished.

Tied but free, your fate is yours, it whispers on the wind as my hands glow a soft green.

And then it's over. No blood, no flashing lights, no countless threads. No one watching but me and Ollie and the stars overhead.

I jump into Ollie's arms. He barely has the chance to catch me. Wrapping my legs around his waist, I bury my face in his neck. "Did you see that?" I screech.

He laughs and kisses me. "Yeah, I saw it. That would be kind of hard to miss."

I squeeze him tighter, laughing in disbelief. My hands glow again and the cloud above us bursts, sending rain sprinkling over us.

"You're making it rain," Ollie says, his voice filled with wonder. Even after everything he's seen, after everything he's done, he's still filled with wonder. "You're making it *rain*. Amazing," he says into my ear.

I take a deep breath and inhale the scent of the rain on the dry desert ground. I can feel everything around me—the shape of the mountains, the pull of the wind, even the slow growth of the plants surrounding us. I can feel the energy required to use this power fluctuating with whatever my gaze lands on. Some magic is big, and some magic is small, but all of it asks something of me. It just depends on how much I want to give.

It's like a switch has been flipped, and my eyes have been opened.

Then, a soft silver thread gleams on Ollie's hand, timid at first but fully shining seconds later. I unhook my legs from around his waist, and he sets me down gently on the ground.

His brow is puckered and uncertain as he looks at the thread. For someone who was just waxing poetically about missing his magic and everything that comes with it, he suddenly looks a little camera-shy.

"Go on," I say, poking him in the side. "It's your turn. It's time to choose your fate."

CHAPTER FORTY-SEVEN

OLLIE

ALL I CAN think about in this moment are the words Ellen said to me when I was twelve years old and couldn't sleep because I was worried about the stars. Life and death, death and life.

"Nothing ever ends, Ollie. Not in the way you think. It just changes into something new, that's all."

Something new.

The silver thread coils in my hand, almost like a ball of yarn waiting to be unraveled. I hear the hum, the whisper sliding off the edge of the cliffs, tumbling down and all around us. It fills my ears; it empties me out.

Claim your magic. Make your choice.

Again, the thread splits. Purple, green, and golden, all in the palm of my hand.

I should be focusing on this choice, on this life-changing decision in front of me, but instead, my mind travels back to how different this is from the last time I was Claimed.

Last time, I felt so scared and confused. I was alone in my room, sweating and shaking and thinking I was losing my mind. I couldn't believe that Gemma had never told me the truth. I couldn't believe that magic was real.

But this time? I'm not alone, and I'm no longer confused. Now there are no secrets between me and Gemma, and I am most certainly a believer—in magic and in us.

I shake my head and roll my shoulders, telling myself to relax and focus, to be in the present moment. The three threads gleam in my hands. Three questions, one answer.

Focus.

I spend most of my time and nearly all my days waiting and wishing, trading the present moment for a past memory or a stolen glimpse of the future, imagining what could've been and longing for what's next. And then there's the worrying—so much worrying.

But every once in a while, my eyes are opened and I *see.* Tonight, this is going to be one of those moments; a perfect memory in the making.

I close my eyes and remember how it felt to hold the threads in the Dreamscape whenever I tied off a Claiming. I felt the power of each branch, but that was always from the outside looking in. A Threader of magic, nothing more. I never asked myself what I really wanted.

The threads wiggle in my hands agitatedly, as if they're annoyed that I'm taking so long. As someone who hates making decisions on the spot, this is basically my nightmare.

Gemma chuckles from behind me. "Any day now, Cade."

I bite my lip and say what's been waiting in my chest since the moment I saw Gemma split the threads and Claim what is hers. "Casting," I say softly. "I Claim Casting as my magic."

"I *knew* it," Gemma calls out. She grins and shakes her head. "You're such a nerd." Then she cackles in delight. "Milo's going to freak out."

"Gem, you're kind of killing the moment."

"Right, sorry. Carry on."

I laugh and turn back to see the green and purple threads vanishing, leaving the golden thread gleaming brightly in my hand. It slowly wraps around my wrist in a simple loop. I expect to follow the pattern, to hungrily memorize a complicated knot, but now I don't feel any pull to the threads.

I just feel warm and right at home. It feels easy.

And then it's over.

Or maybe it's just another beginning.

As the golden thread disappears into the night, I swear I can hear the final notes of Carmen's song, a wistful sound lost to time and legend. But I don't wonder if my soul is Claimed or if fate has any tricks up its sleeve. This magic feels freely offered now that there isn't someone behind the scenes, pulling the strings. Fate can unfold as it always wanted to, unencumbered and tangled up in the wild mystery of magic.

I turn around to face Gemma, and as I do thousands of words float in and out of my mind as if they're drifting by on a breeze. There's a ruggedness to the Language, something otherworldly and unknowable. It's rich and melodic and nearly impossible to describe, but I guess I have my whole life to try.

A beautiful, unending word search. The possibilities are limitless, and now they are mine.

When my eyes lock onto Gemma's, her name shimmers around her, iridescent and rosy, humming like the opening notes of my favorite song. *"Gemma,"* I whisper. Her name rolls around in my mouth, sounding different and familiar all at once. *"Gemma."*

She straightens at the sound of her name in the Language, her mouth dropping open. But nothing else happens. No sparks flying or other dramatics.

No—it's just her. *She* is the magic.

I reach over and take her by the hand, opening and closing my mouth uselessly as I try to think of something to say.

"For someone who quite literally has a gift for words, you seem to have lost them all." Gemma squeezes my hand and laughs.

I just shake my head, part of me still wondering if this has been the longest and weirdest, most elaborate dream I've ever had. A dream seventeen years in the making. About a boy who fell in love with a girl who showed him that magic, in every sense of the word, is *real.*

Gemma stares at me, her eyes soft and full of all the words I can't bring myself to say. "What?" she asks, leaning in closer, a smile on the edge of her lips and sparks on the tips of her fingers. Lightning flashes once in the background, a bright streak against the midnight sky.

I pull her in and press her lips to mine. Like I've done a thousand times. Like I will a thousand more.

Even if I sorted through every available word, every single nuanced variation, I'd never find the ones big enough or grand enough to capture how this feels.

But maybe that's the whole point.

If this is a dream, I think I'll stay asleep.

Wouldn't you?

THE END

ACKNOWLEDGMENTS

I N CASE YOU haven't heard, writing a sequel is kind of complicated (haha), which means that my writing process for *A
Memory Made Real* included quite a bit of wallowing (at my desk,
in the shower; you name it—I'm sure I've wallowed there). But
I'm thankful for the struggle because it brought me to my knees.
Each book I write teaches me something I need to learn, and this
one taught me to surrender to the Ultimate Creators, my Heav-
enly Parents and my Savior Jesus Christ. Each word of this story
was painstakingly fought for, earnestly prayed over, and ulti-
mately given to me through Their unending grace. So it is to
Them that I offer my first and biggest thanks.

Thank you for telling me not to quit and for showing me time
and time again that it's all about the journey. You are so good to
me.

To my amazing husband and my darling girls: you make my
life spectacularly messy, and I am forever grateful for that. Thank
you for always being in my corner, especially on the hard, chaotic,
what-am-I-making-for-dinner days. I hope you know how much I
love and cherish you. I feel so lucky to call you mine.

Thank you to my parents, who continue to raise me. I'm so
grateful for your constant support and guidance. I know I tell you
this all the time, but really—I don't know what I'd do without
you. I definitely got the best of the best. A huge thank you to my
wonderful siblings and their spouses. Thanks for listening to me
talk about this story for the past three years and believing I could
finish it before I ever did. I love you guys. A big shoutout to all my

in-laws; I adore you. Thank you for always treating me like one of your own. I love being a part of your family.

Thank you to the many incredible friends who make me laugh and listen to me cry. Maddie, our friendship took off faster than a green light, go. I'm just so grateful you're less than two ATW1os away. Thanks for watching my kids while I chipped away at revisions, for endlessly dissecting Taylor's lyrics with me, and for dealing with my angst when it's nearly Edward Cullen-level. I'm a lot, I know. But you love me anyway.

Sheridan, thank you for being one of my first readers of this draft and for your emoji-filled Google Doc comments that gave me life when I really needed it. Thank you for hashing out the plot with me and rereading this book so many times. You are a tremendous friend and a safe place for all my crazy schemes. Ollie, Gemma, and Milo love you just as much as I do.

Danica, you are one of the most genuinely supportive people I know. Thank you for being so generous with me and for offering your skills as a reader and writer. This book is better because of your kindness and expertise. I can't wait for your words to be out in the world, my friend. I'm always cheering for you, too.

To my other fantastic beta readers, Tammy, Annalee, Blair, Shalee, Kara, and my mom. Thank you for reading this book with such care. I hope you know how much I appreciate your notes and suggestions and all the little hearts doodled next to your favorite parts. This story is stronger because of you and your insights.

To Sara, Erin, Kara, Amy, and Joanna, my local writer friends who just make this whole thing a lot more fun. You guys are world-class storytellers and human beings, and I'm so happy to have you in my life. And to all my other talented writer friends, both near and far, thank you for your encouragement and empathy. The writing community I've found online has lifted my spirits more times than I can count. Thank you for understanding the strange problems that come from having so many voices inside your head; we're a delightfully weird bunch, and I wouldn't have it any other way. I love reading your words and thank you for reading mine.

Thank you to the creatives who helped me turn *A Memory Made Real* into an actual book. Paige Poppe, your beautiful cover design captures the heart of this story with so much color and wonder. I feel so lucky to work with you; you inspire me. Thank you to my editor, Emily Klopfer, for asking the hard questions and making me dig deeper, not to mention helping me iron out the wrinkles in the magic (not an easy thing to do). Thanks to Katherine Stephen for proofreading and catching those sneaky typos and Phillip Gessert for formatting this stunning book. Big hugs to Lyndsi Earle for writing such a lovely poem for the epigraph; you have a gift. And a special thank you to Jody Moore and Brooke Snow, who help keep my head and heart grounded through the powerful work they put into the world.

To my incredible readers: thank you for dangling off the cliff with me for the past few years. I hope this ending was worth the wait; it was for me. I'm so grateful for every single one of you. Thank you for reaching out and telling me how much you enjoy my books. I don't think you'll ever understand how much it means to me. It's such a joy to share my stories with you. Here's to many more.

And to Brooke, my best friend. Losing you changed me, and it certainly shaped this story. Even though you've moved on from this life, your friendship continues to impact me in monumental ways. Thank you for being nearby while I wrote the funeral scene and for reminding me that goodbyes aren't forever. In truth, they are simply another chapter in the story that never ends. Our memories are some of my most favorite, and I can't wait to make more with you again someday. Thank you for teaching me to look for the magic in the everyday.

photo by Emma Montgomery

NICOLE ADAIR IS the author of *A Tangle of Dreams, A Memory Made Real,* and *Voted Most Likely.* She lives in Arizona with her husband and three daughters. Nicole studied Political Science at Brigham Young University but decided that writing teenage love stories is much more fun. When she's not writing, she spends her time reading, running, and having dance parties with her girls.

You can find her online at writenicolewrite.com and on Instagram @writenicolewrite.

www.ingramcontent.com/pod-product-compliance
Lightning Source LLC
Chambersburg PA
CBHW011121190726
48289CB00012B/2859